THE
AMERICAN LAIRD

BIOGRAPHICAL NOVEL
ABOUT
AL (LAWMAN) ECKSTRAND
MEMBER
DRAG RACING HALL OF FAME

BY

DONALD MANDICH

1stBooks - rev. 12/10/01

FOREWORD

1) The American Laird is generally based upon the life experiences of Dr. Elton August Eckstrand, Eighteenth Laird of Penkill, Girvan, Ayr, Scotland. *(Duncan Alan Fleming in this biographical novel portrays Dr. Eckstrand.)*

2) Dr. Eckstrand was a prominent attorney in the United States, and also during his racing career (1960-1973) a major racing driver for both the Chrysler Corporation and Ford Motor Company before becoming an independent professional. During the last years of the Viet Nam conflict he was the guest of the U.S. Department of Defense touring U.S. military installations with his racing cars entertaining the troops throughout Southeast Asia.

3) Dr. Eckstrand did purchase Penkill Castle in Scotland in 1979 with all of its contents.

4) As described in the book, the castle was intimately involved in the mid-1800's with the group of artists called the Pre-Raphaelite Brotherhood, many of whom visited, lived, and worked there and left behind many of their works.

5) The artist William Bell Scott was a longtime resident of the castle and mentor to various members of the Pre-Raphaelite Brotherhood. The King's Quair mural in the castle tower stairway is signed as his work. It is protected by the Government of Scotland under the Scottish Listed Buildings Regulations, as is the castle.

6) Dante Gabriel Rossetti, the famous poet and painter, was a frequent visitor to the castle and his sister Christina Rossetti visited for two extended periods. There are numerous ghost stories about them and others at the castle.

7) There is a secret passageway in the castle.

CHAPTER I

Duncan Alan Fleming, an American, brought his Chevrolet Corvette to a stop at the heavy, wrought iron gates of Kirkwood Castle in Ayrshire, Scotland. If things proceeded as planned, in the next hour he would be the owner and 18th Laird of Kirkwood Castle - the title passing with the deed. The closing for the sale was set for 8 a.m. He was slightly early and found the gates closed. However, a large man in a kilt appeared on the inside and moved first one gate and then the other. He motioned for the car to enter.

As the car eased through the opening, the Scot waited at the side of the curved lane and walked beside the car as it wove through the gravel road until it got beyond the trees screening the castle from the road. He signaled the car to stop. The castle was slowly emerging from the fog with the light of the morning sun coming from the side.

Fleming lowered the window. The Scot pointed to the castle with his knobby walking stick and addressed him with a broad Scottish accent, "Sic (such) a beauty, Duncan Fleming, ya kin be sonsie (jolly) proud to be the new Laird. I've waited a long time for ya to be comin.' I'm always aboot if you should need me." With that the Scot walked off into a patch of fog.

Fleming switched off the engine and admired nature's art - a private showing - as patches of fog moved about and more and more of the castle and its large tower emerged into view. A small rabbit ran toward the car from the fog in the garden and froze a short distance away. Five or six sparrows flew about chirping and foraging for their breakfasts, a delicate contrast to the massive structure of stone.

He was puzzled by the old man's statement that he had waited a long time for him to be coming. There were so many legal problems in clearing the title that Fleming himself didn't know if the purchase would happen until a few days ago.

Two cars passed through the gates interrupting his reverie. He started the engine and moved to the front entrance of the building. There he greeted Cameron MacKim, solicitor for the outgoing Laird and his two associates. No one answered their ring, so MacKim pushed open the massive, unlocked, oak door, and they walked into the large entrance hallway.

"Hello. - Laird Semple!" MacKim's voice echoed in the large hallway and up the open tower stairway.

"We'll go and find him. Please walk up to the third level," suggested MacKim. "The old boy wishes to hold the signing there where the wall is lined with all the portraits of the Lairds for the last two centuries. In a manner of speaking he wants to say goodbye to the former Lairds and introduce them to you."

Fleming climbed the curving stone stairway to the third level and shortly was followed by the others, two of them supporting the enfeebled Laird. They placed him in a heavily carved chair and pulled up others in a circle around a small table.

The closing ceremony was to be brief. All of the legal documents had been prepared and approved in advance. Two bank drafts were to be given in payment - one for the land and building, the other for the contents. As they laid the papers out on the table, Fleming looked about the room; dust was on everything, and it rolled on the floors.

While MacKim was arranging the papers, Fleming asked, "Who was the old timer that opened the gates when I came in this morning?"

MacKim looked up. "There's no help here. No one left but the Laird. Must have been someone walking on the road."

Fleming thought for a moment. "But he was on the inside of the closed gates."

The old Laird didn't say anything and MacKim just shrugged.

Fleming looked at the portraits of the former Lairds on the wall and focused his attention on the portrait opposite his chair. "Funny," he said, "the old Scot I talked to outside looked a lot like the one in that portrait. The same tartan and he had a walking stick like the one in the picture." And he thought to himself, I'm almost positive he addressed me by my name.

MacKim glanced up at the portrait, but returned his attention to the documents. The old Laird weakly pointed to the picture and said in a shaky voice, "He was the Twelfth Laird." After some seconds he added, "That walking stick is downstairs in the umbrella tub at the front entrance."

In less than twenty minutes the formalities were concluded and MacKim handed Fleming a folder. "These are your copies. I'll take care of the recording of the deed, and so forth. You are now the Eighteenth Laird. Congratulations."

They proceeded down the tower steps and assisted the old Laird out the front door and into a car. One of the men returned and in a few moments carried out two modest sized suitcases. He remarked to the new Laird, "Nothing in these but his personal clothing. I checked."

Fleming nodded and followed him out to the cars. He offered his hand to the old Laird. "I wish you well, Sir. Anytime you'd like to come back and visit, you're welcome."

The old Laird gently took his hand and just nodded. He exhibited no sign of emotion, had no tears in being the last of the family line who found it necessary to give up the ownership of Kirkwood. He was physically and emotionally exhausted and would now be driven to a nursing home where he would spend the remaining days of his life.

Fleming watched as the cars drove up the lane and disappeared beyond the trees. He reentered the castle and closed the great outer door with a thump that echoed throughout the entrance hall. There was no one else in the building, but he was expecting to be joined shortly by his butler Granville (Harrison Hay Granville) and his gardener and general factotum Jeffrey, who were driving the Laird's Rolls Royce and Land Rover from the Laird's manor home in the Midlands of England. The new Laird couldn't decide where to wait, so he unconsciously pushed some of the dust off from some steps with the side of his hand and sat in the front entranceway.

The Laird had several objectives for today, and the list was very short: security, staff, and maintenance.

A locksmith was expected shortly to change all the locks. After Granville arrived he would put together the initial staff and begin to organize them. And thereafter would follow the massive job of cleaning the inside of the castle and restoring it where needed and of course the immediate thirty outdoor acres of grounds. After ten years of neglect there was much to be done.

Kirkwood Castle had been in the Semple family since it was built in the early 1400's. The family had always been known to have substantial wealth until the Sixteenth Laird died ten years ago without issue, and the castle had been left to the only known distant relative, a resident of York and virtually a stranger, who had worked and lived as a clerk all of his life. Seventeen, then sixty years of age and unmarried, was excited with his inheritance and left his job to take up residence in the castle. He had no idea of the cost to operate such a structure day to day, or even to heat the endless number of rooms. The inheritance included only the castle and land - no money. In less than four years his savings had run out and with it his health had deteriorated from anxiety, so that he had little energy and simply moved from his bedroom to a chair in the Great Hall where he took his meals and then back again to the bedroom. At the point when he had to discontinue his day help, his sister's step daughter and her husband, John Riddall, had come to visit for 'just a few days' and they had stayed for more than five years until the 'nephew' died suddenly and strangely a few months ago.

Both the nephew and his wife were rough and simple minded and had no idea how to run a grand household, nor did they have any respect for its age, its history, and the old and valuable contents. At the outset the niece had told John Riddall, "Listen. I didn't come on holiday to be a skivvy." And other than putting together a pretense at meals she washed the dishes every few days and that was pretty much it.

Inasmuch as there was no cash, John Riddall decided to try to pawn things from the castle, but there were no pawnshops in the area. So he wandered into an antique store in the nearby large town where the proprietor was more than willing to help him dispose of some of the old "junk" that abounded in the castle. His new 'friend' also knew someone in the book business who might help Riddall get something for those old books "which no one reads anymore" and also someone to help dispose of some of the old paintings - "which, as everyone knows, few people want." Riddall found it easy to deal with the gentleman and they disposed of numerous things at a fraction of their true value - but nevertheless enough to include a 'rake-off' for himself, to what he felt entitled for the services rendered to the uncle. While the uncle was either in his chair in the Great Hall or in his bedroom, he was unaware of the frequent traffic of dealers exiting with items of value.

The event that triggered the sale of Kirkwood Castle was the sudden death of John Riddall. He had brought an art dealer into the building to look at a painting of the Twelfth Laird over a fireplace. The dealer said, "It has no art value, but I'll buy it for the frame."

The large frame was bolted to the wall, and when the dealer started to pry it off with a poker he saw on the frame the inscription "MOVE NOT THIS PICTURE. LET IT BE FOR LOVE OF THOSE IN EFFIGY." The dealer had heard stories about ghosts in Kirkwood Castle and stepped down from the stool and announced, "I want no part of this picture."

The dealer left the room and walked down the stairs. Riddall grabbed the poker; he was determined to get at least the value of the frame and began prying it off the wall. He suddenly started gasping, and he yelled, which brought his wife running into the room to witness her husband choking, and at the same time he seemed to be grappling with someone and trying to tear invisible hands away from his throat. He suddenly turned limp. She tried to support him as he slumped to the floor. He had stopped breathing and was dead. She shook him, but to no avail. She ran to the telephone and summoned the local doctor.

Doctor Magnus MacLaine arrived from the town in less than fifteen minutes. After examining the body he assured the hysterical young wife that there was nothing she could have done; her husband had been strangled to death. The police were summoned and an autopsy was performed. There was no question about Riddall being strangled by someone with large, strong hands. That left the wife out of the equation and also the art dealer who was a person on the frail side. And likewise the Laird in his weak condition was not a suspect. The wife insisted that she was sure it was the ghost of the Laird in the painting. Doctor MacLaine didn't believe in ghosts, but he had heard enough stories over the years that he didn't disbelieve in them either, and in looking at Twelve in the picture, he certainly would have been powerful enough to have done it.

The niece was frightened and determined to leave posthaste, which was no disappointment to the Laird. She had always been snippy with him and was slovenly in caring for the castle as well as in her personal appearance. Having no financial resources and no one to care for him, the Laird put the castle up for sale. It wasn't sold easily, however, as he had borrowed considerable money from several sources and had executed various documents, each of which purported to give a lien on the property; and although they were not in proper form and never recorded, they placed a cloud over the title. Additionally, the nephew's wife possessed a document which was supposed to be a deed to the property conveying title to Riddall and his wife, although it was on ordinary paper, not in proper legal form, never witnessed, and the Laird's signature looked like a forgery.

After leaving the sale with an estate agent for some months and no potential buyer wanting to get involved because of the possible problems with the title, the agent gave up trying to effect a sale.

A solicitor, Cameron MacKim, was recommended to Seventeen, and he proceeded to clean up the legal mess. He not only marshaled all the outstanding debts, but he noticed the spaces on the walls where pictures had been removed, vacant spaces where furniture was obviously missing, and almost half of the books missing from a library of nearly 10,000 volumes (he could see where books had been on the shelves which had not been dusted after the books were removed). He checked around the likely second hand dealers in several of the surrounding towns and cities, and he learned of items for sale from Kirkwood Castle and hence enough about the backdoor dealing of Riddall and his wife that he confronted her and demanded to see the bills of sale - which she declined to produce. After he warned her that there would have to be a police investigation, she became very willing to surrender the so called deed to the castle.

The new Eighteenth Laird, himself an American attorney, had been patient in following MacKim's efforts to untangle Seventeen's affairs and after several months was able to obtain clear title to the castle and its contents. He didn't know until near the time of closing on the purchase that in Scotland the title goes with the property, and he would be the Eighteenth Laird.

The purchase included all furniture, a tremendous amount of artwork, over five thousand books - mostly in leather bindings - many of considerable age - and every closet, cabinet, desk, and storage room filled with personal possessions, some of which dated back for hundreds of years. In the lowest level was a large storage area with countless boxes, including twenty large wooden cases - coffers that contained documents of the castle and the personal papers of each laird.

Upon purchasing Kirkwood Duncan Fleming had decided to change his life style. He had owned Thorpe-Castle House in the Midlands for five years, which had the remains of a castle on the property. He had restored both, but had spent very little time there. He was now determined to try to spend as much time as possible at Kirkwood and give attention to the restoration. Over a relatively few years he had accumulated a large law practice and had developed a sizable firm. It would be impossible to quit abruptly, as many things were unfinished. He would try to taper off.

The outdoor bell on a pull chain clanged. A new sound; Eighteen would have to get used to it. Simultaneously, the telephone technician and the locksmith had arrived followed closely by Granville the butler and Jeffrey, the young, loyal, general handyman. Both had been his employees at the manor house for the last five years.

CHAPTER II

Granville, dressed in a conservative dark gray suit, and black bowler, emerged from the Rolls Royce he had driven from the manor home in the Midlands; he was carrying a large briefcase. (He looked more like a laird than the Laird himself, who was dressed in a dark plaid sport shirt, corduroy slacks, and brown loafers.) Followed by Jeffrey, who was dressed identically to Granville and who had driven the Land Rover, he passed the workmen and addressed the Laird. "Sir, I apologize. We're twenty-five minutes late. There was an accident up the road, and we had to wait while the police cleared the wreckage. I'll take charge of these two men."

Turning to Jeffrey, he said, "Would you go to the gatehouse and bring the people who are waiting there. After I talk to them you can make a survey of the grounds and make a list for the outdoor cleanup. Fortunately, it's still spring and we can shape the direction of things before summer."

He took a sheet of paper from his case and handed it to the telephone technician. A second sheet was handed to the locksmith who would be changing locks and installing an electronically operated system for the main gates.

Jeffrey returned from the gatehouse with four women and one man, Mrs. MacOster, the gatekeeper, and Mr. and Mrs. MacDuffie and their two daughters.

Mrs. MacOster, a long time widow, had been the gatekeeper for many years and also had done all the baking for the castle in the gatehouse. However, the former Laird had discharged her when he had run out of funds. He had hoped to sell the gatehouse as a separate parcel of property, which had proved to be impossible legally. So the gatehouse had remained empty, and thereafter the gates were randomly open or shut. Mrs. MacOster had lived with a relative during the last five years.

The MacDuffies lived a mile away down the road that bounded the castle on the east side, and for more than 150 years members of the family had served in the castle. This had given them a special status in the community, and they had respected the privacy of the lairds, and had never divulged any confidences - which could have resulted in permanent discharge if such had gotten back to a laird.

Mrs. MacDuffie, a portly matron, was in tears and she started out, "Oh, Sir, its been over six years since we've been here, and it feels like coming home again."

Mr. MacDuffie, a stocky well-built man, took the hand offered by Granville. "Sir, 'Ah'm happy to be of service. I know every nook and cranny of the castle. And aside from tending my farm I used to come to castle everyday and take care of any problem with heating, electricity, plumbing, and small repairs. And in a building like this there's aye something to do."

Granville took his new charges inside and sat them on the steps in the front hall. The butler, now just over forty-five, had spent most of his life on the stage. His speech to the staff had been carefully rehearsed in his mind.

Granville paced back and forth as he orated. He started by looking each person squarely in the eye. "Mrs. MacDuffie, Mrs. MacOster, Mr. MacDuffie, MacDuffie, MacDuffie, Jeffrey. I know you all have had some or a lot of experience, but the Laird and I have our style of running a household. First of all, we shall have in writing a description of each job—how it shall be done and on which days. All orders shall come from me and any questions you might have will come to me; you will never bother the Laird.

"You will never initiate conversation with the Laird other than to say something like 'it looks like it will be a nice day, Sir, or it looks like it might rain, Sir' - or you can address him as My Lord, if you prefer. If he asks you a personal question like 'where do you live,' answer in eight words or less - don't take ten minutes to explain the map of Scotland. If he asks if you have any brothers or sisters, answer in ten words or less - don't give the family history for the last one hundred years. Whenever the Laird or any houseguest addresses you, you will stand. And you ladies, I will instruct you in how to give an abbreviated form of a curtsy to be used when appropriate.

"Regardless of whether you think there is someone around or not, there is to be no shouting or whistling or singing anywhere inside of the gate to the premises. Talking will be only in low tones, as necessary."

He paused for emphasis. "I do not object to joking or laughing or giggling (he paused to look at the two MacDuffie girls) or your enjoying your work, but that is to be done only in the servants' quarters.

"Immediately, we shall be ordering the appropriate clothing for each person for each type of duty, whether it be cleaning or serving at table. The local tailor and his seamstress shall be here tomorrow morning to measure you. Women will wear no makeup, no jewelry, other than a wedding band, and no perfume.

"If you are here at mealtime you are welcome to participate in the same foods that are being served to the Laird and his guests, unless it be something unusual like caviar. And of course there will be absolutely no drinking of any type of alcoholic beverages on the premises - ever! You will see me tasting wines before they go to table, which is part of my responsibility. And there is to be no smoking inside any of the buildings.

"There are many important households in this area, and shortly we shall be having guests, most likely several times each week for luncheon, dinner, or tea, and later on overnight guests. We shall exhibit perfection to the point that we shall become known as the most impressive staff in Scotland, and perhaps be the envy of the other nobility and gentry." The latter thought pleased the group and they all grinned.

"I am sure that you'll find that everything will work better if we stick to these few simple rules. There will be other specific details as we go along. For serving at table we shall have some rehearsals to learn our style with me posing as the laird."

He handed Mr. MacDuffie a piece of paper and a pencil. "I want you first to look the whole place over and make a list of everything that needs to be done and a list of things to be

11

purchased. I'm sure we shall need a supply of things like light bulbs, fuses, and so forth. Jeffrey will bring in cleaning materials from the Land Rover and Mrs. MacDuffie, we shall first attack the kitchen and insure that we can prepare some simple meals for a few days. You'll have to scrub and disinfect everything. The young MacDuffies can start to vacuum and dust the Laird's room and change the bedding - you can throw out the old - except the coverlet with the coat of arms on it, and also scrub down the bathrooms from floor to ceiling and after that we shall work on the rooms in the servants' quarters. Needless to say this will only be the first pass, as everything shall have to be scrubbed and freshly painted and the wood paneling and the furniture shall have to be revived from years of inattention. I'll make a list of the priorities, and then you'll go through it room by room.

"Jeffrey, after you make a list of the things that need attention on the grounds, including the greenhouse, see if the garage is suitable for the vehicles or whether it should first be cleaned.

"And now - everyone - there's a lot to do - let's go to it."

When Granville finished, there could be no doubt in anyone's mind as to who was boss and whom they were working for. Later Granville would repeat everything to the Laird. Being an American, the Laird was egalitarian in nature, and his friendly demeanor sometimes didn't fit Granville's English ideas or the Scottish culture. He could be as open and charming with the lowest maid as with any of the elite. Granville wished to isolate him from the administration of the household, because he felt that any reduction of formality with the staff by the Laird would diminish Granville's status and make his job more difficult, and it also would give a poor image of the household to visitors.

Just as Granville was dismissing the group, the front doorbell rang. He opened the door to find two young men. "We're from the Ayr Sentinel Newspaper and are doing a story about the new Laird." They pressed forward to enter.

They found Granville to be a stonewall; and he said, "Gentlemen, it simply is not convenient to receive you at this time. We've only had possession of Kirkwood Castle for a few hours, and we have much to do. If you wish to come back at a later date, please call for an appointment."

The spokesman for the two started to push forward into the doorway again and said, "You needn't bother about us, we'll just walk about by ourselves and take a few pictures and later we might ask you a few questions."

Granville thought, 'So, they'll just wander through the building as if it was public property, like the town library.' He held his ground. "I'm sorry, gentlemen, but there's much confusion here at the moment; you'll have to return at a later date." He motioned to Jeffrey. "Please escort these gentlemen to the front gate." And as Jeffrey passed him, he said in a low voice, "And be sure they leave the premises." Before he closed the door the man with the Speed Graphic camera pointed the box at Granville and a flash bulb lit up. Because of Granville's dress and regal manner, they had assumed he was the new laird, and the next day the Sentinel had a brief story about Kirkwood and with it a picture of Granville as the Laird.

Granville assured himself that each staff member was busy, and then took the Land Rover and drove into the village to purchase groceries. He wanted to check out the vendors personally. In the future he would ask for delivery or send Jeffrey. He later returned with a massive amount of food, which would carry them through the next several meals. He was satisfied that the local butcher was excellent and that the local grocer could supply everything else they would require and could order specialty items when requested.

After tea Granville met the Laird in the Great Hall. He closed the door and began his report, "All the new locks have been installed and seem to be working properly." He handed the Laird a ring of castle keys and explained each one. "The telephones seem to be in working order, and the fax machine is in place.

13

"Mr. MacDuffie has a long list of repairs and it will take him at least the next two weeks, but he says he'll stay with it, Sundays included.

"Mrs. MacDuffie had a near stroke when she saw the kitchen, but I think she'll recover. I let her know that as soon as possible we shall be installing a new kitchen and also new bathroom fixtures throughout.

"The MacDuffie girls seem well behaved and good workers. With a bit of training they should work out just fine.

"Jeffrey reported that the cleanup of the grounds would be a several month job. It looks like the former residents threw rubbish out the back door and down the embankment toward the river, and all that mess should be cleaned up, but it's going to be a major effort as it's so steep that workers will have to use ropes like mountain climbers to move up and down. It's about a forty-foot drop on the east by the road and a drop of at least eighty feet on the west at the tip of the finger of land. He's going to try to find some casual help down in the town.

"This group should form a good nucleus, and after we get a second cook for the kitchen and an assistant, and a man to help with the heavy cleaning of walls and floors, that should pretty well complete the team.

"And finally, we had a brief visit from the local press. I think they'll be back to interview you at a later date."

"Thanks, Granville," acknowledged the Laird. "As usual you have things well in hand. I took a walk through the entire building during the day, room by room. At first I was going to make a list, but I gave up. We're going to have to hit the important living areas first and then go at the other rooms one by one.

"The place is loaded with art work, and I don't think any of the paintings have had any attention for over a hundred years. Some are in good condition and others are quite fragile - in need of cleaning and retouching.

"I took a look into some of the large wooden boxes in the lower storage area that have all the old papers of the former

Lairds. At first blush I thought that we could use the paper for starting fires in the fireplaces. But after looking more closely, some of these maybe should be given to a museum or university library. They might have historical value. A lot of them seem to be in Old Scottish, and I haven't the slightest idea what they mean, and some are in Latin. I think before we do anything with that stuff I'll try to get someone from the university in Edinburgh to come and take a look."

CHAPTER III

The oldest part of Kirkwood Castle was built in 1426 as a military fortification under the aegis of the ruling Stuart monarch. It was originally a 'peel' - a square stone tower - four stories high with the entrance on the second level which was gained by a ladder which could be withdrawn in case of siege. The original dungeon exists today. The castle is on a promontory of 30 acres above 1200 acres of forestland to the west. At the outset the castle lands included several thousand acres. The 1200 acres to the west was granted by the Sixteenth Laird to the government as a nature preserve; although in perpetuity the Lairds of Kirkwood Castle have walking rights on the land.

The thirty acre promontory is at the top of a fairly steep incline rising eastward from the sea less than one mile from the North Channel connecting the Irish Sea and the Atlantic Ocean. The Irish coastline is less than fifty miles away and on a clear day can be seen from the upper floors of the castle. Directly offshore due west is a small island called Pirate Island which has a natural harbor on its west side and the remains of a castle. For centuries it was used by pirates, which prompted the establishment of Kirkwood Castle to protect the inhabitants along the shore and also to carry out punitive actions against the island and its occupants.

From it's beginning the Semple family, and later its descendants, occupied the Castle. For their loyalty to the Stuart monarchs the Lairds were generously compensated and awarded the honor of wearing the Royal Stuart tartan. As time passed the principal occupants of Pirate Island, the MacBroom family, which referred to itself as a clan, (which it was not and even the 'Mac' part of the name was fake), moved onshore and built a sizable castle on a large tract of land adjoining the Kirkwood property. As the centuries passed they later claimed to have operated privateers under license from the crown, which was debatable, and they also operated slave ships. The wealth of the MacBrooms was considerable and at one point after it built the onshore castle it launched two separate attacks on Kirkwood Castle in retaliation for past actions, which were in turn repaid with attacks on the MacBroom stronghold. It was rumored that one of the attacks on the MacBroom castle relieved them of much of the substantial wealth accumulated by centuries of piracy and other nefarious activities, and while much of the wealth was delivered to the crown, the Semples were rewarded with a significant share which apparently sustained them for over two centuries, as there never was any visible sign of commercial or farming activity at Kirkwood Castle. Yet the Lairds lived in high style until the Sixteenth died.

The MacBrooms maintained their feud against the Semples, and over the years there were numerous unpleasant incidents. This ended when the Eleventh Laird married the heiress and last of the MacBroom line. As fate would have it, the two young people were each walking alone in woods somewhere between the two castles. They met and struck up a clandestine friendship, which flowered and eventually ended in marriage. At first a marriage was bitterly opposed by both families. But the MacBrooms relented because the family fortunes had declined considerably with some of their ships being lost at sea, and they condescended to let their only child marry a Semple to regain some of the fortune, which was once taken from the MacBrooms illegally by deceit and force, as they claimed. The Semples were more liberal, and finding that the MacBroom girl, despite her heritage, was a good person, they consented to the marriage.

The site selected for construction of Kirkwood Castle was well chosen. The building itself is on a finger of land, which stems from the base of an irregular triangle. The Kirkwhapple and Kirkwharry Burns flow sharply down the hill on the north and south sides of the property, well below the table of land on which the castle rests, and as the water flows westward it joins into one stream at the foot of the finger forming a deep whirlpool, referred to as The Devil's Punchbowl, and the overflow continues on downward through the village and into the sea. To further protect the castle, a dry moat had been dug long ago on the east side of the finger, but it was filled with dirt sometime during the last century.

During the last 150 years the castle was augmented first by extending the original square building into a large rectangle, tripling the size, and adding a five story tower at the juncture of the old and new parts of the building. Later in the 1850's the Great Hall was built on the ground level adjoining the tower - this was used for large scale dining and as a day room for the laird, as it looks out onto the gardens. The room is about sixty feet by one hundred and twenty feet, three stories high which includes the open cathedral ceiling supported by large cross beams; there is a massive fireplace at one end.

On the grounds is a gate house inhabited by the gatekeeper, Mrs. MacOster, a large greenhouse, and near the front gate is a long, one story building, originally a carriage house, but converted to an artist workshop in the 1850's by the Fifteenth Laird, a woman. The remainder of the grounds includes a large spring fed pond near the road on the east and a large area that had once been elaborate gardens. The gardens were overgrown with weeds, the greenhouse was empty, and the pond was a swamp filled with dead leaves and branches and trash.

During the period that Eighteen was negotiating for the property, he had several conversations with Seventeen and attempted to obtain information that might be useful. Most of the conversations were fruitless. Seventeen had little interest in the history of the castle or the surrounding countryside. His shortage of money seems to have preoccupied him totally.

Eighteen was only able to glean two potentially useful bits of information. One was that there had been periodic experiences with ghosts, particularly a woman ghost; he thought he remembered her name was Rossetti, and one of the earlier lairds appeared on occasion.

"What were the experiences?"

"Well, you'll find out."

The other thing was that, although Seventeen had never taken the time to search thoroughly, there was supposed to be a Green Book somewhere in the library, which would tell about the history of the castle, and give other important information, and Eighteen might want to look for it.

CHAPTER IV

The next day the staff was on the job early and continued to clean the rooms that would be used immediately. The tailor and his wife appeared and took measurements for the staff uniforms. When Mr. MacDuffie arrived, he had in tow an elderly man, undoubtedly in his eighties, who was introduced to the Laird and Granville as MacFergus.

"What's your given name," asked the Laird.

"Fergus."

"What's your whole name?" questioned Granville.

"Fergus MacFergus, but everybody just calls me Fergus. And beggin' your pardon, Sir, I stopped by to say that I worked as gardener here since I was a boy 10 years old and my father before me and his father before him. One day five years ago the young man Riddall - Laird he insisted on being called - discharged me for no reason and with six months back wages due me - and said he'd put the dogs on me if I ever entered the property. But they had nae dogs. Course ah ken that's none of your business, but I wanted to come by and offer to give any advice that I can. I can't work on the ground anymore - arthritis in me knees. When I look around at this place it near puts tears in me eyes. It used to be a showplace - both the grounds and in the greenhouse."

Mr. MacDuffie interrupted, "Aye, Fergus is well kent 'roun' here and everybody asks his advice about flowers and gardens."

"Aye," said the old man, "and I'd be happy to come and help you to restore the place, just for the memories I have of working here with my father and grandfather. Ah got nae weans, and me wife is deed long ago."

And as he talked his eyes shifted to the grounds. "You see over there, back by the road? The pond full of rubbish? If you clean out that mess, it'll fill up with water. I'll get you two pair of ducks and they'll live in the pond and multiply, and we'll use the water from the pond to water the plants - you won't have to buy fertilizer, and you'll also have plenty of ducks for the table. And we don't use any of them fancy chemicals around here; if bugs come we just give them a spray of salt water and they go and eat somewhere else. Over there - in the middle - is a croquet lawn. That's going to take a lot work to get it in shape. And all the flowers - I know where each kind likes to be."

Granville, the natural skeptic, interrupted, "And how much are these flowers going to cost?"

The old man shook his forefinger from side to side. "It dinnae work that way about here. You go and buy seeds or plants from a garden center, and you don't know how they'll do here. Naw. Ah'll visit me friends - every gardener and farmer for fifteen miles in every direction is me friend. They'll give me seeds and plants from things that have been grown near here in our kind of soil and in the salt air. Many of their plants came from Kirkwood because we grew the best, and their children will just be coming back home."

The Laird was touched by the genuine interest the old man had in plants and his obvious love of the gardens. He suggested, "Granville, I think we should introduce Fergus to Jeffrey and tell him he can come as often as he would like, and if he's here at mealtime, we would like him to break bread with us." The Laird also had in mind that if the old man proved to be as valuable as it seemed he could be, he would give him his back wages to restore the honor of the castle.

The Ayr Sentinel came out in the morning and by mid-afternoon the castle was flooded with phone calls wanting to sell, as Granville said, 'everything from insurance to window washing.' The interesting calls were those offering to sell things, which the callers claimed to have been purchased from the former Laird.

This definitely was of interest to Eighteen, but he decided to call the solicitor Cameron MacKim and ask him to handle the offers. MacKim might be able to negotiate better with the locals. There were some pieces of furniture that he would like to retrieve, and some oil paintings that would mean nothing to anyone outside the castle but were part of its history, and hopefully among any books that were offered the Green Book might turn up. He had searched the library the previous evening with Jeffrey, and since most of the books were in brown leather bindings, it would have been easy to spot a green one. With the nearly five thousand books that the Laird would be bringing from the manor home in the Midlands, he wouldn't be buying a lot of books, unless they were of relevance to the castle; however, he would buy some to keep the offers flowing.

MacKim was pleased to be retained by the Laird, a prestige client. He also agreed to contact the Edinburgh University for guidance on the documents and papers in the coffers. Since most of the offers of items for resale to the castle were coming from Edinburgh, he suggested that in a few days they visit the university and also inspect some of the items for sale. He also suggested that the Laird visit the Lord Lyon King of Arms who was in charge of the granting of coats of arms in Scotland and arrange for a grant of arms, to which he would be entitled as the Laird. MacKim would make the arrangements.

Late that afternoon the Laird made three visits in the village below the castle.

The first was to the bank. The manager MacNab was visibly surprised when the Laird walked in and introduced himself, "According to my predecessors, Sir, the lairds never had any bank accounts; they always paid everything by cash - that is until the last laird. He had an account with us for a couple of years until there were some - ah - irregularities, and what he did after that I don't know."

The Laird explained, "I've always dealt with Barclays in the Midlands, but I'll need accounts for myself and for the household. If you'll prepare the necessary papers I'll have funds forwarded."

As the Laird was leaving, he asked, "Could you direct me to the office of Doctor MacLaine?"

MacNab walked him to the door and pointed. "Straight down the street and the first building to your right as you turn the corner. Quite a man, Doctor MacLaine, respected and liked by everyone, worries about the people in the village as if they were his family, especially the children."

MacLaine, in his middle sixties, was an impressive man, just over six feet with a strong build. He had a full head of gray hair, which was neatly cut, as was his small, gray moustache. He was wearing a clean, white, starched clinic coat, and with his serious and somewhat formal demeanor, he gave an immediate impression of thorough medical competency.

The Laird offered his hand. "I'm Duncan Fleming - your new neighbor at Kirkwood. I wanted to stop by and get acquainted in case we had an emergency among anyone of our staff."

MacLaine gave him a firm handshake. "Sit down. And welcome. Already I've been hearing good things about Kirkwood. I suppose you have heard some of the recent history and the death of the Laird's nephew, Riddall. Very strange. A mystery."

Fleming nodded. He took an immediate liking to MacLaine. "I've heard one version of the story. And I'd like to hear yours sometime. But I must apologize for making this visit brief." He stood to leave.

On his way to the door, Dr. MacLaine asked, "Would you happen to be a chess player?"

The Laird hadn't played chess in years, but he thought he would enjoy getting better acquainted. He replied, "I'm a neophyte at the game, but, if you can put up with that, we might try it one day soon."

"Good," acknowledged MacLaine. "Call me whenever you're free; my time is pretty flexible here, subject to handling emergencies of course." After they shook hands at the door, he tapped the Laird's protruding stomach a couple of times with the back of his hand, and suggested, "You could do with a bit less of that."

As the Laird left the office, he resolved to start watching his diet and get back on his exercise routine, which he had let slide in the recent months. Beginning tomorrow he would jog, providing it didn't rain.

His third stop was at the Presbyterian Church Manse. The young Reverend MacTaggart greeted him at the door. "Laird Fleming. Oh, yes indeed. I read about your purchase of Kirkwood. So nice to make your acquaintance. Please come in and sit down. According to my immediate predecessor, we haven't had a visit from anyone at the castle since he conducted the burial services for the laird before the last one."

"That would be the Sixteenth Laird. I'm the Eighteenth," prompted Fleming. He continued to stand inside the doorway. "I'm sorry that I can't stay. I just wanted to say hello, and you can expect me in church on Sunday. I grew up going to a Presbyterian church in the United States."

The young minister was elated at the thought of having the Laird in his kirk. It would be a feather in his cap to attract him, and it would bring other curiosity seekers to the kirk, which was usually only half full on any given Sunday. "Of course, I'm new here, and I'm still sorting things out. Would you and your wife stay and have lunch with me on Sunday, immediately after the service?"

"I would enjoy having lunch on Sunday very much. But there is no Mrs. Fleming. Never has been."

This information was even more interesting to MacTaggart. This unmarried Laird might attract to the service every unmarried woman over the age of eighteen from a radius of twenty-five miles. "That makes two of us," replied the minister. "So my housekeeper will cook something suitable for two bachelors. Oh, and you should be aware, there's a pew in the church reserved for the laird and his family, which doesn't include members of his staff. It's in the front row. I'll have one of the elders look out for you and take you to the correct pew."

The Laird offered his hand, "Until Sunday then."

MacTaggart shook his hand warmly. "Until Sunday."

After dinner that evening the Laird asked Granville to accompany him about the castle, directing him to bring some blank paper, and suggested, "Let's hit the important rooms from bottom to top and make a list of things to be done."

At the end of their tour they entered the Laird's room - a long room with windows on two sides, a sleeping area on one end near the door with a massive four poster bed with a carved squirrel mounted on each post at the foot; a sitting area on the other end with a sofa and two overstuffed chairs and lamp tables, and on one side of the room a large antique desk.

On the Laird's desk were two photographs in crystal frames - one a 5" by 7" picture of his former fiancée, deceased, (the crystal reflected light onto the picture making her look very angelic with her blond hair) - and the other an enlarged snapshot of two small children, ages around four or five, between two older women at a table - all behind a birthday cake with lighted candles - everyone was smiling. There were two large armoires and a closet in the section adjoining the old part of the castle and another closet in the new part of the castle, and the bath and dressing room were on the far side in the newer section.

When they entered, the Laird closed the door. "Come over here, Granville." He walked into the closet in the old section, reached up and twisted a large curved wall hook. He pulled back the wall paneling revealing a platform at the top of a passageway with stairs descending downward. "I discovered this when I was putting some things in the closet. I was hanging a jacket when it dropped on the floor, and after bending over for it I straightened up and reached for that hook to keep my balance. The hook turned in my hand and the paneling moved outward. As you can see the stairway is filled with gravel, and it would be one heck of a job to clean it out - really make a mess. It looks like the passageway starts to turn to the left, and it's in the old section of the castle; probably goes down somewhere in the dungeon area. We'll have to check it out."

Granville studied the opening for some moments and nodded his head in agreement. "I would also guess that it goes somewhere down in the dungeon area. And now, Sir, could we go to the kitchen and servants quarters?"

There was a first level entrance to the kitchen area and servants quarters from a door off the front entrance hall, as well as an entrance from the outdoors in the rear of the castle. Additionally, the quarters could be reached from interior stairways in the newer addition.

The Laird knew by tradition that he would rarely go into the servant's area; only when invited - maybe for a piece of cake for someone's birthday or to see a little Christmas tree and have a cup of eggnog. Otherwise, it was off limits to him - as would be the Laird's room to everyone else. The only time any of the staff would enter the Laird's bedroom would be while he breakfasted in the Great Hall. Each morning the two girls assisting Mrs. MacDuffie would vacuum the room, change the bed linens, and clean out the bathroom and leave. Mrs. MacDuffie would supervise them and only she herself would do the dusting, being careful not to break anything. Everything in the room and all items on the furniture would be replaced with precision - not only because the Laird wished it so, but also when Granville walked through each room for inspection he could see if anything was missing.

The entrance to the servants' area had a hallway shaped like a "T." One entered at the very top of the "T" and going straight ahead it would go directly out to the rear door of the castle, but near the top was a double door entrance to the kitchen. If one stayed at the top of the "T" and went left it would go to a two-room suite, which were Granville's quarters; and if one went to the right it went into a larger area, which split into two sections, each with a lounge and four small bedrooms - one section for men and one for women.

The Laird marveled again at the Victorian kitchen, and Granville confirmed that an architect would be in the next day and a modern kitchen would be installed as soon as possible. As to the rest of it, he would see that new bedding and anything else needed would be installed in the servants' quarters. The Laird glanced around the kitchen, and they left. His next visit there would be to see the new kitchen when completed.

CHAPTER V

Duncan Alan Fleming, of Scottish ancestry, was born and raised in America in the suburb of a large midwestern city on Lake Michigan. He was six feet tall, of solid build, and had sandy colored hair. He had a clean cut and healthy appearance, which together with his warm personality and easy smile caused everyone, especially women, to categorize him as a handsome person. He was in his middle forties and had never married.

His father had been a building contractor, and, as his son was growing up, he had him helping on various jobs, and in essence had him apprenticing in turn as an electrician, a carpenter, a plumber, a mason, and a painter. If the son was going to follow him as a contractor he had to know the elements of a good workmanlike job. Another major contribution to the boy's practical education from the father was that he had bought Duncan an old Model A Ford when he began to drive at age sixteen, and he encouraged his son to fix it up and learn how the engine worked. All of these activities contributed to making him a perfectionist in everything he undertook.

The Model A Ford was a love affair with 'Dunk' as everyone called him, not only because the car extended his world, but he was captivated by the fact that the inert pieces of iron and steel could come to life, and depending on how they were handled would perform better or worse - just like human beings. The car was in the garage more than on the road as he experimented on improving its performance.

In high school Dunk was quarterback and captain of the football team, and in the spring he played shortstop on the school baseball team. In school he had weighed 175 pounds - trim for his height. In recent years he had added over forty pounds - mostly on his waistline.

In college he didn't engage in sports other than intramural. He obtained a degree first in classical studies and then another in history - focus on British history - and afterward a degree in law - 'Juris Doctor.' All three degrees were with high honors.

He hadn't planned to practice law in a law firm, and he didn't want to go into his father's contracting business. Yes, he loved the creativity of building, but even more he loved books and ideas. His first job out of college was as an attorney, but primarily as an assistant to a senior vice president of the one of the country's major manufacturing companies. He had expected to do a lot with corporate law, but soon found out that he was more of a general aide to the officer, and that he also had to oversee his personal financial affairs.

One of his early assignments was to update the officer's will and set up some family trusts. The exercise was so successful that soon the boss was 'lending' his services as a favor to others to prepare their wills and trusts.

Another event that shaped the direction of his life was that the company was involved in stock car racing, and that came directly under his boss, who one day asked his aide to go over and see if he had any ideas to get some results for all the money they were spending. He went to the track where they kept the cars and exercised them. One look at the carelessly assembled engines and a few brief conversations with the mechanics and their driver who were sitting around drinking beer at nine in the morning, and Dunk left shaking his head. He told the boss that they would never get results until they got some mechanics and a driver who were motivated. The boss told him that he was nagged constantly by the top brass about this racing 'fiasco,' and anything Duncan could do would be welcome.

The first thing Dunk did was to discharge the mechanics. There had to be good people who worked for the winners and maybe there might be someone that wasn't appreciated. He found just such a person.

The new master mechanic was named Butch (Isadore) O'Malley, born and raised on the streets in the toughest part of Brooklyn. He had an ugly scar on the side of his face, which he had gotten in a street fight as a kid, and he looked like a 'tough mug' - an image he encouraged. He told Dunk, "There's no friends in this business. We don't trust nobody. We let nobody in here where we work on the cars - nobody. And when we go somewhere to race we take everything with us, gasoline, water we drink, everything, and we sleep with the cars. And I got a system of putting tools around the cars, and in one step of anywhere is a hammer or jack handle or tire iron. Because some day a couple of tough guys are gonna come through the door and we gotta be ready. If some guy walks in and tries to talk friendly, I tell 'em 'get your ass out of here, I ain't got no time for talk.' And nobody drinks any hard stuff while we race cars - gasoline and whiskey don't mix."

Dunk had readily hired Butch with that understanding. Butch also told him that the large mats they had for sleeping near the cars when they traveled would be used for some practice. He said that everyone on the team would have to learn how to disarm some goon with a knife or tire iron that might try to hurt them or the cars. Nothing fancy. But if two goons came in through the door, don't wait for them to attack you. Be sure you get in the first punch. Get to the side of the nearest one and kick him in the scrotum and duck while the other takes a swing at you, and then grab the arm with the weapon, throw him to the floor while twisting his arm behind him and then stomp on the back of his elbow and break the joint clean apart. He conducted daily drills with Dunk and his two assistant mechanics; maybe one day it would pay off. (Later when Dunk raced as a professional they carried handguns to protect their winnings, as the prizes were paid in cash from the gate receipts.)

Within days after Butch arrived everything under the bonnets of the cars looked as new. Dunk regularly stopped by early in the morning to check on things and again later in the day. He also began to take the cars onto the track himself to see how they responded - a new experience for him as they were sensitive, and it took some practice to get the feel of using the shift to accelerate and decelerate. Butch was a good teacher; he knew a lot about racing. For Dunk it was exciting, and he never felt so much that he was driving the car to demand speed, but rather letting the machine show what it could do with all of the care it was receiving.

From the outset the changes with the mechanics didn't go over very well with the driver. He resented Butch who nagged him about his drinking. He no longer felt in charge, and from the first day he rejected all overtures from Dunk to talk about racing and the team. It was apparent to Dunk that the man had a problem with the bottle, and although things were improving, he didn't seem to get the potential out of the cars, not even as well as Dunk had done in a few of the time trials when he was working with the mechanics to test the engines.

As might be expected, the inevitable happened. The driver disappeared for three days on a drunken spree and showed up on the morning of a race looking like death warmed over. Dunk was angry, and his boss, who was to be there that day with some of the top brass and their families, was livid, but unreceptive to dropping out of the race. He told Dunk on the phone, "I want our people to see that car in the race even if you have to get out there and push the damn thing around the track."

Dunk drove the car in the race and finished third, as well as they had done in a long time, and as a fast learner he could think of a number of things he might have done differently, and also the dirty tricks that were played on him by the other drivers. Yes, today, but not the next time he got out on the track.

Dunk's boss was elated and everyone was congratulating him, and the chairman of the company was saying to Dunk's boss, "Why the hell don't you have him drive all the time. We can't trust that other damn drunk of a driver. The big race is in four weeks. If we could win or at least beat the car from our major competitor, I'll give you a good bonus and maybe another stripe." It was not only a challenge, but the chairman's remark was tantamount to an order. On the program that first time Dunk had driven they had entered the change of drivers and had put him in as Al Fleming. He asked Butch how he came up with that, and he replied, "Duncan's too classy, not tough enough."

For the next several weeks 'Al' drove the cars every day, including each of the three Sunday's that they were in races. Their strategy was not to take a lot of risk and win, but for him to continue to get the feel of the two cars and to learn how to interact with the other drivers.

On the day of the big race he had chosen the car that he felt handled best, and had constantly told his mechanics that it was their car and he would only be the driver for a couple of hours. They had the machine tuned to a fine edge. When he arrived at the track they pulled the cover off the car, and he saw that during the night they had painted in large letters on both sides 'LAWMAN.' Again, all the brass and their families were there, and the chairman stopped by the pit to offer his encouragement.

As the race opened up it was obvious that every driver was feeling out the others and trying to get the feel of the tempo. It was also soon obvious to Dunk that the man driving for his chairman's adversary not only wanted to defeat the Lawman, but if possible force his car into the retaining wall. At first it annoyed him, but when the driver had gestured at him with his middle finger, he pulled himself together and reminded himself of what Butch kept saying, that this was all a matter of mechanics and physics, and don't let your emotions become self defeating. He would just have to be careful and maneuver himself at the right time and leave the other guys behind.

After a few laps he knew his car could move faster than anything on the track; he had no trouble keeping up with the pack and the engine had a lot left to spare. His strategy was not to try to lead the pack, but to force the one car to stay back with him if it was indeed stalking him. He had had a similar experience in other races where the word had gotten around that he was the new kid on the track and as green as grass. So he had practiced a maneuver hundreds of times during the last weeks and now the opportunity to use it might be materializing.

As they came out of one turn, Al intentionally placed his car in the outside lane near the wall, and there were two empty lanes on his left and two cars abreast to the left of that. The stalker was slightly behind and began to accelerate and pull alongside on his left as they headed for the far turn. As he pulled up alongside to hold Al straight into the turn and the oncoming wall, Al touched the brake, shifted and whipped around to the rear left of the stalker and began to accelerate - all in one fluid movement.

The stalker glanced to his right and not seeing Al's car was slightly perplexed and then looked behind and then to the left. They were now in the turn and Al held his direction for an extra split second before he began to take the turn; it was long enough to ride the stalker into the cement wall. The front edge of the car caught the wall and spun it around three-quarters of a turn and it headed straight across the track and crashed into the inner wall. Two men rushed out and extracted the driver before the car burst into flames.

The field was slowed until the wreckage was cleared. After speed was resumed Al pulled up just behind the leaders and trailed them until the last two laps when he easily let the car pull ahead and away from the field.

The team from the stalker's car registered a protest with the judges, claiming that Al had intentionally run their man into the wall. But the judges were 'old pros' at the game. They had seen everything many times, and responded that their man had obviously stalked the Lawman, that he would be fined, given a suspension, and also an official warning, and if he received another negative citation he would be banned from racing in the United States.

Al's boss and the chairman were elated. They rushed down to the track after the race and patted Al on the back, and the chairman kept calling him son. Al had only one thought when his car stopped and that was to tell his mechanics, "You guys did it. You won, and I thank you for giving me such a sweet machine." (The following week he went into a trophy store and bought each member of his team a facsimile trophy of the one they had won in the race with each man's name on it. And he continued the practice every time they won a race, which ultimately numbered 72, and in one year the Lawman did not lose a single race.)

The chairman told him, "Son, you've not only made my day, but my month and my year." And a little later, "Son, I'll see that the Board of Directors awards you a nice bonus for today's work." And later, "Son, plan to have lunch with me and some of the other senior executives on Monday." And a little later, "Son, my granddaughter is graduating from college and we're having a little celebration at my home next Friday evening. Plan to be there. You and my granddaughter have a lot in common." Al learned later that the chairman had sent his counterpart at the competing company, which had sponsored the stalker's car, a bottle of Old Crow Bourbon with a note saying, "To my dear old friend. You're not supposed to drink this stuff. You're supposed to eat it."

Al couldn't think of what he and the chairman's granddaughter could possibly have in common, except that both were unmarried. This was the beginning of numerous invitations to meet potential marriage partners. Being a celebrity generated many invitations and opened many doors, including the doors to many bed chambers - oftentimes those of the wives of prominent men.

Al wasn't ready for marriage. He had been in love with the girl next door, literally, the girl who lived next door to his childhood home. Carolyn had been his sweetheart in high school and college, and they had planned to get married as soon as he had settled into a good job. When he took up racing it upset her greatly, as her father had died in an automobile accident. Al, on the other hand, tried to assure her it was safe enough if your equipment was in good condition and you used your head. His plan was to do it for a few years and save money to buy a home and get married.

After the second year of racing Al decided that he was risking his neck for very little and turned professional. The success of his team was almost phenomenal. In addition to the United States they raced in a number of countries in Europe and

Japan, and he became one of the handful of top drivers in the world. Each member of the team watched his personal collection of facsimile trophies grow and grow.

Sometime late in his first year of professional racing a competing car suffered a mechanical failure during a time trial, and the driver lost control. The car sideswiped Al's, knocking it into a wall from which it bounced and rolled over several times, bursting into flames. Luckily, he managed to get out and ran from his car, but his clothing was in flames and a considerable amount of skin was burned off his left arm. He should not have continued to race that day, but after receiving first aid he smiled his way past the inspecting physician and went back on the field to drive and win. The newspaper picture of him running from his car with his clothing in flames was captioned, "And he came back an hour later to drive and win."

It was reprinted in his hometown paper, and when Carolyn saw it, that was it. She telephoned him, "Either you quit driving immediately or we're finished with each other - forever!"

He tried to explain that his racing commitments continued almost a year ahead, and he would quit when finished; his team depended on it for their livelihood. But she was piqued, and in two weeks she married Darwood Konrad Courtiss IV, scion of one of the most prominent local families - someone who had chased her for years and whom she had never even dated.

CHAPTER VI

The Courtiss family (pronounced Curtiss) was one of the early settlers in the area and had made money in real estate, manufacturing, and retailing. Socially it was one of the most prominent. Carolyn's father had been born in the area, but not of money. However, he had achieved prominence as a writer, which automatically opened the doors to many mansions. Her mother and Mrs. Fleming, Duncan's mother, were lifelong friends, and it was no accident that they had built homes next to each other. There was no fence between the houses, and they were in and out of each other's home every day. This close friendship had existed as long as Duncan could remember, but he never paid much attention to Carolyn until they were in high school. And what she mostly remembered of those early years was that he was always taking apart a car and had the pieces all over the garage and driveway, and that he usually seemed to be smeared with grease.

Duncan was shocked and crushed when Carolyn married Darwood Konrad Courtiss IV. He heard about it when his mother had telephoned him in Europe and said it was to be a very short engagement. He tried to telephone Carolyn, but she wouldn't accept his calls, and before he returned to the United States she was married.

The marriage was a disaster from the start. Carolyn didn't realize that she had only been another conquest for her husband, and he had expected that there would be some money in her family, which would fall into his hands. The death of his grandfather during the last decade had cut the Courtiss family fortune by more than half, and they had to sell valuable properties to pay the estate taxes. And his father had not been open- handed with him and had wanted him to settle down and learn a job in one of their companies. But he was undependable. He had never been a serious student in school as he felt he would live off family money. He was invited to leave prep school after the first term; he was a poor student, and worse he had intentionally injured another student in one of the sports. The headmaster believed he had an uncontrollable mean streak.

Carolyn wasn't aware that he was an open philanderer during their first year of marriage, or maybe she refused to acknowledge what was obvious. They first had a boy, Darwood Konrad Courtiss V, and while she was pregnant with their daughter Victoria, it was then that she realized he was chasing anything in a skirt, often during working hours when he should have been at a desk in a family company.

It was also during the second pregnancy that Mr. Courtiss III died suddenly of a heart attack. This reduced the family fortune by more than half again. But the father had carefully planned his estate. His wife had predeceased him and the estate was divided among three children. One-third to his daughter, a serious girl who was married to a young doctor, and they would make good use of the money and be good members of society. The next third went to his younger son - a business that manufactured office furniture and retailed the line along with related items. The final 1/3 went to his namesake; he had been strongly tempted to put it into a trust and only give him the income, but he felt this would cause strong resentment against the other two children, so he settled on him directly the ownership and control of the real estate company.

The real estate company was the easiest to run and the father had left the son a letter:

'Let Charlie (the executive vice president) and his team run the company and keep Mr. Candler to handle the finances and you'll have no problems. And don't retain ownership of any property too long. Sell it while things are going well and the maintenance is reasonable. Charlie will advise you as to when the time is right.'

After taking over the real estate company, Charlie had briefed him fully. The company had never borrowed up to the hilt and always was able to ride out the business cycles. He suggested that the new owner take the same salary as his father had and let the rest of the earnings go to pay down debt or into reserves. All of this was contrary to IV's expectations. On paper he was worth several million dollars, but from a cash flow standpoint he would only be living on a salary.

The Courtiss family, despite their social prominence, had tried to keep a low profile and had been conservative in their business affairs. But when IV took over the real estate company, he insisted that they make a news release announcing his presidency - which he drafted himself, indicating that dramatic plans for expansion were being formulated, and later stating verbally to a reporter the phrase 'after years of overly conservative management.'

He was determined to increase the profits and the cash flow from the business. He was unhappy with his inheritance; it was too modest, not what he felt he was entitled to. He resented having to share with his brother and sister. He hated the government and taxes. He hated the trust company that handled his mother-in-law's affairs. He hated the responsibility for his wife and children.

His wife and children - IV felt no compunction about his extramarital activities. Although he and his wife continued living together, they were estranged, as she well knew about his philandering. In his mind he reasoned that her needs were no different than his, and that she surely must be active with men behind his back, which justified his duplicity. He couldn't fix the date, but he had had no contact with his wife for a long period, and he conveniently reasoned that the children probably were not his. They had blond hair like their mother and her old fiancé Duncan Fleming. Yes, in his wishful thinking the odds were heavy that Fleming was the father, and why should he worry about them and their future.

His greatest pleasure was the next sexual conquest. He frequented the cheap pickup bars each evening. He would select an isolated girl and give a waiter a few dollars to go over and tell her who he was - his prominence. When the waiter nodded to him, he would approach the girl and she would say something like, "Gee, Mister, I didn't think someone like you would even talk to someone like little me."

He would smile benignly and wait for her next statement, which would be something like, 'How may I serve you.'

His payment of money to the prostitutes didn't detract from his feeling of conquest. He looked upon it as helping someone that was less fortunate - an example of his good heartedness, a charitable act. He gave nothing to organized charities. When approached, he would simply say that he was too deeply involved with his own private charities.

His determination to expand the real estate company triggered a parade of developers looking for backing for every conceivable type of deal, and it not only annoyed Charlie, but also it caused serious disagreement between the men - Charlie because the deals were 'flaky,' and IV because Charlie would have to realize that IV was boss and things would be different now.

Several weeks after he assumed control of the company IV received a letter on pink stationery from a woman asking for an interview - she was sure that she could run his finance department. Having little to do all day, IV received most of the 'flakes' that asked for appointments, and the woman was admitted. She was a handsome woman of even more handsome proportions (practically falling out of her tight jersey dress the secretary noticed as she showed her in). The interview continued until the lunch hour and the pair went to lunch together. IV didn't return the rest of the day nor did he go home that night, phoning his wife that he had an urgent problem in Chicago and would be back in a few days.

He hired the woman to run his finances and simultaneously terminated Charlie and his staff. On her advice he proceeded to undertake a number of new projects and to leverage all properties up to the maximum. She showed him how to save money by contracting the maintenance on a bid basis, which the company had never done before - they always had opted for quality. She also improved the cash flow by paying bills more slowly, which masked her expenditures for purchases of furniture for her home, plus jewelry and numerous other personal items. In addition she took cash advances from the company of over $200,000, as well as entering falsified expense reports. She drove a Cadillac which the company purchased and which she titled in her own name, which IV did know about and felt was an appropriate payment for her numerous favors to him personally. IV had the company buy a jet airplane, and he and his new financial v.p. jetted all over the country spending time in Florida, New York City, and Palm Springs, California. He also partied with other femmes that she didn't know about.

With his lack of skill and inattention to the business, in less than four years the company was in serious financial trouble. Tenants were exiting their properties because of the lack of good maintenance. They had over-expanded when interest rates were low, the new financial v.p. having chosen to borrow at short term rates which were cheaper than long term rates, and when interest rates skyrocketed they found themselves with unfinished projects and in an impossible cash bind, and the company was forced into bankruptcy. The receivers uncovered the lavish expenditures of the financial v.p. and advised IV to sue for restitution, as there would be little left after the company was liquidated. Upon confronting the woman she countered that she had functioned much as his wife in this family held company. He had introduced her to clients and others as his wife numerous times, and she would be suing him for breach of promise. She had retained copies of the hotel bills where he had registered them as husband and wife and a list of the people to whom she had been introduced as such. His attorney advised him to drop the whole thing.

Duncan only saw Carolyn once all those years. She was in the rear yard of her mother's house when he was visiting his mother. The two children, now ages four and five, were playing in the back yard. He said, "Hello, Carolyn. Those are beautiful children."

She looked at him with a sad expression and replied, "They should have been your children."

Her husband rarely visited his mother-in-law, but he was in the house that day and saw her talking to Duncan. Duncan noticed that Carolyn's face had an ugly bruise under one eye and was going to ask her about it when her husband opened the back door and yelled, "Carolyn, get your ass in here." Duncan was tempted to go and smash his face in, but that would only make trouble. He heard a scream after Carolyn entered the house, and next IV ordered the children in from the yard, and being children they did not react immediately until a second stern order, and as they went through the door he gave each a vicious slap.

It wasn't long afterward that IV was driving himself and his wife home from an evening reception where he had imbibed too much. He lost control of the car on the lakeshore road and it struck a tree. The car was totaled and Carolyn was killed instantly, but he received only cuts and bruises. The local police didn't test him for drunkenness - they knew well the Courtiss name, and the local papers played it up a tragic, freak accident.

After the accident the children were at their grandmother's home often, and Duncan usually saw the children each Saturday afternoon when he was in the city and made his weekly visit to his mother's house. The children called him uncle, and he took little gifts to them and gave them attentions that they never received from their father. Their grandmother died the spring just before the children finished high school - the girl was bright and had skipped a grade, so that they finished together. The grandmother had constantly worried about the father who had been a wife beater and had also beaten the children frequently for no apparent reason. Before she died she had told them that if they ever had a problem to go to Duncan's mother for help.

On the Saturday after the two children had finished high school, by coincidence Duncan was at his mother's house the afternoon that they had arrived on their bicycles greatly frightened. They related that Victoria had been at home reading in her room when their father had awakened after being out somewhere all night, and he had started drinking. He had walked unclothed to Victoria's room and announced that the time had come for him to teach her how to be a woman, and he started to paw her. She had been agile enough to slip away from him and ran down the stairs with him close behind yelling, "Come here you little slut!!"

Her brother Darwood had just returned from the library with some books and had entered the rear door and walked through the kitchen to check out the noise in the adjoining room where she was circling the dining table with the drunken father staggering after her. His sister at that moment decided to run out of the house through the kitchen. He was holding Michner's book **Texas** in his hand and seeing his father naked and his sister screaming, he surmised what was happening. He waited for his sister to run past him and when his father came through the door he swung the whole State of Texas as hard as he could directly into his face, smashing his nose and causing blood to gush forward and blinding him. The father covered his face with his hands and dropped to the floor on his knees in excruciating pain. He screamed. "You bitch, I'll kill you for this."

The son followed his sister out the back door and lifted the car keys off a hook by the door. The two took their bikes and pedaled the two miles to Duncan's mother's house. Darwood also added to the story that the father had recently been making strange advances to him and some of his friends who had come to the house.

Duncan was infuriated. He was fond of the two kids and felt that now was the time for action. There may be some risks, but he was willing to take them.

"O.K.," he announced firmly. "Uncle Dunk is going to take care of you. First of all, you're never going to live in that house again. Secondly, you're both going to go to a good college where your father will never find you. So get in my car. We're going to go to the house. I'll guess that your father'll be going to the hospital for some emergency treatment, and while he's away you'll have twenty minutes to pack a suitcase and take whatever clothes and things you can cram in, and what you forget Uncle Dunk will get for you later."

They got into his car and drove to the children's house. As they turned into the street they saw an ambulance leaving the house in the opposite direction. He waited until the ambulance was well down the street and pulled into the driveway. He reminded the children, "Remember, no more than twenty minutes."

When they returned Duncan was fishing through his dispatch case and pulled out his personal phone book He telephoned a business acquaintance. "Gene? I've got an emergency. Are you using your private plane this weekend? I need it for a mission of mercy. I have to go to Pennsylvania. No problem? Thanks, and your crew will be standing by? O.K. We'll probably be at the airport in say no more than two hours." As an aside, he said to the young people, "We can use his private jet."

The next number he phoned was a longtime college pal who was now Chancellor of Penn State University. "Tony? Dunk here. I need a big favor. I know this is the last minute, and summer school is starting soon. I've got two fine students for you. No, they're not my kids, but, well, they practically are. Anyway, I want you to do an old pal a favor and admit them and get them some dormitory space. Yah, I've heard that; kids don't want to live in dormitories these days like when you and I went to school, so dormitory space is available. O.K. I'm flying out tonight, and say hello to Maude. What? Tomorrow's Sunday, you know. Well that's very nice of you. You're sure it won't be a problem? O.K. We'll come to your house for dinner tomorrow around noon, and then we can go and look at the school afterward. Great. See you tomorrow noon."

The two children were speechless: "You two are going where your father cannot possibly find you. It's a great school. And I'm in and out of Pennsylvania every few weeks, and I'll come by to see how you're doing."

Victoria said sadly, "Father refused to discuss our going to college, even though our aunt and uncle said they would pay for it. He said that he hadn't needed to go to college, and we didn't need it either."

Duncan knew very well the risks of transporting minors out of state, but he was ready to take some risks. The children didn't know that Duncan had acted as their grandmother's attorney and was co-trustee with the bank of their grandmother's trust for them, and that income would be paid to their father until they were of legal age and the payments would include additional money for college expenses. The father wouldn't complain about the children being gone. He would be relieved of the burden of caring for the children, and he would spend the money, including their college money, as he pleased.

Duncan headed straight to his apartment to pick up his suitcase, and they continued on to the airport. As he drove, he said to himself and hopefully to Carolyn if she were somewhere where she could read his thoughts, 'Carolyn, I'm doing this for us and these children that should have been our children.' He knew that for the rest of his life he would belong to Carolyn's memory; her death haunted him; he felt partly responsible for causing it.

CHAPTER VII

The Laird awakened the next morning to the sound of his alarm clock. He had to orientate himself as to where he was, but by the dim light he could see the heavy posters at the foot of the bed with the two squirrels standing as sentinels. He hadn't slept very well. As often happened, especially when he was overtired, he would have dreams about racing, and he would live or relive a race and wake up more tired than when he had retired. He glanced toward the heavy draperies at the windows and the bright outline of light around the edges. Probably a nice day. He remembered that he had resolved to start jogging this morning - if it didn't rain. He debated whether to postpone it another day or grit his teeth and do it. The decision was inevitable; he would jog.

He dressed in a gray tracksuit and Nike running shoes and headed out the front door and up the lane for the main road. He passed Jeffrey at work with Fergus at his side and two other young men that he hadn't seen before. They had started to accumulate a pile of rubbish at the side of the drive. When he passed them they all stood and Jeffrey greeted him, "Good morning, Sir; looks like its going to be a nice day".

"Morning, my Lord," added Fergus, touching a knuckle of his hand to his forehead. The other two young men said nothing.

The Laird acknowledged their greeting and moved out through the gate. Mrs. MacOster, the gatekeeper, had seen him coming and had it swinging open. He nodded to her as she stood in her doorway and stopped on the road just outside the gate to decide which way to go, left or right.

The road slanted gently downward to the left and upward to the right. He decided it would be more sensible to start off slowly and first go downhill about a quarter of a mile and then return to the point of the gate and continue uphill another quarter of a mile and finish up with an easy jog back downhill, altogether about one mile. Later he would gradually extend the distance.

The road was macadam, dun colored from age and weathering. Other than the castle there were only two homes to be seen in either direction - the farmhouse adjoining the castle property to the north on the other side of the Kirkwhapple Burn; he would pass it going down hill and a second house to the south of the castle property on the east side of the road, and he would pass it when he returned uphill beyond the castle gate. As far as the eye could see everything was hilly, slanting westward down toward the ocean, and the hillsides were dotted with animals - cattle and sheep. The weather in the local area was ideal for raising either sheep or cattle. The grass grew abundantly to a length of eight inches or more and bent over, giving the countryside a lush green appearance. An animal would have to move very little distance in its lifetime for its food.

The Laird took a deep breath of the moist morning air; he could smell the green grass; and he started down the hill feeling virtuous for having honored his resolve to start exercising. When he got part way he was passed by a girl (he was sure), a little taller than average, in a blue jogging suit, and wearing a blue baseball type cap, but with a longer peak. A red ponytail protruded from the rear of the cap. She ignored him and sprinted in the opposite direction up the hill. As he was returning upward he met her coming downward. He stopped opposite the gate of the castle to catch his breath. Mrs. MacOster swung the gate open, assuming he wanted to enter. But he motioned for her to close the gate. At that moment the girl jogger stopped. Both were perspiring from the exercise, and the Laird was puffing slightly.

Despite the beads of perspiration on her face and her flushed cheeks, his impression was that she had a healthy, attractive face with lovely green eyes. She greeted the Laird with a dazzling smile and a crisp English accent. "Do you live in here with the new Laird?"

"Yes, I do," he replied.

Detecting his American accent, she said, "Oh, you're a Yank too, like the Laird. Is he easy to work for? How long have you worked for him?"

"Well, I guess I've worked for him most of my working life. Sometimes he's easy, and at other times I guess he can be frustrating."

"What do you think the Laird's going to do with the castle? Is he going to keep it, or just live in it until the novelty wears off and then sell it?"

Duncan was surprised at the questions, but the Scots can be direct in their speaking and he liked it. He replied, "Miss - ah?"

"Kerrie, Kerrie Bramwood."

"Kerrie," he mused. "Sounds Irish."

"No. It's an old Scottish name. It's spelled C-h-e-r-r-i-e, but the Ch is like the Ch in Christian, and it's pronounced Kerrie."

"Well, Kerrie, you can never tell what the Laird's going to do. Some people say he's unpredictable. Sometimes he surprises even me. So, I guess I can't tell you what he's going to do with the place. But right now it looks like he's going to spend a ton of money fixing it up." He enjoyed the repartee with her direct manner and crisp English accent.

"And what might your name be?" she asked.

"My friends often call me Al."

"That's all, just Al? Don't they call you something else?"

"Well, they call me Lawman too."

'Strange name,' she thought, 'Al Lawman, but many Americans do have funny names.' "Well, let's be very American, and I'll call you Al, and you can call me Kerrie."

"Sounds great to me - Kerrie. And where did you get that English accent, what with your Scottish name?"

Her voice turned guttural and using broad a's and rolling her r's she replied, "For sure ya dinna know, but I lived here as a young wean, and then me athair moved to England, and I lived most of me life there. And now I've come back to the auld sod and live nearby here, I do"

"Fascinating," was all the Laird could respond.

Back to Oxford English again. "Do you think someday you might show me a bit of the castle, maybe when the Laird isn't there?"

He smiled. "Well, the Laird has strict rules about a lot of things, but nobody breaks his rules more than I do, and I think it could be arranged."

"I'd be so delighted. I jog out here almost every morning, rain or shine, and when you think the time is right let me know." She started to turn away, and stopped. "Do you play tennis?"

"Do I play tennis? Yes, I guess I do. Although I haven't played much lately. Tell me where do you live?"

But she had already taken off like a shot up the hill and was out of earshot. He decided to finish his jogging. Maybe he would see her again. As he jogged up and down the hill he kept glancing up from the road. She was nowhere to be seen.

Mrs. MacOster was at the gate waiting for him as he jogged into the castle yard. He stopped and asked, "Who was that girl that I talked with on the road?"

"Her. She be Kerrie Bramwood. Lives alone in the wee house on t'other side of the road, just at the end of the castle property, this side of the brig (bridge). Moved in a few weeks ago. But the Bramwoods has owned the house more than a hunder years. Knew her mither well. Gude people. Used to come in summer for holidays. House was empty rest of the time."

A tradesman was tinkering with the motor on one of the castle gates, and he approached the Laird. "Sir, I came by to be sure all was in order. And your Mr. Granville asked me about an alarm system for the castle. I told him that it wouldn't be practical to put an alarm system into something of that age. I suggested that you get one or two dogs."

The Laird nodded. "I like German shepherds, always had one when I was a boy."

The tradesman advised, "Because of the wars with Germany we call them Alsatians. If that's what you like, there's a good breeder just this side of Ayr on the main road. You can't miss their sign. Got a dog's head painted on it."

The Laird thanked him and continued walking down the lane toward the castle at a good pace. He noticed that the four gardeners were over near the greenhouse, listening to Fergus, who was pointing at something in the garden.

He liked the girl jogger. She seemed like the type that could be a good friend. He didn't have the slightest romantic notion, and of course she might be married; although Mrs. MacOster did say she lived alone. He preferred to meet people by chance that didn't know him. Having been a celebrity, he felt that everyone he had met who knew who he was, was trying to work him for something; so he was cautious when introduced to people.

After the Laird showered and finished his breakfast, Granville approached him. "Sir, the fax machine has been active, and we have over fifty pages of material that came in during the night from your law office in the States. And Counselor MacKim telephoned this morning. He said that, if you're able, he's arranged the appointments tentatively for tomorrow in Edinburgh - I told him that your schedule looked pretty good for tomorrow. And he wants to know what time would be convenient to start in the morning."

The Laird began, "Tell him 8 A.M., right after breakfast." He stopped. "No, tell him 9 A.M. I'll be jogging tomorrow morning. And, Granville, what do you think of the idea of getting a dog, a guard dog for the castle?"

"Splendid idea. Security man advised it," answered Granville.

The Laird spent the rest of the day at his desk reviewing the faxed legal documents and had several long telephone conversations with his law office. He had hoped that as he spent more time overseas that his partners would shoulder more of the burden. But the demands for his time seemed to be increasing.

After dinner alone in the great room, he went into the storage area below and dug through some of the papers in the coffers to get a better idea of the contents for the meeting with the man at the University Library in Edinburgh the next day.

CHAPTER VIII

Kerrie Bramwood, thirty-two years old, lived alone in the house just east of the castle property. The house was early 19th century, larger and better built than the typical local farmhouse. There was a garden and a sizable garage, which must have been the carriage house at one time, and a sizable area of trees and grass, the whole covering about twelve acres.

She had lived the early years of her life in the house. Her father was a civil engineer. When she was ten he took a job in London and the family moved there. After grammar school she studied for four years at the University of London, majoring in the history of the British Empire - emphasis on Scotland. Afterward she spent two additional years at the University of Edinburgh for intensive study and research in Scottish history. Her ambition had been to write books on Scottish history. There seemed to be a lot of unanswered questions. Her first job was working as an assistant editor for a book publisher in London. Her associates discouraged her from trying to write the 1,000th book on Scottish history. Unless she could uncover some new material, no publisher would touch her book.

Her own family was closely tied to Kirkwood Castle. The Thirteenth Laird in the early 1800's had sired a child by a local girl who worked in the castle as a maid and kitchen helper. The relationship was active and he built for her the house across the road where she lived and raised the child - a boy. After the death of his wife, Thirteen began proceedings to adopt him. There was no issue from his marriage and the boy would have become the Fourteenth Laird. Kerrie had heard all of her life from her parents that Thirteen had instructed his solicitor to draw up the necessary papers. Unfortunately for the boy, the Laird died suddenly, his mother disappeared, and the legal proceedings were not completed. Kirkwood Castle passed to the Laird's brother's daughter.

As a child, Kerrie had often fantasized about gaining ownership of Kirkwood Castle. She had seen the letter to the attorney, or a copy of it, which had become grimy and dog-eared over the years, but it had disappeared somewhere with others of her father's papers.

Kerrie had any number of male friends throughout her school years. Her first serious attachment was a young professor at the University of Edinburgh while she was pursuing her postgraduate studies. She had once mentioned to him an ancestral tie to the Semples and Kirkwood Castle, and he had taken it to mean money and status. He pursued Kerrie so vigorously that she felt she had found true love. He talked of marriage. When he learned more specific details of the ancestral connection and that there would be no money or social status, he shifted his attentions to another student. This hurt Kerrie deeply and left some scars, and it made her cautious about accepting male attentions.

When Kerrie took her first job in London, she lived with her parents. During that first year, her parents took an inexpensive tour to Egypt and North Africa, and when they returned both had contracted hepatitis complicated by amoebic dysentery. Both were virtually bedridden and her father was unable to work, and that winter he died. Her mother had survived until six months ago, but had never recovered her full strength. Kerrie took care of her for six years. After the mother died she gave up the rental flat on the outskirts of London and moved to the house next to the castle. The work she did could be done at home, and she traveled to London and back by train once every three or four weeks.

While she was a student at the University of London a friend had introduced her to a tennis coach; he was one of the trainers for the British Olympic Team and also had a number of professionals with whom he worked. Kerrie was an above average player, but had no interest in pursuing tennis seriously. He needed an assistant at the time - someone to hit the balls back and forth with his students and clients and there was a modest compensation that she could well use.

For hours at a time she would hit lobs to every part of the court or feed the backhand of a player from every part of the court. Or serve to a player putting 'English' (Irish the coach called it) on the ball; she learned to create spin in any direction. The coach emphasized that the condition of the legs is as important as the arms, so she frequently paced players for their running exercise. In truth, while she was training others she was being trained.

At one point the coach asked her if she would like to work toward being a professional tennis player. But sports were not her priority. She did enjoy the exercise and the contact with the players, but her first loves were history and research.

Despite her disappointing love affair and the long siege of caring for her sick parents, she had always maintained her positive personality and enthusiasm for life. She well knew the difficulties of living on a tight budget and sometimes wondered what it would have been like to live like a laird in Kirkwood Castle.

While Kerrie did her editing, a part of the job was to verify dates and facts, and for these she would visit a major library - now that she was in Scotland the University Library in Edinburgh. And while in Edinburgh she might also wander through some of the stores in the city.

Shortly after her move to Scotland, on her first trip to Edinburgh she had passed a bookstore, and on the street in front was a cart with a number of used books and a hand printed sign that read "any book on this table 50p."

A small green book caught her eye; the title on the outside was printed by hand in white ink or white paint - "KIRKWOODENSIS." She well knew the name Kirkwood and picked up the book and scanned it. It was clearly a homemade type of book with typewritten pages and pictures and drawings pasted in. She scanned the text and noted that someone had written details about the construction of Kirkwood Castle and its secret passages, and it indicated that the castle was built on a large finger of land directly over a cave or several caves.

She purchased the book for fifty pence and took it home for further study. Despite some missing pages, there was enough information in the book to describe the interior passageways - two separate and distinct networks which connected with the cave or caves below and two outside accesses to the caves - one from the west and one from the south, both on the steep hillsides above the rivers that flowed past the castle grounds.

The poverty and penury of the Seventeenth Laird was common knowledge and gossip in the village. Even his 'nephew' Riddall had talked openly about it to shopkeepers in the village and bragged how he was supporting the old man, and how he would be the next laird. She and the other local people couldn't understand how the Sixteenth Laird could have lived in total luxury, entertained large numbers of people regularly in grand style, and yet Seventeen was so poor. The wife of Sixteen had appeared in church wearing the Kirkwood emerald (it was worn by a number of the wives of Semple Lairds for generations and could be seen in the oil paintings in the castle) just a few weeks before her death and the assumption of the lairdship by Seventeen. The emerald was the size of the old large English penny and was surrounded by a cluster of sizable white diamonds, and it was rumored to be worth enough to buy a castle. She was convinced that Seventeen had not found it, and the emerald and other valuables were still hidden somewhere in the castle.

Now that she had the 'Green Book' her plan was to gain entrance to the castle through the underground caves and search for the emerald and other valuables. There might still be some of the original wealth taken from the MacBrooms centuries ago; rumors to that effect still circulated. If she found anything she would simply take what was her birthright. If there was enough, she might buy Kirkwood Castle when the Yank got tired of it. However, she had to get into the castle and get a feel of the room layout; the interior was not totally clear as some of the pages were missing from the 'Green Book.'

She had originally expected to cope only with three people in the castle, and when she read in the local paper that the castle had been sold, it introduced a totally new problem - there were more people inside the gates with a parade of tradesmen streaming in and out. Kerrie's fortunate encounter with 'Al Lawman' might, however, be playing right into her hands. If she could get a tour of the inside, it could be a giant step forward on her plan. She had already checked the outside of the hill on the west side. But the entrance was closed in. It had either collapsed or had been dynamited.

The access on the south side was not readily apparent. The spot where the entrance would be located was covered with bramble and brier and that would take closer exploration. She would have to learn the habits of the new occupants and enter the castle grounds when they were away. There was a sizable opening in the outer fence by the road, and she could enter the grounds without passing the gatehouse, but that might be repaired in due course and the sooner she acted the better.

She didn't feel that it would be a theft if she found valuables that the present owner didn't know existed. Theft was depriving someone of something; but how could you deprive someone if they didn't know they were being deprived? She was determined, and she would see that her plan played out.

CHAPTER IX

The next morning the Laird awakened and immediately got into jogging togs and headed for the outside road. Kerrie Bramwood must have been jogging back and forth near the gate when he exited, as she was right there to greet him. "Hello, Al Lawman," and "Hi, Kerrie," and as he started jogging down the hill, she fell in alongside him.

He liked the company of someone else running alongside - made it seem easier. And he had to admit to himself that the rhythm of their bodies moving together was quite pleasant. It took his mind off the effort he was expending, and the two seemed to float together side by side. They went first down the hill and then all the way up and back to his starting point without speaking a word. She had paced many a professional tennis player, but today she would just run along and not push him too hard. When they stopped, he was puffing and perspiring generously; she was barely winded.

When he seemed to be getting his breath back, she asked, "Where did you live in the States?"

"In the Midwest, on the shore of a large interior lake - Lake Michigan."

"Is that where you were born and raised?"

"Born and raised there."

"Where's your wife from?"

"I don't have a wife. I guess I've been so busy, that I haven't had time for one."

She volunteered, "I'm in the same boat. I'm too busy studying and working to fit marriage into my life."

That placed things openly on the table for both. She clearly was not on the hunt for a spouse, and neither was he, but he thought she nevertheless could be a pleasant jogging companion.

She was itching to get back to playing tennis and asked, "How would you like to play tennis one day?"

"Where do you play?" he asked.

"There's a place over by the school in the town, and if we go while school's in session, the courts are open."

"I warned you that I haven't played in quite a while, but if you're game, I'll try it. I'll have to pick up a racket first."

"That's no problem," she volunteered. "I've got a couple of extra racquets."

They agreed on a meeting for tennis three days hence. The Laird thought that while he hadn't played much, he usually didn't have much trouble playing tennis with women. Most of them were not strong players. He would pick up a racquet today in Edinburgh. Also, if things worked out like they did in the Midlands, he should begin to make the acquaintance of some of the local gentry pretty soon, and they might let him use the courts on their estates; he had seen several nearby while he was driving about.

MacKim was waiting for him when he finished breakfast, and they rode in his car. Today they would cut northeast through the moors and several small villages; no major motorway, but an easy two-hour trip. Along the way MacKim pointed out landmarks and things of interest.

"Before we visit the library, let's talk about the papers in the coffers," suggested the Laird. "I've looked through them several times. They're a giant hodgepodge, and just sorting them will take months. Maybe the people at the library could recommend someone to help. And most of the lairds seemed to have kept diaries, particularly Thirteen who left numerous diaries, usually more than one book for a single year, and although I only quickly flipped through a number of pages, it looked like many of his entries were in a kind of code."

"Thirteen," mused MacKim. "Wasn't he the judge? The High Court of Session Judge? He was famous. We had to read some of his opinions when we were students. If his diaries are extensive, they might contain some interesting information. And by the way, as your lawyer, I would advise you to keep a diary of your daily activities- especially your whereabouts. A person in your position - there's always somebody out there who's going to want to get into your pockets. If you have a clear record of where you are at all times, it's useful as a defense. Some strumpet might come along and claim you took her to a hotel in Glasgow and abused her, but if you've entered in your diary that you were in the castle that night and had so and so to dinner, that could be all important." It was good advice, and at the first stops in Edinburgh he purchased a large diary, a couple of tennis racquets and a generous supply of tennis balls.

Next they went into an antique furniture store that had contacted them about several pieces of furniture - a long side table and two chairs -that the Laird was very sure were from the small drawing room, and also a bed which had been in the fourth floor bedroom, undoubtedly the bed in which Christina Rossetti had slept. When the dealer first named a price, MacKim frowned. "For this old stuff? It's going to take a fortune to restore it. Maybe someone else will be happy to deal at your price."

The Laird stood off to the side while MacKim negotiated. He saw him shaking his head 'no,' and he started walking to the door, motioning for the Laird to follow. Before he got to the door, the dealer was at his side and agreed to deal at MacKim's price. They arranged for delivery and payment. On the street the Laird remarked, "I'd hate to be on the other side of a court battle with you as my opponent."

MacKim answered in a matter of fact tone, "You're forgetting that I'm a solicitor, not an advocate, but I do a bit of court work from time to time. Let's go to the book dealer and see how anxious he is to get rid of the books."

They got in the car and drove a half dozen blocks, and parked in front of the bookstore. As they walked toward the entrance, they passed a cart with used books; the sign said, "any book on this table 50p." MacKim advised the Laird, "This doesn't look like the typical shop where one would expect to find expensive books and fine bindings. Looks more like a shop for popular novels and paperbacks."

When they entered the store, MacKim again took the lead, asking if he still had the books that were supposedly from Kirkwood Castle. The shopkeeper walked to a room in the back of the store and returned with two books, which he placed, on the counter. He opened the covers to reveal the castle's bookplates.

The books were old novels whose authors were unfamiliar. The Laird leafed through each of them, looked at MacKim and shook his head 'no.'

"Do you have any more?" asked MacKim.

"I did have more, but they're gone. Sold," replied the shopkeeper.

"Thank you, anyhow," said the Laird and they left.

"And now let's have lunch," suggested the Laird looking at his watch, "so that we can be on time for the appointment with the Lord Lyon."

They drove a short distance up the street to the George Hotel and parked the car. From there it would be a short walk to their next call. They ate in the hotel restaurant where MacKim was well known.

The visit to the Lord Lyon's office was pleasant. The Lord Lyon himself received them. He advised the Laird that technically he was a 'sub-vassal' of the queen, and that he was indeed entitled to a grant of arms. They spent some time talking about what might be appropriate for the design. The Lord Lyon was not only a judge, but also a very cultured gentleman - very interested and knowledgeable in heraldry and Scottish history. He took them to the artists' workroom, which adjoined his office, and they watched one of the artists, a lady, painting a magnificent coat of arms on leather vellum. They left, being promised that within a few weeks they would be receiving a proposed sketch.

The last call was at the University of Edinburgh Library, where they were received by the Chief Librarian himself, a Mr. Robert MacDonald. He was quite interested in their offer to work together. He commented that most people wouldn't offer to share historical information with anyone, or for that matter, be interested in exploring the possibility of historical value in a cache of old documents. He impressed them with his integrity by saying that he had had one of his assistants check their archives, and that there were a number of old documents from Kirkwood Castle in the library, and that the correspondence indicated that they were on loan for some research that had been done many years ago, and that they were indeed the property of the castle and would be returned anytime they wished.

MacDonald offered to come to Kirkwood Castle when they began their study of the coffers and felt he could save them some time by suggesting things that might be of historical interest. It was an exciting project for him, and he talked over an hour about the history of the area near the castle.

The Laird advised him that there were literally thousands of items, to be examined and studied, in Latin, old English, old Scottish, and modern English, and if he could suggest someone to help they could get started anytime. MacDonald excused himself for five minutes and came back with an envelope, and handed it to the Laird. "Here's the name and address of a person in the nearby area of Kirkwood Castle who might be interested; you can try. If Kirkwood Castle were closer to Edinburgh you could use some of the graduate scholars at the university, and that's still a possibility, but only during the summer months. This type of project should be handled only by a trained person. An amateur would miss too many things."

The Laird put the envelope in his pocket. They were invited to stay on for tea, but they begged off and set a date for MacDonald to visit the castle the following week. None of the party envisioned it at the time, but MacDonald would become a regular monthly visitor at Kirkwood Castle.

CHAPTER X

The Laird loved dogs. As a boy he always had a German shepherd. He was hoping to find a nice animal at the kennel recommended by the locksmith. He jogged that morning, but didn't see Miss Bramwood. She must have been out at the usual time, and he had been half hour later than usual.

After breakfast he took the Land Rover and head for Ayr. He returned a couple of hours later with a nine-month-old female Alsatian that had been trained as a guard dog.

The Laird spent the rest of the day introducing the dog to the rest of the staff and walking the dog about the castle property, inside and outside. He was impressed that having introduced staff members as 'friends' only once, the dog remembered and allowed each person to approach and pet it. Everyone was delighted with the dog, and it appeared that it would make a good addition to the household. And the dog's new name was Ogier. The castle dog had always been named Ogier.

CHAPTER XI

The next day was Sunday. The Laird assumed that his jogging friend would be taking a day off, and, if he were going to church and having dinner with the Reverend, he would need the rest of the day to review legal briefs that were piling up.

He became absorbed in his legal work and almost missed getting to church on time. He walked in as the service was about to begin, and he noted the relieved expression on Reverend MacTaggart's face as he was sitting down in the front pew to which he had been escorted. Despite the many empty seats, he could detect a buzzing around the room as he sat down. He glanced across the aisle toward a seat on the right; a lady in a large hat was looking directly at him; she nodded and smiled.

The service took about an hour. It was familiar to him, except for the sermon. The young minister had selected what the Laird might term a modern or offbeat theme for his sermon; it was built around the 'Sayings of Confucius.' As he got into it, the topic clearly had some messages for the new Laird, particularly that the elite class had responsibilities to fulfill for the rest of the people, but also they should take unto themselves the rights and privileges and customs of people with their status, as the rest of the world expected it, and society functioned better with a structure, and it also gave people something for which to aspire, or words to that effect. The Laird didn't quite catch all the thoughts. But he got the message, 'he should act like a Laird, do it in style, and he also had some responsibilities.'

At the end of the service he followed the people out, and from his front row seat he obviously was last. It was clear that several people had lingered expecting to be introduced to the new Laird - the provost of the small town and his wife, and Lady that, and Baronet this, and Dame that.

The signal event that happened in those few minutes was when Baroness Auldlay, the lady in the large hat, approached him. "My husband and I would be pleased if you would have dinner with us some evening, perhaps this coming Wednesday if you're free? There'll be just a small group."

The Laird had been through this routine when he had purchased the manor home in the Midlands. He responded, "I'd be delighted to join you." In effect this would be his local 'coming out party' where the local lords and gentry would get a chance to look him over, and after that the telephone would either ring regularly or it would be silent.

The church manse, like the church, was from the Victorian era, and the principal rooms were all paneled with heavy mahogany. The dinner was pleasant and well prepared. At one point the Laird remarked about how much he was enjoying the leg of lamb - the best he had ever tasted. The housekeeper was in the room and heard the comment. Without a doubt she would relate his remark all over the village for the next two weeks.

The Laird found the minister to be a broad-gauged young man and well educated. He had come from a prominent family north of Ayr. His family home, almost a castle, and the lands were passed down to his oldest brother. He related how he had felt resentment until he watched his brother try to maintain the estate with the income from raising cattle and sheep. What had been a lucrative piece of property in former generations was a millstone around his brother's neck - they were property poor. The Reverend seemed reconciled and dedicated to his chosen profession, and appeared determined to do more than just provide Sunday services.

The conversation at the dinner table was general, mainly learning each other's background. Afterward, they moved into the library for coffee, and the topics became more serious. First off the Reverend asked, "What was your reaction to my sermon?"

Not wishing to be other than complimentary to his host, the Laird was non-committal. "It was very interesting. Maybe you could expand on your thoughts. I would enjoy hearing more."

"Well, I was trying to make two points. First off, let me say that despite my relatively short tenure here, it's very clear that the people in the village take a great interest in what goes on in the castle, and in a way whatever happens in the castle reflects on the pride of the whole village. For example the last laird..."

"That would be Seventeen," interjected the Laird.

"Yes, Seventeen. Some of the stories about him and especially his niece and nephew were shameful. No one was sorry to see them leave. The previous laird - Sixteen? - had grand parties, important people coming to visit, a lot of foods supplied to the castle from the village, extra help all the time, - the whole village gets the picture and they feel proud that they are indirectly part of it. And a lot of the villagers' ancestors were a part of the castle in its early history; some fought for it in distant days when it was under siege. Now they can tell from the number of tradesmen going in and out that the castle is pointed again in the direction of its former grandeur.

"And what did I mean by fulfilling some responsibilities? I'm not really sure. But there is sadness in this town - something pervasive. I think it's because the world's changed and the economy is no longer mainly agrarian. And you know in the past the little seaport was active when ships were smaller; and there were numerous fishing boats before there were quotas. Today that's all gone. I have two wishes for the village. One is how to find jobs for the young people so they don't leave as soon as they finish school. The other is that we have some young people who have superior intelligence, and it won't be utilized. Our school system categorizes the students too fast. They'll wind up being laborers when they could be scientists or professionals in almost any major field. I'd like to find some way to spark and unleash that potential. If you have any thoughts on this, let me know. I'm not talking about scholarship money; I'm trying to think of a way to make the lamp burn brighter in some of these youngsters before the light goes dim and burns out before they're in their twenties."

The conversation next shifted over to the Laird's projects of restoration of the castle building and the grounds and of sorting and studying all the documents in the coffers. The latter was particularly fascinating to the young minister, and he said, "Before I decided on the ministry my college studies were concentrated in history. I'd love to come over some time and see what you have. I'm an amateur on the subject, but I've never lost interest."

They spent the next hour talking about Scottish history, and it was obvious that the minister was not a rank amateur. His memory was photographic, and he talked on like an encyclopedia. It was after three o'clock when the Laird glanced at his watch. "I'm sorry, but we'll have to continue this conversation sometime at the castle. Let me call you and we'll fix a date."

After the Laird left it was only a few minutes up the hill from the village and a right turn, and his Chevy Corvette was in front of the castle gate. He slowed to turn, but on impulse continued up the hill. When he reached the house of Kerrie Bramwood, he started to turn into the lane and came to a dead stop with the front tires just off the main road. He wondered why had he stopped there; maybe the car had a mind of its own? He backed up and continued up the hill.

Inside the house Kerrie heard the car motor and looked out the window and saw the Laird. Her first impulse was to improve her appearance, but he backed up and drove off. When he reached the top of the hill, he turned around and went back down and again drove the car just off the road into her lane. Once more he found himself wondering, 'Just what am I doing here? I shouldn't bother people on a Sunday to talk about—to talk about what?' He lingered a few moments and again she looked out the window to see him back out and continue on down the road. She was puzzled and thought about it on and off throughout the rest of the day. He was annoyed with himself, because he couldn't conclude why he had ventured into her yard in the first place.

After arriving at the castle, he spent the rest of the day clearing away the pile of legal work. At one point he glanced at the envelope on his desk that had been given to him by

MacDonald the librarian. He opened it. The possible research assistant they had suggested was Miss Kerrie Bramwood.

CHAPTER XII

The next morning the Laird bounced up promptly when the alarm sounded, dressed in his jogging outfit and headed straight for the road. He started down the hill on the first leg of his routine. Kerrie was jogging up the hill, and when they met she fell in beside him and they finished his routine together. Outside his gate, he motioned for her to stop.

He paused to get his breath, smiling at her a few times; Kerrie returned each smile. She concluded that he had something on his mind and undoubtedly that's why he had stopped in her driveway yesterday.

Finally, the Laird spoke. "Kerrie, you mentioned that you wanted to visit the castle, and I think I can arrange it. What's a good time for you?"

She pretended to look at an imaginary watch on her wrist, pursed her lips slightly, and said, "I think I can fit it in my calendar anytime during the next month, starting about one hour from now."

The Laird smiled. "How about coming over at ten o'clock this morning. This will take some time. Just to see the principal rooms is pretty much an all day effort. We'll tour for two hours and take lunch at noon. Then start again around two and go until teatime. And I'll be frank. We have a number of things to organize in the castle and may need some help for a while. Don't be surprised if I ask you to help us - for pay of course."

What kind of job he might be offering her, she couldn't visualize. But she could use some extra cash; the house she was living in had only been used as a summer retreat for many years and needed quite a few things to make it more livable. She held out her hand, "It's a date. Ten sharp. I'll be there"

The Laird took her hand and his mind suddenly wandered to another place and another time. After part of a minute she said sweetly, "If you want me there at ten o'clock, you'll have to let me have my hand."

His face flushed. "Oh. Excuse me. I was thinking of something else. See you at ten."

When she arrived at ten o'clock, he was waiting outside the front door. She had debated what to wear and fully expected to meet the Laird. The weather was cool and she opted for a shapeless two-piece suit of Scottish tweed with a longer than average skirt and a bulky jacket. Since this was going to be an employment interview she decided no makeup, and she fixed her hair in a bun at the back.

It was the first time the Laird had seen her in other than jogging togs, and trying to think of something complimentary, he offered, "I like your suit. Hand made Scottish tweed?"

"Made the suit and the tweed myself. I have one of those little looms. As you might know the looming of Scottish tweed is a cottage industry. I don't sell any. I just make it up in different colors for myself. It's very practical for this weather, and wears like iron."

Entering the front door they were met by Ogier. The Laird patted Kerrie on the arm and said, "Friend. Friend."

She asked, "What's that about?"

He explained the routine with Ogier's training.

She said, "Do that again."

The Laird repeated the routine. This time tapping her arm five times, repeating the word friend. And he explained that now she could pet the dog if she wished. The dog was a new dimension in her plan to explore the castle clandestinely, so she accepted the offer to pet the dog. The dog must have gathered that she was a special friend, maybe the way he said the word friend, as she not only let Kerrie pet her, but after a few moments rolled over on her back.

"You've really made a hit with Ogier," observed the Laird. "She's usually cautious with strangers."

He decided to first show her the place and get her excited about the castle, and offer her the job afterward. And while they were touring, he would of course interview her as to her qualifications. But his instincts were that she was probably well qualified, and she had been recommended by MacDonald the librarian.

They started in the lowest level - the dungeon. It had twelve small cells, each a cubicle of about five feet square plus one larger cell. Most of the doors were missing from the cells, probably used for firewood at some time or other, and pretty much the whole area looked to be a receptacle for ordinary rubbish that should have been tossed out long ago. Arrangements had been made for a large skip to haul away the rubbish.

Walking about the keep, the Laird continued, "We don't have an armory as such, but I think there's enough of a collection of old pikes, swords, maces, battle axes and what have you in the storage area so that we can make quite a display on the walls in here and turn this area into a veritable museum. That open area over there - I can't guess what it was used for, but there's a big wooden figurehead from the prow of a sailing ship, and it could be mounted on that wall and make an interesting conversation piece."

They proceeded up to the main level, the level of the front entrance hallway.

"This is a beautiful front entrance hall, but it's almost completely empty, like a barn. Down in the storage area there's a large coat of arms carved out of wood, about four feet square. That will be cleaned up and mounted on the wall directly opposite the entrance, and we'll put a few lances or pikes or halberds around it to make a statement to anyone coming through that door that they have indeed entered a medieval castle."

They next moved over to the Great Hall - still on the first level. The Great Hall was pretty much in tact with furniture, paintings on the walls, and many types of curios and pieces of china on cabinets, sideboards and shelves. Kerrie wanted to inspect every item carefully and speculate on its age and origin. The Laird had to prod her gently to keep moving so that they could cover the whole castle within the day. "In here," announced the Laird, "I've decided that there's nothing that needs to be done but clean up the place and restore the wood."

They walked up to the next level into the original main room. It has a massive, carved stone fireplace six feet high. "We'll use this as a small drawing room. A suit of armor is being brought from the Laird's manor house in the Midlands. It'll be put over there by the wall next to the window." He opened a cabinet door on the outer wall. "This was the original entrance, but now it's nothing but an empty closet. It will be lined with heavy cork and turned into a liquor cabinet and bar. On the back side of the room we might place a large open cabinet and place in it a collection of old china or glassware, of which there's an abundance throughout the castle"

As they went from room to room, he explained the plans for renovation. He tried to focus on the few items in each room that he thought might be the most important. But she pointed out items that might at first glance seem unimpressive or innocuous, yet were of definite intrinsic value and likely historical interest. Before they had proceeded very far along, he had taken her by the arm and gently guided her, so as to keep the tour moving. It quickly devolved into the two of them finishing the morning physically connected, arm in arm. Her level of excitement continued to build, and it became mutually infectious. The Laird was beginning to feel that here was someone that appreciated what he was trying to accomplish and could be a good helper.

Moving about they passed Granville in the hallway in his morning outfit with the gold and black striped vest. The Laird introduced her. "Miss Bramwood, this is Mr. Granville. Next to me, he's the majordomo in the castle."

Granville was pleased to see the Laird talking excitedly with his visitor. It was rare for him to be so lively and animated. He bowed slightly and gave her a friendly half smile, and said, "Madam."

As they walked away, the Laird whispered to her, "Sometimes I wonder if he isn't even more important than the Laird around here."

They passed Mrs. MacDuffie. Mrs. MacDuffie had known Kerrie since she was a child. Not well, but she knew her and where she lived, and Kerrie likewise knew her and greeted her cheerfully, "Good morning, Mrs. MacDuffie."

Mrs. MacDuffie noted that she was in the company of the Laird, on his arm, and he was obviously addressing her as an equal. She responded, "Good morning Miss Bramwood. It's a nice day isn't it?"

"It's a lovely day," enthused Kerrie.

Later they passed Jeffrey, and he addressed her exactly like Granville.

As they had gone from floor to floor, they used the tower steps which were quite wide, undoubtedly originally built to allow two people to pass, maybe even carrying trays, because of the old dining room on the third level. He walked next to her and supported her up the stairs. After two hours they had barely gotten half way through the planned tour. He guided her back to the tower steps and downward for lunch in the Great Hall.

During luncheon he stopping talking about the castle and asked about her background and schooling. He kept her talking about herself during the entire meal. She was impressed with the courteous service of the staff, but she thought it overmuch for two people - one of whom was an employee and one who might be.

At one point she inquired, "When do you think we'll talk with the Laird?"

He thought for a moment. "Right now might not be a good time to unveil the Laird. But I'm sure that'll happen in due course."

At two o'clock the Laird looked at his watch. "I think we'd better continue the tour if we hope to finish today."

Upon reaching the third level he continued, "There are only three rooms on this level which are very important. First, the old main dining room. This room is so far from the kitchen, that one has to wonder why it was used as a dining room. I guess labor was cheap and they didn't mind having servants run up and down the stairs. I don't think we'll use this as a dining room very much, maybe for teas if we're setting up the Great Hall for an evening dinner."

Kerrie was taken with the tapestries on the wall. "Aubusson?" she asked. "Magnificent, but it looks like they need a bit of help."

"Good question or guess," responded the Laird. "These two look like Aubusson, sixteenth or seventeenth century, but they could be imitations, and it would take an expert to tell. If any one of these were genuine, they'd be worth a fortune. They should be moved down into the Great Hall on the first floor. There is an inventory and an appraisal of the contents, which was made for the Seventeenth Laird. It's titled Appraisal for Purchase - made by a local dealer. More and more I'm wondering if he might have undervalued everything so he could buy things cheaply. But we'll get Christies up here sometime and determine the real values. And now the library."

They walked into the next room, the library. The walls were covered with richly carved wood paneling and shelving which went up to ten feet in height, requiring a ladder to reach the upper shelves. "This is a spectacular room, and I think it will easily hold all the additional books we'll be bringing up from the manor house. After it's thoroughly dusted out, we'll have to restore all this wood and the leather bindings on the books will have to be restored. Now to the fourth floor.

"We're only going to go into this large corner bedroom. It's in the oldest part of the castle and has windows opening on three sides - ideal for a principal guest room. Everything looks to be in the proper place here, including that little desk by the window - there's a beautiful view of the surrounding countryside. I understand that this was the favorite room of Christina Rossetti, the famous poet, when she was a visitor to the castle in the mid-eighteen hundreds, and that she wrote many lines of her poetry at that very desk.

"As to the rest of the bedrooms and small rooms we'll have to decide what to do with them later on."

Most of the interesting parts were in the older section of the castle, and Kerrie tried to focus on the entrances to the secret passageways that she had memorized. It was difficult, because the story of the castle and its possibilities was captivating, and so was the manner of 'Al Lawman' with his open, friendly, American manner. She enjoyed being with him - not only the conversation, but also she sensed beneath the friendly, charming manner a strong inner strength. She hoped she would be offered some kind of connection with the castle for a while. It could be pleasant work.

They had pretty well completed the tour of everything except the coffers by teatime. Both were weary from standing so long, but the enthusiasm had never waned. They were chatting nonstop as they entered the Great Hall. At this hour Granville was in his afternoon costume, as were Mrs. MacDuffie and her daughters and all four were involved in serving the tea. Again this seemed a bit much to Kerrie. But she didn't say anything.

When tea was nearly over, one of the MacDuffie girls had offered the Laird more tea, and he had declined, but as she walked away, he turned and spoke to her, "MacDuffie, I've changed my mind. I will have a little more please."

She turned and replied, "Yes, my Lord."

Kerrie looked at the girl puzzled, and she looked at the Laird. It flashed through her mind that 'Al Lawman' had spoken so authoritatively about everything that maybe he was the Laird.

But after the tea had been poured and MacDuffie had exited the room, the Laird explained to her, "She's just practicing. Granville is right behind that door, and he's training the new staff, and they've been serving you and me like we're the Lady and the Laird of the castle. He's a perfectionist, which you will learn if you join our little family." He paused. "And now let's go and view the piece de resistance." They left the Great Hall and walked down into the lower storage area.

When Kerrie saw the coffers and the Laird exhibited some of the documents, her first reaction was that this could be something that she could lose herself in, and it would probably take years to get through it all and make sense out of it. She momentarily forgot her original mission, and when the Laird said, "Now what do you think about helping us go through all this and seeing what should be saved, what should be tossed, and helping develop a plan for the things that might be of genuine historical value?"

She didn't hesitate. "When do I start?"

"You didn't ask what the pay would be," he teased.

She was bubbling with excitement and made a grand sweep with her arm in the direction of the coffers. "This is very exciting. The pay isn't important. I'd do this for nothing, well, almost."

"Let's go back upstairs and talk some more," suggested the Laird. They walked up to the small drawing room on the second level. As he supported her up the tower stairs, she felt that she needed it, as she was feeling a little giddy.

In the small drawing room she sat on the green leather chesterfield facing the fireplace, and he sat on an armchair at the side. "Let me outline further what I have in mind," he began. "The job has several dimensions. First of all the coffers. We should probably make several passes at it. Initially, we want to get a general idea of what's in those boxes. Then we should probably look at the things that might be of greatest interest, and at some point get at the things that need translating from Latin, and Old Scots and get some help with that."

She interrupted, "I'm quite familiar with translating old documents that relate to Scots history. I wouldn't be worth my salt as a researcher if I weren't."

"Great!" he continued. "That's even more than I had hoped for.

"The second part of the job is to make some sense out the library. There are over five thousand books on the shelves, as you saw today, and there are roughly that many more coming up in a few days from the house in the Midlands, and we might be buying back more that were sold out the back door of the castle."

She nodded in understanding.

"And one more thing we would appreciate is that we'll be shipping in more than a dozen filing cabinets from the last home. Part relate to the Laird's law practice in the States which he still supervises, part have a lot of memorabilia from his automobile racing days, and the rest have a lot of things that were saved over the years, including some manuscripts of things he's written, and all this should be sorted out and organized. Just as he's been meticulous in keeping the legal files, he's been meticulously disorganized with the others."

She nodded again in understanding. She would eagerly take charge of it all. (When she replayed the description of the job to herself later in the evening at home, she couldn't remember if he had spoken in the first person; he had been so authoritative. She finally decided that the Laird was lucky to have someone like this working for him. The salary he had offered was generous, and she had simply answered, 'Thank you.'

The Laird escorted her to the front door of the castle, and Granville was there holding her coat. The Laird walked out the door with her and up to the front gate. While they were walking he suggested, "You can start tomorrow if you wish, anytime after eight o'clock, but I'd really prefer to jog with you first. On second thought, just to accommodate an important member of the Kirkwood staff, I would be glad to jog at seven A.M., if you wish."

She thought for a moment, "Let's compromise and jog at 7:30 and I'll get over here as soon after 8:30 as I can."

When the Laird looked at his mail that evening, there was an invitation to dinner on Wednesday, from Baroness Auldlay confirming the conversation in the church on Sunday.

CHAPTER XIII

The next morning he went out to jog and met Kerrie who had already completed most of her longer routine. She told him that she had hardly slept all night thinking of all the possibilities of the new job, and as they jogged together she unconsciously paced him faster than she realized, and he had to ask her to slow down, adding that the job will wait until she gets there. When they finished his mile, she didn't stop to converse and sprinted to her house.

When she arrived at the castle, they had to decide where she would work. The lower storage area simply was not satisfactory the Laird told her, and after eliminating all possibilities, he suggested, "Why don't you sit in the wide hall on the third level, the 'Rogues Gallery,' opposite the library. The lighting is good, and you'll have a nice view of the gardens and the countryside. There's a washroom down the hall, and we can set up a routine with the MacDuffie girls to carry your stuff up or down at the beginning and end of every day." Her worktable was placed just opposite the painting of the Thirteenth Laird, her reputed ancestor. Next to the table were placed a sofa, an easy chair, a couple of straight chairs, and a small table with a tall lamp.

'And,' thought Kerrie, 'just down the hall next to the washroom is a room that has an entrance to one of the secret passageways.'

Kerrie spent most of the day looking through the coffers and the library and making notes. At one point she was approached by the Laird together with Granville asking her how she would go about getting someone to do some resurfacing of the stone on the outside of the building. She thought for a moment and said, "Let me work on it, and I'll solve it."

She made a number of phone calls, and by late in the day she had a good recommendation and had checked a couple of the references. Before the day was over Granville had come to her for advice on the placement of furniture in one of the rooms.

"Before we start to rearrange anything, I'd really like to make a drawing and inventory of everything in each room," requested Kerrie. "If we approach this whole project like an archeological dig, I think we'll learn a lot more about the history of the castle and its former inhabitants. I understand that some things have been here for the better part of two centuries. It's like excavating a modern Pompeii, and we're only beginning to clean away the top layer of ash."

Granville breathed a sigh of relief. "Miss Bramwood, I can't tell you how pleased I am to have you take this responsibility off my shoulders. You make the decisions and I'll see that things are done properly. Jeffrey was sent to the manor in the Midlands and should be returning by Wednesday with a large lorry load of furnishings, books, and so forth. When they arrive you can decide where to put them."

"Well, Granville, this falls into the category of contamination, albeit elegant contamination. I think we should carefully inventory everything old and everything new to the castle, and be careful not to mix them until we have a clear picture of the past."

That afternoon the Laird took a walk in the garden and noticed that in less than a week the major cleanup and cutting had improved the appearance 1,000 per cent. He found Fergus kneeling in one section and planting some new stock. He managed to get to his feet, and the Laird chastised him, "Fergus, with your arthritis, you're not supposed to be down on the ground."

Fergus smiled. "Yes, my Lord, but I feel better getting back to working with the plants." He pointed to the far rear corner of the garden. "We've got two men planting the kitchen garden. We should get plenty of vegetables out of there this year."

When it was teatime the Laird asked Kerrie to join him in the Great Hall. It was an opportunity for her to let him know how things were going. And he would welcome her company for tea.

When she sat down at the table, she began, "Al, I've got so much to tell you that I don't know where to begin. But I don't want to talk about the coffers yet. That would be like a doctor making a diagnosis before he's done all the proper tests. As to the coffers, I can see that if we're going to organize things we're going to need a variety of acid free envelopes like libraries use and we must segregate the things on bad paper that are contaminating other documents. And we should create a catalog system for everything.

"But talking of cataloging; let's talk about the library. Do you have any idea how long it will take to catalog 10,000 or more books? If a person spends only the bare minimum of ten minutes per book, including the typing of the catalog card, that's six an hour, or ten months of time just to enter the titles and the authors. However, if a library is going to be useful, the cataloger could spend anywhere from fifteen to forty-five minutes to develop cross-references for a single book. Looking at the present mix of novels and serious reference type books, my estimate is that the cataloging job would easily take a year and a half, if the person works a full five-day week.

"The coffers? I've no idea, but there's undoubtedly a minimum of several years work to get the material properly sorted and identified and evaluated.

"And then there are the Laird's personal files. I think that if I spent an hour a day, they could be put in pretty good shape in a matter of weeks."

The Laird listened intently until she was finished. "Well, I think we want to do it carefully; so let's spend whatever time is necessary."

"But what's your priority, the library or the coffers, or should I work on both each day?" queried Kerrie.

The Laird thought for a moment. "I like your thought of spending a little time each day on the personal files. In the long run it'll save time if things are organized. As to the other things, I hate to wait a year or more to attack the coffers while the library's being organized. Maybe you could work on both simultaneously. The real excitement is in the coffers, I think. Yet the Laird would hate to leave the library in a mess for an indefinite period. Give it some more thought."

CHAPTER XIV

For the next ten days no one took any time off from work except on Sunday. There was an endless list of things to be done. Progress was being made, but after a decade of neglect, things were being uncovered daily that needed attention. It was a massive job for Kerrie to evaluate the work to be done with the documents in the coffers. Granville seemed to be on the telephone constantly, and found it convenient to go to Kerrie each time he had to find a tradesman or when the housekeepers had a problem.

Two days after Kerrie joined the staff at the castle, fresh and potted flowers appeared. A large fresh arrangement was put into the Great Hall, a smaller one in the old main drawing room, some potted green plants in the front entrance hall, a bud vase with a single flower at Kerrie's workplace and an identical one in the Laird's room. At Granville's instruction Mrs. MacDuffie each day would place the single flower in the Laird's room on the night table on the far side of his bed - the side on which he didn't lie. Each day the Laird would move the flower onto his desk next to Carolyn's picture.

When Granville first saw the flowers he demanded of Mrs. MacDuffie, "Who ordered all of these flowers?"

"Fergus gave them to me to put around the house," she answered.

He next challenged Fergus, "Where did all the flowers come from? How much did they cost?"

Fergus was all smiles. "Miss Bramwood mentioned that the castle looked so cold that some flowers would make it more homelike, so I got some from ma friends. Didn't cost anything. Over the years Kirkwood had so many extra flowers that we shared in all directions. If I live another eighty years I can call in what they owe us for flowers. Pretty soon we'll have our own; they'll be even better." After that they had flowers regularly in the castle.

Another duty that Kerrie was drawn into was menu planning. After she was there a few days she approached Granville. "The food in the castle is not just good, it's excellent. However, I think that it's perfect for someone like you and the gardeners who are on your feet all day. But for those of us who are sitting all day, you'll soon have everyone up to twenty stone (280 lbs.)."

Granville nodded. "I'm weighing more than I should. I'd welcome any ideas for menus. Oftentimes I struggle to come up with something different." After that conversation Kerrie did the weekly menu planning.

A few weeks after he had taken possession of the castle, the Laird came out of the Great Hall after breakfast one morning and found the entire staff gathered in the hallway. The two MacDuffie girls were sitting on the steps leading to the tower - their faces ashen. "Sir," Granville began, "the young MacDuffies were going to enter the fourth floor bedroom in the old part of the castle, and they saw a woman sitting at the desk. When they entered she stood up, looked at them, and then evaporated into thin air."

The Laird looked at the two girls. Obviously, something had frightened them. He calmly asked, "Why don't you tell me exactly what you thought you saw?"

The two girls started talking at once. The Laird interrupted, "One at a time. And slowly."

The older of the two spoke, "We - we - were going to go - into the room - room - to tidy up like we usually do - do, and this woman in a black d-d-dress, was sitting at the desk. She g-g-got up and smiled at us and then d-d-disappeared into the air."

The other girl added, "And that's exactly what happened."

Mrs. MacDuffie took over the discussion. "It was her - Miss Christina Rossetti. I didn't want to frighten the girls. So I never told them that we all had seen Miss Rossetti many times when I worked here before. She never bothers anyone, except someone that might want to hurt the castle or someone in it. You might say that she doesn't haunt the castle - she tends it!

"She likes to sit at that desk, and if you move that black covered book of her poetry somewhere, you'll find it back at her desk the next morning. I didn't tell the girls because I thought maybe she wouldn't be here anymore." And looking directly at the girls she admonished in a firm voice with a thicker accent, "You've not' to worry. A ghaist she be. But, a gude un."

"Can you tell me more about your other experiences with Miss Rossetti," asked the Laird.

"Well, I can tell you all I know about ghosts here in the castle," offered Mrs. MacDuffie.

"Please," requested Granville.

"There's also two other ghosts. One is the Twelfth Laird, was a soldier. I never saw him, but Mrs. MacOster says she's seen him many times at night. He walks all around the grounds, and sits on the bench by the croquet field. He looks just like the painting on the third floor. A big man. Wears a kilt.

"When Sixteen was Laird, and I worked here at the time, two men tried to break into the castle one night when nobody was here. Used a ladder to get to a window on the second floor. One man went in first and when the other was at the top of the ladder, he saw someone in a kilt that looked like the Twelfth Laird standing inside the window, and he threw the first man out the window and into the yard twenty feet from the building. And they said that a woman in a black dress, could have been Miss Rossetti, she pushed the ladder backward. Both men had broken bones and were found when people came back to the castle a few hours later. Police said that only a very strong man could have thrown a person so far from the building.

"And the other ghost - and we never see this one, only hear him - is supposed to be Mister Dante Rossetti, Miss Rossetti's brother. When Mister Rossetti's wife died he put a big roll of his writings in her coffin. Later he wanted the papers, but the law wouldn't let him open her grave. He often came here to the castle - when Fourteen was Laird. Someone here told him to go up to his bedroom and open the window and breathe some fresh air and shout out the lines he could remember and the rest would come back to him. Sometimes people in the castle can still hear him shouting. I've heard it myself a number of times, and when we go up to his room, the window's open, but nobody's there. It happened one time when the minister was visiting here; he heard it too."

"Very interesting," commented the Laird. "But I think what I'm hearing is that these are friendly ghosts. So we needn't worry. And, girls, since your mother has experienced this many times, I think there's nothing to fear. If anything, they're going to protect us. If you see anything or hear anything, let me know right away. I'd like to meet them - particularly the Twelfth Laird." When the Laird reflected on the incident later, he wondered if by chance the large man in the kilt that had opened the gates for him that first morning was the ghost of the Twelfth Laird?

Granville clapped his hands twice. "And so, back to work." The two girls began to climb the tower stairs, holding hands, and peering around the curve in the stairway as they proceeded cautiously.

Later that morning Jeffrey drove into the yard in the Land Rover followed by a large lorry loaded with furniture and books and other items from the manor home in the Midlands. Kerrie had seen the truck enter the yard from her work table by the window on the third level and walked down to be sure that things wouldn't be mixed in with the castle furniture. When she arrived at the door she could hear one of the two removal men suggesting to Granville and the Laird, "Guv, since you don't know where you're going to put these things, why don't you just put them somewhere on the ground floor and later you can pop them here and there when you're ready. Kerrie glanced into the open doors of the truck, and could see some large pieces, and it would be a lot easier to hump them down the steps than up. She walked out and joined the conversation.

"It's really a hot day," she observed. "And you two good gentlemen must be quite weary having driven all the way up here. Why don't you go and sit over there in the shade, and I'll have someone bring you each an ice-cold lemon squash. And we'll get someone to move these things right off the truck and into the building for you."

The older trucker glanced at the younger man at his side and winked. "Certainly is a hot day ma'am. And thank you very much."

They started to take a few steps toward the bench in the shade when they heard Kerrie addressing Jeffrey who was walking up just then. "Jeffrey, would you go over to the school and ask the headmistress if we can borrow two girls, any two girls. Tell her we have to move some furniture." The two men stopped dead in their tracks.

"And Granville, may I borrow your pencil to take the telephone number of the company from the side of the truck. I think I shall call them and cancel the next load and get someone else. These men simply are not up to this kind of work."

At that point the two men were back in front of her. "Ma'am we didn't mean we wouldn't move the furniture. We'll put it anywhere you say. On top of that tower if you want."

And the second man protested, "We like to move furniture. Do it all the time. Yes ma'am. Just tell us where you want it."

Kerrie put one hand under her chin. "Hmmm, let me see. I think we want every bit of this on the fourth floor except those filing cabinets. They'll go on three. I'll show you where. And Jeffrey, would you please monitor these two while they move things up the tower stairway? Make sure they don't put the smallest scratch on the mural."

She turned to face the two movers. "There's a mural on the stairway walls. Quite valuable. National Trust. Do you know what that means?"

The two men nodded.

"If," she continued, "you put the tiniest scratch on that mural, you'll have all the National Trust people after you, plus the police, plus Scotland Yard. But you needn't worry about them, because before they get here I'll have chopped your heads off myself."

The two men were thoroughly cowed, and both answered softly, "Yes, my Lady."

When she walked back into the house, she was followed by the Laird and Granville. "Bravo," whispered Granville into her ear.

The Laird followed her down the hall, and remarked, "That was quite a show you put on with that pair."

Kerrie looked at him and said in a voice filled with resignation, "If the Good Lord hadn't intended for buildings to have four floors they wouldn't have four floors, but they do. I hate those kinds of disagreements. But sometimes we do what we have to do. Later on if we have to move things, it'll be a lot easier to hump them down rather than carry them up. And by the way, we'll inventory everything coming off the truck, and add it to the inventory of everything in the castle that I've started to prepare."

The Laird shook his head from side to side, "You certainly are a person of many talents." He walked off, and Kerrie returned to her third floor work area.

That week the Laird attended his first dinner party at the estate of Baron and Baroness Auldlay. The title was one of the oldest in Great Britain. The 'small' party had almost thirty people, which seemed to be all of the prominent local gentry. It was not only a superb dinner in an elegant setting, but the people were friendly and made the Laird feel welcome. Several remarked that they heard he was restoring Kirkwood Castle and were anxious to see it.

After the dinner the entertainment was provided by a man and woman who were folk singers. They sang old Scottish and old English folk songs to the accompaniment of their two guitars and soon had the guests singing along with them. The Laird learned that the routine was always the same - dinner plus some kind of entertainment.

When the evening was over, a number of the people said they hoped to see him again soon. He would find out in a few days. And indeed, as hoped, within forty-eight hours he received another two invitations to dinners the following two weeks. He had passed 'muster.'

CHAPTER XV

Kerrie busied herself during the first week and a half with her primary duties, as well as getting deeply involved in the household problems and routines. Granville welcomed her help, and in an establishment that size there was a lot to do. She enjoyed being a part of the Kirkwood family. They were good people. She was wondering when she would meet the Laird, but didn't have too much time to think about it, and her assignment, as instructed by Al Lawman, was very clear.

Her location on the third level was ideal. She didn't mind walking up and down the stairs several times daily, and being near the windows gave her a lot of light and a good view of the outdoors. One afternoon after her first few days in the castle, she made sure no one was on the third level, and she checked on the entry to the hidden interior passageway from one of the rooms in the old section. The sliding panel entryway worked easily, despite its age. She had no torch with her, but the opening looked clear, except for dust and cobwebs. Further exploration would have to wait until the staff had its weekly afternoon and evening off - probably next week Thursday.

Each day she took her lunch and tea with Al Lawman in the Great Hall. They had plenty to talk about, but she held off on her analysis of the total project until she could get a better reading. After a week she was ready.

"Al, I think I'm ready to make some recommendations. First, there's a librarian in the town. Her mother lives with her and is an experienced librarian. Used to work at the large Mitchell Library in Glasgow, but had to take early retirement. Some kind of problem with her legs. For a modest fee we can get her to do the book cataloguing. Either I or, if it's agreeable, Jeffrey, as he goes in and out of town almost every day, could drop off the books and pick them up.

"And that brings me to my second recommendation. If we're going to do a reasonable job of cataloguing books and the many documents in the coffers, we should consider getting a small computer and also a good copy machine. And with the computer we could also create an inventory of all castle items. I have already mentioned getting acid free envelopes and boxes, and I have an initial supply on order."

"Don't go any further, Kerrie. I've already been thinking about both a computer and a good copy machine. Let's get going on those right away. I think we could get either in Glasgow or Edinburgh. But didn't you say you have to go to London periodically? Well, I do too. So let's go together for a day. I'll make all the arrangements. I always stay at the Connaught, and so will you, if that's alright."

"Do you think the Laird would object?" she asked.

"Definitely not. The Laird's very progressive. Loves computers - any kind of machine. He'd applaud our thinking. So put it down on your calendar. Next Thursday. We'll try to arrive in time for dinner, and then do our shopping on Friday."

CHAPTER XVI

The first of the Laird's social invitations after the evening at the baronial estate of the Auldlays was from Lord and Lady MacKenzie. It was in some ways a carbon copy of the memorable dinner the previous week, and the guests were much the same list - the 'who's who' of the area near Kirkwood Castle. Overall the Laird had found the group to be interesting and well educated; almost everyone had had some part of his or her education in England - a few in schools on the continent. Two things made the evening quite an experience for the Laird.

At dinner the Laird sat next to a married lady who was pleasant, but who directed most of her attention to the partner on her other side. The lady on his other side (probably carefully planted, as the Laird decided later) was Saundra Morthland, spinster in her thirties and member of one of the wealthier families in Great Britain. A beauty she was not. She had the shape of a girl in her pre-teens; her hair was straight and cut off squarely above the shoulders, and she wore no make-up. Her sheath dress was suspended from two straps over her shoulders, without which it would have dropped to her ankles. Her only distinguishing feature was a bracelet of sizable diamonds - bespeaking her family wealth.

Again the dinner was sheer opulence - an elaborate table with flower arrangements, fine china, five crystal glasses at each place for the fine wines to be served, and almost as many liveried waiters as guests. As they took their places at the table, the Laird held her chair and introduced himself, "I'm Duncan Fleming, a new resident in this area."

"How do you do. I'm Sandy Morthland. So nice to meet you." When they were seated, she asked, "Please tell me about yourself."

The Laird gave her a sketchy background of himself. Each time he paused she would say, "How interesting," or "How very interesting."

He wasn't sure she was really listening, because she looked somewhat detached. When he felt he had told her more than enough about himself, he asked, "Now tell me about you." He waited for her reply.

When he stopped talking, she answered, "How interesting, how very interesting."

He knew that she hadn't listened to a word he had said. Putting together her appearance and her total lack of personality, he concluded that he could understand why she was unmarried, despite her family's wealth.

The hostess, Lady MacKenzie, was interested in the supernatural and whenever she had a dinner party there was always a séance. Some of the guests participated because of a genuine interest, others were simply curious, and others drifted off into the library or billiard room. It was her eccentricity and didn't seem to bother anyone. It reminded the Laird of a saying he had once heard: 'A Lady is always to be treated like a Lady, even if she swings on the chandeliers.'

The hostess took the Laird by the arm as they exited the dining room. "You must come and join our séance. We have a most distinguished medium tonight. She's from Glasgow and very hard to book. And who knows, she might have a message for you."

The Laird replied, "I've always wondered about the supernatural, and I'd be delighted to join you."

They went to a small sitting room which had a round table set up with a dozen or so chairs. The hostess placed the Laird next to her.

The medium was a woman in her late fifties or early sixties. She looked like a person one might pass anywhere on the street, totally undistinguished in her appearance. After the lights were dimmed, she asked everyone to hold hands to heighten the emotional transference and bent her head forward to concentrate. After a minute, she lifted her head, reached down on the floor, and took a gray wig like an advocate or barrister might wear and placed it on her head. After another minute she stood up and

89

began to speak to individuals at the table. Her voice was entirely different and she had a professional manner.

The hostess leaned over and whispered to the Laird, "She's been taken over by a deceased advocate, a woman, who was one of the first women to become an advocate in Scotland."

Most of her messages purported to be from a deceased relative and was something like, "I am well and happy, and I'm glad to see that you and the family are doing fine." She seemed to know her audience and this undoubtedly made her job (or act) a lot easier, or so thought the Laird.

When she came to his side of the table she put her hands on his shoulders and said, "Ah, I see I have a fellow lawyer here."

'That's no secret, the world knows I'm a lawyer,' thought the Laird.

"I have a several messages for you. The first is from a large man in a kilt. He says that he was your forerunner. He likes what you're doing, and that he'll help; you are not to worry."

'Sounds like she's referring to the Twelfth Laird,' Duncan thought. 'But if she knows the territory and has done her homework, there's nothing unusual in her message.'

"He also has a message for someone who lives with you in the castle, a woman with red hair. He says that you are to tell her to 'Look up'." That message was most cryptic, and the Laird decided not to bother to remember it.

The other person wishing to contact you is a handsome lady in a black dress, and she has a black book in her hand. She says you know her. Her message is, 'Someone very near to you loves you.'

'Oh, oh,' thought the Laird. 'First they plant Miss Morthland on me and now they give me a push. This clever lady with the wig also probably knows that Christina Rossetti haunts the castle.'

"Is there anyone you would like to contact?" asked the medium.

The Laird thought a moment and decided to throw one at her that she couldn't possibly know about. "Yes. My old chief mechanic, when I used to race automobiles. Name was Butch."

She appeared to concentrate for part of a minute and then said, "I have here a Butch who says he knows you well. Has a bad scar on his face. What would you like to say to him?"

The reference to the scar was a shocker to the Laird, but he wanted more proof of the contact and said, "Just tell Butch '72."

She repeated the message, waited and then repeated, "Butch says that he misses the old days and that he's still waiting for 72. Says you can send it to him by Federal Express,—and now he's laughing and fading out."

Number 72 was to have been the last facsimile trophy for the last race in which they had worked together. Butch had died before the Laird had number 72 made. The medium was asking the Laird if he had any other messages. But his mind had drifted off to the time Butch had died very swiftly of a heart attack. He didn't know that Butch had doctored for several years for heart problems, and it was a shock when he had died in bed one night. Duncan had attended the funeral and had gone back to his home afterward for a dinner with the family. He had never been in Butch's house before, and he was impressed that the living room was his trophy room. The walls were lined with the 71 facsimile trophies that he had given Butch from their numerous victories together. His wife told him that Butch was happiest if the grandchildren would point to anyone of them and ask to hear the story about that particular one, and he would be good for the next hour reliving that particular race.

Someone snapped on the overhead lights and the Laird was aware that the séance was over. His hostess remarked, "I'm pleased that the medium did have some messages for you. I hope you found them interesting."

'Indeed. I found them very interesting," remarked the Laird. "I would like to thank her."

"You needn't bother," explained the hostess. "She doesn't remember a thing after she takes that wig off."

The group moved into a large library and joined the remainder of the party for a nightcap and further conversation. Miss Morthland's brother approached the Laird. "So nice to be with you tonight, Duncan Old Boy. Sandy enjoyed your company at dinner. In a few weeks we shall be having a long weekend with friends at a little place our family has in the Highlands. Hope you'll be able to join us. A lot to do there. Fishing on a couple of lakes, riding, shooting, and so forth. Do join us, if you can. Sandy would like it."

Sandy was standing at his side, and if she was enthusiastic about the invitation, she didn't show it. She was watching a mosquito circling overhead, waiting to see who would be the selected target. The Laird could envision the whole scenario. Already it was 'Old Boy,' and if he took the bait, he could be wed to this lady very quickly and relieve her brother of the responsibility for her life. The family owned several private companies, and next would come an invitation to sit on the boards 'just to look out for Sandy's interests,' and the board fees would provide a handsome income aside from the dividends on her stock, and the rest of his life would be an existence of disinteresting, decadent luxury.

He would have to accept the invitation if given, so he replied, "That's kind of you. A weekend in the Highlands would be very pleasant. I hope I'm in the country at the time. I do go back and forth to the United States quite regularly." He learned later that the 'little place' in the Highlands was over 4,000 acres.

CHAPTER XVII

In the second week of Kerrie's employment at the castle things began to settle into a routine, and on Thursday everyone finished work for the day after the lunch hour. The Laird headed for a chess game with Doctor MacLaine and everyone else had somewhere to go. This would be Kerrie's chance to start her search for the castle treasure, which she was even more certain existed after having spent time in the castle and seeing first hand how former laird's lived and the tremendous wealth they must have enjoyed.

She went to her home after lunch and changed into a dark colored jogging outfit. She watched from her window as each person left the castle grounds, and then slipped across the road and entered the property through a break in the fence, undoubtedly made by some lorry backing up to turn around in the road.

Once in the castle grounds she looked about to be sure no one was present. She was certain that Mrs. MacOster was in the gatehouse, but she wouldn't be able to see across to this side of the grounds. She peered down over the embankment of the Kirkwhapple Burn. The cave opening should be about twelve to fourteen feet below the upper ground level in a straight line with the rear wall of the greenhouse. When she looked down, she could see nothing but a tight growth of bramble and brier.

Not to be deterred, she went to the tool shed and pulled out some ropes and pruning sheers, and a pair of gardening gloves. She took a stout knife and a pole three feet long in case she ran into any critters in the cave. She anchored a rope to a tree above the supposed opening and carefully lowered herself. As she got into the wild growth she cut the cane and kept tossing it into the river and it floated down and away - headed for the firth. She scratched herself numerous times, but she kept focused on her goal. After an hour she had cut away enough to place her opposite the expected opening, and she had reached a ledge on which she could stand. It looked like the ledge ran alongside the hill in the direction of the road and the bridge near her house.

She studied the side of the hill where the opening was supposed to be. Either it had been filled in, or the whole thing was a joke. She climbed back up, returned to the tool shed, and pulled out a small shovel and a metal stake about eighteen inches long. She lowered herself again to her foothold and started probing the side of the hill with the stake. At the predicted spot the stake sunk in easily, and she began to dig with the shovel. Earth had accumulated in the entrance, weeds had rooted and the entire opening was covered. In half an hour she had the accumulation cleared away. The growth of the bramble around her masked the opening from every direction.

When she opened the entrance she found a space enclosed by rock the size of a public phone booth. She was tempted to believe she had found the wrong spot, but she pointed her torch upward and saw an opening, which might lead into the supposed cave. She studied the wall of the enclosure; there were crevices into which she could place her feet. Carefully she inched her way upward and looked into the opening. Her torch revealed a large room.

She continued moving upward and pulled herself forward on her stomach. Below there were large boulders upon which she could descend into the cave. She slowly scanned the room with her torch; other than dust and rocks strewn about, it seemed empty. She stood and listened. First she heard a groan, then a low whistle. She searched in all directions with her torch, but no sign of life. Again a groan. Again a soft whistle. The cave seemed totally devoid of any sign of life. No bats or animals.

She could see little streaks of light near the outer wall and concluded that the sounds were made by air passing through the crevices. But the sounds and the moving shadows from her light gave her an eerie feeling. She noted that the cave was dry despite the sound of water moving somewhere to the right - in the direction of her house.

She moved forward, avoiding stalagmites and stalactites, and when she got about 100 feet away from the entrance, there was a solid wall. All of the walls were pockmarked with holes and cracks of all sizes. She edged along the wall and found an opening and kept moving in the direction of the castle.

She entered another small room. It seemed to have a choice of two openings. She choose the one that was in line toward the castle, and quickly it opened to another chamber, but it was larger, and there were piles of large stones which had left several openings. It struck her that the piles didn't seem like natural formations; they were too carefully arranged. She selected an opening and continued through. After another hundred feet she hit a solid wall with no opening to continue farther.

She retraced her steps, she thought, and entered a room and came upon another solid wall. She didn't remember this room, and decided to go back to the piles of rocks and again start there. An hour later she hadn't found the rock piles, and it struck her that she was in a maze - an intentional maze. The batteries in her torch were getting weak, and the light was starting to flicker. She began to panic. She could feel her heart pounding. If she hoped to find the entrance she would have to do so quickly.

She turned off her light and sat down on the rock floor to think. But it was hard to concentrate with the groans and whistling which seem to come from all directions. If she lost the use of light she reasoned that she could go forward and just keep turning right or left each time she found an opening. As she sat there thinking, she heard the sound of running water in the distance. Maybe it was the water she had heard when she first entered the cave. She turned on the weak torch and moved toward the sound of the water. Each time she reached an opening she stopped and listened for the water and suddenly, to her great relief, there was the light coming from the opening where she had entered.

She retreated to the opening and climbed out. After resting briefly, she took a few deep breaths of fresh air and climbed the rope to the top. It was late afternoon. As far as she knew, people would not be returning until the evening. She decided to return home and get a fresh supply of batteries and a generous supply of weaving yarn.

When she returned a half hour later she carried a duffel bag of necessaries, including a compass and some bread and cheese. This time she entered the cave with more confidence. She started by tying the yarn to a stalactite near the entrance, and then by exploring each opening systematically she found her way to very near the castle dungeon in less than an hour. There was no doubt that there was an intentional maze. The whole cave area continued to be devoid of any creatures, living or dead.

When she was close to the castle she ran into an opening filled with a barrier of heavy iron bars, like a portcullis. Upon close examination it was obvious that the bars were immovable. Had someone permanently closed the cave off from the castle? Why such an elaborate structure? A cement or masonry closure would have been easier. She could see through the opening and the entrance to the castle had to be close beyond.

Having come this far she was frustrated and annoyed to find the barrier. She decided that she wouldn't leave until she explored every possible alternative. Maybe there was an entry from another path in the maze. She retraced her steps part way and selected another opening that she felt would go in the general direction of the castle. She found herself facing another blank wall, but her compass and her instincts told her that the castle entrance had to be close on the other side.

She studied the numerous holes and pockmarks in the wall. She carefully searched for a place where someone could place feet and move upward into an opening. Finding such a spot, she climbed up and placed her torch into the hole. There was an 'L' shaped opening in the rock and when she climbed into it and moved forward she found herself inside the area closed off by the immovable 'portcullis;' the barrier of iron bars was obviously a decoy to confuse an intruder, or a place for a lookout.

She moved forward along the next wall and found a wooden doorway, which opened easily and quietly, despite its unlikely use for a long time. Once inside the entrance to the passageway she found herself in familiar territory. It fitted the schematic in the 'Green Book.' She moved upward in the stairway.

Slowly, she worked her way through the passageway and visited every room. She found a small slide opening to observe each room, including the larger rooms in the servants' quarters. Every panel moved easily and without noise.

She entered the Laird's room and looked about. It was the first time she had been in it. She saw the flower vase on the desk next to Carolyn's picture. She guessed she must have been a previous wife; reportedly he wasn't married. She also saw the picture of the two older ladies with two small children and thought the children might be his. It crossed her mind that she still hadn't met the Laird; he certainly was reclusive; he seemed to spend all of his time in this room.

She looked in the desk and spotted his diary. He had already entered his experience for the previous night. He had met Saundra Morthland - and he wrote that he definitely was not interested.

She went to the closet and opened the panel to reveal the other secret passageway and the rubble that filled it. This opening and passageway connected to an entirely different section of the underground caves, and the exit for it was on the north - the exit that had collapsed. For the moment this should not be of concern. Any possible treasure had to have been accessible to the Sixteenth Laird, and she felt sure that Seventeen hadn't been the one to put the rubble there - not with his penurious life style.

She spent over two hours in the castle exploring every route of the secret passageway, and finally when she thought she heard someone entering the building she retreated into the walls and watched through the peephole in the servant's quarters and saw Jeffrey enter and go into his room on the far side.

She descended to the cave and followed her yarn to the outside. She stood on the ledge and resolved that each time she would come she would cut away a few feet of bramble until there was a path all the way to the bridge. She climbed up onto the garden level to find herself greeted by Ogier. Jeffrey had let her out. She petted the dog and commanded, "Go to Jeffrey." The dog ran off. She replaced the ropes and other tools in the shed and returned home.

It had been a satisfying first experience in her exploration for the treasure. But how next to look for it? There was no obvious place, and it certainly was not in the passageway anywhere. Would they have left it in the cave? That wouldn't make sense. It would be safer to keep it somewhere in the confines of the castle itself. She would make a systematic plan and go over everything inch by inch.

CHAPTER XVIII

The Laird also had a satisfying day. To his great pleasure the scheduled session with Doctor MacLaine was more than the chess game. He found the elderly gentleman to be a wealth of knowledge about everyone in the area, and since he was the fifth generation of the medical family in the area, he was a storehouse of anecdotes about former lairds and everything else of interest in the county for the last 150 years. The Laird found the Doctor to be judicious in the way he talked about people. He might say that so and so were an outstanding family - pillars of the community, or that some others were a good family, or that family X were (only) interesting. If the Doctor was outspoken at all, it was usually something that was common knowledge, or references to ancient events where the people were long gone.

The Doctor told the Laird, "The reason that the Sixteenth Laird never had a family was that his wife was infertile - she had a structural problem that could not have been cured with the then known techniques of surgery. The Thirteenth Laird, the famous judge, had never had children by his wife, but my ancestor never knew whether his wife was capable; she seemed to have had severe mental problems. It was also common knowledge at the time that Thirteen had one or more mistresses. Fourteen, the Lady Laird never married, but undoubtedly was in effect the mistress of the famous painter William Bell Scott, who lived at the castle for many years; as you might have seen, if you've visited the Semple mausoleum in the cemetery at the bottom of the hill on the castle road, the grave of William Bell Scott is placed immediately next to the Fourteenth Laird. My ancestors visited the castle regularly for all of their medical needs; Scott's legal wife was an invalid for many years; she had had typhoid fever and it left her mind childish. They kept her comfortable in an interior room in the castle until she died. All these bits of information came out between chess moves.

The Laird asked, "What made you decide to be a doctor and to work here?"

"Never thought of having a choice. My ancestors were doctors here since the 1700's, and from the time I was a boy I expected to be the same. And I wouldn't want it any other way. The only concern I have is that I had always expected that my son would join me. But there's not enough activity around here to support two doctors. He's prolonged his studies. He finished his training in internal medicine and now is near the end of a second residency in cardiology. I'm afraid he'll wind up in one of the big cities."

They played on for another hour and skipped about in their conversation. Several times the Doctor had to excuse himself for ten or fifteen minutes to attend a patient.

When the Doctor returned from one of his exits the Laird said, "You know I've been thinking about your son and a problem that I have. I've been wondering what to do with the large building on my property near the gate. This was an artists' workshop and living quarters for some of the young Pre-Raphaelite artists that were supported by the Fourteenth Laird and William Bell Scott. It was also used for refugees during the two great wars. There are living quarters on both levels, and a large open area that was a general workshop.

"I'm thinking that a likely activity would be to move your office there and turn it into a clinic. And specifically what I have in mind is that a growing business in the world today is annual physical examinations for corporate executives. This is something that's not covered by the National Health Service, and I think we could attract executives from all over the United States and Europe. We have one of the world's great golf courses a few miles away at Turnberry; we could even tie the experience in with a tour of several of the famous Scottish courses.

"If you're interested, I'll take care of the construction. We shouldn't need too much in the way of fancy equipment. You'll be doing physical exams, not major treatment."

The Laird's enthusiasm infected the older man. "Duncan, this could be very interesting. It's worth a try at least. Let me discuss it with my son, who by the way is a serious golfer, and I agree that it shouldn't take a big investment in equipment."

The Laird continued, "You've got a beautiful stretch of beach here, many places to stay, and more than a few things for tourists to see, including things of interest for wives if they should accompany their husbands."

They never finished the last game, but talked on about all the positive aspects of such a venture. The Laird could envision that it would be a pleasant experience to go into a joint venture with him, except that the Laird wasn't really interested in profit, but more in something that would benefit the community. It would create some jobs, what with people needed for reception, nurses, cleaning, and kitchen help.

It was after six o'clock when the Laird asked, "What about the little pub off the high street? Is that a good place to get a light supper?"

The Doctor thought for a few seconds. "Food's excellent. But you might find yourself an object of curiosity." He thought a few more seconds and added, "but go ahead and give it a try. Can't do any harm."

When the Laird had lived in the Midlands he had discovered a charming old pub with a lot of interesting regulars. It was almost like a private club. This little pub was tucked away on a back street and most likely didn't draw too much of the tourist trade that frequented the beaches.

They shook hands at the door. "I'll call you in the next day or so; soon as I can get a reaction from my son," promised the Doctor. "In the meantime let's schedule chess again for next week."

The Laird held out his hand. "Until next Thursday. And thanks for the sherry. It was excellent."

The Laird got in his car and drove the few blocks to the pub, 'The White Corbie.' The sign was small and unlit, and the windows were likewise small and covered with heavy curtains obscuring the interior to passersby. When the Laird entered it was as he had expected. The customers were obviously the local townspeople; no tourists; he could tell by their dress and the quiet atmosphere. On the left the room was filled with tables, and on the right there was an aisle going to the rear from the entranceway. Halfway back there was an opening to the side, which had the bar; a few people could stand there, but not more than five or six. The entire room was paneled in dark stained wood, as was all the furniture. Above the opening to the bar alcove was a stuffed white corbie (crow).

As the Laird started to walk to the rear of the room he noticed the local provost, whom he had met at church. He waved to him and the provost half rose from his seat and waved back. Toward the rear of the room he selected an empty table and sat down. The owner came from the back of the bar in his long white apron and greeted him, "Evenin' Sir. Would you like to see a menu?"

The Laird responded, "Good evening. Yes, please."

The man returned. "We especially recommend tonight the roast lamb, always good, or we have a few pieces of turbot - brought in from the ocean this morning."

"I'll have the turbot, please, and you can start me out with a glass of dry sherry, Tio Pepe, if you have it."

The man disappeared in the back and in a few minutes a woman appeared with a white tablecloth and napkin and a setting of tableware.

While the Laird was sipping the sherry he glanced around the room. There were several other stuffed birds, an enormous stuffed salmon, a few trophies of some kind, and some framed prints of old golfing scenes. After he had become seated the people at the other tables had lowered their voices and kept glancing at him. It might have been a mistake for him to come.

When the food was served he found it to be excellent. The fish was very fresh, a treat. As he was eating, a big young man in a leather jacket came in and went to the bar and asked for a pint of bitter. The owner said, "That will be 75p, please." He made no move to draw the beer.

The burly young man said, "What's the matter, don't you trust me?"

The owner reached behind the bar for a piece of paper. "No. Not until you pay me the more than ten pounds that have been on your slate for over three weeks now."

The young man turned and looked into the room and walked over to a small, elderly man. He grabbed the man by the front of his jacket and demanded, "Give me the ten pounds you bet me on yesterday's football match. I won."

The little man looked at him incredulously. "What? I never bet you or anybody on any football match in my life."

The bully shook the little man. "If I say you bet me, you bet me. If I say you lost, you lost."

There was silence in the entire room. Nobody made a move to intervene. The Laird was sorry for the old man, and he was annoyed that it was disturbing his dinner. He folded his napkin, laid it on the table, got up, and approached the bully.

"Young man. You're disturbing everyone here. This gentleman is a friend of mine, and if he says he hasn't bet you any money, I'm sure that he hasn't. I must ask you to take your hands off him and behave properly."

The bully pushed the old man back down in the chair, and turned toward the Laird. "And just who might you be to be tellin' other people what to do? Do you think you're a lord or a duke?"

"It doesn't make any difference who I am, but these people are my friends, and I'm asking you to behave like a gentleman."

"Why you bloody—," the big man swung his large first at the Laird's face. He never finished his epithet. The Laird ducked to the side, grabbed his arm and twisted it upward behind the man.

The bully screamed in pain.

The Laird released the pressure slightly and began pushing him toward the door. He glanced over his shoulder. "Would someone please open the door? This man wants to leave," and to his adversary, "Out and don't come back 'til you're ready to act properly." He pushed the man out the door and closed it. He walked to the bar and asked the owner, "Where's the washroom? I'd like to wash after touching that scum."

The owner conducted him to the bathroom in the rear of the building in the family living quarters. While he was giving him a clean towel he said, "That man comes from somewhere in England, just south of the border. Doesn't do anything; just hangs around; makes trouble all the time. We'd be better off if we never saw him again."

The Laird thanked the owner and returned to his table. Everyone in the room was talking, creating a general hum. The Laird had known what he might expect when he got into the middle of the row, and he knew it might not yet be over.

He continued to eat his dinner, and as he anticipated the bully soon came in the door, and this time his right hand was behind his back. The Laird rose promptly, and walked toward the man. He waited for him just opposite the bar alcove. The bully's eyes were wild. He started again, "You bloody—" and he swung from over his head a tire iron.

The Laird had selected the arena for the contest. He stepped backwards into the bar area, grabbed the man's forearm and at the same time slipped his leg in front of the man, providing a fulcrum. He let the forward thrust of his weight take himself over the Laird's leg and onto the floor, the iron flying from his grasp as he landed face down. The Laird twisted his arm behind him and when he came to rest the Laird had his foot pressing down on the back of the man's elbow.

The bully screamed in pain. "Stop! Stop! Somebody, stop him! He's hurting me!"

The Laird eased the pressure on the joint and said, "If I wished I could break your arm in two." He applied a little more pressure.

The man screamed again. "Stop! Somebody call the police!"

The Laird continued in an even voice, "If you ever come into this room again, or if I ever hear that you are anywhere in this town, I will personally come and break both of your arms. Now get up and get out." He leaned over and moved the man's arm up behind his back and guided him onto his feet and to the door. There was someone already at the door and the whole room burst into applause and laughter. The bully was the laughingstock of the pub.

The Laird gave him a forceful push, "Out now. I said out. Out of this town. Now! And don't ever come back!" He closed the door.

He walked back to the bar again and addressed the owner, "I guess I'll have to wash the rot off my hands again."

He returned to his table and slowly finished his meal, forkful by forkful. When he was finished he asked for his check. The owner protested, "Sir, 'twas an honor to have you, and you're my guest for the dinner."

"Sir," the Laird responded, "that's nice of you, but I feel uncomfortable in accepting. And I couldn't come back unless you let me pay. The dinner was excellent. Best turbot I ever had."

The owner thought for a moment. "Well, since you put it that way, it's five pounds even."

The Laird fished in his pocket and laid six pounds on the table.

Before he rose to leave the provost came over to his table. "Sir, may I speak to you for a minute? I can't tell you how much all of us appreciate what you've done. That man's a troublemaker, a real bully, and I hope he'll take your warning and get out of town." He lifted his arm and pointed to each man in the room and introduced him by name to the Laird. As the Laird had suspected, these are undoubtedly the local businessmen and in effect this was their club. "We're so happy that you've taken over Kirkwood. We hear nothing but wonderful things happening there. Would it be too much to ask you to come and speak to this little group? We call ourselves the

Booster Club for the village. We haven't done much boosting in a long time, but we keep meeting and trying to think of ideas."

The Laird reflected on his years in the manor house in the Midlands and the protocol of his relationship with the local townspeople, and there was no such tradition here as far as he could tell. But he wished to have a good relationship with the town people. So he offered, "How would your Booster Club like to have a meeting at the castle? Say in a month or so from now? We're still getting settled. I'll show you around the place, and then you could be our guests for dinner. I'm not sure what I would have to say for a speech, but I'll give it some thought."

The group was obviously pleased. The provost said, "If you have such a meeting at the castle it'll be the highlight of the year for us."

The Laird rose and shook hands with the provost. "I'll be in contact with you to set up a date." He glanced around the room. "Good night, Gentlemen."

They rose as a body and in unison said, "Good night." And they spontaneously applauded.

The Laird was careful when he left the building to be sure the bully was nowhere in sight. He got into his car and drove back to the castle. Another productive day. He wondered if everyday in Scotland was going to be like this. He wondered what Granville and Jeffrey were doing on their first night off. He also wondered what Kerrie Bramwood was doing. He would have to remember to get up a little earlier tomorrow to get organized for their trip to London.

CHAPTER XIX

While the Laird was playing chess and during his famous visit to The White Corbie - a visit that would be recounted for years by the townspeople with embellishments - other members of the staff spent their time off differently.

Miss Bramwood did a bit of shopping and attended the usual chores that are necessary for the maintenance of a house. Afterward she worked on editing some book material, as she did most evenings.

Jeffrey took the van and headed straight for Glasgow. His mentor, Granville, had once told him, 'Jeffrey, education never stops. What you learn after your schooling is extremely important. Aside from being a perfectionist in your job, remember that you are associating with people who are familiar with the finer things in life, which includes the arts. And for yourself you cannot too much read good books, listen to good music, or look at good art - which of course includes good theatre.' In the Midlands and now in Scotland Granville knew what was playing at all theatres within a reasonable distance, and he always seemed to be able to arrange free passes with a telephone call. So today Jeffrey would be heading for the art gallery, a bookstore to find books about the classics, and to the theatre.

Granville first went to Ayr for some personal shopping, and near dinnertime drove to a small village inland and almost twenty miles from the castle, far enough away that no one would know him. He had been searching for a pub to have a good dinner and some spirits, and the butler at the home of Baron Auldlay had suggested that he might try 'The Wallace and The Bruce.'

When he arrived at the pub he found his friend and, as he had hoped, there were another eight of the same profession, most of them with their wives. They occupied several tables and all were dressed in casual, but carefully selected clothing. He could feel as he was being introduced that this was similar to the group he had been part of in the Midlands - a small network of superior professionals from the better houses. They got together for socialization plus the exchange of useful information, which would enhance their stock in trade. Most of them had other training; one was a concert pianist until he had injured a finger; another had trained to be an accountant; another had been a teacher in an exclusive boy's school, and so forth. The one thing they all had in common was that they aspired to be good at their work. All of their wives performed some function within their places of work.

Granville was invited first to sit at one table for a drink; he next had dinner with a different group; and afterward a drink with a different group. The conversation evolved not too differently than the Laird's conversation with the doctor. They spoke about visitors to their respective places and using words like fine people, good people, or interesting, they were categorizing them. And since they all worked essentially the same group they offered little tips to Granville like when Lady Z announces that she would like 'just a small glass of sherry,' she really means a sherry glass full of Glenlivet malt whiskey, neat. And Lord Y is an alcoholic and you needn't ask his choice, just give him a glass of orange or grapefruit juice. And Baronet X is allergic to champagne, but would enjoy a glass of sparkling hock, and you might want to keep a supply of that in your wine cellar. And Lady W is allergic to flowers, so never put her near a floral arrangement at the dinner table. They also named the handful of real wine connoisseurs who would appreciate seeing the label on wines being served. On and on they went: so and so liked only Knockando scotch, another Johnny Walker Black Label, another Famous Grouse, and you didn't ask - just hand it to them during cocktail time. Terribly valuable information, and Granville made notes.

After dinner the former pianist was inveigled to get up and play something on the piano in the middle of the room. He knocked off a few requests, and when asked to sing 'When I was a Lad' from Gilbert and Sullivan's H.M.S. Pinafore, he apologized that tonight his throat was scratchy and he would have to skip the singing. Granville, unthinkingly, leaned over to the lady on his left and remarked, "I wish I had tuppence for every time I've sung that song."

The lady promptly stood up and announced, "Ladies and gentlemen. Ladies and gentlemen. Tonight we have direct from the Savoy Theatre in London (little did she know), the famous actor and singer," she leaned over and asked him what his full name was again, "the famous actor Harrison Granville who will now sing for us."

Granville didn't want to be too forward for his first evening with this group to which he had taken a liking, but he stood up. "Friends, I think this lady has grossly exaggerated my singing ability. But after several glasses of wine, I've lost my good judgment, and I shall honor her request, even if I make a bit of a fool of myself."

Everyone applauded, and there were a few 'bravos.'

He walked up to the pianist and announced his key, turned his back to the audience, and when the musical introduction was over he turned and 'made his entrance.' He had all the humorous body moves and expressions and an excellent voice. There was no doubt that he was professional, a very good professional. The group applauded and insisted he do it again. He sang a couple of other numbers from Gilbert and Sullivan, and then protested that he had run out of voice. He knew it would be wise to leave a little bit wanting for another night.

A sidelight to the event was the wife of the owner of the pub. She was a woman about thirty years old and of generous physical proportions, at least 15 stone - maybe 17 (210- to 238 pounds), but she had a pretty face and large sincere eyes. She functioned as the chef and actually ran the whole place. She was born and raised on a local farm, and the local talk was that her husband had married her to obtain a 'free' cook; he was an alcoholic and spent all his time in the back in his own miserable alcoholic world.

When Granville sang and acted, she was captivated. She sat at a table, put her elbow on it with her chin in her cupped hand. She couldn't take her eyes off him. Such talent; such poise; what a contrast to the sodden excuse for humanity that she had for a husband. Afterward she rose and said to Granville, "Thank you so much. You were wonderful."

As the group parted and left the pub to return to their home territory, everyone congratulated Granville and obtained his assurance that he would join them again the next week. He was the last one to leave the room, and the wife of the pub owner was waiting for him at the door. "My name's Patricia - Trish, I'm the owner. Anytime you want to come and sing, your dinner and anything you drink is free. You were so handsome."

He leaned over and kissed her hand while she breathed an "Ooohhh."

Granville knew from long experience he had a 'stage door Jenny,' and still holding her hand he replied, "Madam, you have a superior establishment. The cuisine was excellent, matched only by the charm of the hostess. Good night, and until next time."

As she watched him walk down the street to his car, she uttered a deep sigh. Then she returned to her mundane world of closing the pub, cleaning up, and coping with her drunken husband.

For Granville the evening had been successful in many ways. For someone hooked on the profession of acting, even the small performance tonight was gratifying. He had been away from acting too long. He was itching to return to it.

Granville had started in theatre as a young boy - sweeping the floors and moving props around the stage. He came from a poor family that lived in the Soho district of London, and he had started hanging around the theatres for something to do. Eventually, he was hired for small jobs, and watched the actors perform. He was a born imitator and would practice imitating every part in a play. He learned instinctively who was good and who was second rate. In due course he was used in crowd scenes, and then short speaking parts, and finally when he was only twenty he was the understudy for the male lead in Romeo and Juliet.

On the day of the dress rehearsal for Romeo and Juliet the male lead stumbled over a stage prop and twisted his ankle so badly he couldn't stand. The impresarios, the famous Bradley brothers, Garrick and Bankhead, searched for a substitute. None was to be found. Bankhead (Banker everyone called him as he ran the financial side with a tight fist) was all for canceling the opening, but Garrick, the artistic talent, told him he thought Harry Greep could do it, and reminded him, "In our first production, when we started out on a shoestring, we didn't have a single known name in the cast. We always went for talent, Banker, and I know Greep can do it."

They went ahead with the opening and it was a success. Greep, who had adopted the stage name of Harrison Hay Granville the first time his name had been printed in a program, was heralded by the critics as a great new talent, and the Bradley brothers were praised for their genius in developing a new star.

For years Granville had acted the parts of young men. As time passed he should have gone on to more mature roles. But his big step upward in life had been in youthful roles, and he refused to accept the fact he was aging. After he refused offers of parts too many times, the offers stopped coming, and he was down at the heels when he had agreed to take on the job of butler temporarily for Duncan Fleming. Temporarily had lasted over five years. He enjoyed the work (which in a way involved acting) and the relationship with the Laird, whom he had found to be an unusual person.

Whenever the Laird focused his mind upon something, things happened. He was a doer, and anyone that got involved with him profited from it. Granville had decided that when things got settled he would move on. But it took them a few years to renovate the manor house in the Midlands, and he also was worried about the Laird in general, very busy, but no real life of his own, always doing things for others. Then the Laird had bought Kirkwood Castle and things were starting all over again for restoration, but on a bigger scale.

Granville knew he would return to the stage someday, but he wanted to fulfill a personal vow of getting the Laird settled into a good pattern of life. Old age would creep up quickly, and he wanted to see the Laird well situated; he deserved it.

CHAPTER XX

At nine the next morning Jeffrey drove the Laird in the Rolls Royce to Kerrie Bramwood's yard. She was waiting at the door and came out with a small overnight bag.

Jeffrey saluted her. "Good morning, Miss Bramwood. I think it's going to be a perfect day for your trip." He took her bag and held the door while she joined the Laird in the back seat of the car. After placing her bag in the boot along with the Laird's, he carefully backed out of the yard and started for Ayr. The Laird had raised the glass divider and any conversation in the rear would be totally private.

The Laird smiled as she joined him. "Good morning. Are you ready for a train ride?"

She replied with enthusiasm, "And a very good morning to you, Al. It's a beautiful day, and I think I'm ready for almost anything."

It was only twenty minutes to Ayr and they reviewed their plans for their time in London. They would return the following afternoon.

They changed trains in Glasgow and settled into their reserved seats in the first class carriage. The train ride was just under six hours, and they never ran short of conversation. Mostly it centered around the restoration of the castle, in which Kerrie was very much involved, and her progress on the contents of the coffers. The train arrived on time. They took a cab to the Connaught Hotel, dropped their bags, and each went in a different direction, agreeing to meet in the hotel lobby at 7:00 for dinner.

The Laird headed for the brokerage office of Merrill Lynch, and Kerrie headed for the publishing company to drop off some material, and afterward she went to the University of London Main Library where she had been a frequent and well-known visitor.

At the library she approached one of the old hands and asked him, "Do you have anything on old British homes - particularly things like security for valuables?"

The librarian smiled. "You mean old castles with secret passageways and secret hiding places? I suppose you're editing a book with the plot centered in an old castle. I've got just the book for you."

He took her back in the stacks and pulled one book forward for her. "This whole shelf might have something that would be helpful. But this is a book for the professional architect, and it has a section with many examples and instructions for building safe places to hide valuables."

He left and she took the book to a little table near a window and began to read. The book was exactly what she was seeking. It indicated that the best places are indoors where people are always about. A master bedroom is good because it is usually occupied at least 35% - 40% of the time. It went on to describe how hiding places can be constructed under floors, in walls, behind baseboards, behind door frames, in furniture, in ventilators, and a long list of other places, all of which she copied. She thought she had found all she might need for her next quest for the treasure. Now that she had begun to search, it had become an obsession - its existence a certainty in her mind.

After returning to the Connaught she only had time to freshen up, add a bit of light make-up, and meet Al in the lobby.

He was waiting for her when she got off the elevator. "Did you have a good afternoon? Did you get everything done that you had hoped to?"

She smiled. "A productive afternoon. I accomplished more than I'd hoped."

"Now," he took her arm and guided her to the door, "I didn't know what you prefer, and since we are only here one night I thought we might shoot the works and go to the main dining room at the Savoy, unless you have another thought?"

She looked at him and said, "I'm totally in your hands. Whatever you say."

They were there in less than ten minutes by cab. They walked through the opulent lounge area, but agreed to skip cocktails there and go directly to the table. The Laird insisted on ordering a bottle of champagne to celebrate their progress at the castle. Kerrie had tasted champagne only once or twice in her life, and she remembered reading somewhere the old warning, 'It's a wise virgin that muddles her champagne.'

She asked the Laird, "Why do people muddle their champagne? I mean, is it a good idea?"

He thought for a few seconds. "I wasn't aware that people did muddle their champagne. That would destroy the bubbles, and after all that's what champagne is all about - something gay and festive and bubbly."

She accepted his explanation and sipped on the wine. It really was very good. The dinner was leisurely and excellent, and with it they consumed an excellent bottle of Bordeaux - a 1970 Chateau Cheval Blanc.

"I don't drink wine very often," she remarked, "but this is so good I could keep drinking it all night."

The dinner conversation was light. They talked about the food. The Laird gave a run down on the restaurants that he enjoyed visiting in London. They looked out the window at the lights across the Thames Embankment, and while they perhaps didn't realize it themselves, they were having a good time simply being with each other.

After dinner they watched the people dancing, and she inadvertently remarked, "It's been a long time, years, since I've been on a dance floor."

The Laird stood and smiled, "We can correct that right now."

"Oh no," she protested. "That just slipped out of me. I wasn't asking you to ask me to dance."

He was still smiling, "Well, I'm asking you to ask me to ask you to dance." He walked around the table and took her hand and led her to the floor.

He was not a bad dancer. With her athletic ability she was agile and as light as a feather in his arms. They continued dancing until the musicians stopped for a break.

He suggested that they should stay a little longer, dance a little more, and drink some more coffee. He told the waiter, "Two Irish coffees."

She had already drunk more alcohol than she was accustomed to, but she didn't feel lightheaded. She decided that she felt - well, she just felt like she was having a wonderful time.

In his mind they were just friends having a good time. That first morning he had met her, or was it the second, no matter which, she had announced very clearly that she had no time for a mate in her life, and that was precisely his attitude. So they were just having a bit of relaxation together - she his employee and jogging friend.

When the music finally stopped and the musicians were removing their instruments from the bandstand, she said, "Oh, are they finished already? It's so early."

"Early in the morning," corrected the Laird.

When they got to the street she suggested, "Could we walk back to the hotel?"

"We could," he said, "but not at this hour of the night. I feel perfectly safe in London, but it's not a good idea to walk dark streets late at night anywhere in the world. But we could walk through the Strand down to Trafalgar Square and take a cab from there."

They started down the street toward Charing Cross. She took his arm. "I think I'm feeling that Irish coffee. Is it O.K. if I use your arm for a life preserver?"

The Laird took her arm and put it under his and held her hand and announced, "In your case that's why there was an arm attached to me right here."

They slowly strolled down the street and she leaned on him and pulled herself close to him. She had felt so good dancing with him. She had admired that feeling of inner strength, which he had conveyed to her since their first meeting, and she felt she could just place her life in his hands. She thought, 'He probably would have a good bedside manner if he were a doctor. And would make a good solicitor too.'

When they reached Trafalgar Square she begged, "Let's go in the Square and watch the pigeons for a few minutes."

They crossed into the Square, walked around it, and then sat on a bench. A street performer was roaming about playing a small accordion, and he walked over to them. He might have been a gypsy; he had that sensitivity of analyzing his targets, and he said, "You two lovers look to me like Americans on a vacation. Your honeymoon?"

The Laird whispered to Kerrie, "Tell him in your accent that we're Scottish."

"Sahr, we are Skawts, di-rect from Skawt-land, the auld sawed."

Immediately, the stroller launched into the Scottish air, 'I Love a Lassie.' Duncan had heard it many times when he was a boy when his father had taken the family to dinners and functions at the St. Andrew's Society. He unconsciously started to sing along, and after you get past the lines 'I love a lassie, a bonnie, bonnie lassie,' the very last line names the girl, any name one wishes to insert, and he sang 'Kerrie me Scots bluebell."

The musician said, "Very good Guv'nor, but you sound like you're not so proud of Scotland or your lady. Let's do again like we mean it." And he launched right back into the tune full force.

With that challenge the Laird let go with a more lusty baritone, and sang it all the way through again, this time looking at Kerrie, and again ending with 'Kerrie me Scots bluebell.'

When the music stopped he was looking into her eyes and she at his. Finally, the musician interrupted their silent tete a tete. "That was much better Guv'nor. Should we do it again?" He was waiting for his tip.

The Laird reached in his pocket and flipped him a pound. The stroller saluted with his finger and moved on.

"I think it's our bedtime," he said softly, looking at Kerrie.

She felt her body tingling and thought, 'I wonder what he means by that?'

They stepped out of the square and into the next cab that came along and were at the Connaught in minutes. The Laird picked up their room keys from the concierge and escorted her to her door. He opened the door, and closed it behind them. He walked into the bathroom and looked about. "Plenty of towels," he observed. Then he went over to the window and closed the drapery a bit more. Next he walked over to the bed and pushed up and down on it with his hand. "Seems to have a nice spring to it." All the time he was walking about, she was following a half step behind him. Next he walked over to the telephone, picked it up and told the concierge, "Wake up call at 7:00 a.m., and please hold any incoming calls; no interruptions during the night." Then he walked to the door.

At the door he turned the bolt shut with a snap and slid the chain in place; then he turned around. She was standing less than a foot from him, and she could feel electricity arcing from her body to his at several points, and she thought she could feel the same coming in her direction. She was breathing in short rapid breaths. She leaned slightly forward and tilted her head back and started to close her eyes. He spoke: "I think everything looks comfortable and secure here. It's been a nice evening. See you at breakfast downstairs at eight o'clock."

Her eyes snapped wide open. He lifted the chain off the door and opened it, and he handed her the key. "Be sure to keep your door locked with the chain on. Good night"

He closed the door behind him. She stood there for the better part of a minute. Somehow she had misread things. She went over to the bed and sat on the edge and reflected. It had been such a wonderful day from the beginning, and she couldn't remember when she had had such a lovely evening. He was like a man of any girl's dreams; at least for her it was developing that way. She thought maybe she'd better take a cold shower. Maybe she was acting like a schoolgirl. She reminded herself that she was on a treasure hunt, not a manhunt. And after all, Al

Lawman was really her immediate boss, and it would not be a good idea to get romantically involved with him. As she thought about it more, she wished he had kissed her, so she could find out where her true feelings lay.

When she finally got herself into bed, she tried to focus on the good luck she had had in finding the architecture book and how it would help her in the treasure hunt. But try as she might, her mind kept going back to her companion - Al. 'It was a lovely, lovely evening. One of the best I've ever had.' And the tune of I Love a Lassie kept repeating over and over in her head until she dropped off to sleep.

When she went down to breakfast the next morning the Laird was already at the table drinking a cup of coffee. He rose and greeted her, "How's my bonnie lassie this morning?"

She dropped a half curtsy. "Almost alive. I was out most of the night with a wicked man who filled me full of champagne and danced my legs off. I won't have to jog this morning or the next three. What do you recommend for breakfast?"

"I've already ordered for myself. A compote of mixed fruit, an omelet, English bacon, Danish pastries with butter, coffee with cream, and also some fruited yogurt. We can double that order if you wish?"

The waiter was waiting. She ordered, "Half a grapefruit, dry toast, and black coffee please." After the waiter left, she advised the Laird, "This lassie wouldn't be so bonnie if she ate the same breakfast as you." She also thought to herself, 'He'd better enjoy this breakfast fit for a woodcutter, as he'll be eating something more like I ordered when we get back to the castle - at least as long as I'll be planning the menus.'

Their first stop was at a computer super store, and since they knew what they had in mind, it didn't take them very long. Not surprisingly, they were told the order would be delivered from the Glasgow Branch.

The next stop was very brief. They entered the store of the Minolta distributor and purchased a copy machine. Not the smallest, but slightly larger with the ability to collate.

When they had made their purchases the Laird suggested, "Let's grab a quick lunch in the little dining room at Fortnum and Mason's, and then we'll have just enough time left to catch the train for home."

Over luncheon and all during the journey home they continued their vigorous interchange. The Laird was 'just as charming as he had been during the lovely evening at the Savoy, and during the entire trip,' she thought. 'He certainly knows how to handle women - and how to keep them guessing.'

When they arrived in Ayr, Jeffrey was waiting to drive them back to the castle. It was dinnertime and the Laird asked Kerrie, "Would you like to stay for a simple dinner tonight? I don't know what we're having, but I'm sure you'd be welcome."

"Today's Friday and you're having liver. I understand the Laird likes liver, and this is his once a month splurge in cholesterol."

"How'd you know that?" he asked.

"Well you know that I frequently pass the kitchen and often stop for a glass of water or something, and the week's menu is right there on a bulletin board."

"Oh."

Dinner was served to them in the Great Hall at the smaller table on the side. The Laird insisted that they have a bottle of wine to go with the dinner. He explained, "It's my duty to sample the wines once in awhile and make sure they're O.K."

The dinner was well prepared, and they were served by one of the MacDuffie girls and Jeffrey, who had changed from the livery that he wore when driving to a tuxedo - with a white tie. The pair continued their good fellowship throughout the dinner, and near the end, Jeffrey entered and interrupted, "My Lord, Lady Auldlay is on the telephone and is asking if she can speak to you for a moment."

The Laird took a deep breath and rolled his eyes slightly, and said, "Excuse me for a few minutes." He would have to explain away Jeffrey's use of My Lord when he returned.

While he was gone, Kerrie asked Jeffrey, "What did you call him?"

He looked at her half surprised and said, "My Lord, like I always do, unless I call him Sir."

It hit her like a rock on her head. 'Of course. He had always been so authoritative about everything; he couldn't have been just an employee. How could I have been so dumb?' She recalled that over the years references had been made to the Lairds of Kirkwood as if they ranked in importance just after the Queen. There was an aura, a mystique, and they were on a pedestal. She found it hard to reconcile all of this. Al Lawman - the Laird, one and the same. But he was so open, so informal, so likable. She was still trying to sort out her feelings when he returned to the room.

When the Laird rejoined her he started to say, "You know the staff is still practicing..."

But she interrupted. "Jeffrey and I had a little talk, Sir. I don't know why I didn't realize you were the laird, and here I am addressing you by one of your Christian names. In the future I shall be more respectful."

"Kerrie, don't be ridiculous. We know each other as Al and Kerrie. Let's please leave it that way."

She desperately didn't want to give up her job and her relationship with the castle, so she avoided any hint of being angry, but she declared in a pleasant tone, "Sir, I think that since I'm your employee, it would really be better if I addressed you more formally and you called me Miss Bramwood."

She didn't know why, but she could feel tears starting to well up in her. It had been such a wonderful two days, but such an unhappy ending. She was worried about making a fool of herself at the table, so she said, "I think I've had more than enough dinner, and I had better go now. Thank you for everything."

The Laird rose. "I'll take you home."

"No. Please don't." She turned her back and walked out of the room rapidly. She couldn't hold the tears back any longer.

She walked out the front door and on up the lane and down the road to her house.

The moment she left, the Laird rang for Jeffrey. "What the hell happened in here while I was gone?" he demanded.

Jeffrey knew that when the boss used that tone of voice he was upset. "Nothing. She just asked me how I usually address you, and I said I called you either Sir or Lord."

The Laird grimaced. "Damn." He looked out the window and watched until Kerrie, her head down, slowly walked out of view.

CHAPTER XXI

The next morning the Laird got up at his usual time and went out to jog. He hoped that Kerrie would show up, and later in the morning they were to go over to the Auldlay's to play tennis on their court. He hoped that yesterday's misunderstanding wouldn't spoil everything.

When he got out onto the road, she was near and came over to join him. She was her usual bright self and greeted him with a cheery, "Good morning, Sir. Are you ready to work off some of those calories you collected in London? And don't forget, Sir, we're supposed to play tennis this morning." She had resolved to call him only 'Sir,' never Lord - he wasn't a Semple - he didn't deserve to be the Laird of Kirkwood.

He thought to himself, 'Damn it, she's still piqued, but it'll wear off; women are that way sometimes; so I'll go along with her little game until it passes.' And then pleasantly to her, "Good morning, Miss Bramwood. It couldn't be a nicer day for tennis. I'll race you to the bottom of the hill."

After breakfast he drove into her yard and picked her up, and they drove the eight minutes it took to reach the Auldlay estate. He went to the door to announce their presence. The butler appeared and told them to go to the courts and stay as long as they wished.

They left the car near the front door and walked to the tennis courts. "Beautiful. Just perfect," observed Kerrie. She was eyeing the clay court and next to it, separated by a fence and some bushes, was a grass court. "They're immaculate."

There were four children hitting tennis balls back and forth on the grass court and when they walked up the children stopped and introduced themselves. They were the children of the Baron, a boy seventeen, his twin sister, and two younger girls sixteen and eight. They were very courteous, and the boy said, "You can have either court that you want; we're just playing around. We're really not tennis players. Do you mind if we watch?"

"Of course not," said the Laird.

Kerrie suggested, "Why don't we do this right, and each of you will watch the net or the lines, and that way we'll all be in it. And whatever you call 'in or out' will be it, just like at Wimbledon." And looking at the Laird, she continued, "There word will be the absolute law on what is in or out. And no arguments." And she thought to herself, 'and in that way they'll also learn a little about the game.'

She knew from the first half minute that the Laird was an amateur at tennis. But he did have some qualities on which she could build. He was still agile and fast enough to move around the court. Also, whatever made him a good shortstop in baseball would help in tennis, because he had a sense of anticipating where the ball would be when it came off her racquet, and he always was in good position, and he also had strong arms.

She worked on moving him all over the court and feeding his backhand. Finally, she taught him only one thing for the day and that was how to get more wrist action and racquet speed in his serve. She pretended that she had just read an article on the subject and was working on the same thing herself, although she had been serving to him very gently. She didn't want to lose him after the first time out. And she gave him just enough of a workout so that he would feel invigorated.

The children had a good time chasing the tennis balls for them, and being very firm in yelling 'let' or 'out,' with the two adults having no appeal.

After a little more than an hour the Baroness came walking down to view the game. She was followed by two servants carrying large trays of refreshments, which they set up on a table under an umbrella just outside the courts. She was pleased to see her children involved and clearly having a good time.

After they had had a cool drink, Kerrie said, "These four tennis judges look like they would make good players. Who would like to have a go at it for a little bit, and we'll teach you some of the basics?"

In unison four hands went up. So she showed them some basics on how to hold the racquet and the stance one should take and how to stroke the ball and where to aim. Then she and the Laird split up and spent a half hour with each child, one at a time. They were full of enthusiasm, but when Kerrie worked with the seventeen-year-old boy, it was obvious that he had a lot of potential for the game. He was already over six feet tall with long arms - a distinct advantage. He had excellent concentration and coordination. After she had worked with his younger sister for her turn, she invited the boy back and said, let's try to work on the serve a little bit more. She reviewed the basics of the swing and then emphasized, "Never, never, serve without putting a lot of spin on it," and she showed him how. After he tried it a dozen times he was delivering some vicious serves to her.

Kerrie told him, "You practice these things and I guarantee that you'll be so good that no one will want to play tennis with you."

By the time they finished it was almost lunchtime and the Baroness insisted that they stay for lunch. They protested that they weren't properly dressed, but she said, "It's going to be out on the terrace, casual, and the children will be there. So please do stay." They had no choice. It would have been rude to refuse.

The four children bolted their lunch despite admonitions from their Mother, and returned immediately to the courts to practice their new skills. After the luncheon Kerrie and the Laird walked back to the courts to see how the new players were doing. The older brother had one of his sisters just retrieving the balls from his serves. Kerrie watched for a couple of minutes and then went over and gave him a spot to aim for above the net and helped him make some adjustments and it was like instant coffee.

She walked back to the Baroness and said, "I really think that young man has natural talent. He ought to pursue the game."

The Baroness was visibly pleased. "His father played rugby and cricket in school, and Ramsay is too much of a string bean for rugby and cricket bores him. If he did develop a good hand at tennis he might salve some of his father's disappointment in him. He's actually a bright boy, a top student, and some day will be an asset in the family businesses. But so often I do wish they would be closer to each other. He's already seventeen."

Kerrie yelled at Ramsay, "Good serve - vicious. You'll kill everyone with that, but remember rhythm, let the racquet speed do the job - don't try to strong arm it."

The Laird was impressed with Kerrie's positive manner in talking tennis - like a coach. He asked, "Where did you learn so much about tennis?"

She replied without looking at him, she was watching every move of her new protégé. "I don't know so much. I just like to read about it and memorize basics. I wish I could play the game as well as I can talk about it." And without interrupting the flow of her speech she called to Ramsay, "That's good. Very good. Now turn just a little more this way - perfect."

The Baroness looked at the Laird and shook her head from side to side almost imperceptibly and just smiled.

Kerrie walked over to Ramsay. "If you think you really like this, I'll bring over a box of tennis balls. I've got loads of them, and whether your sisters are around or not you can practice serving them and then go to the other side of the court and do it again."

"That would be super," he replied enthusiastically. "There's also a wall next to the tennis courts at school where I can practice by myself."

"I have one more request to make if you and I are going to work on tennis together," said Kerrie in a low voice. "You mustn't listen to or take instructions from anyone else. I don't want you to do too many things too fast or get confused with different techniques. Someday I'll tell you who plays the kind of tennis that I'm showing you, but you have to promise not to tell anyone, especially Laird Fleming."

They began their thank yous and started to leave when Ramsay approached the Laird. "Sir, I know you know a lot about motor cars. Could I take five more minutes of your time to show you a car here and get your opinion on it?"

"Of course," answered the Laird. He expected to see an old junker that the boy was trying to run or maybe his well-to-do parents had bought him a new Jaguar.

The Baroness seemed not at all disappointed at their staying and turned to Kerrie, "Why don't you come back to the house with me. I want to show you some things."

While the three girls banged tennis balls back and forth the Laird was led to a large garage, which at one time was obviously the stables for the estate. The boy opened one doorway, and walked forward and pulled a sheet off a silver colored vehicle. It had the number 17 painted on the side in large letters.

The Laird's face lit up. "Do you know what you've got here? It looks like a racing Vauxhall from the twenties or early thirties. They made very few of these. This is a classic, a collector's item. Look - at - that - aluminum - body!" He walked around the car and he kept touching it gently like it was a fragile museum piece. He opened the hood. He was totally captivated, and he kept repeating, "Beautiful. Just - Beautiful."

Ramsay replied, "It was my great-grandfather's. I think it's a 1927 Vauxhall. As far as I know it's been sitting here for years - ever since I can remember. Do you think we could start it? I can get some petrol over in the garden shed?"

The Laird leaned over and studied the engine. "It looks like everything is here. But I don't think it would be fair to this old lady to make her run until we gave her a bath inside and outside, greased her joints, and put some new shoes - tires - on her. And by the way, I know exactly where we can get tires for it; if they don't have them they'll make some for it. Have you got a light of some kind, maybe on an extension cord?"

"Just a minute." The boy ran out. In a few minutes he returned with a light on a cord and plugged it in the wall.

"Let's take a look underneath," suggested the Laird. They pushed the sheet under the car and the two slid under to take a look. The Laird had on his white tennis outfit and the boy his khaki slacks and a light colored sport shirt.

In roughly half an hour from the time they had left the tennis court they were under the car when Kerrie and the Baroness came walking into the garage to find four legs protruding from under the car.

Kerrie ventured, "Gentlemen, there's more light up here, and I think we have overstayed our welcome."

The Laird and Ramsay slid out from under the car, both smeared with grime on their clothes and their hands and faces. Kerrie and the Baroness burst out laughing. The Baroness said, "If you really want to make that thing run, why don't you call the men at the garage in town, and they'll come and take care of it."

"Oh no, Mother," protested Ramsay. "Lord Fleming thinks we can make it run, and it's not the sort of thing you turn over to just any mechanic. He says this car's a priceless beauty, and he and I are going to work on it together."

The Baroness announced, "You've just saved this so called priceless beauty from the fox farm, because in the coming weeks we were going to clean out this old barn and that thing was tagged to be pitched out. It's been sitting there on those blocks for better part of a half century. But if you want to have some fun with it for awhile, go ahead."

The Laird said to Kerrie, "If you'd like to leave, I'll have Jeffrey come and pick you up. We're making a list of things to get. There are some tools here, but we'll need a few more to make the job easier and safer, and we've got to have some safety goggles. I should be finished in another half hour."

The Baroness took Kerrie by the hand. "We'll be back in half an hour."

An hour later the Baroness walked back in the garage followed by a servant with a big tray. They were still under the car. She leaned over and said, "I think you two mechanics should stop and have some tea. We'll just leave it here for you, and we'll be back in a little bit."

It was finally 6 p.m. when the Laird and Ramsay had completed their list. The tea tray was untouched. They walked back to the house, deep in conversation. He was pleased to see that Kerrie and the Baroness hadn't run out of things to talk about. He explained to the Baroness, "You really have a very unusual vehicle there. I could think of a dozen people that would give their left arm to have that car. Ramsay and I have discussed what we could do with it. One is, we could just make it run. A little more is, that we could clean it up inside and outside and make it very presentable - that wouldn't be a whole lot more work. The ultimate would be complete restoration; this would involve some real experts and when finished, you'd be reluctant to take the car out of the garage in case it might get scratched or a drop of rain might fall on it. That wouldn't be any fun. So Ramsay has opted for the half way measure.

"The cost will be negligible except for the tires which I will donate on the promise that you'll let me drive it once in a while, and the rest is mainly elbow grease which Ramsay will provide under my supervision."

The Baroness shrugged. "As I said. Go ahead and do with it what you will. It was headed for the scrap yard."

The Laird smiled. "I can think of several people that would pay at least 100,000 pounds for that beauty, just as she is."

When Ramsay had turned his back and was discussing something about tennis with Kerrie, the Laird assured the Baroness, "Don't worry, I'll supervise this carefully. And while that old baby might easily do over one hundred miles an hour when we get it tuned up, I'll put a governor on it to keep it under forty."

The Baroness walked them to the front door after sending for a clean bed sheet for the Laird to put under his clothing in the car. When they got to the car she said to Kerrie and the Laird, "You two are wonderful. I've never seen the children so animated. I love to have them home on weekends, and so often we just don't know what to do with them. And I hate their sitting in front of the T.V." She kissed Kerrie on the cheek, and then reached under her sleeve and took out a small lace handkerchief, cleaned a spot on the Laird's face, and kissed him there.

"Please come and use the tennis courts anytime. No one here uses them." The Baroness waved goodbye as they drove off and Ramsay returned to the garage to work on his car. The Laird had given him a list to begin the cleaning process.

On the way back to the castle Kerrie was elated. "That old girl's amazing. So interesting to talk to. I can't believe she's almost fifty. When I talk to her she seems like someone my age."

The Laird nodded in agreement. "I've seen it so many times in the business world - people can be relevant whether they're twenty or eighty; all depends on the person."

Kerrie forgot herself for the moment and said, "Al, it meant a lot to the Baroness for us to spend some time with her children. She would be happy if we went over next Saturday, and she wants us to stay on for dinner. There's a natatorium in their place where we can shower and take a dip if we wish. The Baron always plays golf on Saturdays, but she wants us to stay on and have dinner with all of them - in other words make a day of it. And I do enjoy her company so much."

The Laird pretended to think for part of a minute. "O.K. Kerrie. I think Ramsay and I might be able to extricate ourselves out from under that car by dinnertime."

"Oh, and I've had one other thought," said Kerrie. "I have a feeling that Ramsay may just be a natural tennis talent. We'll know in a few weeks if he has the determination to stay with it. The Baroness told me a lot more about his relationship with his father. I have a scheme wherein we might just get him ready for the Glasgow Masters Tennis Competition in August. He'll slide under the wire age wise in the junior men's division. And I know that the tournament is more one of social tennis than serious tennis. No self-respecting serious player would be caught dead there. There's a husky entry fee, and the trophies that are awarded are impressive. That might get his father's attention. I know you're busy, but I'll try to get there earlier on Saturday's to keep pushing him on his technique."

"Are you free for dinner tonight?" asked the Laird as he pulled up into her yard.

"No, Sir. I'm afraid not. I've got a lot to do. But thank you for playing tennis with me. See you at work Monday." She was just as pleasant as she had been all day, but she was placing things back on a formal basis.

He smiled and echoed, "See you at work Monday." And to himself, he thought, 'Damn. She's back to that Sir stuff again. I thought for awhile that the effect of a nice day had erased all that.'

CHAPTER XXII

Although the new tenants were barely settled into Kirkwood Castle, the following weeks became a heavy schedule of cleaning and restoration, inside and outside. Kerrie Bramwood was occupied with the numerous tasks of organizing the household in which Granville had involved her, and she worked to sort out the Laird's personal records and organize the items in the coffers, which as yet she had not had time to look at.

Doctor MacLaine's son was enthusiastic about the project of doing executive physicals in a clinic located on the Kirkwood property and the renovation of the building to be used had begun. If there was enough response to their initial mailings and advertising, the building would be ready by September 1st and the first patients could be received at that time. If the response were poor, they would refurbish the interior in some other way. Kerrie was drawn into the project from the beginning. She kept after the workman to keep the construction site neat and clean so that building materials and trash would not invade the rest of the castle property, and she made a daily inspection.

The Laird's weekly social engagements included the regular dinner parties of the elite circle of friends into which he had been accepted. The hostesses continued their efforts to attach him to one of their lady friends.

It was the turn of Lord and Lady Q. The Laird arrived solo as usual, and at the dinner table he was seated next to Countess Pantland, widow of the deceased Earl of Lochmoor. She was an attractive woman in her forties and her gown generously revealed her abundant proclivities, bordering on the edge of acceptability.

The Laird held her chair. "I'm Duncan Fleming."

"I'm Catherine Pantland." She leaned over and put her face close to his. "But call me Kitty." And she whispered, "Or Kitten if you prefer." She gave him a sultry half wink. He caught a whiff of an elegant perfume.

Throughout the dinner the Countess interrogated the Laird on his life experiences, and never offered a thought or experience of her own. All she contributed was her physical self as she leaned more and more onto him as the dinner progressed.

When the dinner was over, the hostess announced, "Everyone is invited to the library. The big game hunter in our family has some exciting movies to show."

The Countess said to the Laird, "Please wait for me outside the library while I powder my nose."

He waited while the others took their seats. Finally, after the lights had already been dimmed, she appeared and took the Laird by his arm and they sat by themselves in the very rear. Despite the dim light, the Laird noticed that she had adjusted her dress by pulling the bodice down even lower, revealing a cleavage worthy of a centerfold in a men's magazine.

Throughout the movie and the narrative which went on for an hour and a half, putting most of the audience to sleep, the Countess kept whispering little obvious comments about the pictures, and she kept leaning well into the Laird until he felt that if he leaned back another few inches she would be on top of him. She also kept her hand on his thigh at positions he felt were indiscreet.

When the movies were over, the party broke up, and the Countess raised the bodice of her dress. As everyone was walking to the door, the hostess approached the Laird. "The Countess seems to be without transportation tonight, would you be so kind as to drive her home? Only another ten minutes or so further than Kirkwood."

"Of course," responded the Laird. "My pleasure."

When they got into his Chevy Corvette, she was adjusting her gown again, and he was glad that there was a divider between the seats. However, that caused her to lean over even further, almost spilling out of her gown. The Laird had no desire to get involved with this type of woman. She was vigorously vending her physical attributes, and she was indeed attractive, but she didn't seem to have a single serious thought in her head.

They had to pass Kirkwood Castle and when they reached the castle gate, he turned and drove in. At the door, she started to get out of the car. "I've always wanted to visit Kirkwood Castle," she cooed. "So nice of you to invite me in for the night."

The Laird held up a finger. "Please wait here for a few minutes."

She settled back in the seat, expecting him only to be making sure the coast was clear for her to enter. After a few minutes Granville came out of the door. "Madam, the Laird is suddenly feeling unwell," he said. 'I'll have to drive you home in the Rolls."

The Countess looked disappointed, but she got into the Rolls. She hadn't readjusted her gown.

At what hour Granville returned to the castle, the Laird never found out. He didn't ask.

CHAPTER XXIII

Kerrie Bramwood had her next treasure exploration at the castle the day after the Laird's encounter with the Countess. She entered through the cave, again being cautious for any critters, and followed her stretch of yarn. It took only a few minutes. Once inside the building itself, she went directly to the Laird's room.

Her first act was to go to his desk and read his diary. She noted several interesting entries: 'C.B. is working out very well in her job at the castle. She seems to be appreciated by everyone.' And, 'C.B. has really added a lot of life to Kirkwood - a breath of fresh air.' And, "C.B. and I had a most successful two days in London. She is charming to be with. Some young man will be lucky to get her for a wife some day.' When the Laird had penned this entry, he had tried to think of who might be a suitable husband for Kerrie. He had listed on a separate sheet of paper her qualities: honest; physically healthy and attractive; intelligent and well educated; positive personality; quite athletic and getting better at tennis with practice; solves any problem tossed at her. He ticked off many men that he knew; none seemed worthy; he concluded that someone would eventually turn up.

She also was very interested in the entry for the previous evening: "Last night I met Countess Pantland. Whew! What a voluptuous female - one of the most beautiful I have ever met. Exciting! And she almost broke her back to get me to drive her home after the dinner party.' He omitted whether he drove her home or he didn't. She thought, 'He must have. He's such a gentleman.' But she wondered what happened when he got there. What was the 'whew?' She had never met the Countess, but she had heard rumors about her reputation, and she hated her type. The Laird was so open with people and so trusting, almost a boyish innocence. She would have to find a way to warn him to stay away from her; yes, definitely stay far away from her.

She would have to help protect him from himself. She thought, 'Whew!—Yuk!'

She sat at the desk longer than she had expected and reread the diary entries several times. Finally, she reminded herself that her mission was the treasure hunt.

She scanned her notes from the architecture book. Floor boards - there weren't any. The only paneling was in the closet where the two passageways entered with a section between. Both passageways opened by turning the coat hooks at the top. The one she used needed two hooks to be moved simultaneously, and the other only needed one hook. She first opened the two passageways. Neither had a fine finish on the walls. She began exploring the one through which she had entered. There was a lot of bulging mortar and cracks, and some crevices. She tested each by tapping with a hammer. Nothing; the walls were all solid.

She tried the other passageway, which had been filled in with stone rubble. When she opened it she found that the Laird had put a small floor safe on the landing. It was unlocked and contained nothing. He also had placed two shotguns and two handguns in the opening. Again she inspected the walls; more cracks and openings; some big enough to get her hand into; but nothing proved to be a storage place.

There was a stretch of paneling between the two openings. It had five hooks on it. She tapped all about the wall and it sounded solid. She first tried one hook at a time and then two at a time, using all possible directions and combinations. It couldn't require three hooks to be moved simultaneously, she reasoned, as they were too far apart for one pair of hands. She gave up on the section of paneling. So much for the closet area and the passageways.

The floor was entirely stone. She crawled over every inch of the flooring looking for any possible crack suggesting an opening. In the new section the pointing was very tight, and in the old there were numerous small cracks, but nothing suggesting that any stone could be moved. She tapped every stone and was satisfied that there was no likely hollow space beneath.

The door frames. She doubted that the frame on the door to the front hallway would be a candidate for a hiding place. The only other frame in the room was in the old part of the castle for the closet door. That was barely a frame; the door was more of a screen, maybe a late addition, but she checked the edges carefully and concluded that there was no hiding place. Next the relatively newer doorways in the new section. Again no indication that the frames could be unscrewed or otherwise removed.

The furniture. She first studied the large armoires, measuring the inside and outside dimensions. It was doubtful that there were any false sides, but she tapped them all and could feel the hammer impacts on the opposite sides with her hand. She checked the massive desk, taking the drawers out. No false panels in the desk, but she did find a false bottom in one of the drawers. It contained an assortment of paper currencies - a few French francs, a few Swiss francs, and some Italian lire, probably the remains of a tour on the continent. She looked at the dates - over a hundred years old; probably worth more as collectors' items than the exchange value. But at least she was making progress. The lairds, or at least one of them, believed in hiding things.

The bed was heavy, but she moved it and checked in and all around it. Where else to look? She looked at her notes and saw 'bed posts.'

She went to the foot of the bed and tried to remove the squirrel on one of the posts. It seemed to turn a little, and suddenly it moved a full half turn. She tried to turn it more. It wouldn't move. She was about to give up and return it to its original position when she tried to lift it. It came out easily. She laid the squirrel on the bed and looked into the opening. There was a wad of paper in it. She pulled out the wad - English pound notes; she had never been so pleased to see Her Majesty's picture. She thumbed through them - there appeared to be well over thirty thousand pounds, nearly forty. She checked the dates. They were all over ten years old; undoubtedly belonged to the Sixteenth Laird, and Seventeen had slept in that bed every night for ten years and undoubtedly didn't know they were there.

She looked again into the opening. Nothing more. She stuffed the notes back into the post. They were hardly a treasure. It was undoubtedly the cash box for day-to-day expenditures. The bigger cache would have to be somewhere less obvious.

She tried to remove the squirrel on the other side of the bed. It was stuck more firmly, and after persisting she lifted it out of the opening. She reached in and pulled out two passports, those of the Sixteenth Laird and his wife. Also, she found a piece of jewelry - a ring with a large ruby. It was not the sort of thing women wore in these modern times, but the paintings of the former wives of the Lairds all portrayed them with this ruby ring. She looked in again, hoping to find the Kirkwood emerald. But there was nothing else. She returned the passports, slipped the ring into her pocket, and closed the opening.

There were heat ventilators for the central heating, a relatively late addition. She climbed on a chair and looked into one. Nothing. What with Mr. MacDuffie coming in every day to solve any problems with heat, electricity, and other things, she doubted if the ventilators were candidates for hiding places.

She sat on the sofa in the room and looked about. What had she missed? She was sure that at various times the next large room down the hall had been the bedroom for the spouse of the laird. But would that be a likely hiding place? She was doubtful. It was starting to get dark and she would have to use a torch or the lamps. She decided she had better leave, lest someone returning would see lights in the room.

She looked around to make sure things were as she had found them and left through the passageway. She continued on into the cave and out in the open air and home. She was satisfied that there was progress, and she had the ruby ring in her possession. It was undoubtedly worth a substantial sum. She would return and search the Laird's room again carefully and also check the other possible rooms.

The next day when the Laird went to receive his daily briefing from Kerrie, she had the ring lying on a piece of paper on her table. "I found this in one of the coffers wrapped in paper - the coffer of the Sixteenth Laird. I think it's the one worn by the lairds' wives in the various paintings about the castle."

The Laird was impressed. "What should we do with it?"

"Well," she responded, "It's yours. You own everything in the castle. Put it away and someday when you find that special woman," she smiled, "you can put it on her finger when you marry her."

The Laird grimaced. Talking with her about his marrying some unknown woman felt awkward. But he thought 'This lady certainly is trustworthy. The ring is extremely valuable; she could have kept it and no one would have known the difference. What to do with it??? I could give it to her as a gift for her honesty. But that'd likely be misinterpreted. So I'll just lock it away in the safe.'

CHAPTER XXIV

The second week that Granville returned to be with his new friends at The Wallace and The Bruce he was greeted warmly by them and also the wife of the owner. The latter was dressed a little more carefully. She reminded him, "Remember that you're my guest tonight - that is if you'll perform something. You will perform won't you?" she begged.

He said, "Good lady. If you wish me to do so, consider it done." The pianist had not appeared that night as he had yielded to the cold that plagued him the previous week. Granville could play the piano a little, but not enough to be called professional, so he had planned for that eventuality and would do Hamlet's soliloquy and maybe some thing from Romeo and Juliet - his great acting triumph. On inspiration he said, "How would you like to try your hand at acting and speak a few lines with me?"

Trish lit up. "Me. Me act? Do you really think I could do it? With you? Ohhh. I'd just love to! Where are the lines? I'll start memorizing them right now."

"No need," Granville replied. "We'll do something from Romeo and Juliet. You'll be Juliet. You'll sit right here on this table. No not with your legs crossed, that would command too much - ah - attention - and this will be in Act Two, Scene Two where you will begin by just saying 'Ah, me.' Don't put any emotion in it; just speak in a flat voice."

She looked at him questioningly. "Like this—Ah, me."

"Perfect. And after a bit, when I pause, and I lift my hand like this, you will say, 'O Romeo, Romeo! Wherefore art thou Romeo.' Again in a flat voice, like the 'Ah, me." He didn't tell her that he would be skipping a number of Juliet's other lines, but in the spirit of fun, he would use her as a prop.

The dinner again was useful, and he learned more things that would be helpful in making guests feel much attended personally and would place Kirkwood among the distinguished households. One other item was mentioned that was helpful. The informal leader of the group, the butler in the Auldlay household, suggested a date for Kirkwood to take its turn in entertaining the local peers and gentry. "Granville, we've selected a date when we know most of the likely guests will be in residence, and we know they're all anxious to visit Kirkwood. And if there's any help we can give you, let us know. At large parties we're always willing to assist or at least lend out kitchen and serving help."

The date suggested was shortly after the date that the Laird planned to invite the Booster Club from the village. Maybe they could use some of the same entertainment for both. He had a plan in mind.

At the end of the dinner a lady, the same one as the previous week, rose to announce his expected performance. "Ladies and Gentlemen. Last week, we were all privileged to have one of our friends perform - very admirably I might say - some little ditties from Gilbert and Sullivan. I've been making some enquiries and found that we have in our midst the famous thespian Harrison Hay Granville, who appeared more than five thousand times on the London stage and acted in over fifty productions of everything from comedy to tragedy to musicals, and most of them were starring roles. Reportedly he never missed a curtain call. We do not ask him to perform tonight, but we do beg him to perform for us please. Anything he might wish to do."

There was applause and several bravos. Granville stood up. "I confess. I'm unmasked. I'm totally unprepared. But for good friends, I will try."

Again applause.

He walked to the front of the crowd. There were numerous other patrons at other tables. Trish walked to his side, tapping on a glass with a spoon. "You might have not heard what the lady just said, but please be quiet. We have one of London's great actors here, and he's going to perform something." She looked around the crowd with a pretended pugnacious look as a warning that they should be quiet.

Granville began, "I think we'll start out with a bit of Shakespeare. Something from Hamlet." He turned his back to the crowd for part of a minute, and when he faced them again he was Hamlet. There was a burst of applause when he was finished. A number of voices were saying, "More. More."

"Yes. If you wish," answered Granville. There was more applause. "Ladies and gentleman and friends, not meaning to say that friends are not ladies and gentlemen." He paused until the chuckles subsided. "To end on a lighter note and since this seems to be a Shakespearian evening, we shall do something from Romeo and Juliet. I have asked a fair lady to assist me in the performance." Everyone was looking around the room, but Trish just stood there at his side.

"Now we shall ask this sweet young lady to just sit - here." She stepped back and sat on the edge of a table. "And I will stand - here. And now - we shall begin." He bowed his head and when he looked up, he nodded at Trish and she said in a flat voice, "Ah, me." That was all; just, 'Ah, me.' There was a mild tittering around the room, and then there was total silence as Granville took command. He was again the young hero of the stage of two decades ago, and he was performing the role he had acted hundreds of times. You could have heard a pin drop.

When he paused again, Trish said in her flat voice, "O Romeo, Romeo, Wherefore art thou Romeo?" There was no laughter this time. Not only had Granville captivated the audience, but also the amorous look that Trish had on her face bespoke total love, and it was sensed by the audience, and they forgot her portly figure and otherwise non-stage appearance. At the end they applauded vigorously, and when Granville pointed to his co-performer they applauded with enthusiasm.

Granville thanked the audience, indicating that the performance was over. Not long afterward the crowd began to break up and people left to go home. Granville's associates thanked him and invariably said, "See you next week. For sure?"

Before he left the pub, Trish approached him. There was no one near. "Mr. Granville, that was the most exciting night of my entire life. Thank you so much."

Granville courteously replied, "You did very nicely. I can see that you have natural acting talent." He knew exactly what had happened. She had captivated the audience by her demeanor, and what he had expected to be a bit of a spoof turned into an intense love scene.

"And one other thing," she whispered blushing, "I've never said this to anyone before, but everything in my house is yours, anytime you want it, everything."

Granville was touched by her offer. But he never poached on anybody's territory, despite innumerable offers when he was regularly on the stage. With other unmarried women and particularly actresses? Yes. Regularly. It was routine, like brushing your teeth before you went to bed each night, and the relationship with that night's partner meant just about as much. He held her hand, and said gently, "Dear lady, I'm flattered by your offer, and much as it tempts me, you are married, and I wouldn't sully your good reputation for anything." He kissed her hand. "Good night."

She placed the back of her hand against her cheek and watched him walk to his car, and thought to herself, 'That's a man I could change my life for.' And she resolved to begin by dieting and losing some weight.

CHAPTER XXV

Mr. MacDonald, Principal Librarian of Edinburgh University, made his first visit to the castle, accompanied by an art historian, who was particularly interested in the Pre-Raphaelites. The visit was scheduled to begin around ten in the morning.

When they arrived the Laird greeted them in the front entryway. "Gentlemen, so nice to have you. Welcome to Kirkwood. I've asked Miss Bramwood to show you about. I'll join you for lunch."

He walked with them as they started on their tour. For her first time delivery of the castle story, Granville had suggested that she wear the Semple tartan - skirt and jacket, that is the Royal Stuart tartan, and for this occasion the hunting plaid, which was mainly green, and would set off her red hair and fair complexion.

As Kerrie gave the tour the Laird was not only interested, he was captivated. He thought she did it better than he could have. She had many interesting facts at her fingertips, and in her tartan outfit she looked and talked like she was one in the direct line of the pantheon of Kirkwood Lairds. Despite his earlier plans to do legal work, he never left the group. He stayed with them until lunch, had lunch with them, and continued on into the afternoon.

He loved watching Kerrie talk, and the way she touched things. It made them seem so much more important and valuable. Not a good idea to get too fascinated; after all she had declared that she was determined to be a spinster. And a voice inside him said, "And what about Carolyn?" 'Yes,' he thought, 'What about Carolyn? I likewise am definitely not in the marriage market. But whoever gets her will certainly be a lucky man.'

They took the visitors out to the workshop. Although construction had begun on the outside to make the walls and roof sound, the inside was yet largely undisturbed. As they showed where some of the Pre-Raphaelite artists had worked and lived, the art historian declared, "I can almost feel the presence of those artists here."

There was no obvious evidence of the history of the artists' lives in the workshop; it was over 125 years ago. However, there was a large, covered, wooden bin about five feet high, five feet deep, and ten feet wide. It might have been considered a rubbish bin, except that it had been painted with a floral design, and it had a hasp with a snap bolt. The historian lifted the lid and looked in expecting to find nothing or perhaps firewood or rubbish. However, he discovered a number of cardboard boxes, and looking inside of one of them he pulled out a roll of drawings. He proceeded to lay them out on the floor.

"My God!!!" he exclaimed. "I can't believe it. Look what we have here, the original cartoons for the The King's Quair mural in the castle tower!!"

They continued slowly to pull things out. MacDonald marveled, "This is like the discovery of King Tut's tomb!" They pulled out sketches for paintings, some of which he recognized. They found the pieces of raw wood for a chair tied in a bundle. It had never been assembled. MacDonald marveled, "Unless I miss my guess, this is a duplicate of a William Morris chair in the Victoria and Albert Museum which was designed by Dante Rossetti. This might have been the prototype."

A box of papers was pulled out from the bin. MacDonald started reading the handwritten lines. "Unless my memory is bad, I'm sure these are drafts of some of Christina Rossetti's work in her own handwriting." He turned over more pages. "And these definitely are drafts of her brother Dante's work. Did someone save these from the wastebaskets? These would be most interesting to a student of poetry."

They would have spent the rest of the day examining the contents of the bin, but Kerrie finally intervened. "Gentlemen, we have a lot more to cover today, and we haven't yet looked at the papers in the coffers, which was one of the main purposes of your visit. I promise you that I'll inventory everything in this container and send you a copy. I hate to dampen the excitement of discovery, but we do have a lot more to cover today."

The librarian kept shaking his head from side to side, "I can't believe these things stayed there all those years and were left untouched."

The Laird commented, "I can believe it. Wait until we give you a taste of the other things we have in the castle. The accumulation spans at least 200 years."

They walked back to the castle and went below to the storage area with the coffers. Kerrie had laid out a number of things for them on the tables that had been placed there.

The librarian glanced at a few items and flushed with excitement. He looked about, saw a chair and sat down. Then he reached in his pocket, took out a pillbox and placed a pill under his tongue. He took a handkerchief and mopped his brow. And after a minute, he said, "I'm alright now. Too much excitement. I have a heart problem, but I feel all right. Do you realize what you have here? You've got some of the rarest documents in Scottish history. The government's copy of this one was consumed in a fire some years ago. These things are priceless. Look at this seal of Queen Mary of Scotland, in quite perfect condition, extremely rare."

Kerrie kept showing him one item after another, and he just kept saying, as if he were numb, "I can't believe it. I just can't believe it"

The Laird excused himself for a moment and went over to the telephone and dialed the kitchen. In minutes Granville came down with a tray of glasses and an assortment of spirits.

The librarian downed a glass of cognac in one swallow, and after he had had a second, he started to regain his normal demeanor. "Lord Fleming, Miss Bramwood. Just from the few things I've seen here, you have treasures that could keep one or more scholars occupied for a long time. I hope you'll share at least copies with us and other libraries. This is more than I expected to find. In my briefcase I've brought a suggested scheme for organizing all of this, but I think I'll have another go at it and broaden it somewhat. I'll give it top priority and get it to you within the next few days."

Kerrie showed him one of the diary entries that were written in code. "Have you ever seen anything like this? Any ideas for translation?"

He looked at it. "Yes, I have seen things in code, but usually they're all different. I really don't have any quick suggestions except that you'll have to experiment with trial and error."

Kerrie replied, "I've already done that and it's not a simple substitution of one letter for another. At least I don't think so."

The Laird interjected, "I think we'll have to find some expert on codes and let him work on it."

They looked through more of the documents. The Librarian suggested that they be careful about fire. The Laird declared, "No smoking is permitted anywhere in the castle. It's truly a museum. Fortunately, this has not been a problem so far, and I hope it won't be a problem when we begin entertaining."

After the guests had been given tea they reluctantly began their journey back to Edinburgh. In their car the professor remarked to the librarian, "I think you're going to have to add 'D.C.' to the string of degrees you have after your name."

"What does that stand for?" queried the librarian.

"Dan Cupid. Didn't you tell me that you were the one that suggested Miss Bramwood for the job at Kirkwood? As an old married man of two score years, she looks to me as the absolute Lady of the Castle already, and when you watch how the Laird looks at her, he may not realize it, but she has him totally wrapped around her little finger."

When the Laird and Kerrie walked back into the castle, he complemented her, "You did a beautiful job of leading our guests around and telling the Kirkwood story, at least as far as we know it. Much better than I could have done. I think you should be the one to do this all the time, if you don't mind."

Kerrie smiled. "I'm at your disposal for whatever you want during the hours I'm here. Every day that I come here, I fall in love with this place more and more."

They reached the foot of the stairs and were going to part when the Laird concluded, "Well, I hope you never stop coming here." When he re-entered his own room he wondered, 'Maybe that was too strong of a statement. I hope she doesn't misinterpret what I said. On second thought, it wouldn't be so bad if she remained a spinster. She could spend her working career right here. She's a good employee, and good help is not so easy to find.'

He sat at his desk and tried to read a lengthy legal brief. But it was difficult to concentrate. The day had been exhilarating, and Kerrie's personality and enthusiasm were still echoing inside him. He looked at Carolyn's picture - her cool, platinum blond hair. But the aura of Kerrie's Titian red hair kept blocking out her image.

Kerrie would work for another hour or more at her station on the third floor. She too was excited from the visit of the two specialists, and she enjoyed sharing the hosting with the Laird.

CHAPTER XXVI

A few days after the visit of the men from Edinburgh the Reverend MacTaggart was invited to luncheon and for a tour of the castle. Again Kerrie gave the tour and again the Laird stayed with the pair throughout, enjoying it all as if he were hearing it for the first time. Spiritually, he was in tandem with her every word and every move of her body, and he just followed her about like Ogier might have.

(Ogier. It must be reported that she had become a valued and appreciated pet and guard dog by everyone in the household. She made the final rounds with Granville every night. She was quick to spot an open window or an item on the floor that shouldn't be there, and alone she checked the entire outside grounds before asking to get in for the night. She would alert Granville if the gates were left open, if there were anything unusual lying anywhere on the grounds. During the night her favorite spot was right outside the Laird's door, but she would run to any part of the castle if she heard a noise.

An interesting thing about a dog's perception is that, being a pack animal, a dog can sense easily who the top dog is, and the pecking order. At the outset if the Laird and Granville were together, Ogier would stand immediately to the side and slightly behind the Laird and face Granville. If Granville and Jeffrey were together, she would side with Granville, and so on down the line. At the lowest end were the MacDuffie girls and the assistant gardeners. The interesting thing was when Mr. and Mrs. MacDuffie were together; she stood behind Mrs. MacDuffie. A shrewd observer might wonder who wore the kilt in that family. And not too long after Kerrie Bramwood entered the household, Ogier fitted her into the pecking order immediately after the Laird and before Granville. Kerrie was definitely a great favorite of the dog who spent many hours each day on the floor next to her feet.)

The minister's visit promised to be valuable to the study of the diaries of the former lairds and their frequent references to other people. He announced at one point, "We have all the old local church records going back to the 1600's. That includes what are now the ruins of the church at the bottom of the hill on the road just behind the castle when it was the local church. The original church that was there, likely a wooden structure, predated this castle and the woods here was literally the Kirk's woods, and hence the name Kirkwood castle, I'm sure. I'll be glad, actually delighted, to research the dates of any baptisms, marriages, burials, and so forth. It might help to eliminate confusion. Often, children have the same names as their parents, and you can't always tell who is who. And if you want anything checked in any other parish, I can also get that done easily - professional courtesy."

Aside from the intellectual exploration into the castle research project, the minister took the opportunity to do a little recruiting, and he said to Kerrie, "I haven't seen you in church on Sunday. I hope the reputation of my sermons isn't that bad? With that beautiful red hair of yours, you'd certainly help to brighten up any service."

Kerrie apologized, "I've only been back in Scotland a matter of weeks, and now that I know who's delivering the sermons and how brilliant they must be, you can expect to see me on Sundays when I'm here. Sometimes I do go to London for long weekends."

"Good," concluded the reverend, and unthinkingly he added, you can sit right down in front with the Laird, and..." he stopped. A contretemps. He looked upward with his eyes, and she could see him fumbling for words.

"If you look in your records, you'll see that I was baptized in your church a number of years before you were born, Malcolm, and I know very well where the Laird sits. I think I'll just sit in the pew right behind him and poke him if he should doze off at any time during the service. Sometimes he stays up very late at night, when he should be home in bed at the castle."

The Laird thought he detected a hint of iciness when she said 'in bed at the castle.'.

Kerrie did begin going to church on Sunday after that visit and true to her word she came early enough to get the pew immediately behind him. When the congregation sang a hymn he could hear her. She had a clear, sweet voice, not trained, but pleasant. He preferred not to sing himself, but rather listen to her. On one occasion he was waiting for the next verse to continue the hymn when he felt a tap on his shoulder. He turned around. Kerrie was smiling and pointing down at his seat. The music was finished, and he was still standing alone, and the minister was waiting in the pulpit to begin his sermon. MacTaggart nodded to him when the Laird sat down, as if to say 'thank you.'

As the Laird moved about the castle during the following weeks, he would occasionally see the minister with Kerrie, and he would announce to the Laird that he had just popped in with some things that he was checking for her. They seemed to be getting along famously judging by the 'Malcolm this' and 'Kerrie that.' If there hadn't been a significant age difference between the pair, he would have kept a closer eye on things - for her protection. Ministers are human too.

And the minister wasn't the only visitor who surprised the Laird. He walked past Kerrie's area one day, and discovered a visitor who thereafter was quite regular, to be precise - every weekday from around ten a.m. until just before tea time, if that fits the use of the term regular, Saundra Morthland.

The Laird was passing Kerrie's area, and actually looking at Kerrie when he heard a different voice say, "Top of the morning to you, Duncan." He was amazed to see Saundra sitting there, and this utterance was more in words and personality than she had exhibited in the contacts, now numerous, that he had with her at the local dinner parties.

"Sir," Kerrie addressed him, "Miss Morthland and I met at the library in Edinburgh recently when I went there to check some things, and I discovered that she's intensely interested in

Scottish and local history, and actually quite learned on the subject, and she's offered to come as a volunteer and help sort out some of the thousands of things we have in the coffers. Already today, she's come up with some ideas that I hadn't thought of. Her education is similar to mine, and she's not only good, but you can add the big 'D' when you say she's good at it."

What could the Laird say? "That's awfully nice of you Sandy. Kerrie, I mean Miss Bramwood, can introduce you to everyone and everything, and please feel at home here."

"History's my passion, Duncan," she said, "and what's particularly attractive about this is that it's not like reading a book about it. These things bring one closer to the actual time and events."

The Laird walked back to his room. 'Damn,' he thought. 'First my friends push this little dame at me and now someway somehow they got the lady camel's nose inside the tent, my tent. Hell, it's not just her nose. It's all of her now on the inside. Always problems.' He was determined to believe that her presence wasn't accidental. Most likely Kerrie was in on the plot.

Another visitor, this time one of Granville's old friends - Regina Godfrey, Director of the largest theatrical costume house in London - came by for a visit. She had been on a business call to a client in Glasgow. This lady was well into her sixties, and was a person of stately character, beautiful appearance - wore designer clothing, and an interesting conversationalist; she had been everywhere and seemed to know many important people, some of them heads of state.

Regina Godfrey had been in women's high fashion clothing all of her life. She was an artist with a photographic memory. In her early years in the business she had worked for one of the famous fashion designers as a 'spy.' She attended the showings of other designers and after leaving the show would accurately sketch all of the gowns from memory. Later she did original design, and among her clients were numbered many internationally prominent people, including politicians and heads of state, who do a lot of acting and posing and need the ideal 'costume' for each situation. When she had accidentally become involved as a consultant for theatrical clothing, she found that this was far more challenging and interesting. If clothes made the man, she could make him a king or the Hunchback of Notre Dame. So she joined the largest theatrical costume house in London and soon became its director.

The Laird was pleased to have Mrs. Godfrey be a guest of the household and take all of her meals with him if she wished. Soon she was drawn into the project of identifying the hundreds of items of clothing in the storage areas of the castle - women's and men's - and that included uniforms. She was immediately hooked when she saw some of the old gowns of the former ladies of Kirkwood.

"These are priceless," she declared. "Handmade fabrics many of them, one of a kind. And this gown - these are not beads; these are all semi-precious stones. With alterations for current styles, many of these would be stunning today."

She also knew that historical objects were a lead-in to history, and she couldn't hear enough about the Kirkwood history. She loved the castle and thereafter became a regular monthly visitor for a few days.

CHAPTER XXVII

Two of the greater pleasures for the Laird were the project of 'fixing up' the old Vauxhall racing car at the Auldlay estate, and playing tennis with Kerrie.

Between jogging and tennis and a leaner diet, the Laird could see that he was definitely trimming down and getting back into shape physically. He felt quite virtuous that he had the self-discipline to restrict his diet to sensible foods and to keep up with the exercise program. His tennis game was getting better by the week, and he noticed that Kerrie was improving also, so that they played pretty much even.

Tennis was once during the mid-week for just the Laird and Kerrie. On occasion they saw the Baroness, and often they didn't. But Saturdays evolved into an all day affair. Kerrie went over early and worked with Ramsay for two solid hours, and afterward spent some time with the girls who were destined simply to be social players. After the Laird and Kerrie completed their tennis session, they were joined by the Baroness for refreshments, and for the rest of the day Kerrie and the Baroness would go back to the house while the Laird and Ramsay worked on the car.

They were unsuccessful in getting a parts catalog for the Vauxhall; one might have never existed. There were very few of the cars made. It was virtually a hand made vehicle, and each one that was produced could have been slightly different. The Laird suggested that they take apart each component carefully, clean the pieces, and lay them out on a white sheet, photograph them, and make their own parts list. In the process they could uncover any broken or worn parts and he would arrange to have them replaced.

Springs became a big topic of discussion, especially the many springs in the moving parts. They were over half a century old and the technology had greatly improved. Many of them were brittle - what is sometimes called metal fatigue. But the

Laird had them copied by a company that specialized in parts for custom restorations.

When the Laird brought a camera to take a picture of the first group of parts, Ramsay offered to carry the film to the town for developing. The Laird shook his head. "I've got a better idea." They went back to Kirkwood Castle and the Laird introduced Ramsay to the process of developing and printing black and white pictures and immediately gained a new convert to the hobby.

Most of the metal parts were in good condition. The Laird guessed that the car had been driven very little in its lifetime. After some weeks school was out for the young people and summer vacation began. At that point Ramsay gave his full time to working on the car, and Kerrie would stop by a couple of extra days in the late afternoons to work with him on his tennis. He was improving rapidly, and she knew it was only a matter of practice to gain consistency, and he would be very competitive on the courts.

The interaction between the inhabitants of the Auldlay Estate and Kirkwood Castle became almost daily. Ramsay was often over at Kirkwood to consult with the Laird on some detail about the car or to use the darkroom, and his twin sister, who was rarely far away, went along as did the younger two.

His twin sister, Rhonda, was taken in by Kerrie and Sandy Morthland who showed her what they were doing on the research project. The girl was going to college the following autumn, and she was unsure about her course of study, but as the weeks went by it was obvious that history was going to be the principal subject - maybe not English or Scottish history, but history nevertheless. She was also pleased that the two older ladies were not condescending toward her, and treated her much as an equal partner which spurred her on to ask questions and receive suggestions.

The sixteen year old sister, Lesley, started out on the history project, but when they touched on the period of the Pre-Raphaelite artists, she wanted to stay with that. She also wanted to try her hand at some drawing and painting. Did they have any of the necessary tools for painting, such as an easel? They had numerous things from the time of the Fourteenth Laird, but most fascinating to her was the entire painting box with tubes of paint and brushes that bore the initials 'D G R.' (Dante Gabriel Rossetti). Sandra Morthland had been well schooled in painting, although she was not a great talent. However, she showed the girl how to manipulate the colors and launched her into a hobby that consumed most of her waking hours. If not painting she was reading books about painting and painters with particular focus on the Pre-Raphaelites, and she eagerly pursued the project of assisting Kerrie in identifying and making an inventory of all the works of art in the castle.

The youngest girl, Susan, only just beyond eight years was the outdoor type. On one of her first visits to the castle Fergus showed her the garden and explained how plants grow. On her next visit he took her for a walk in the woods below the castle and suggested that she make a little drawing of each kind of leaf and tree.

The Baroness frequently popped in for a brief visit, which often resulted in an impromptu invitation to luncheon or tea. She said that if she wanted to see her children on many days she would have to go to Kirkwood.

In due course the tires for the Vauxhall arrived. The Laird brought them with him when he returned from one of his periodic trips to the United States. And also the other replacement parts kept trickling in. The Laird guessed that by sometime in mid-summer they would have the machine running. He and Ramsay were becoming firm friends.

On the Saturdays at the Auldlay estate the Laird cleaned himself up for dinner, and whereas Ramsay would go back and work on the car until his bedtime, the Laird and the Baron would sit and talk while the women were elsewhere. Like so many of the Laird's business clients, the Baron had no one to talk with. He was chairman of the several family companies, and it was a lonely job; there were few people with whom he could talk in complete confidence. He found the Laird to be a good listener and easy to talk with and his counsel most worthwhile. The Laird listened to what the Baron knew he should do about some of his problems and simply encouraged him to follow through with his plans. Also to strive for quality, in people and facilities. In today's world it was not enough to have capital and to keep out of trouble. There was too much competition. One had to be proactive.

One evening the Baron was struggling with a particular problem, a personnel problem. They had a position to fill at the top of one of their companies, and his brother-in-law wanted it very badly. "But Duncan, he simply isn't qualified, and worse yet he'll be in so far over his head that I'm afraid it'll kill him. And if he doesn't get the job, it'll make a big problem in the family."

How many times had the Laird heard similar comments in family businesses? He asked, "Lord Auldlay, if you had your way, just what would you have your brother-in-law do?"

Without hesitating the Baron replied, "He's a nice chap, but not really the business type. He shouldn't be leading people. He should be doing research and development."

The Laird had heard enough about the Baron's businesses over the weeks that he felt that they were probably running what in the States would be called a good old boy operation - very risky in today's world. So he suggested, "Sounds like the perfect person to create a new title of Deputy Chairman or Assistant to the Chairman and create a new planning department for him to oversee. You can surround him with some strong types that can push the numbers and do the scientific stuff. And there's a lot of good material around on the techniques and formats for planning. I can get you an armload of that stuff."

The following week the Baron implemented the Laird's precise suggestions. As the weeks progressed the interaction became more and more intense and detailed, and in effect the Laird was acting as a friendly business consultant. The Laird's philosophy was very simple: first decide what you should do, and then plan, plan, plan, go for quality, and keep measuring performance against plan. Yet every time they turned over a new problem, those ideas seemed fresh and unique. One evening the Baron told him, "Duncan you're the only friend I have that I can rely upon for good counsel." They were becoming close friends.

The Laird was concerned, however, that Ramsay and his father were somewhat distant. He was a fine young man and the Laird wished they had a relationship like the Laird had with the boy.

CHAPTER XXVIII

The wives of the Laird's social circle seemed to be intent on finding a suitable life partner for him. At one of the weekly dinners he was partnered with a most attractive woman in her late thirties. When they were being seated at the dinner table, the Laird noted the name Elspeth Stokesdale. He held her chair and said, "I'm Duncan Fleming."

She smiled. "I'm Betsy Stokesdale," and sat down. When they were seated she leaned over close to him and said, "Hello, Lawman. I've always wanted to meet you."

He wondered, 'How did she know he had raced under the name Lawman. Had she done a little research or what? Obviously a different type of person.' He asked, "How did you know my racing name?"

"Oh, I know a lot about you. Over a hundred races in fourteen countries. 72 wins. Never out of the money. One of the top money winners in both stock car and drag racing for six years. Owner and restorer of the famous Thorpe Manor in the Midlands, which received architectural prizes. Prominent attorney. And now Laird of Kirkwood. And I forgot to mention - world famous for a recent little incident at The White Corbie."

The Laird shook his head. "I suppose you've seen my baby pictures too?"

She looked him up and down and smiled mischievously. "No, but I think I can envision what they looked like."

"Where'd you get all the racing information?"

"I've read Racing Magazine for years and years, and I used to do a little racing myself."

The Laird looked at her more closely, and looked again at the place card. He mused aloud, "Betsy Stokesdale, Stokes— Betty Stokes—. Say, you aren't Betty Stokes the lady driver? Raced at Daytona? You came on the scene just about the time I stopped racing."

She smiled, giving him a profile pose. "One and the same. Yes, I raced at Daytona among other places. I had to use an alias, because my father threatened to disown me if I used the family name."

After that start they talked about racing and all the people they knew. She had only raced for three years and for a while employed one of the mechanics on the Laird's team. She told him, "I heard so much about you and a mechanic named Butch, that I feel I really know you both intimately."

The Laird said softly, "Butch died a couple of years ago. He's now in racer's heaven."

"I'm so sorry to hear that," she said. "And by the way did you know that STP (Stanislaus Thaddeus Pryszczinski - Editor and Publisher of Racing Magazine. Everyone called him STP for short) is going to open a racing hall of fame in Florida, and you and I are both going to be in it. It's scheduled to open sometime this autumn; I'll keep you informed. Maybe we could go to the opening together. And big news for you - I talked with STP a few days ago; told him I expected to see you; he said to say hello; and he told me they're going to have a life sized picture of you in the exhibit, the one of you running from the car with your clothing all in flames. You poor darling let me see you arm."

The Laird obeyed and lifted his left hand, but he didn't unbutton his shirt cuff. She looked at his hand, and said, "Looks as good as new - better than new." She kissed the top of his hand. "And one other thing. You won't believe this, but they'll have a piece of the side panel from that car on display right next to your picture. Your mechanic that worked for me saved it as a souvenir, and when the appeal went out for things to put in the Hall of Fame, he donated it."

The Laird was fascinated. He had never met anyone as beautiful and intelligent and interesting as Betsy Stokesdale. She undoubtedly fit very well into his category of the type one might call a Wonder Woman.

When the evening was over and they were parting, she had him by the arm, of which she had taken possession when they left the dinner table and had kept it until they were separating at the front door. "Lawman, I've also done a bit of competitive horse riding and they're going to have an important competition in London in a couple of weeks. If you could get away for a few days, there's a very heavy round of receptions and parties every night. I won't be riding, but it'll be a lot of fun - a lot of people you would enjoy meeting. We could stay at our family penthouse in the Savoy Hotel. And don't worry. My Aunt will be there to chaperone. It'll all be very proper."

The Laird was captivated by Betsy Stokesdale. She was an enchantress. He felt he would enjoy more of her company, and they had only scratched the surface in talking racing. He didn't hesitate. "I accept. Just name the dates."

CHAPTER XXIX

As had become habit, the day after the Laird's night out at the elite dinner parties, Kerrie would read his diary. She was interested to find, 'At last I have found her, Betsy Stokesdale, a Wonder Woman. Truly one of the most amazing women I have ever met. She can do anything. Can't wait 'til we meet again.' This gave Kerrie a vicious wrench in her stomach. Why? She wondered whether it was because she might be jealous. She tried to dismiss the thought from her mind. His interests in women were his business, and they only became her concern if he was going to introduce another woman at the head of the Kirkwood household, which might complicate things, particularly if she were not interested in history and everything related to the castle.

But back to business. Kerrie continued over the weeks to retrace her steps in searching the Laird's quarters for any secret hiding places. She searched all the other connecting rooms from the passageway. The only hiding place she found was in the library behind one of the shelves. There was a panel about ten inches wide and shelf high. It had looked suspicious when she first looked for cracks and lines in the paneling behind the shelves. She looked for a button or release and finally pushed on it; it snapped open. When she moved it back on its hinge, it revealed an old Scotch whiskey bottle. It still had a small amount of liquid in the bottom. That was all that was in the opening. She speculated as to who might have kept this secreted there, when anyone could have simply rung for one of the servants and they would have brought anything requested. Did someone, maybe a servant, have a problem and hence the secrecy?

As the weeks wore on she became less and less certain of finding the treasure, but she never doubted that such existed. The side benefit of all her meticulous searching into every likely floor, wall, and piece of furniture was that she discovered numerous little things that should be repaired or improved, and she had started early on to make a list for each of the rooms. Later when she worked with the housekeepers or checked on the work of the tradesmen, they found her to be most exacting. She could point out the smallest hairline crack or scratch they had missed. She would point to a piece of furniture, and say, "I'm sure there's something on the back of that piece by the wall that needs attention." And when they moved it out, she was always right. Did she have x-ray eyes?

She took her luncheon and tea each day by herself at her work place on the third floor. The Laird took his in the Great Hall at a small table by the window looking out to the garden. He usually finished tea quickly and then walked up to her area. It was the time of every day when she would brief him on the work she was doing, not only with the research projects, but also the restoration of the building and its contents, which really were part of the history of the place and were part of her responsibilities.

That time of the day was the highlight for both of them. It would have been patently obvious to anyone passing and seeing the interaction that they were not only deeply involved in the subject matter, but also with each other. The conversations ranged far beyond work in the castle and included topics like 'do you like fish and chips?' or politics, or religion, or personal experiences each had had in his or her youth, or any and everything that came to their minds. Sometime Kerrie just listened to the Laird as he talked about some of his legal cases and in effect lent an ear while he was working out solutions in his mind; she liked hearing about his concerns for the human aspects of the legal contests. They were gradually getting to know each other very well, their likes and dislikes, and their whims.

When the Laird was away, the day was a dull one for Kerrie. He likewise, might be somewhere in the States, and he would look at his watch and think, 'Teatime would be just about over at the castle. I wonder what Kerrie would have to show me today?'

The little briefings were meant to be only fifteen or thirty minutes, but they usually went on for two hours or longer. Both would lose track of time. They might have people in and around almost anytime during the day, but after teatime they were always alone. Undoubtedly, the servants had arranged it that way.

Much as Kerrie resisted the idea, she had to admit to herself that her relationship with the Laird was important to her. Intensely important. She knew it wasn't because the likelihood of a treasure being found was dimming. She had found that the hours that they spent together were the hours that she lived for each day and thought about later when she was at home by herself. She tried to think of a way of getting the relationship back on a first name basis. But he seemed so definite about calling her Miss Bramwood; there would be no way without losing face. She couldn't bring herself to say, 'From now on let's drop all the Sir and Miss Bramwood stuff.'

Whenever they played tennis, even on warm days she always wore long sleeved shirts and leggings to protect her from the sun. And for work she always wore loose fitting two-piece suits with long skirts. On one of her trips to London she picked up an American tabloid newspaper named The Comet in the train station. An article caught her attention: 'Twelve Ways That Guarantee He'll Propose'. She bought the newspaper. The article started out saying that no man is going to enter marriage until he sees the merchandise he is getting. It then went on to list things like going to the beach and wearing the briefest bikini. Oh yes—just say to the Laird, let's go to the beach today. Ridiculous. Another was that when he took you out to dinner and you went back to your apartment afterward, tell him you want to be more comfortable and slip into a sheer negligee. Great, she thought, first of all I have to get him to take me out to dinner. Where? The White Corbie? And afterward take him to my modest house? Plus I don't even own a negligee. She speculated on maybe wearing a miniskirt to the castle one day and putting it on just for their session after tea, and she could wear a tight open blouse. But after she thought about it for a while she felt she would be embarrassed to do it. Not that there was any part of her body to be ashamed of, but it simply wasn't her style of behavior. And besides, if she stripped down naked, he probably wouldn't notice it; he always seemed to be mainly absorbed in the restoration of the castle and the research project.

The cataloguing of the books was coming along very nicely. Jeffrey would take a load of books to the house of the librarian for her mother to catalog and later would pick them up and deliver another batch. At first it started out as a weekly delivery, and soon it became a routine every other day. He had found the daughter to be a most attractive companion. Also, he had been made to feel very welcome in the household by both mother and daughter. Despite his lesser education, they found his manners to be most courtly, and they were impressed with how well read he seemed to be. The daughter worked with books every day, but Jeffrey seemed to have had more exposure to what was in them.

CHAPTER XXX

Tennis was important in the lives of Kerrie and the Laird. Both were receiving the benefits of the exercise, and she was leading him along bit by bit, and he was developing into a better than average player. He would never be as good as Ramsay was promising to be, but he was now well above the typical social player.

There was a houseguest at the Auldlay's for one week. He was the head of a large American company and had come to Britain to conclude a sizable contract with one of the Auldlay companies. Afterward he was invited to Scotland as a guest. He was greatly interested in tennis, and considered himself a superior player and regularly invited leading professional players to his large estate to rest and practice and play tennis on his courts. He would brag to any listener, "Of course I'm not a professional, and of course I have to work in my office every day, but I have to admit in all modesty that when I play these professionals I do win my share of games." He had brought along his racquet and asked the Auldlays if there was anyone that might be interested in playing. The first person that came to mind was the Laird, and at the weekly dinner they took along their houseguest and introduced him to the Laird.

The Laird told him that to play the next day would not be possible; he had a long conference call scheduled for the morning and an afternoon appointment, but he would try to send over one of his employees who liked to play.

The next morning Kerrie showed up as arranged. The day was overcast, but the rain held off. She didn't wear her cover-ups that day and looked very attractive in her tennis shorts. He was disappointed that he might just be hitting the ball back and forth over the net with her, but at least the scenery wouldn't be bad. She took out a pink racket, and as they were unpacking, he gave her his speech on how he played the professionals and got his share of the games. She pretended to look impressed and offered, "I hope I don't disappoint you. If it gets too boring, let me know and we'll stop."

They started off by just hitting the ball back and forth to warm up. Kerrie could tell in the first minute that he was of doubtful ability, at least not at the level he claimed. When they started playing she pretended to let a ball hit first on the rim of her racket and another on the handle. He shouted, "Keep your eye on the ball." And a little later, "Try to keep your arm straighter."

Despite her seeming ineptitude, he found himself scrambling all over the court. Several times she thought she might have to ease up on the old geezer so that he wouldn't have a heart attack. She concluded that his serve was far from professional; his backhand weak, and he moved too slowly to achieve good position for returning the ball.

He assumed that he must have been suffering from jet lag. It was obvious to him that this little doll of a lady was bumbling around the court, but he really had to work to gain his points. If he had been a little more observant he might have noticed that in five minutes, he was wringing wet and she wasn't even winded. She allowed him to win each game by one point, just barely. And after they had played four sets, she looked at her watch and said, "Well, I guess that's it. Back to the salt mines for me."

He was on vacation and had nothing but time, and he was sure he was loosening up, so he asked, "How about one more set? Winner takes all?"

She accepted. "O.K. Winner takes all?"

They played another set. A lot of tie breaking points, but she let him win each of the first two games barely. She edged him out for the third and let him have the fourth."

As they were packing and getting ready to leave for the second time, he said, "I should give my host and hostess a break. How about having dinner with me somewhere tomorrow night and afterward we'll go back to your place and crawl between the sheets together?"

Kerrie blushed. She thought to herself, 'So he wants to play with me some more.' She replied, "I'll challenge you to another set. Winner takes all."

She had acquiesced to his request for an extra set, and he had to agree. And he was hoping that her desire to extend the friendship had prompted the request. "O.K. Winner take all," he agreed.

This time she pulled a different racquet out of her bag and carried it to her side of the court. She announced, "My serve."

The first serve she aced him. He wasn't sure he even saw the ball go by. The next she gave a vicious slice, and he couldn't back away fast enough to get his racquet on the ball. And so it continued. When he served she gave him shots that were difficult if not impossible to return, and if he did return them he was far out of position for the next one.

After three games he had only taken a few lucky points. He was angry but hopeful that he could get something out the day's experience. He said to her, "I think I've been had by a ringer. You're professional. What's your real name?"

She smiled sweetly, "No. I'm just a social player. Remember. Winner takes all. And I won't be available tomorrow night or any other night. I'm taken. Permanently."

Jeffrey had come to pick her up and witnessed the last set. He was impressed, and he told Granville about it who later repeated it to the Laird, who said, "Well, it's hard to judge the progress of someone, but I've worked with her pretty steadily for weeks, and practice makes perfect."

The Laird was scheduled to play with the visitor the next day. Kerrie reminded him in the afternoon of his appointment for the game. She decided to give him some incentive to win. She told him, "This chap thinks he's a hot tennis player. And I think he's also a little overheated otherwise. You would do me a favor if you cooled him off a little."

"What happened?" asked the Laird.

"In the annals of Scottish history it will never appear, but suffice it to say, I want you to give him a lesson tomorrow - a tennis lesson."

"Isn't he supposed to be pretty good?" asked the Laird.

"He's not as good as he thinks he is. He has a weak backhand and a short temper. You're going to let him beat himself."

"Keep going," said the Laird.

"Most players have a weak backhand, particularly amateurs. He knows it. What I suggest you do is keep returning every shot to his backhand. And he'll soon know that you know his Achilles heel. And that will make him angry. Also, you're a very courteous and predictable player on your serve. He's a very nervous and impatient receiver of serves. I would suggest that after the first couple of games when you see that he's getting annoyed with your feeding his backhand, that you begin to alter the timing on your serves. Bounce the ball a couple of times and then stop and do it a couple of times again. Keep varying the pattern. Once or twice lose the ball and make him wait while you pick it up. This will throw him off balance and his temper will continue to build until you have him totally out of stride, and then he's yours."

"Is that what you've been doing with me?" asked the Laird.

"Yes and no. But you're very patient and even-tempered and an excellent receiver of shots, rarely out of position. And no, I can't say in effect you were ever mine." She repeated to herself, 'No. You never were mine.'

"Where'd you get all this strategy?" questioned the Laird.

"You know that I edit books, and I've done a couple on tennis, and I do read tennis magazines."

The next morning the Laird went out and followed Kerrie's instructions. The visitor thought he could tell from the beginning that the Laird was nowhere near as skillful as Kerrie, and expected to carve him into little pieces. But as the play progressed, the Laird was quick on the court and always ready to return the ball and always to his backhand. 'Damn,' thought the visitor. 'Doesn't he have any other shot, except to my left?' As Kerrie predicted, he began to get annoyed, and he began to lose his coordination and tried to smack the ball harder and harder. In a few words, the Laird walked away with the match. As they were packing up, the visitor asked him, "What was the name of that pro you sent over here yesterday. She claims she's one of your employees."

"Pro?" questioned the Laird knitting his brow; he was thinking. "She's far from a pro. She works for me in the castle. She's a record keeper. Takes care of the library and does some filing. I've actually been helping her work on her tennis game, and she's improved quite a bit in the last few months."

"Yahh," said the visitor.

That night at dinner the visitor asked the Baron. "About that Miss Bramwood that was over here yesterday. Is she a tennis pro?"

The Baron thought for a minute and looked over at the Baroness. She just shrugged her shoulders. The Baron said, "Impossible. I think she takes care of his library and some family records. Sometimes she comes over here and bats the tennis balls around with my children. I'm sure she's just a very ordinary player."

"How about Fleming?" asked the visitor.

The Baron was anxious to champion his friend's cause anytime, and he answered, "Fleming. Let me tell you, that man is brilliant. Anything he gets interested in, he tries to become the best. Yes. In his case I suspect if he decides to play tennis, he can play as well as anyone. Man's a competitor. Was one of the world's most famous racing drivers for a number of years."

The Baroness added, "Miss Bramwood does more than just books and records for Laird Fleming. She helps him get his blood circulating the first thing every morning, and takes care of anything he needs anytime every day."

At that point the visitor decided he 'had been had' twice. First by Kerrie and then by her teacher, who had pretended to be an amateur. Later, as he reflected back on it, he envied the

Laird. He would like to hire a cute doll like Kerrie to take care of the few hundred books in his household library and his family records and play tennis with him or whatever else he might want. He'd never get that one past his wife.

Two important things happened in late summer. The first was the unveiling of the Vauxhall, which had been reconditioned and was ready to roll. Every part had been cleaned and oiled or greased, and all questionable parts were replaced. The two 'musketeers,' Ramsay and Duncan had had the engine running on and off a number of times. On the day of the 'unveiling' they had invited Ramsay's parents and grandparents and aunts and uncles and cousins, altogether over thirty people. And of course Kerrie and the Laird were there.

The Laird and Ramsay pushed the car out into the yard. And then they put gasoline in the tank as if it were for the first time. "I hope this starts," said Ramsay. The Laird put one thumb up in the air and gave a turn on the crank. Nothing. He gave another turn. Nothing. Then Ramsay, who was sitting in the driver's seat, turned on a switch and on the next turn the engine roared and quickly settled down to a smooth purr.

The Laird announced, "I know that everyone wants a ride in this magnificent chariot, so we have here some slips and everyone will have to draw and go in number order. Only three passengers at a time."

While Ramsay drove the first passengers out to the gate and back, the Laird remarked to the boy's father, "That's quite a son you have there. Good mind and a lot of 'stick-to-it-ness.' He actually did all the work on that car himself. I was only the consultant. That piece of junk that was headed for the scrap pile is now worth several hundred thousand pounds. And a lot more, if he decides to put just a little more work into it."

In the father's world, pounds and pence were the real measures of value, and he was impressed. "Well, I guess all the year's of training I've given the boy are starting to pay off."

The Laird nodded his head. "It's obvious he's had a lot of good training somewhere long the line."

The second important event was the following week - the Glasgow Masters Tennis Competition. Ramsay had been entered. It was an all week affair. The field was large, and Ramsay would have to play seven times if he reached the finals. Kerrie received permission from the Laird to go there with him each day, and while there she would scout his opponents.

The Laird was anxious about the whole endeavor. "Are you sure," he asked Kerrie, "that he's ready for this sort of competition?"

"No doubt about it," affirmed Kerrie.

"But he's only played tennis with you."

She pretended to look hurt. "Yes, and I only play tennis with you. And you're a whole lot better than you think you are."

That logic sounded incontestable. The Laird shrugged his shoulders and accepted her answer.

The final instruction Kerrie gave Ramsay was, "Remember. There are no friends on the tennis courts. Don't feel sorry for anyone who looks like he wants pity or pretends he has a sore arm or whatever. You take every single point you can get. It could just be that on the next volley you might twist your ankle, and you'll be sorry for giving away points."

In the first four matches, Ramsay breezed by his opponents. He simply blew them off the court. Kerrie's scouting was of great value. Each player had his strong points and his weak points, and she could spot them quickly. The opponent for the fifth match, the quarterfinals, had watched Ramsay play his fourth match and was convinced that he was a 'ringer,' a professional. He refused to play him and registered a protest with the judges. The judges took the protest seriously as the boy was totally unknown to any of the tennis clubs in Scotland. It was easily established, however, that he was the son of the Baron Auldlay. But maybe he had played elsewhere as a professional under another name.

Kerrie intervened and suggested they contact her former boss in London, who was still the most notable tennis coach in the country. Upon reaching him he asked, "Who did you say was his coach? Kerrie Bramwood? Best teaching associate I ever had. I tried to get her to become professional. She wasn't interested. If she had, there's no one that could have beaten her. She's both athletic and an intelligent player. But aside from that, she can teach."

With those credentials Ramsay's status was no longer in question. The final two rounds were to be played on Saturday and Sunday. They hadn't mentioned to his father that he was in the tournament. His father was uncertain as to what was happening, but he was persuaded to go to Glasgow to watch for the last two days. Again on Saturday it was hardly a match. The competition was tougher, but he was tough - too strong a player for amateur tennis. Why? Because from the first minute of his first lesson, he had been trained for professional tennis.

His father was elated, and as he could see his son in easy control. He couldn't restrain himself, and turned to other spectators around him saying, "My son out there. Good boy. Good at everything he does."

After the Saturday game Ramsay's family and the Laird and Kerrie all had dinner together. Kerrie showed him the local papers from the last few days and from the space allocated to the tournament, it was clearly an important event - at least in Glasgow. The Laird asked him if he had played tennis himself.

"No," he replied. "Rugby and cricket were my games. But I believe that if you're good in one you can be good in another. It's in the genes. Athletic talent runs in the family."

On the final day there had been a bit of light rain in the morning and the ground was a bit heavy. Kerrie had scouted the opponent, and she told Ramsay that the man was a nervous player - impatient. She gave him the same instructions that she had given the Laird when he had played the visitor from the United States. Bounce the ball irregularly and throw him off his timing. Also she put a strip of lead tape on the side of his racquet, and instructed, "Keep this on the right side of your racquet. This is going to give you more spin to the right. Don't even think about it being there. Just play your usual game."

The final was hard fought, but Ramsay handled the opponent like he had the others, and he was cool as a cucumber throughout. Later, Kerrie asked him, "What impressed you most about all the matches?"

He thought for a moment. "That little piece of lead tape you put on my racquet. How many more tricks like that do you have up your sleeve?"

She smiled. "Oh, a few more."

When Ramsay received the trophy, it was over two feet tall. He took it and handed it to his father. Later he and his father posed for the picture, which would appear in the newspapers. The trophy had to be engraved, and when it was delivered the following week, his father asked to take it to his office where he put it right in the middle of his desk, and everyone that came into his office would have to notice it and listen for fifteen minutes while he told him about his son and the tennis match. "And let me tell you, he made mincemeat of his opponents. Bright boy. Good at everything. Good student. Can't wait 'til I get him in here to help with the business. And you ought to see the racing car he restored. He's already a genius with machinery."

CHAPTER XXXI

On one Friday after the Laird and Kerrie had their usual two hour afternoon session, he told her, "Miss Bramwood, I won't be about next week. I have to go to London. Some business matters."

She replied pleasantly, "I hope that it's not all business, and that you'll have a good time, perhaps be with some friends?"

She had read his dairy, and she thought, 'I know damn well he's going to be with that Stokesdale female - a Wonder Woman, and I wish he didn't lie about having to do some business. Lie or not. It hurts. A lot.'

On Sunday afternoon the Laird met Betsy Stokesdale at Prestwick Airport as she had instructed. She was waiting for him along with a private jet owned by her father. She greeted him with a hardy embrace and whispered in his ear, "We're going to have such a good time."

When they arrived at Heathrow airport there was a limousine waiting, and they were soon delivered to the Savoy Hotel where her family kept a penthouse suite year round for their exclusive use.

She showed the Laird to his bedroom, and said, "You'll have to dress for dinner tonight, Darling, and I'll meet you in the sitting room a few minutes after six."

The Laird so far hadn't seen any sign of the aunt who was to be the chaperone.

At six promptly he was waiting in the sitting room, dressed in black jacket, and he had started to look at a magazine. A slender, leggy, and handsome young lady in her early twenties in a lovely dress with a short, tight skirt walked into the sitting room, obviously from somewhere inside the suite. She stopped when she saw him. "Oh, you must be the famous racing driver I've heard so much about."

The Laird rose. "I'm Duncan Fleming if that's whom you mean. And your name is?"

She strode directly toward him and stood face-to-face, "I'm Eudoxia Stokesdale, Betsy's Aunt - really. I'm always glad to meet her young friends." And, embracing him, she pressed herself firmly against him and proceeded to give him as deep a kiss as she could execute - catching him totally by surprise.

At that moment Betsy walked into the room. "Eudoxia. Behave yourself," - this in a calm voice, as if she were saying, 'Eudoxia, stop slurping your soup.'

Without releasing her embrace and without looking at her niece, she replied, "I'm only trying to make your friend feel welcome." And again she began to explore the Laird's mouth, which was hanging open in amazement.

"Eudoxia, your fiancé is waiting for you downstairs. Or shall I invite him up and tell him to sit here on the settee while you finish greeting my friend?"

Eudoxia released the Laird. Licking her upper lip she said, "You are so tasteful in selecting your friends." She sauntered out the door of the room deliberately swinging her hips.

"Brat. Strumpet." Betsy muttered. "She'll never live until she's twenty-five. Somebody in the family, like me, will do the world a favor and kill her first. Wait here while I get you some tissue to wipe the lipstick off your face."

The reception was held in the Royal Automobile Club in St. James. It was obvious to the Laird that this was a privileged set. There was no one there that he knew. Betsy seemed to know many people - mostly men. And she greeted everyone as 'Darling,' and most of the time had four or five men standing around her. She was very beautiful, and if you have beauty and a lot of money, it attracts men like bees to honey. 'But she has much more than that,' thought the Laird as he listened to her talk to each of the men about their occupations or special interests.

One was a merchant banker with a prominent old house in the City of London. "Peter," she said. "What a brilliant maneuver that was in your takeover of the Stromboid Corporation last week. But from my mathematics, it looks like you stole it. It's easily worth another fifty million pounds. Your competitor in the bidding missed the boat."

Peter took his cigarette out of his mouth and stared at her for a moment, "Betsy, either one of our partners has been talking or you've broken into our file room."

She smiled and said sweetly, "Elementary my dear Watson. Elementary."

To another gentleman she said, "Whom are you betting on in the competition? I know that Bohun Chinah is the favorite, but I'll take Hyland Dancer and bet you a hundred quid against any horse you select."

The challenged replied, "I know better than to bet against you, Betsy. Thanks for the tip. Now I know where to place my bet."

The Laird admired her as she went on and on like that all evening. 'She really has it all.' But as the hours wore on, he also felt more and more like an acolyte and less and less an escort. Clearly it was important to her to be surrounded by men - as many as possible. She enjoyed being the center of attention.

When they returned to the apartment she said, "Darling, walk out on the balcony and look at the lights across the Thames. I'll be back in a moment."

The Laird opened the French doors and stood in front of the stone balcony and admired the view across the Thames Embankment. In a few minutes Betsy returned in a negligee that she had neglected to tie around her. Tying it would have been superfluous as it was very sheer. She slipped between him and the rail, facing him. "How do you like the view?" she asked.

The Laird swallowed. He had already made up his mind earlier in the evening that this relationship had to come to a dead end. He said, "I do think it's bedtime."

She embraced him and kissed him. "I agree," she whispered.

They left the porch. He walked to his bedroom and she to hers. He was relieved that the parting had been accomplished so easily without any embarrassment.

The Laird walked to the far end of his bedroom and took off his clothes and draped them over the chair near the bed. He felt like he needed a shower. There had been so much smoke at the reception.

He took two steps toward the washroom when the door opened and out walked a naked and very attractive Eudoxia. Her evening had not ended as she had expected. At the dinner party they had attended they were talking with some people and her fiancé had bumped her arm causing red wine to spill from her glass all over her legs and shoes. This had triggered a spat and to punish him she had gone home alone in a taxi. But she was programmed to finish the evening with a male, and she had decided to wait for the Laird to return, and she would surprise him by waiting for him in his bed.

When she saw him standing by the bed, she put her hands on her thighs and slowly drew them up to her breasts and while she lifted her breasts in the air toward him, she said in a sultry voice, "Lover, I've been waiting here all evening for you."

Just then Betsy walked into the room. She had removed her negligee and it was hanging behind her back on the crook of a finger. She had clearly interpreted the Laird's last words to her as an invitation. "Eudoxia! What are you doing here?"

Eudoxia looked at her smugly. "I could ask you that. My lover and I plan to make torrid love, and you are intruding."

Betsy glared daggers at her, "Eu-dox-i-a. That is exactly what he and I agreed to do just minutes ago. So go collect your teddy bear and get out of here."

The Laird was standing there listening to the debate between these two beautiful unclad creatures, and to his embarrassment his autonomic functions dominated, and he was doing his best to disguise it.

Eudoxia was not about to give up the prize easily, and she declared, "Elspeth. As your aunt, I'm supposed to be here to chaperone you. So trot off to bed like a good niece. And have a glass of cold milk. It'll not only help to cool you off, but it's supposed to be good for the geriatric set."

The last few words cut too deeply, and Betsy tossed her head and replied, "Oooff." She turned on her heel and walked out of the room.

The Laird stood in his tracks. It had sounded to him like two sisters had found themselves pulling on the same dress on a bargain table, and they were coolly but firmly debating who was going to gain possession. 'At least they didn't agree to take turns using it,' he thought.

When Betsy left the room, Eudoxia took several leaps across the floor squealing a loud "NOW," and she pushed him onto the bed and fell on top of him. She then proceeded to join herself completely to him and after she had achieved whole possession of his masculinity, she placed her arms around his neck and ran her moist tongue back and forth over his lips.

All of this had happened so quickly that the Laird hadn't recovered his composure. He found his mind stupidly speculating, 'Had Eudoxia achieved a wrestling fall? Or had he fallen? Should he resist the pleasant onslaught of this leggy nymph or let his conscience take a recess for the rest of the evening?'

While he was cogitating and Eudoxia was coiting Betsy walked back in the room.

She was wearing the negligee and now had it firmly tied about her waist. She walked up to the side of the bed and studied the pair, and said coolly, "Well, I see you two have become quite attached to each other."

Eudoxia ignored her and continued her conquest. Betsy tried to get her attention again and sang, "Eu - ^{dox} - ^{i} - a."

Just then a flash bulb popped. Betsy had brought her camera. Eudoxia looked up and over her shoulder. Betsy said, "I think your fiancé would be interested to know that you have such diverse talents."

Eudoxia jumped off the Laird and the bed. "Let's negotiate."

Betsy was walking swiftly out of the room closely followed by Eudoxia.

The Laird lay on the bed trying to replay and assimilate what had happened in the last few minutes. Something had happened, but nothing had happened. Neither of the two returned to the room. After a while he got up and went to the door and looked down the hallway. He saw and heard nothing. He closed the door and started for the shower. He paused a moment, and then walked back and set the bolt on the door.

The next morning the Laird walked into the dining room of the suite. A maid appeared and took his breakfast order. When she returned she handed him a note:

"Al, Darling, Something dreadful has come up, and both my Aunt and I have to rush to the home of an elderly relative who has been stricken very suddenly. See you soon in Scotland.

Love and Kisses. Betsy.

P.S. The invitations for the whole week are on the desk in the sitting room. Please use them and have a good time. B.

P.P.S. There was no film in the camera. B."

When the maid come back with more coffee, he asked, "Is anyone else still here, or am I alone?"

"They're both gone, Sir. Left early this morning. Oh, and I forgot. The young lady also asked me to give you a letter." She left the room and returned with a sealed envelope. The Laird opened it. With red lipstick Eudoxia had firmly placed the outline of her lips on the paper. In the center was a phone number. At the bottom she had written:

"Be sure to give me a call soon. We have some unfinished business to attend to."

The Laird packed after breakfast, called the castle for a pickup at the airport and took the next plane out for Glasgow. In the late afternoon he walked into Kerrie's area and said cheerfully, "Ready for our afternoon visit?"

She responded enthusiastically, "I've never been so happy to see you." She was startled, having expected he would be gone the whole week. 'Something must have gone wrong between him and Wonder Woman,' she thought.

The Laird liked the welcome, but he wondered, 'Why so happy now rather than any other day?' He sank into the chair opposite her and concluded, 'Being right here with Kerrie is like - what?' He thought some more, and words like 'home, decency, unaffected beauty, complete integrity,' and he could have gone on and on, but she was talking. He sat back in his chair for the next two hours and relaxed, more accurately basked in drinking in her personality. He would only occasionally nod, or say "A great piece of work," or "Terrific" or "Truly interesting."

When it was the usual time for her to leave, he was strongly tempted to ask her to have dinner with him. She was hoping he would ask her for dinner. But he reminded himself that she was the one who insisted that they be Sir and Miss. When she left he went down to the Great Hall for the next hour and awaited dinner. He sat and looked out the window and watched as it slowly darkened outside.

CHAPTER XXXII

Not too long after the London - Stokesdale experience the Laird was walking past Kerrie's area on the third floor (and it had become a habit for him to walk by several times daily, only saying 'Hi' or maybe stopping by momentarily if she had something particular to show him or ask him. He noticed the routine in himself, and concluded that it was good for him to get up and walk around a bit, and also it kept the employees on their toes to see him walk by once in awhile).

Often Kerrie would be involved with Granville, or sometimes Jeffrey, or one of the MacDuffies, or on the telephone with some tradesman. In the morning he might see the Reverend MacTaggart. Around ten Sandy Morthland would come and stay until just before tea time, and any time during the day he might see anyone of the Auldlay children or the Baroness herself having a tete a tete with Kerrie. The place was as busy as Piccadilly Circus at any hour of the day or night, it seemed to him.

On one of those ordinary days he was walking by when he saw a someone that he didn't recall seeing before. She was talking with Kerrie and the two of them just acknowledged him with a pleasant "Good morning" and returned to discussing the document they were looking at.

The Laird was puzzled. The stranger he was seeing was familiar and yet she wasn't. He stood there staring. When they paused and looked at him again, Kerrie said, "Sir, is there something we can do for you?"

He just kept staring.

Kerrie looked down at herself and at the guest and then around the room. "Is there something wrong?"

The Laird swallowed and cleared his throat. "Do I know our guest?"

Both the Ladies laughed. The guest said, "Duncan, it's me, Sandy. Saundra. Don't you remember me?"

The Laird was still staring.

Sandy offered, "Saundra Morthland? Scotland? The twentieth century?"

He recognized her voice, and he finally managed, "Of course, Sandy. Forgive me. My mind must have been a million miles away. I was having a mental block. Nice to see you today, and that's a pretty dress you're wearing. I've got to hurry on. Expecting an important phone call."

Granville had been at work, and he had enlisted Regina Godfrey and her mastery at dress and costuming.

Regina was a wonderful person and a motherly and sisterly type to everyone. How often she had had 'to hold the head' of a young actress or actor that was anxious about his or her forthcoming role. How often she had convinced them that she would make them into the role of the princess or prince charming or whatever.

She had schemed first with Granville and then with Kerrie and had managed to take Sandy aside and told her, "Miss Morthland, I've watched you from the distance, and you are a beautiful person. But you don't use your best qualities to let the world know how beautiful you are."

All of Sandy's life she had been teased by her father and mother and siblings about her 'plain looks,' and she had always been a wallflower at every social function. Mrs. Godfrey's words brought forth a lifetime of tears and while she wept, Mrs. Godfrey talked about the real meaning of beauty and told her, "The fish takes the bait initially for its appearance, but its really of the substance of the bait that fish really wants. My Dear, give me a chance, and I'll have the big fish lined up begging to nibble at you. You are a beautiful person. I've made leading ladies out of toads that couldn't hold a candle to you."

They sat together that day for several hours. After the first hour Sandy acquiesced, "I'm in your experienced hands, Mrs. Godfrey".

Mrs. Godfrey went on, "Granville, in my opinion, was one of the great actors on the London stage. Why? Because he knew every part of every person in every play, and not just the words, but how they should look, what their every move should be, and how they should walk and speak. Granville should be directing plays right this minute."

"What?" Sandy questioned. "Granville an actor? Are you sure?"

"Trust me," said Mrs. Godfrey. "I want you to work with Granville and take everything he says very seriously, and I guarantee that magical things will happen. Ninety-nine percent of the people are very ordinary in the role of the particular person they are destined by Mother Nature to play on this planet called earth. Granville can train you to be in that other one percent."

Resolutely, Sandy hugged Mrs. Godfrey, "I'm in both your hands. I'm ready to be reborn and try a new me. The old me has been unhappy for years. When can we begin?"

"Right now. Let me get your measurements. And then we'll call Granville."

Granville had been standing by, and when they rang for him he joined the two in the guest suite where they had been talking. He was most professional. He knew it would take empathy and patience and yet a professional demeanor to get her to stay with the project.

"What we're going to do in the next few weeks is transform you into the real you," began Granville. "Try to think of Mrs. Godfrey and me as teachers or advisors. Forget anything else about us. And forgive us if we speak frankly, but we'll be giving very specific instructions, and we wish to do this in a few weeks, not a few years.

"First off, you are a beautiful person. Very good material to start with. I've done wonders with infinitely less than you bring to the party." Granville opened his make-up box. "First let's wash the stains off your face. You do have a very pretty shaped face. Most people don't know what to do with make-up. It can turn the same woman into a crone or a beauty. What we're going to do gradually over two or three weeks is emphasizing your strong points, and you have plenty of them. We don't want people to notice. It will be gradual enough that they'll think you've always been this way." He made up her eyes, eyebrows, cheeks, and lips.

"I'm going to give these cosmetics to you to take along. You see what I've done to emphasize your pretty cheekbones, and your eyes; you do have beautiful eyes, but we have to outline them a little, because you are so blonde. For the daytime we'll use brighter tones to give you color, but for the nighttime we'll use darker tones to make you look a little mysterious. And your lips; we're going to make them just a little larger. Do you like it?"

She looked into the mirror and nodded and smiled.

"And, by the way, whenever you talk to someone, make eye contact. You'll hypnotize them.

"All this will take a few days of practice. But do your best, and we'll adjust it after you come tomorrow. And tomorrow I want you to wear a shoe with at least a medium heel. You have youthful legs - very pretty, the type many men admire. But we'll do two things with them, one is to change their shape with a higher heel, and we'll also do some work on walking and standing. Is this posing? Yes. But so is slinking if people do that. You have a lot of natural poise, and we'll just let it take over and not hide it.

"Also, you have beautiful teeth. Let me see you smile. That's it. Lovely. Is there anything you can think of that always makes you smile? Don't tell me what it is. That's your secret. We'll talk about when to turn on the charm and how to use it to maximum advantage. And now that's enough for one day, and Mrs. Godfrey will take over." Granville left the room.

"My Dear, let me tell you that there is no such thing as the perfectly shaped human being. We can teach people how to act, but they can only look like what Mother Nature has given them - that is until Aunt Regina gets hold of them.

'You're lucky that you have a teenage build that will keep you looking svelte into your eighties when other women will blow up like balloons and walk around in dresses like Mother Hubbards. But we're going to make you look like you'll appear all the rest of your life - chic and shapely. So let me take your measurements. In anticipation of this secret little meeting I've brought along a couple of things that I'll fit to you, but I'd like to visit your home tonight and see if there are things that we can adapt to the new you."

What the Laird noticed that day was Sandy a week into the process. After three weeks the new Sandy had her hips and breasts padded out, exquisite make-up, her straight hair pulled back and clasped on one side, and on the other she let it fall slightly over the front of her face. Instead of always receding into the background of any group, Granville had her walking and standing as well as any leading lady he had worked with, and as she smiled more and more, she felt the reciprocity that it generated, and she loved her new self and found that people were reaching out to her.

The Laird had walked back to his room that day convinced, 'Somebody or somebodies have worked on Sandy, and she looks pretty good. In fact she looks very fetching. But are they just gilding the lily to bait the trap for this old, confirmed bachelor?'

CHAPTER XXXIII

The clinic project was launched with advertising in golf magazines in a number of countries, including Western Europe, the United States, and Japan, as well as mailings to the chairmen and directors of personnel at the 1,000 largest corporations in the world. A brochure was mailed with the qualifications of the physicians and color pictures about the other amenities while at the clinic - golf, golf, and more golf. Several older professionals, their names still remembered, were hired to be about the clinic and give lessons as requested, or just talk golf. A putting green was to be installed at the rear of the building and a practice range with a green for chipping and practice from the sand bunkers was set up across the road on the Bramwood property; Kerrie was glad to rent the property for a small fee, and their maintenance would be an improvement to the land used in the historical past as a pasture for a small number of cattle for the castle.

The response was more than anticipated. The first six months were quickly subscribed with a waiting list, and they had to add another physician to the staff. The initial staff was to be twelve people in total, a nice shot in the economic arm of the village.

They had not anticipated that many of the executives wished to bring their wives and had requested examinations for them. This would add new dimensions and skill requirements for the staff, and it was planned to add that in the second six months. And there were numerous requests for dental care.

Weather should not be an obstacle. That area of Scotland enjoys a fairly mild climate. For inclement days they had indoor driving nets and a putting carpet. Also there were numerous videos of tournaments, individual slow motion analyses of the techniques of famous players, and golf lessons in general.

The opening date of September 1 was firm.

CHAPTER XXXIV

Granville was a regular, a popular one, with his butler friends at The Wallace and The Bruce each week on the staff's night off. On occasion when the Laird was away in the States, he would visit there and be received with a warm welcome by Trish, the proprietress, and invariably would find a few of his friends who were enjoying similar respites.

On one evening when he entered the pub Trish greeted him heartily and whispered, "When you can, come back into the living quarters, maybe at closing time."

All evening every time she walked near him and caught his eye she gave him a knowing look. At closing time Granville lingered and followed her into the rear of the building into a living room, Victorian in style. When they entered she closed the door and took off her apron and tossed it into a chair. "I have the most wonderful news. Night before last, my husband was drunk as usual, and he walked out the front door and into the street and stepped in front of a big lorry. Killed instantly. Funeral's tomorrow."

Granville was taken aback by her matter of fact way of talking of her husband's death, and he wasn't sure what kind of reaction she wanted from him. He felt awkward. Usually, people expect sympathy at a time like this. There are tears and regrets. Yet, here she was as happy as if she had won the Irish Sweepstake. He managed to say, "I'm so sorry to hear about your husband."

She continued in a matter-of-fact manner, "Best thing that could have happened to him. He was a dead man anyway. Drunk all the time and lately he's been in and out of the doctor's office every other week, and the doctor kept telling him his entire system was closing down - especially his liver - and it'd only be a matter of months before he's finished if he didn't stop drinking immediately. And the doctor told me personally that his condition was hopeless; he had abused himself too much.

"So, Mr. Granville, I'm not married anymore. Remember what you said some months ago? Since then I've lost over two stone, and I'm going to lose another two."

Granville had noticed her weight loss and the outline of her true facial and body features were re-emerging. He hated sordid conversations and welcomed the change of subject. "Yes, I've noticed very much your weight loss, and I compliment you. You've looked different each week, and it hasn't detracted from your natural beauty in the least. However, I must ask if you've been consulting your doctor, so that you don't lose too fast? If you haven't, we have a superior medical man in my area. I'm sure he'd be glad to monitor your progress, and I'd be happy to introduce you to him."

She looked at him with her innocent sincerity. "Mr. Granville, I've been losing this weight for you, hoping some way, some day, that," she paused and blushed and put her hands over her face. "I don't know how to say it."

Granville took her by the hand. "Sit down here next to me on the sofa." He didn't say anything for three or four minutes. Just held her hand. The emotional trauma of the death, the unknown change in her future, and now the man she adored sitting with her and holding her hand was too much. She wept.

Granville didn't say anything. He reached in his pocket for a handkerchief, unfolded it and handed it too her, and then pulled her head on his shoulder and let her sob until she stopped.

While she sobbed, he thought about this woman and how he had observed her in the pub. She ran a place that was always neat as a pin, like a private home. Her food was superior - everything cooked and baked right there in the kitchen. The customers related to her like a friend. She checked every plate brought to the tables. And if customers hesitated in choices, she would bring a small complimentary portion of their second choice. And all this she did quietly and simply. Despite her naiveté, she had an aura of calm and dignity. She was liked and respected by everyone.

"Trish, you've carried a big cross and carried it longer than anyone should. You deserve better. You're one of the most genuine and sincere persons I've ever met, and you'll get a crown in the next world, a gold one, for your loyalty to your husband all these years and running his business. But after tomorrow that chapter'll be finished, and you can throw that book away."

He paused for over a minute. "You don't really know me very well, and in truth I'm not sure I know who I am myself. Most of my life I've lived with people in the theatre. Sincerity is a rare commodity among them. Almost every sentence they speak is a line from a play they've been in, and as I've gotten older I've thirsted more and more to have relationships with genuine people. You're one of the most genuine I've ever met. But not in your favor is my age. I'm quite a bit older than you. How old are you?"

"Twenty -nine. But it won't be very long before I'm thirty," she added hopefully.

Her head was still on his shoulder and he gave her a hug. "I'm nearly half again as old as you."

She lifted her head off his shoulder, and looked into his eyes. "When I've heard you speak and act, I've seen a man of every age. I don't want a youth. I want someone like you. I want to taste it all. Mr. Granville, you can have me anytime you want me."

Granville pulled her head back on his shoulder. "Let's go slowly. First of all you can stop calling me mister; Harrison Hay Granville is my stage name; actually my legal name - I changed it after I went on the stage. You can start by calling me by my childhood name, Harry."

"Harry," she repeated. "I love it." She looked up at him and then snuggled her head down on his shoulder again.

"Sundays are pretty quiet at the castle, and I can be away, and also several evenings during the week. I think we ought to take a few months to talk a lot, get to know each other, and after that time if you feel you want to get tangled up with the likes of me, we can take the next steps."

As he talked she nodded occasionally. He leaned over and kissed her gently on the forehead. She lifted her head and looked into his eyes appealingly. He leaned over again and kissed her on her closed mouth for a long while. When they stopped she pulled his cheek next to hers and held it there while she slowly caressed the back of his neck.

"Harry, please take me now," she whispered. "I've dreamt for months of giving all of myself to you. Please. Tonight."

Granville didn't answer for some minutes. He reflected on his life, and how he had never had a close relationship with anyone. He didn't want a relationship with a leading lady - those things rarely worked out - each competing to be the top star. And he didn't want a supporting actress either. And definitely not someone from the theater, but a person he could count on being genuine, someone whose thoughts and words could be depended upon. He wanted someone different, someone who might be good in other things. Trish could well be the type of person he could live with and admire and respect.

He whispered, "There must be mutuality in a true loving relationship for it to last. You have to get as good as you give. You're a precious person. You could be very easy for me to love."

She took his head between her two hands and kissed him very deeply. When she returned his head to her cheek again, she was breathing rapidly. She took his hand and put it over her breast. He didn't withdraw it. After a few minutes she reached down and unbuttoned the top of her dress and slid his hand directly onto her breast. He didn't withdraw it. After a little longer he began gently to caress her breast. She opened all the remaining buttons on her dress, at the same time whispering to him, "There's nothing underneath the dress - just me. I was praying this would happen."

He reached up and tuned off the light on the table lamp behind the sofa. Then he hesitated, the ever-practical Granville. "Who's going to lock up the place?"

"The cook. She always locks the doors behind her when she leaves. Very dependable. She should be gone by now."

He continued where he stopped. Shortly, she uttered two words, "Ah me." Nothing more, just, "Ah me." And after that silence for the next several hours, except little sounds of enjoyment during which time they got acquainted and a little later reacquainted.

Before he left they talked at length. He asked, "What are you going to do with the pub? Continue to run it?"

"I could. I've been running it for ten years, and I've trained the help so that I just supervise. But I'm going to sell it. Too many unhappy memories here."

"What do you want to do after you sell it?"

"I want to do whatever you want to do, Harry."

Granville said, "I've got some thoughts for changing my life and things we could do together. But they're too complicated and detailed for a long explanation tonight. We'll talk further tomorrow night. What time is the funeral tomorrow?"

"First thing in the morning. And it can't be too soon for me."

"Let's get started on your new life right away. I'll call you say around eleven and by then I'll know if its possible for Doctor MacLaine to see you. I am worried about your losing weight too fast. And let me be emphatic - I'm more interested in your health than in your becoming smaller as soon as possible. Besides, the way you are there's more of you to appreciate."

When Granville left at the wee hours in the morning, they had more than a mild commitment to each other. What had happened was not a one-night stand, he thought. He felt the beginning of something lasting and satisfying.

He phoned her the next morning and Doctor MacLaine saw her early in the afternoon. Shortly afterward MacLaine called him and reported, "She wants me to give you the full story about her visit. Do you want it on the phone, or do you want to come to my office?"

"I can be in your office in minutes if that's convenient."

When Granville was ushered into his office, MacLaine said, "I hope I didn't cause any anxiety for you. I have nothing but good news. First of all let me say I think she's in good health. I didn't give her a complete physical, but I did some non-invasive tests and took some blood and interviewed her at length. Also I called my colleague down in her area. He attended her mother when she was born and hasn't seen her in his office since. She apparently hasn't had a sick day in her life. Says she comes from a very solid family - no inherited defects.

"I do want her to be careful of her diet as she loses weight, and I gave her some exercises to keep her from getting flabby. She's still young and resilient and that's on her side. And I also gave her a prescription for birth control pills."

Granville wasn't a prude, but in surprise he couldn't help exclaiming, "You what?"

MacLaine continued in his even tone, "I gave her a prescription for birth control pills. She very much hopes there'll be a marriage in the not too distant future, and I told her to take these pills for a month and see if they agree with her. Sometimes they don't, and that can put a damper on a honeymoon and start things off on the wrong foot. If they don't work, there are others we can try. She was worried about buying them from the chemist now and creating gossip. I told her not to worry about the chemist here, but if it made her feel better she could drive up to Ayr. I think she headed that way when she left.

"She doesn't object to my letting you know that she's had very little experience with intercourse. Apparently, her husband had kept his alcoholism well hidden before their marriage and immediately after the wedding he celebrated and was on a binge that lasted over ten years. She only had three contacts with him, all unsatisfactory for her. So you might have to be a little patient until she gets the hang of things."

Granville reflected on the previous evening, but said nothing, He thought, 'She may not have had much experience, so she's obviously a natural talent. And what a talent.'

"Doctor MacLaine, thank you. I can't say for sure right now that there will be a wedding. I'm quite a bit older than she. In my own mind I hope there will be, but I want to give her time to be sure. And of course there should be some proper interval after a funeral before a widow remarries. I'm not sure how long that ought to be. We'll get that detail worked out."

"Granville, Old Boy, my colleague, their family doctor, told me that the whole countryside in her area knows the hell she's been through these many years and her loyalty to her husband, and if you married her by sundown today, they'd all be saying bully for her."

They shook hands and Granville left much encouraged. As he thought about it, it struck him that this lovely lady might have suitors lined up at her door, beginning like tonight, and he better get his oar in first and strengthen the commitment. Instead of driving straight back to the castle, he looked at his watch and decided he might still find the shops open in Ayr. He would buy a suitable engagement ring with the understanding that he could come back if it weren't the right size and also that it could be made smaller if her hands got smaller as she lost weight. He was old enough to know what he wanted. If she decided to break the engagement later, he would try to understand.

As he drove to and from Ayr, he made plans for the future. It felt good. He didn't feel like he was drifting anymore. He resolved that he wouldn't try to teach his future bride how to walk and talk. He was going to keep her exactly the way she is. The only exception was that after she had lost the additional pounds and her weight stabilized, he would have Regina Godfrey work with her and they would drape her and make her up so that it would cause heads to turn when she walked by. Every woman was entitled to that. And after all, the wife of Harrison Hay Granville should look more beautiful than nine out of ten women that ones passes on the street, or better yet lovelier than ninety-nine out of a hundred.

That night after the pub closed, he joined her again in the living quarters. They sat again on the sofa and held hands. She was hoping they would repeat the intimacy of the previous night. For more than five minutes nothing happened. He started out to speak by clearing his throat several times. And finally, "Trish, I have something to say, and I'm having a hard time finding the right words." Every phrase that came to his mind was from some play that he had been in, and he rejected the words, as he wanted to be sincere, as sincere as the fine woman who was holding his hand.

She was apprehensive. He had something to say. He couldn't find the words. She was girding herself for the worst when the words finally tumbled out of him, "Trish, you're a precious gem, more than I think you realize. If you'll let me try, I want to make you happy. I'll do my damnedest to make you happy." He fished the ring out of his pocket and said, "If you'll accept this we can be engaged, and I want you to know I've never been engaged or married because I never found anyone as special as you. I think we should wait a few months, and if you decide it's been a mistake, you can just send the ring back to me or throw it away and let me know, and I won't ask any questions. I'll understand."

She held her hand outward, and he slipped the ring on her finger. She closed her hand and covered it with the other hand. "Nothing could ever get this away from me, Harry. I told you yesterday that you can have me whenever you want, and I'll marry you tomorrow if you wish."

They embraced, two people believing they had finally found true happiness and were starting out together for the rest of their lives. They sat for an hour basking in the good feelings of their mutual commitment. Finally, she whispered, "Doctor MacLaine told me that because I've had so little physical experience in my married life that you'll have to be patient with me until I learn all the things a good wife should know." She got up and started towing him toward the bedchamber. "Let's practice right now so that when we get married, I'll be the perfect wife."

Unreluctantly, Granville allowed himself to be towed along.

CHAPTER XXXV

The Laird had been postponing the promised reception at the castle for the village Booster Club, and also his turn to entertain the local gentry was due in a few weeks. The invitations had been printed and were ready to mail. He and Granville had discussed numerous possibilities for entertainment and finally conceived the plan for an evening that could be used for both groups.

The Booster Club was only thirty people - the backbone of the town - the professional and business people. The Laird didn't want them arriving at different times, so a bus was arranged to pick them up at the center of the village and bring them all to the castle gate just before dusk. They were asked to wear their kilts and the Laird greeted them in his.

The bus parked just inside the gate, and as a group they walked to the open area facing the garden. Fog was beginning to settle in between the trees on the south side of the garden. When everyone seemed ready, a bright spotlight went on a short distance ahead of them and they saw Kerrie in a skirt and jacket of dress Royal Stuart tartan and wearing at a jaunty angle a Kilmarnock bonnet with a long pheasant feather.

She put her fingers up to her lips. "Shhhh, brithers. Some of our ancestors are joining us tonight. We're turning back the clock to 1472, and we shall witness part of the battle of the siege of Kirkwood Castle. We are standing on sacred ground, stained with the blood of our ancestors. Let us watch with reverence."

At that point an amplifying system began to play the background sounds from a sound track that Granville had borrowed from his friends at the BBC. First the MacBrooms and their men began arraying themselves around the edges of the castle grounds. The fog kept opening and parting in patches, and Kerrie advised the spectators in a hushed voice with her Scottish accent, "Tis the dead of night and a surprise attack is beginning."

At a signal fifty men rushed forward to begin the attack. Some were carrying scaling ladders. They were a motley lot in dun colored clothing. Almost simultaneously, an equal number poured out of the castle and met them head on and a hand-to-hand battle ensued. Steel clashing on steel, screams, shouts. In a short time reinforcements came to the castle rescue through the woods from the direction of the town and drove the attackers back into the fog. The charge of the MacBrooms had spent its fury and was steadily beaten back, and finally those yet standing took to flight. After the last sounds of the battle subsided, bagpipes were heard from the fog playing Scots Wha Hae, and the victorious troops emerged slowly from the fog into the yard, carrying the wounded and ushering prisoners into the castle dungeon. They walked on past the spectators to the rear of the castle where an encampment had been set up.

The symbolic reenactment of the battle was moving for the audience. More than a few eyes were moist, and everyone remarked that they had one or more ancestors who had participated in the defense of the castle. One said he had ancestors on both sides of the battle.

The visitors were invited to follow, and reaching the rear of the castle they found a whole Black Angus steer roasting on a giant spit. The actors were many of the local young men together with several pipe bands. They began to take turns in playing the pipes and performing Highland dancing. The visitors watched for a bit and then moved inside into the dungeon area for the first part of a brief tour of the castle.

In the dungeon they saw prisoners from the battle in chains in the cells, and it all looked very real. Off to the far side the figurehead from the bow of a ship was mounted on the wall, a woman - a hag - in a gray hooded cape, which only left her ugly face exposed. The man who claimed people on both sides of the battle exclaimed upon seeing the statue, "My God, The Sea Witch. I thought she was at the bottom of the ocean. One of my ancestors sailed as a pirate with the MacBrooms, and that there lady - witch - was on the prow. It was said that she had witnessed enough blood to float a ship. I've still got a Jolly Roger flag from The Sea Witch, and if you like you can have it to put it on the wall right there to keep the lady company."

Kerrie, who was helping to lead the visitors about and would be giving the remainder of the tour, said, "We weren't sure where The Sea Witch came from, and we're glad to know her name, but as you might know, the last of the MacBroom family married a Semple and very likely this was part of the keepsakes that wound up here at Kirkwood."

After she conducted a brief tour of the principal rooms of the castle, the guests went to the Great Hall for dinner. In addition to the entree of the beef, haggis was served and presented with Robert Burns "To a Haggis," recited by one of the locals before he plunged his 'skean' into its 'gushing entrails.'

After a generous amount of whiskey and wine and good food, the provost rose and proposed a toast to the Laird, ending with, "and if at anytime you ever need help to defend Kirkwood, to a man we'll all come and, if necessary, die trying."

"To the Laird," rang out the voices in unison. "To Kirkwood Castle."

The Laird accepted the toast. He rose. "Gentlemen, I toast each of you and your families and your ancestors, and thank you and them for all you've done for Kirkwood and the town and Scotland." He paused while he took a sip of wine, and set down his glass. "I'm particularly happy that you're here tonight, because our lives, as neighbors and friends, over the centuries have been and are intertwined.

"I've had the privilege of getting to know some of you and learned a little of the problems of the area, and I've given it a lot of thought. The one problem I heard mentioned over and over is that the young people all leave the town when they finish schooling, as there's little opportunity for employment here. The first thing in deciding what can be done to solve any problem is to take stock of what we have to build upon.

"First of all we have a group of fine families. Secondly, we have a long stretch of water with good beaches and fishing. And we have the remains of a fortress right on the water at the edge of the town. Plus there's Pirate Island just minutes away offshore, which has the remains of the ancient pirate stronghold.

"I've consulted with my butler, Mr. Granville, and I might mention that for many years he was a prominent actor on the London stage, and we have some ideas.

"First of all I think we could consider restoring parts of the fortress at the water's edge and make several of the rooms into a restaurant with a pirate theme. I'm not talking about rebuilding the fortress, just enclosing what's there from the weather. Sir Bruce MacEachern has a massive pile of building stone on his property from the renovation they did some years ago. We can have the materials just for removing them. A lot of this work can be done by volunteers.

"Granville thinks he has an ideal person to handle the supervision of the food. And he personally will work on the decor, the costumes, service, and so forth.

"Also, we could do some work on the remains of the structure on Pirate Island, and fix it up into an outstanding theme park, as it was a real pirate stronghold, and we can sell the beach tourists a boat trip out to the island.

"I'd like to suggest that the Booster Club appoint a committee to work on the project, and Granville and I would be glad to help and bring it to fruition. If you agree, I say let's get going tomorrow.

"I thank you again for coming. And now Mr. Provost, I'll give the floor back to you."

The men all stood and applauded the Laird, and comments were heard like, "When can we get started," and "Let's get going tomorrow."

Kerrie hung on the Laird's every word. She was bursting with pride in him. And when he said, 'Let's get going tomorrow,' she loved his direct approach.

The provost rose. "All in favor of the suggestion raise his hand."

It was unanimous. Before they left the Great Hall a committee had been appointed. And then the guests exited to the courtyard where the piping and singing and dancing were fully under way. Everyone would have stayed through the night, but after a couple of hours Kerrie went around and said to almost every one of them, "Bedtime Sir, or Laddie," and, "The Laird has enjoyed this so much I think he'll want to make it an annual event." And reminded the new committee members, "The Laird has invited the committee to meet here tomorrow morning at ten o'clock."

The Booster Club reluctantly got back on their bus, and the others stayed to put out the fires and decamp. It was the wee hours when Granville sent out Ogier to check the grounds and he finally secured the castle for the night.

CHAPTER XXXVI

The following Wednesday evening, it was the Laird's first turn at hosting the local elite. Enough of the castle had been placed into decent shape, and apologies would be limited. With few exceptions the invitations were accepted, as there was more than a little curiosity about the castle, which many had never visited. The battle routine of the previous week was repeated with some changes to smooth it out.

The weather cooperated with patches of fog at the side of the garden. The guests arrived almost simultaneously. And Kerrie once again did the introduction and short narrative. She would also this night give the tour inside, but it would have been irregular for her to sit at the table with the guests as she had the previous week.

One of the guests was Sir John Haynes, a retired Brigadier, formerly of the Scots Guards. He was now well into his eighties, and often a bit forgetful. But nevertheless, he was a good friend and long time favorite within the local elite. The Baroness Auldlay approached him immediately after the battle as they were walking to the rear of the courtyard. "John, tell me, don't you think the young lady who did the narrating is a sort of prototype of what you men were fighting for in all those battles?"

Sir John gave Kerrie a studied look across the yard, and nodded. "Yes, by Jove. Exactly." He worked his way to where she was standing and took her by the hand. After that he led her around to just about every guest and keep repeating, "And if you wondered what those men were fighting for, here she is." Kerrie just kept flashing her beautiful smile.

He finally got around to the Laird. "Duncan, Old Boy, I don't know where you found this beautiful lassie, but she reminds me of exactly what all the boys were fighting for when we were in all those battles. Yes. And I don't know where you have her at table tonight, but I request that you move a few cards around and place her next to me. If I were a year or two younger, I'd probably propose marriage to her before the night was over. Might do it anyhow."

The request couldn't be refused and by the time all went into dinner, Kerrie was at the table next to the General. As they sat down Baroness Auldlay noticed that Kerrie came to the table on the arm of the Brigadier and imperceptibly nodded in self-satisfaction.

There were no speeches at dinner, except a toast was given to the Laird for helping most of the people in the room to remember more strongly their Scottish heritage. After the meal they returned to the courtyard.

The guests stayed for over two hours watching the piping and the dancing and the singing. The General escorted Kerrie out into the yard and walked her in among all the young 'soldiers' and kept repeating, "Men isn't this what you were fighting for?"

Although the Laird was fond of Sir John like everyone else, long before the evening was over he was a little weary of the General parading Kerrie about like a prize cow soliciting confirmation of her beauty from everyone on the grounds. He thought, 'After he runs out of people here, he'll probably take her down to the High Street in the town and stop the cars going by, so he can keep repeating the clever little joke that he thought up all by himself.'

After the guests left Kerrie stayed behind to help Granville supervise the removal of things indoors. The Laird noticed that a number of the young men kept walking up to her and saying, "The old boy was absolutely right." And, "You are what I was fighting for." And, "When can I fight for you again?"

He reflected to himself, 'All these comments are shallow and inappropriate. I'd better save her from further embarrassment. Besides she has work to do tomorrow. And we're supposed to jog and play tennis.'

He approached Kerrie. "Come on. It's late and dark, and I don't want one of the ghosts from the battle to bother you on the way home. I'll walk you there."

She handed her clipboard to Mrs. MacDuffie, pointed out a couple of things for her to check, walked back to the Laird and said, "Ready."

As they walked back, Kerrie wished that she could think of any excuse for holding his arm as she had that time after the evening at the Savoy several months ago. Nothing came to her. She said, "I think that all of the guests had a good time. Surprisingly, quite a few asked me for a copy of the address to the haggis."

The Laird agreed, "I think they all did have a good time. Especially, Sir John."

Kerrie smiled. "He is such a dear. Do you know, he invited me to go with him as his guest to London next month to attend the annual reunion of his army unit." She didn't elucidate any more on the invitation.

After waiting a few moments, the Laird said nonchalantly, "And when is it that you're going to be attending that reunion?"

She replied, "He didn't have the date with him."

He paused a little longer. "Are you going to go is what I mean?"

"I haven't decided. I was going to consult with you. After all, he's your friend, and I wouldn't want to offend him or you by refusing."

The Laird grimaced. She had put the thing in his lap. He replied, "It's entirely your decision, but we're so busy around here, I wonder if you'll have the time?"

"Well, I do go to London for a day every month or so, and I might work it in together." She thought she might also add another barb to the already biting issue, so she said, "Besides I was going to ask you if I could take a few days vacation - without pay of course. Some of the fellows in the pipe bands said there's going to be a big festival of pipe bands in Edinburgh in a few weeks, and thought I might like to see it. I did think that they performed admirably, didn't you?"

He couldn't decide why he was annoyed. This lady was a free agent. So he choose to let the whole subject drop and suggested, "If you want to take some vacation, just let Granville know."

When they got to her door, there were still a few of the pipers and dancers pulling their cars out of her yard. Several handsome young men approached her. "We're looking forward to seeing you in Edinburgh. Don't forget" Being so late, he stood and talked with her until the last car was gone.

"See you jogging tomorrow, and please plan to attend the meeting at ten with the Booster Club. And in the afternoon we had probably better go over your list of 'to do's' as I think I've quite a number of things you might have omitted." He was sure he would have enough for her to do to keep her busy non-stop until the New Year.

CHAPTER XXXVII

Summer was nearly over. Kerrie had virtually given up trying to find a treasure in the castle. Her thinking had also changed. She had surprised even herself when she had found the ruby ring and had promptly surrendered it the next day to the Laird. She knew that she wouldn't be able to keep the treasure if she did find it. It wasn't hers. She couldn't rationalize that it was. Yet, she was absolutely convinced that there was wealth hidden there somewhere. For centuries the lairds had never indulged in any kind of business. There was no indication of any kind of commercial activity in anything she had found in the papers in the coffers.

There was one thread that was interesting if she could find a way to explore it. In the records of every Laird except the Seventeenth there were letters, usually annually, from a company in London: K.T. and C. L. Hoare, Dealers in Old Coins and Precious Metals. The letters were always very much the same, "Thank you for your recent visit. It is always a pleasure to serve you."

Granville was a regular visitor several times a week to The Wallace and The Bruce, and he was getting near to announcing his forthcoming wedding.

Jeffrey was a regular visitor several evenings a week to the home of the local librarian. It looked like something might be happening there soon.

The weekly visits to the Auldlay's for the Laird and Kerrie were becoming more and more like family gatherings. And their children continued to be in and out of Kirkwood constantly as regular visitors.

On one long weekend the Laird was invited to the lodge of the Morthlands in the Highlands. Sandy had become a totally different person. He wondered if she had started taking vitamins or something. She had also apparently gained some weight and was starting to look - no, not starting - she was a very handsome young woman, one might say actually fetching. He couldn't get over the transformation.

He had noted the invitation in his diary. Even though Kerrie had just about given up her treasure hunting, she couldn't resist going into his room once a week and reading his diary. She felt a bit hurt, and jealous that Sandy might be getting her hooks into the Laird. She kept reminding herself that money always marries money. And she was fond of Sandy - a good friend, and if she herself weren't going to be able to attract the Laird, at least a good friend would marry him.

The Laird had a pleasant weekend with the Morthlands. There was no doubt that her brother was anxious to push Sandy at him. But there were a number of other people there from their little crowd, including the Reverend MacTaggart, who periodically was invited to local social affairs.

After the weekend, Kerrie couldn't wait to read his diary and went into his room during the day when she was sure he was at lunch. She read, 'Sandy M. is a beautiful lady. I'm pleased that she has either gained or regained her health. Whoever gets her will be lucky. I totally misread her the first times we were together. Her brother tries very hard to get me interested. But as nice as she is, she's not for me.' Kerrie was relieved. But now she was concerned that someone truly worthy should get Sandy.

The Laird made a trip to the United States every few weeks for a few days, and coincidentally, Kerrie usually had her trip to London at the same time. It seemed that while she was away every project at the castle came to a halt waiting for her to return. Her desk was the absolute hub of all activity at the castle. She arranged for any needed tradesman and insured that the work was properly performed. All of the servants came to her with every problem, including things purely personal. She had unlimited patience and each person felt that she was genuinely concerned for him or her as an individual. In the aggregate it could be described that Kirkwood Castle was no longer just an efficient household, but because of Kerrie it had developed the warmth of a home of a good family. Within it all she found it more and more difficult to do her editing at night and on weekends, as the castle and its activities and the people kept preoccupying her thoughts. She didn't go to the reunion with the general and she didn't attend the pipers' festival in Edinburgh.

Just before schools in Europe and the United States reopened, there was a visitor at the castle from the United States - Victoria Courtiss. She had finished her first year of college and had worked all summer at a job and now was to visit Kirkwood for the first time. The Laird had seen her and her brother numerous times during his trips to the States.

The day she arrived at the castle, Jeffrey picked her up at Prestwick Airport. When they reached the yard the Laird walked out to greet her. Kerrie saw the car drive into the courtyard from her vantage point at the window on the third floor. She wasn't aware of the impending visit and didn't know any of the history of the Courtiss children.

Kerrie witnessed a tall, slender, young girl (lady? - maybe) get out of the car and run over to the Laird and throw herself into his arms and she clung to him it seemed to her for an eon. To Victoria, the Laird was her surrogate father, her savior, and her anchor to a stable life. For the Laird this was a child that should have been his together with Carolyn. They each filled an important void in the other's life.

Kerrie's reaction was quite the opposite. She wondered, 'Who's this young filly that he neglected to mention, or was afraid to mention? If they don't disconnect soon, she'll have him laid out right there in the garden.'

A little later before luncheon the Laird was walking Victoria through the castle and enthusiastically showing her the more interesting things. When they passed Kerrie's area, he introduced the pair. "Victoria, this is Miss Bramwood. She's an important member of the castle family. Miss Bramwood, this is Victoria - someone who's very precious to me."

For the next five days the Laird spent all of his time in and out of the castle with Victoria. The daily tete a tete with Kerrie was omitted, and she felt more than a little jealous of the girl.

She concluded that this might be one of a stable of fillies that he kept in the States. She particularly disliked the girl calling him 'Unkie.' Why pretend he was an uncle.'

At one point the Laird was showing Victoria some rooms in the castle when the tour was interrupted with a business phone call that lasted the better part of an hour. They were on Kerrie's floor, and he asked her, "Would you please continue showing Victoria around. This call might take more than a few minutes. Kerrie found the girl to be very intelligent and despite her questionable relationship with the Laird, she thought that she could be quite likable. She certainly had the Laird twisted around her little finger. Kerrie made a point of asking her, "How well do you know the Laird?"

Victoria innocently replied, "Very, very well. There isn't anything about me that he doesn't know."

After Victoria left, things returned to normal. The Laird continued drifting by for a few minutes several times a day, and their two-hour daily sessions resumed as if they had never been interrupted. He never explained to Kerrie the background of the relationship. She thought he was brazen to bring her right here into the castle for the whole world to witness; even took her along to meet the local gentry at the weekly dinner party. He'd written in his dairy, 'Victoria made a favorable impression on everyone at dinner last night. They encouraged me to bring her often.' At least they weren't sharing the same bed. Kerrie had checked that each night from the secret passageway. If there was something going on between the two, it had to be happening while they were away from the castle during the daylight hours. It was most callow of him. She was sure it wasn't entirely jealousy on her part. It was simply that one can often see frailties in others that they cannot see in themselves.

CHAPTER XXXVIII

Despite the help of Granville and Kerrie - more than he realized from the latter, the Laird also found himself on a very full schedule. The castle was a veritable museum and required the efforts of many, plus his involvement with the clinic, and the projects of the Booster Club were taking an increasing amount of his time. He was thinking more and more each day of discontinuing his law practice in the United States. He felt it wasn't fair to the clients, despite their insistence that they at least wanted him to review or look over the things that were prepared by his partners. Also, he found himself being slowly drawn more deeply into the affairs of the sizable business of the Auldlay family.

Saturday evening sessions became more and more specific with the Baron soliciting his opinion on everything that was on his plate at the moment. The Laird felt that the Baron had good business instincts, but like so many chief executives, he needed a sounding board and someone to encourage him to choose the best routes, even though they might be the toughest. Especially, being a family owned business the pressures were not the same as if they were publicly owned, and one exception could become the springboard for the next.

Occasionally, the Baron would call the Laird during the week for lengthy consultations. He also asked if he would join him on a tour of all of their operations in England, Germany, Belgium, and the United States.

After the famous tennis victory of his son in Glasgow, the relationship of father and son changed overnight. The father retained the trophy in his office on his desk and continued to sing the son's praises to everyone that entered. "Not only a great athlete, but a smart boy too. A natural genius at engineering - made an antique car run. For more than half century no one could even get it started. Purrs like a kitten now. I should get him here in the company as soon as possible. Would be a great addition."

Ramsay was to start college at the end of the summer. The father wanted to bring him into the company immediately. The Laird deterred him from that. He suggested, "Why don't you start him in the mail room or the shipping room and move him around a little so he can learn what and where everything is. Also, the employees know you, but they don't know him, and he'll have to earn their respect, like you did. Maybe let him work mornings in one of those departments and afternoons in the planning area, just to see and appreciate the size and complexity of the Auldlay enterprises."

"That's exactly what I was thinking, but I wanted to hear your opinion first," said the Baron. "As you say, he'll have to earn their respect by himself, like I did."

Ramsay willingly accepted the proposal to work in the company. He still wanted to keep tinkering with his car and liked to spend as much time as possible in the Laird's darkroom. And he also liked to spend time just talking with the Laird - his mentor. Before he went to work in the company, he asked the Laird if he had any suggestions.

"Just keep your eyes and ears open, and use your common sense. Most of business is common sense. And if you think you spot a problem, ask the people involved if things are working right. They often know better than anyone. And when you get into the planning area, I don't know what they'll have you doing, but remember just one thing: It's cash that pays the bills."

The first week he was in the shipping area of the factory, he saw that the packing materials were on the far side and they had to be hauled through the plant causing congestion or fighting it. The workers complained constantly. The factory produced production line machinery, and he watched the men in the shipping department standing and scratching their heads as to how they could lift the machines and crate them. He wondered why the original designs didn't facilitate the shipping.

After mentioning these things to his father, the father walked down to the building department, and complained, "Every time I walk through the plant it bothers me that the shipping department has to drag its materials through the building. Let's have their supplies delivered to that side of the plant. Attach a small storage area to the building; it can be a corrugated steel structure if you wish." Then he strolled over to the engineering and design department and asked, "When you design all these machines, why don't you design the frames with holes and arms for moving and lifting the machines - not just for us to ship the stuff, but also for the customer every time they rearrange their production lines?"

After the son worked in the mailroom a few days, he said to his father, "Sir, we have five small shops in the nearby area. Every piece of mail in and out goes through the Main Office mailroom. Every afternoon someone has to drive to each shop, actually five someones in five vehicles to drop off and pick up mail. That must be a staggering cost. For a small price we can take the incoming mail for each and put it into a box or bag and drop it in the local post office and they'll have it first thing in the morning. For the outgoing mail we can give each of them a postal meter and have someone drop their mail in the nearest box on their way home for the night." Shortly thereafter, that was implemented.

The other major idea that came out of his less than three weeks in the company occurred during the afternoons while Ramsay spent time in the planning area. They gave him worksheets to check the arithmetic and the totals. They were making three to five year forecasts for each product and each factory. Every hour he ran adding machine tapes that he was sure would reach to Lands End and back. But he remembered what the Laird had told him, and he kept looking to see where the cash was coming out of the various efforts. After a week he approached his father. "All these forecasts show a lot of profits from various products and factories. I'm no accountant, but it looks to me like after five years some of them don't produce a pound's worth of cash. Everything is being reinvested just to maintain production."

At the next weekly planning meeting the father reviewed the departments' efforts and after the presentations were finished, he said quietly, "Gentlemen, this all looks very impressive to me. But where is the cash coming out? It takes cash to pay the bills." So back to the drawing boards they went.

In one of his frequent meetings with the Laird, the Baron said, "Duncan, I don't know if I or the company can wait until Ramsay finishes school. He's had more ideas in three weeks than ten of my executives have had in three years. I can use him right now. And, I might add that somewhere in the back of all this I detect the work of a fine hand, something like the hand of someone that lives at Kirkwood."

The Laird smiled. "I wish I could take credit for Ramsay. But he's your progeny. Good or bad, he's yours. And fortunately he's good. But I wouldn't steal his youth from him. Let him go through college; get a liberal education, maybe some engineering, and then some business. And you might consider one of the American business schools like University of Pennsylvania. But don't over-educate him. That might ruin him. Destroy his common sense."

CHAPTER XXXIX

The Pre-Raphaelites. From the first day of occupancy of the castle the term kept surfacing. The Laird and Kerrie independently were long aware that some of the Pre-Raphaelite artists had visited or lived at Kirkwood during the mid-1800's - the period of the Fourteenth (lady) Laird. However, neither was aware of the magnitude of their involvement during those years and the continuing legacy that was extant at Kirkwood. They knew there were a number of pieces of artwork still in the castle. But there was work to be done in developing an inventory of the art, verifying authenticity, and obtaining reliable valuations.

Kerrie was deeply involved in the numerous household projects and overseeing the renovation of the clinic building. As to the contents of the coffers she had isolated all of the diaries, and chose to focus first on the Fourteenth Laird and her involvement with the Pre-Raphaelites. Sandy Morthland focused on the extensive collection of documents assembled by the Thirteenth Laird; she was obsessed with the numerous entries in code and was determined to break it.

The two older Auldlay girls, Rhonda, aged seventeen, and Lesley, aged 16, were invaluable in assisting Kerrie in the project of organizing the art collection and all information regarding the Pre-Raphaelites and their relationship to Kirkwood. When it reached a point that some sort of initial report could be produced, she decided to have a special report session for the Laird. Up until then she had only fed him bits and pieces at their daily sessions. Kerrie also decided that she would let the two girls each deliver parts of the report orally; they had worked very hard and both had produced meaningful results. At the last moment a dinner was arranged and the Auldlay family plus Sandy Morthland and the Reverend MacTaggart were invited.

The reports were given after dinner and Kerrie gave the introduction. "These two young ladies have spent many weeks preparing the reports you are about to hear. Actually, what you will hear is a summary, as the reports themselves are quite lengthy. Sandy and I only gave them some general parameters and what you're going to hear we can say in honesty is mainly the fruits of their efforts."

Rhonda, the older girl stood up. She was dressed in a simple navy blue suit, white blouse, a navy blue string tie, hose, and medium heels on her shoes; that is, looking very professional and businesslike. She tapped the table with the top of her pen several times. "May I please call to order the first meeting of the Pre-Raphaelite Brotherhood Study Society? The reports tonight will be divided into two sections. I will first describe the sources of our material, the origin of the Pre-Raphaelite Brotherhood and tell you something about some of its principal members. My associate and valued colleague," she nodded in the direction of her sister, "will talk more specifically about some of the artwork itself."

Everyone smiled at the formality of her opening remarks. The Baroness leaned over and looked at Kerrie who just raised her eyebrows and opened her two palms very slightly, as if to say, 'I didn't have anything to do with this part.' She then looked at Sandy, who emulated Kerrie's gestures.

Rhonda continued, "First let me invite your attention to the source materials here on this table. This section of eighteen books is from the original castle library, and they are dedicated in whole or in part to the Pre-Raphaelite Brotherhood. Most of them are twentieth century. This group, equal in number, has been acquired since the research began; we have scoured the larger booksellers in England for anything relating to the Pre-Raphaelites and also have asked one to search for such books.

"These boxes contain well over 500 letters written by members of the Pre-Raphaelite Brotherhood and their close associates to the Fourteenth Laird, and/or William Bell Scott - more about him in a moment, and this box of over 100 letters were sent to the castle subsequently by descendants of the original group or people offering or seeking information. By the way, three of the letters from descendants were sent to Laird Fleming quite recently.

"Now for today. We will only talk about what the Pre-Raphaelite Brotherhood Movement was, why it was important, and who the principal personalities were, and of course the involvement with Kirkwood Castle through the Fourteenth Laird.

"What the Pre-Raphaelite Brotherhood Movement was has been described differently by various writers, and from our early research, it even appears to have had a different meaning to members of the Brotherhood themselves. But in its simplest form, and the one thing they all would have agreed upon, it was a revolt among young artists to get away from the stylized form of art that was popular in the 1800's with its wooly landscapes, and an effort to get back to nature as it really is. They choose the great artist Raphael as a point when the drift away from nature began, and hence the name Pre-Raphaelite Brotherhood.

"Attached to this concept of realism, however, were idealistic concepts that for one member meant that the themes and inspiration had to come from medieval poetry or literature; another disagreed and felt it should come from religious sources. But suffice it to say, the art itself should depict people and things as they are in nature and real life.

"One 20th century writer expressed the opinion that photography was developing during this period and that competition from that medium drove the art world to be more realistic. I think my colleague," again she nodded in the direction of her sister, "would argue strongly that art need not be photographic in character to be good art.

"Contrary to the claims of a number of writers in these books," she gestured at the table of books, "the basic concept of the Movement did not originate in England and was not unique to it. Such claims might be attributed to national pride or lack of information. The name Pre-Raphaelite Brotherhood is of course unique in England, but the movement started in Germany some years earlier and was well known. A group of German artists migrated in 1811 to Rome, Italy and painted there, calling themselves the Nazarenes. At least two British painters had earlier started down the road of realism - Dych and Ford Madox Brown, who by the way was one of the people who gave Dante Gabriel Rossetti some art lessons.

"And so on the scene is Dante Gabriel Rossetti, and one cannot mention the Brotherhood without starting with Rossetti - poet and painter - generally considered the principal architect of the Pre-Raphaelite Movement in England. Rossetti is described as being brilliant, persuasive, and able to be an exciting companion. It was he who persuaded persons of greater art talent at the time to take their careers into a direction different from tradition. It is also he who died at a young age, penniless and friendless, a victim of a vicious drug - chloral hydrate, a depressant, initially heralded as a wonder drug, a boon to mankind, but later it proved to be like other drugs of its type - malicious and debilitating. Despite his personal problems, I should mention that we consulted a famous university professor, and he expressed the view that Rossetti was one of the three greatest romantic poets of the nineteenth century along with Coleridge and Robert Browning. This of course makes his art even more interesting.

"The following is a list of the principal people about whom we shall talk in our discussions about the Pre-Raphaelite Brotherhood:

The original three members: Dante Gabriel Rossetti, William Holman Hunt, and John Everett Millais.

The subsequent members:

William Michael Rossetti, brother of Dante, Thomas Woolner, a sculptor, James Collinson, a painter, and Frederick George Stevens, a friend - not an artist.

"Others who strongly aided the movement: John Ruskin, William Bell Scott, Ford Madox Brown, Arthur Hughes, Walter Deverell, Charles Alston Collins, J. F. Lewis, Augustus Egg, William Mulready, William Morris, and Edward Burne-Jones.

"It is interesting to note that various writers refer to many other artists of that era and subsequently as Pre-Raphaelites, even though they were well outside of this group and unknown to them or came to be known in the art world much later.

"At each future meeting of this society we shall on average spend one session on each of the above people on our list, giving his biography and examples of his work.

"But one question that should be answered as we proceed is: what is the significance of Kirkwood Castle in all of this? Are people interested in the artists or simply fond of a given picture? Why does anyone want to know about the artist? To answer these questions we might use an analogy. It's not unlike a man or woman who gives a very serious speech on some topic. The serious listener wants to know who is this person, what did he say, what did he really mean, and why did he say it. And certainly a piece of art can and should bear the scrutiny of the same questions.

"So. We are interested in the people. To gain a window from which we can study the people we arrive at Kirkwood Castle. Unlike 16 Cheyne Walk in Chelsea, outside of London, where Rossetti lived for a long period, and one can go and stand outside the building and wonder what is or was inside, Kirkwood Castle is preserved much as it was in the 1800's when William Bell Scott lived here and Rossetti and other Pre-Raphaelites frequently visited and worked here - the same furnishings, the same pictures, the same objects on the tables, the same clothing worn by those people are yet in the cupboards and storage areas, many pieces of their work were left or donated here, gifts given and retained, and literally a small warehouse full of correspondence and diaries of these people which in the aggregate gives a very rich picture about them as individuals. It's almost as if they walked out yesterday, and we walked in to find everything present and intact to reveal to us their lives and personalities."

She held up a small painting. "Here's a painting of this room from that exact period by the famous Arthur Hughes. The two people pictured here are William Bell Scott and the Fourteenth Laird, and other than exchanging us for the two in the picture and placing a few fresh crumbs on the table, everything is very much as it was a century ago.

"Alice Semple, the Fourteenth Laird was thirty three years old, a spinster, when she started to take painting lessons from William Bell Scott, who was Principal of the College of Design in Newcastle upon Tyne. He was twenty years her senior. Scott's wife had had typhoid fever just prior to their marriage, during their engagement period. This made her mind childlike and apparently difficult to cope with. However, he did go through with the marriage, reportedly out of a sense of moral obligation. Later he is quoted as saying, 'The biggest mistake I made in my life.'

"I have not seen it mentioned anywhere, but I would like to pose a question. Is it just possible that Scott married his wife for an interesting dowry?

"In the various letters and diaries, it's increasingly clear that Scott's wife was around 'somewhere.' But the real relationship is that between Scott and the Fourteenth Laird, not only in their activities and communications, but also in the eyes of their friends and relatives. We also have some correspondence that indicates that one person, alive today, named William Bell Scott, claims he is able to prove that he is the direct descendant of that relationship. There is also in the coffer remaining from Alice her collection of letters, which include some that Scott wrote to her, which bespeak far more than a platonic relationship.

"What did Alice Semple derive from her relationship with Scott? A life mate, albeit irregular, entry into the world of painting at which she became quite proficient, - you'll see some of her work at another session, and a whole new host of friends in the art world which must have expanded her world measurably beyond these very castle walls.

"What did William Bell Scott receive from the relationship? A life mate that from all indications was satisfying, someone with a rather unlimited purse with which they could spend time in London during winter months, and they could endlessly receive and entertain notable persons both at Kirkwood Castle and in London.

"Scott is treated variously by different writers with adjectives like 'dour, critical, outspoken, malicious, carping, pompous, and crotchety.' Yet it was also he who was encouraging to the younger artists, most of them his junior by a couple of decades, and also tolerant of their idiosyncrasies. Rossetti, over the years, lost most of his friends by his highly emotional and scathing outbursts. But it was Scott who stayed by him and even watched over him during periods of illness, and received many long letters from Rossetti communicating his innermost thoughts. We shall talk more of these letters at a later meeting. Similarly, William Holman Hunt turned to Scott for encouragement over the years when he suffered from depression.

"For the nonce I would like to suggest that we withhold final judgment on William Bell Scott. Because of the difference in ages with his younger friends, and we are talking of Victorian times and behavior, he may have seemed parental and disapproving on occasion, which perhaps was not entirely uncalled for with their behavior at times. Let it also be mentioned that it was also from him or through him that they received not only encouragement, but also financial support, and were received extensively in his, and Alice Semple's, homes in London and Scotland for extended periods.

"And now I shall let my colleague take the floor, and when she is finished, if you have any questions, we shall try to answer them."

At this point Lesley took the floor. She was dressed very similarly to her sister in a dark blue suit, but she had a colorful silk scarf around her neck with one end pulled over onto her shoulder and anchored there with a pin, the top of which was a gold colored bee. The scarf undoubtedly reflected her artistic inclination.

She began, "As my associate indicated, there are numerous pieces of artwork in the castle of every type. Today we shall only present a brief overview - a potpourri. We started out here at Kirkwood with the premise that we should first inventory everything and make no assumptions about importance or values. As an example," she held up a small clay figurine, quite ordinary in appearance, "one could easily assume that this is worthless, the effort of a school child or a souvenir of some sort. However, according to correspondence in the coffers, it was a gift to a former Laird from the famous pioneer archeologist Heinrich Schliemann, and this piece, a statue of the God Baal, was excavated by him when he discovered Troy. Lesson number one for us was, don't jump to conclusions too early about anything. If it's here in the castle, it's probably worth a serious look."

She pointed to a portrait on the wall. "That portrait is of William Bell Scott as a young man. It's simply listed in an inventory as a copy of a portrait originally painted by William Rossetti, Dante's brother - no value indicated in the inventory list. However, only the briefest examination indicates that this copy was painted by the most notable Arthur Hughes, and anything with his name on it is likely to be sold at auction for a very substantial price.

"You may have noticed four small tapestries in the hallway before you entered this room. Completely omitted from the inventory, and being unsigned, they might be assumed to be of little value. However, correspondence in the coffers indicates that they were made in the workshop of William Morris, possibly some of his earliest tapestries. Value? Considerable, aside from their being beautiful and enjoyable.

"One interesting set of items is the blue and white pottery scattered here and there around the castle. There are six pieces, two of which are there on the mantle. These were gifts to Alice Semple from Dante Rossetti when he was a visitor. In William Bell Scott's memoirs, it indicates that he chastised Rossetti for overspending his assets to make a collection of this type of pottery, as he was chronically in debt and short of funds. To know that he parted with some of his prized possessions and gave them to Alice Semple, and I guess we should include Scott (or Duns Scotus, as Rossetti jokingly called him), is actually touching, and bespeaks his generosity. The pots by the way are early seventeenth century of German origin. Monetary value? Perhaps not great, but sentimental value considerable.

"Oil paintings? Numerous throughout the castle, a number of them unhung. But we must of course start out with the magnificent mural in the tower stairway - The King's Quair - based on an ancient Scottish poem reputedly written by King James I in 1423." She held up a large sheet of paper. "Here we have part of the original cartoon for the mural. The entire cartoon was recently found here on the castle premises, and also most interesting is William Bell Scott's personal copy of the book containing the poem with his handwritten notes in the margin, reflecting his plans for various sections of the mural." She held up the book.

"Dante Rossetti and his sister Christina are shown in the faces in the mural, as are Alice Semple's brother and also Scott himself. The mural is wholly attributed to Scott, but the question can be fairly raised: 'Was he the only artist that worked on the mural?' Reportedly, he completed the entire painting by working several months during each of three summers, something like the equivalent of one year or a little less. Known to be a slow and meticulous worker, it's very possible that he did have help to complete the work in that relatively short period of time. Since Dante Rossetti posed for a face in the mural and was here at the time, did he do some of the painting? Certainly, Alice Semple might well have painted some of the background and edgings. So far we've found no reference to such cooperation anywhere in the coffers, neither in Alice Semple's diaries nor elsewhere.

"As for the other oil paintings we shall delay until future sessions. We do believe that at this early stage we have in the castle work of the Pre-Raphaelites, which is unknown to the outside world. We definitely have found reference to some of their works in the correspondence to Scott about paintings which were completed and sold to private parties and are not listed in their biographies. Some of these are notable families, and possibly even a phone call might produce interesting information.

"I think I've run out of time. We haven't touched carpets, glass, silver, medieval weapons, and things like the construction drawings for the additions to the original peel tower.

"I will now relinquish the floor back to my associate."

"Thank you Lesley. That was very nice." Facing the audience, Rhonda said, "This is the first time I've heard a lot of this information myself.

"And now we shall close this first meeting of the Pre-Raphaelite Brotherhood Study Society. But first we have a small gift for each of you for your patience in listening to us and also as a token of your being founder members." She lifted a cardboard box to the table from the floor.

"Here is a coffee mug in the style of Rossetti's famous blue pottery collection. We had them made at a nearby pottery. On the bottoms are the initials PRB, which at the outset of the Brotherhood were secret. But you can use this for your coffee or for pencils or whatever, and only you will know what the initials on the bottom mean. Thank you all very much. Are there any questions? (A pause.) There being no questions, the meeting is closed."

Everyone applauded vigorously. Kerrie jumped to her feet and went over and embraced each of the girls, saying, "That was marvelous."

The Laird stood and waited until the compliments subsided and raised his hand. "We have a small item to give each of these young ladies. It's not really a gift, just something practical that each can use. Here is a box of stationery from Kirkwood Castle. As you see it has the coat of arms on it; this one is for Rhonda Auldlay, imprinted with her name and the title Castle Historian. It should be useful as you correspond with dealers and so forth. And this one is imprinted Lesley Auldlay, Castle Art Curator. Likewise it should be useful in any correspondence you might have."

Each of the girls accepted their box of business stationery, shook the Laird's hand and gave him a hug.

"And now," announced the Laird, "to finish the evening I think we should have a genuine Pre-Raphaelite snack, natural vanilla ice cream, made right here in our kitchen by the most natural of Pre-Raphaelite processes, topped with strawberries, and served in blue and white bowls of course."

While everyone was eating their ice cream, the Baroness remarked to Kerrie as an aside, "Yesterday I thought I had two girls for daughters. After tonight I know I have two young women for daughters."

CHAPTER XL

The autumn season of the social circle into which the Laird had been accepted always started off with a large costume ball given by Baron and Baroness Auldlay. In addition to their tight local group many others were invited, and there would be well over two hundred guests. It was considered a plum to be invited, and some guests traveled from as far away as London for the occasion. The Laird had received an engraved invitation a month in advance and had written his acceptance. Granville later reported, "Sir, I received a call from the Auldlays' butler and they would like to know whom you will be escorting to the ball? And from the tone of their man, I would say that it sounds like they definitely expect you to come with someone."

The Laird thought to himself, 'This is it.' He had been invited to every grand house or castle in the little inner circle. It appeared that he had been fully accepted. They have shown him all the eligible females within their set of friends, and now he was being pushed to make a choice. And whoever it is will automatically be invited to the continuing round of dinners and parties, and he would sit between that person and some married woman. It was not what he wanted. He would give it some thought. Since it was a costume ball he could say he was going to impersonate some famous bachelor in history. Maybe the pirate Jean Lafitte; he'd have to check that one out, but it seemed logical that pirates never got married.

The following Sunday as he was leaving church after the service, the Baron and Baroness were waiting for him in the front entranceway. She started out, "Duncan Dear. I'm so glad that you'll be coming to our little party. But you must bring along a lady friend. We're going to give a prize to the couple with the best costumes, and if you come alone you can only win half the total points. And," she added, nodding over her shoulder toward the Baron who was at her elbow, "Preston and I would love it if you were to win the prize. We've already picked it out, and when you see it, you'll know we specifically had you in mind. Didn't we Preston?"

The Baron cleared his throat a couple of times and agreed, "Yes. Yes, of course. Barrel of fun, Old Boy, barrel of fun!"

The Baroness placed her hand on the Laird's arm. "Now, I won't take no for an answer, Dear. We'll just put you down for two. And you can surprise us."

That was it - a command performance. It even sounded like the prize was rigged. He would have to choose someone. But which one? Damn. Why wasn't life simple?

When he got back to the castle he decided to consult Granville and see if he could come up with a practical solution. Granville thought about it for a bit and suggested, "Well, you could hire someone, and since it's a costume ball, no one need ever know who she is. But the question is whom to hire and from where? In London there are all kinds of escort services, or I could easily get someone through the theatrical agencies, or one of my actress friends." He paused and thought some more. "You could take one of the young MacDuffie girls."

That didn't appeal to the Laird. He shook his head emphatically, 'No.' "The MacDuffie girls might be too shy and overwhelmed, and it would be inappropriate to take them to something like that."

"For the same reason it probably wouldn't be a good reason to hire Miss Bramwood for the evening," mused Granville.

"On the contrary, she's much more mature; could handle herself perfectly well," countered the Laird.

"In that case you might hire her. You could go as a king, and she could be your queen. I know where I can get an impressive king's costume, and for her - well, I'll come up with something."

"Hmmm," mused the Laird. "A king. That ought to fit in very well for a ball held in a castle. Why don't you get the outfit and do your best for her."

"Actually, the outfit I'm thinking of is French, and you would be Louis the XVIth, and she would have to be that tragic, little character, Marie Antoinette."

The Laird looked at Granville. "I didn't know that she was so tragic?"

"Of course, Sir, she was guillotined. And she was also a foreigner in the French court, caught in nasty little intrigues from the beginning. But nevertheless we shall do our best to dress her up, and she should make a fitting supporter for Your Majesty."

"Not bad," said the Laird nodding his head slowly as he thought about it. "Do you think she'll want to work some extra hours? You could tell her that she wouldn't have to do much but just tag along behind me and wear the costume."

"I'll do my best, Sir. I'll remind her about duty to country and her employer and all that sort of thing. You leave everything to me. Just keep the date on your calendar, and other than one fitting of the costume for a few minutes, you'll only have to be ready to go out the door that evening."

The Laird liked the idea of Granville taking charge of the whole project. It had given him a headache, and that's what Granville was for - to help him shoulder some of the wearisome burdens.

"O.K. Whatever you come up with is fine with me. I'm dumping the whole thing in your lap, Granville."

When they parted it was already crystallizing in Granville's mind. A lot of the peers of the realm would be there. He was reviewing: what did he have to work with - Miss Bramwood had a beautiful walk - a very nice carriage, and the Laird had—he decided to let him be the supporting actor. They would have to know a few French words. He didn't know if Miss Bramwood spoke French, but that didn't matter, he would get her trained for her part.

The next day soon after Kerrie arrived, the Laird asked her if she would work in the evening on that certain date (the night of the ball), and she might have to dress up specially, and Granville would explain it all to her. And of course she would be paid the usual hourly rate plus something extra for the evening.

Granville was more specific, and got her caught up in the thought of being in a little play - a performance, a chance to do something very different, and at any rate it ought to be a spectacular evening. When she agreed, he had Mrs. MacDuffie take her measurements, and then he got on the telephone with Regina Godfrey at the costume house in London, and the project was under way.

Kerrie could read a lot of French, but her pronunciation was not good. So for the next few weeks he worked with her every day. He would write down a sentence for her in English, and then the experienced master of several dialects spoke it for her first sounding like it was Italian, then German, then English, and then French - only speaking the English words. He explained that while the words were identical, it was mainly a matter of accent and inflection.

"And remember, Miss Bramwood, you must think that you really are Marie Antoinette - a queen. You don't bow to anyone. You only acknowledge introductions to others with a slight nod of your head, turning your chin slightly to the side. And tomorrow you must bring shoes with high heels; I'll show you how you must walk." He gave her a slight demonstration up and down the hall.

'He's amazing,' she thought. And the more they got into the project, the more she became fascinated and interested.

Each day until the ball Granville worked with her for an hour or so. She learned very quickly, but Kerrie was worried that she might not have enough of a good vocabulary in French with the right pronunciation.

"Don't worry. We'll have everyone believing that you are 100% French. If someone addresses you in French, you only need one phrase in French - 'Ah - je vois que tu parles couramment francais' - Ah, I see you speak an excellent French. And then go right back to your French accent, and if he persists, you wave your index finger back and forth, like this, and say, 'You naughty boy, Louis insists that I must practice my English.'

"Yes, but what if it's a woman?"

"I guarantee that won't happen," avowed Granville. "When we have you ready the women won't want to hang around you other than to say hello. No woman wants to stand in the shadow of another."

The night of the ball, Granville was thoroughly comfortable with Miss Bramwood's preparation. He didn't coach the Laird until he was helping him get into his costume. He was sure that he would be much like a male ballet dancer - really only in the act to help the ballerina look beautiful. So, he just reviewed him a few times on saying hello, goodbye, and thank you in French, and that was it.

After the Laird was dressed he looked into the mirror and complemented Granville on a good job. It was indeed a very regal outfit. They then left the Laird's room and walked to the front door of the castle. The Laird looked around, and asked, "And where is Miss Bramwood?"

"She's not here yet, Sir. I've sent Jeffrey to fetch her. I think they're coming down the lane now. And I have a surprise for you."

They opened the door and the Laird stepped out to see an open carriage rolling down the lane. It was pulled by four beautiful gray horses. It had a driver and a footman on the front and two footmen standing on the rear, and in the carriage was seated Miss Bramwood. The men were in livery uniforms - blue with a gold fleur di lis on the left breast. The hats were tricorn - blue with a gold edging. When they pulled up to the door the three footmen jumped down - one held the horses and the other two attended the door of the carriage. Fergus was driving the team and for all the world his commands sounded like they were in pure French. Jeffrey was the footman holding the horses. The other two footmen were young men that helped in the garden. Granville had drilled them in their duties, and they moved with precision.

The two footmen were waiting on either side of the carriage door for the Laird to enter. He, however, was rooted to the ground. Granville had earlier applied the makeup to Kerrie's face and it was exquisitely done, complete down to the false eyelashes. She had on a magnificent gown, a diamond looking necklace, which if it were real would be worth a king's ransom, a tiara fit for a queen, and a lovely wig. He also noticed (particularly) that her gown was quite low cut, not unpleasantly. 'She's got the right parts to wear it,' he thought to himself.

The Laird continued staring at Kerrie and decided, 'Miss Bramwood is Marie Antoinette. She's absolutely beautiful - stunning.' And Kerrie was saying in a sultry voice, "Comb, Lou-eee, and seet by me."

Granville gave him a slight nudge, "Sir, it's a nice evening," and thought to himself 'thank God,' "and it's not that far a distance, and I thought you wouldn't mind the carriage ride."

Completely astonished, the Laird stood and stared at her. She patted the seat next to her with her hand. Finally, he obeyed and climbed in beside her. Their bodies were firmly in contact when he sat down. He liked being near her. She felt stronger being close to him, as she had been apprehensive about the whole routine these several weeks. He noticed a beautiful perfume, and leaned over to take a deeper whiff. She whispered in his ear, "Bal de Versailles, what else should it be?"

When they reached the Auldlay estate, there was a line of cars and limousines waiting to deliver their passengers to the front door of the home. Fergus decided that Kings don't wait in line, so he maneuvered the coach around the vehicles and moved to the front of the line.

They stepped down from the coach with the footmen going through their act again, and then the Laird placed his arm out flat slightly in the front and a bit to the side of himself, as Granville had showed him, and Marie Antoinette placed her arm flat on top of his, and they proceeded to walk in a courtly manner to the door.

230

The host and hostess were receiving guests as they passed through the doorway after a herald had shouted out their assumed names. "Their Majesties, the King and Queen of France." When the Baroness welcomed Their Majesties, she leaned over and whispered into Kerrie's ear, "Give it your all, Kerrie Dear."

Although the evening had barely begun, the Laird was already thinking that this might after all be a nice experience. He would have to act the part of a husband, and she would be his wife, and for the evening they would be the most devoted pair. But suddenly he felt a gnawing at his conscience - Carolyn. It would be disloyal to her memory. But on the other hand, it was just an act for one evening. Actors and actresses did that all the time. So he concluded that he would just go with the flow, and make a good show of it.

There was already a sizable crowd standing about and champagne was being offered from large silver trays. Kerrie accepted a glass of the champagne, but she didn't hold it by the stem; she let the base rest flatly on the palm of her left hand while her fingers curved gracefully up and around the base, the French way. As predicted, it wasn't long before she had a group of men standing around her and following her as they moved about the room. Also, as predicted, they paid little attention to him.

The Laird noticed that most of the men kept their eyes focused more than a little on the cleavage between her breasts - not surprising with the cut of the gown. And when he looked more closely he saw a small dark colored mark - a beauty spot exactly at that point. He looked at it a number of times. He wondered, 'Is that natural or did Granville take the liberty of placing a dab of cosmetic in my wife's bosom?' If he did, he would remind him of his place. Actually, Kerrie had done it herself. She sort of remembered seeing a picture of Marie Antoinette with such a mark somewhere, and while Granville was getting her made-up for the performance and hyping her up mentally, she had on impulse taken one of his fine tipped make-up brushes and dipped it in a dark colored paint and touched the tip to that place. Granville had nodded approvingly, saying, "A good idea."

A few people asked her, "And who are you supposed to be?"

She would bow her head down slightly, and give them an under-look, and reply with her heavy accent, "Mon dieu, and you do not recognize your queen, poor little Marie Antoinette," and then turning to the Laird she scolded, "You see, Lou-eee, I keep telling you that we do not go out from the castle enough."

And one of the men thought to himself, 'If that doll was mine, I'd stay home alone with her every night too.'

The Laird didn't mind all the attention she was receiving. He felt good being at her side with her clinging to his arm as they moved about and pressing herself close to him as they wove through the crowd. And he was King Louis of France and this was his wife, his queen, and he was proud of her, and he was showing her off to the world.

At one point a young man came up in a polo outfit. He was very handsome and very suave. The Laird recognized him. He had seen his picture in the newspapers and magazines a number of times. Polo player, yachtsman, married and unmarried a few times, and each time the Laird had seen his picture he was with a fashion model or an otherwise strikingly beautiful woman. He was Count William Scarborough, son of the Earl of Brimstone, and heir to the Earldom.

When the Count approached, he gave a deep bow, kissed the hand offered to him, and said to Kerrie, "Your Majesty, I hope you'll save a dance for me later in the evening." The Laird was sure that Kerrie gave more than a coquettish flicker of her eyes to him and after that the Count followed her around 'like a puppy dog,' the Laird thought.

Eventually, they sat down to dinner. The room was quite noisy with all the people, and there were two harps playing. The only way one could talk was to put one's mouth up to the person's ear next to you. The person on the other side of Kerrie was talking non-stop throughout the dinner to the lady beyond him and the Laird found it most pleasant when 'Marie' talked to him and brushed her lips on his ear. At least that was the result as he leaned closer to hear what she was saying. The only distraction was that he noticed Count Scarborough staring at Kerrie throughout the meal - didn't take his eyes off her.

When the meal ended the hostess rose and after everyone was quiet, she announced that they would move next to the ballroom and that the prize for the best costumes would be awarded immediately, followed by dancing.

The Laird was not at all surprised when King Louis and Marie Antoinette were asked to come up the bandstand. The prize had been virtually promised if he showed up with a lady. The hostess handed Kerrie a box, which a servant opened to reveal a piece of Edinburgh crystal in the shape of a squirrel about eight inches tall, the symbol of Kirkwood Castle. She handed the squirrel to the Laird, placed her two hands on the hostess' shoulders, and kissed her on both cheeks, and then repeated the same with the Baron. Everyone in the room applauded.

The hostess raised her hand and silenced the crowd. "Since we have a genuine king and queen honoring us tonight with their presence, we should follow custom and let them begin the dance."

The crowd moved back from the middle of the floor leaving a large open space. Kerrie whispered to the Laird as they walked to the floor, "Let's do it right. You make a sweeping bow to me, and I'll curtsy to you before we begin the dance."

The orchestra began a Viennese waltz, and as they executed the bow and curtsy, she said in a low voice, "Let's do a grand waltz - big steps." They whirled all about the floor. No one joined in. They just watched and applauded when they finished.

Afterward the Laird couldn't get near her. Aside from her stunning attraction for the men, the hostess had said to every man that she spoke to that it was his duty to ask the queen to dance. The men were lined up like stags at a coming out party, and Count Scarborough kept cutting in during every dance. The

Laird was getting more than a little annoyed with him. At one point the Count bluntly asked Kerrie if she was married to her escort, and when she answered in the negative, he asked if he could call her the next day, and he would like to take her dinner - tomorrow night.

As he stood about watching Kerrie dance, the Laird visited with a number of the men - mostly the small local coterie of which he was a part. Despite the costumes they all had recognized each other, and every one of his friends asked him who his companion was. He couldn't decide on an appropriate answer, except, "A member of my staff."

A member of his staff. So this is what he kept in his household. One friend gave him a gentle elbow in the ribs and remarked, "You old devil you." Another insisted, "Old Boy, you must bring her to the dinner party at our place next week." Another said, "Fleming, you're being selfish - keeping her all to yourself. We're planning to sail our yacht in the Mediterranean for a few weeks later in the fall. Why don't you plan to come and be sure to bring her along? She'd add a lot to the cruise."

'Yah,' thought the Laird. 'He's not saying it, but he's thinking that she would be pretty exciting in a bathing suit. Well, I'm not going to be parading my wife around like a chorus girl. And this will be the last time she'll go into public with such a shocking gown; next year if we attend this thing, she'll go as a nun and I'll be a monk. That Granville - he was just supposed to get some costumes so that I could show up at the ball, and instead he's gone too far and created a monster of some kind out of Kerrie.' He'd have some words with Granville when he got home.

Kerrie sensed that the Laird was not enjoying all the attention she was getting. But her womanly instincts told her that maybe she finally was getting his attention, and maybe he was a little bit jealous. And this gave her greater incentive, and she continued to pour it on with her act; Granville would have been proud of her if he had witnessed it. After each dance she would be returned to the Laird, and she would call him Cherie, and Darling Louis, and My Sweet. And before he could grab her for the next dance she was being pulled away by someone claiming it was his turn to dance with her. Finally, he pushed his way through the men and declared royal privilege. But they were standing very near to Saundra Morthland, and Kerrie said, "Louis, you must dance with my dear Amie." She pushed Sandy right into his arms.

Count Scarborough was standing directly behind Kerrie and took her out onto the floor. The Laird only said something like, "It's a nice evening" to Sandy, and the rest of the time he kept turning his head to see where his wife and that Count were. All of his life he had usually found something interesting in everyone he met, and he was most reticent to judge anyone harshly. His initial inclination was to be slow to judge anyone as either bad or undesirable. But this Count. He was for one thing too handsome, too suave, and - and - too damn attentive to my wife.

Before the dance was over he didn't see Kerrie anywhere. He escorted Sandy to the edge of the room, pushed her up to a man in an old navy uniform, and suggested, "She'd like to see your ship." Then he started circling his way through the room.

Not seeing either Kerrie or the Count, he began to feel a sensation he had rarely felt - jealousy. He felt strange; he hated the feeling, but he couldn't repress it. He walked out of the ballroom into a large hallway and starting looking into the first room that opened from the hall. A servant approached him. "Sir, can I help you?"

"No, I'm looking for someone - a lady."

"Sir, no lady has come into the hall in the last ten minutes."

He walked back into the ballroom. It was a nice evening and large glass doors had been opened out to balconies on two sides. He first went to one side and saw a few couples standing about, but no Kerrie. He felt a little panicky. Then he stopped. Mentally pulled himself up short. His conscience was reminding him that he didn't own Kerrie, and she really wasn't his wife. But he was feeling indignant, and to justify his indignation to himself, he calculated that he was paying her for her work that night, and he was entitled to her attention. But his conscience reminded him that forty or fifty pounds was little more than tuppence to him. Yet he still felt a right to his indignation; after all it was a matter of principle, and besides she was just barely out of her teens and had never been married, and he was responsible for protecting her from any possible difficulty.

He rapidly walked across the room to the balcony on the other side. He looked out onto the balcony. He saw only one couple. They were on the far side where it was dimly lit. They had their backs to him, but as he walked closer he saw it was Kerrie with the young Count. He had his arm around her with his hand on her bare shoulder. Yes, her bare shoulder! And as the Laird was approaching, the Count slid his hand down her back and below her waist.

The Laird cleared his throat a couple of times to speak, and the pair turned inward toward each other and looked at him. And now, damn it, their abdomens were touching.

Kerrie had been pawed a few times in her life by aggressive men, and she had been ready to slip away from the Count's overly intimate gesture when the Laird's approach had caused her to pause for a few seconds. After she saw him she executed a neat little pirouette to the outward side and away from the Count, and addressing the Laird, she said with her Frenchy accent, "Bill-ee, is just showing me ze moon. Isn't it be-you-tee-fool tonight?"

The Laird thought, 'So already it's Bill-ee - Bill-eee! Damn! Maybe Bill-eee would like a fist-eee in the jaw-eee for putting a hand-eee on my wife's fan-eee.'

The Laird stiffly addressed Kerrie, "My dear It's getting quite late, and—."

Kerrie had only heard that tone of voice once before when he was annoyed, really annoyed, which was unusual for him. She knew he was piqued, and while that might serve one good purpose, she didn't want to spoil their evening together and have him go home angry. So she wrapped her arms around one of his and pressed herself against him and said, "My Darling Louis, you want your little slave, Marie, to return with you to our little nest," and then adding over her shoulder in the direction of the Count, "Louis always likes us to go to bed so early." The last comment had a tinge of that sultry voice again.

They were walking to the open glass doors and she had a firm grip on his arm, and she kept talking away about something with that accent. But he wasn't listening, he was thinking, 'When we get home in the privacy of our own quarters; we will have to have a little talk, maybe not so little, definitely a frank discussion about behavior in public.'

When they passed through the open doorway she shifted her posture to a more courtly style, and they proceeded to find their host and hostess. They said their thank yous, and Kerrie with her accent and said, "I hope you will come soon to visit us at our modest little place in Versailles."

The host and hostess insisted on accompanying them down the stairs and to the front door. When they got to the front door their coach was waiting. The footmen were standing at attention. Kerrie turned and kissed the host and hostess each on both cheeks and thanked them for a wonderful evening.

They got into the carriage and the footmen assumed their positions, but nothing moved. Fergus was waiting for a command. So she said with her accent, "Feh-goo, en avant." Fergus lifted the reins and called out something in French to the horses and the coach began to move. She then leaned forward, looked toward the crowd and nodded a goodbye. She had stayed with the act until the last possible moment - until the curtain came down, so to speak.

The Laird looked straight ahead and just lifted his hand as a tired goodbye gesture. He was still irked, and he said nothing. But as soon as they got out of earshot of the crowd she took his hand and laid it on one of hers and covered it with her other hand. She started chattering away with her normal voice, asking, "Who was that big man who was supposed to be King Farouk? Clever costume, just a fez and dark glasses with his tuxedo. He could also have been a Santa Claus and wouldn't have needed any padding. And that big fat woman in the fairy costume with the little wand she was touching everyone with? As she was tiptoeing around the floor on those pink slippers, I was expecting her to trip at any time, and if she had, she would taken down at least four other guests - like a rugby player." She laughed, and the Laird couldn't repress a smile.

When they got to the main road outside the gate, Fergus stopped the coach and nudging Jeffrey who was next to him said, "All footmen out. It's a nice night for exercise. You can walk home." He had peeked over his shoulder and thought he saw something evolving in the coach, and from the tone of their voices it might be good to let it evolve a little more.

Fergus liked the Laird very much. However, he suspected that inside of him was a hurt, a great big hurt. Like other people that are sensitive to flowers and nature, he was very sensitive to people, and he knew that in the Laird he had a kindred spirit. Fergus had lost his wife over twenty years ago, and it had left a perpetual sadness in him. He knew that the Laird must have had a similar experience. Despite his always friendly and charming manner, he knew that a part of him was hurting inside. Something was happening in the coach; the Laird was a different person. When they got to the first crossroad, he turned away from home, and even slowed the horses a little, and the journey that could have taken a little over twenty minutes went well beyond an hour.

As Kerrie continued chattering, the Laird began to relax more and more. She always had that effect on him when they were alone. Her enthusiasm and magnetism would totally engulf him. And he was sitting tightly pressed against her; she was now his solely. Soon she had him laughing and volunteering other funny things that occurred during the evening, and unconsciously he had taken both her hands in his. Fergus (he hoped that Jeffrey and the other footman wouldn't start calling him 'Feh-goo') liked what he was hearing behind him. When they finally got to the castle gates he turned directly into the lane.

Granville was waiting for them when they arrived at the front door. Like an impresario on an opening night, he had been anxious all evening, and he had to get a report. The Laird helped Kerrie down from the coach, and walking toward Granville she blurted, "We won the prize. Duncan was just marvelous."

But Duncan was standing there beaming and pointing at her. She gave Granville a hug, and kissed him on the cheek. The Laird thought that was a little too familiar and after giving Granville a verbal 'ahem' he said, "Come, my dear, it's time to go in."

He was waiting for her to precede him through the door. She didn't move. He was going to repeat his comment when she said quietly, "But I don't live here."

The Laird stood rigidly still. Reality returned, and the magic of the last hours was being stolen from him. She was no longer his wife, and she had been a beautiful wife for those hours, she was—he felt totally confused. And there was Granville standing and Fergus with the coach. He finally managed, "Let's get back in the coach, and I'll ride home with you."

They were absolutely silent during the five minutes it took to arrive at her house. He walked her to the door. She was tempted to ask him if he would like to come in. Come in to what - her modest house? Hardly a fitting capstone for an evening of being a king and a queen. She turned to say good night. He stood there and then moved up very close to her and started to bend his face forward. She closed her eyes expecting a kiss. But he stepped back, and took her hand and kissed it, and said, "Good night, my queen." He turned on his heel and walked toward the coach. She felt disappointed, and tears were welling up inside her. She went in the house and leaned back against the door. Shortly there was a knock.

She pulled herself together, and opened the door. He was standing there. She managed a smile. He handed her the box with the Edinburgh crystal. "Here. You should have this as a souvenir." He turned and walked back to the coach and told Fergus to go on ahead. He needed a little walk before retiring, and he walked slowly to his castle. Fergus witnessed what had happened, and he felt sad, sad for both of them. How much they needed each other.

When he left her door a second time she couldn't control herself. She walked into the bedroom and flopped on her face on the bed and cried uncontrollably. Her entire body throbbed convulsively. She was in agony. She had felt miserable when the young university professor had jilted her, but it was nothing like this. She so badly wanted to be the wife and life mate of Duncan Alan Fleming, and she wouldn't care if they lived in a thatched roof cottage. The hell with the damn castle, the hell with the damn treasure, if there was one.

After an hour she had no more tears. But her stomach and her body continued to convulse periodically. She got up and looked in the mirror. The tears had streaked the cosmetics all over her face, and she looked a mess. An hour ago on the other side of the door to the house she had been a wife and a queen, and now she was Kerrie Bramwood, spinster. And she didn't mind being a spinster to the world, but not to Duncan Fleming.

She took off the costume and folded it into its box. She washed the makeup off her face and daubed cold water on her swollen eyes. She lay on the bed again and tried to gather her thoughts. She would have to make some decisions. They might not be happy ones, but she would definitely have to terminate her relationship with the castle. She wasn't sure what she would do after that. Eventually, she fell into a restless sleep.

When the Laird entered the castle, he went into his room and sat at his desk and stared into space. The castle seemed empty, a big pile of rock devoid of life, even though he knew the servants were there somewhere. He felt that his life had suddenly become disorganized. He looked at Carolyn's picture on the desk. Their relationship seemed so long ago and so far away, like another life. He sat staring at his desk and the picture for over two hours. He finally decided to try to get some sleep.

He had a rotten night. He relived the worse racing experience he had ever had, the crash when he had had his arm burned so badly, and the message from Carolyn terminating their engagement, and then her sudden marriage to Courtiss. He awakened after a few hours in a state of anxiety.

The covers were helter skelter on the bed and the pillows were on the floor. It wasn't the first time that had happened. He had many such nightmares over the years. Even though it wasn't yet 4 a.m., he decided to get up and shower. He dressed in slacks and a sport shirt and pulled a chair over to the open window and stared outside. It was totally black, like he felt inside. What were his thoughts? He didn't have any thoughts. He physically ached all over, in every muscle and every joint, and his arm felt like it was burning, as if he had crashed again.

Eventually, the sun began to come up, and he watched the fog start to burn off slowly and the landscape to emerge in brilliant color. Everything around him was alive, but he didn't feel part of the re-creation. He felt left out. He could hear Jeffrey and the other gardeners talking somewhere below outdoors. It wouldn't be long before he would be expected for breakfast. If he didn't appear, Granville would be knocking gently at the door, and if he didn't answer, he would use his key to enter and see if the Laird were well.

CHAPTER XLI

The Laird appeared at breakfast at his usual time. He didn't eat much of anything. He broke the toast up and left it on the plate and just drank coffee. It was Tuesday. Because many of the staff had worked the previous night, including the MacDuffie women who had been lent to the Auldlay kitchen for the ball dinner, the entire staff would work only through noon luncheon, and then everybody would have the afternoon and evening off, and he would be alone. He wondered what Kerrie did on her days off. He had never asked her. Then he remembered that he wouldn't be alone - his mind wasn't functioning. He usually played chess with Doc MacLaine on Thursday, but it would be Tuesday this week, and unless he notified him the Doctor would expect him more or less between 1:30 and 2:00 p.m.

He had thought that soon after his breakfast Kerrie would be entering the building, and he would walk up to where she had her work table and say 'hi' and whatever else might come into his mind.

Before he was ready to leave the breakfast table, his law office in the States telephoned. It was the middle of the night there, but they had a couple of emergencies with important clients and they had to make some major disbursements on some trusts on which he was co-trustee and there would be risks - complicated risks. That took most of the morning with several call backs with information that he had requested, and during the rest of the time he was on the phone directly with the clients. Noon rolled around and he never did get to see Kerrie before she left the building.

After Kerrie had come in she had gone directly to her work place and started to push papers around aimlessly. Granville came up very shortly afterward and wanted to hear the whole story of the previous night - every detail that she could remember. She started at the beginning, saying how from the moment they had left the front door that she had felt like a queen, and that the Laird, the king, was really her husband. And she assured him that she tried to create the character and do everything as he had instructed. She told him how she had been surrounded by only the men as he had predicted, and in the telling she repeated things she had said using the accent he had taught her, and he kept nodding approvingly. She even told him about the pass made at her by Count Scarborough without being too specific about exactly what happened, and how irked her husband had been, and altogether the narrative took over half an hour. Granville liked the part about Count Scarborough; it couldn't have been better if he had worked with the Count and rehearsed him on his part of the production.

Granville was satisfied, almost. He had written the script, and they had acted their parts much as he had hoped. The only part of the script they hadn't observed was a part he hadn't 'shown them.' He was sure that the whole evening was going to be an emotional experience for the Laird, and he fully expected them to come home announcing their engagement. In fact he had expected it last night at the front door. But he remembered the Laird standing there so stone-like when she had said 'But, I don't live here,' and he wanted to be like a prompter in a play and supply him with the correct response.

While she replayed the previous evening for Granville, Kerrie came alive again and exhibited a lot of her normal enthusiasm. After he left, she hoped that the Laird would come by. When he didn't come and didn't come, she began to feel depressed all over again. She accomplished nothing, and decided she would go home for a while and come back and try to work in the afternoon to compensate for the wasted morning.

When the Laird finally did go up to her work area, she was gone. He didn't feel like eating lunch, so he told the staff to skip his lunch, and he got in his car and drove down to the waterfront near the town, and stared out at the breakers rolling in until it was time to go for his chess game.

Doctor MacLaine knew the minute the Laird entered the door that he was preoccupied. They sat right down at the chess table, and it was the Laird's opening move. When he opened the king's castle pawn to four, MacLaine knew he wasn't even thinking about the game. After they had each made five more moves, the Laird had made a hopeless hash out of his side of the board, and MacLaine was relieved when the telephone rang. He listened for a minute and said into the phone, "Yes, tell her to relax and try to breathe evenly, and I'll be there in a few minutes."

He returned to the table and announced, "Mrs. MacPherson. She's started labor and if it's like her last delivery this might take a few hours. Let's postpone the game until next week."

The Laird readily agreed. This had happened before, and there was no need to sit and wait. After he got into his car he debated what to do. He decided that the best thing would be to focus his mind on something constructive, and he drove back to the castle. It was a beautiful day outside, very warm, and he was tempted to take a long walk in the woods. But his conscience reminded him that he did have a long list of things to do. So he went into his room, sat down at the desk, and tried to concentrate on bringing his financial records up to date.

Carolyn kept staring at him from her picture, and he had a hard time keeping his mind on the numbers, and he kept making mistakes. He finally threw the pencil down on the desk and told himself that this wasn't working. He stared at her picture, and she seemed to be telling him, 'Why don't you go outside, get some sun and fresh air and you'll feel better.' Wishful thinking on his part, he thought. Instead, he decided to go into the darkroom and work on some pictures. Racing Magazine had been pressing him for some pictures of the castle for a feature story. He had taken a number of shots, and he decided to go and sort them out.

He went into the darkroom and turned on the lights, took the recent batch of pictures, spread them out on the table and started evaluating them. Every picture was of the castle, inside or outside, but he kept seeing the face of Christina Rossetti in each of the pictures, staring at him and smiling impishly, and she seemed to be telling him, 'Go outdoors and get some fresh air and sunshine.' He shook his head to clear it and thought that the ghost stuff must be getting to him. Everyone else had seen ghosts, but not him. Maybe he was starting to crack up. 'Nuts', he thought. 'I give up. I'll take the walk in the woods.'

He returned to his room and started to get ready to go outdoors with a couple of cameras, one for black and white and one for color. Then he remembered that he had wanted some shots from the top of the tower. Change of plan. He stripped down and put on a pair of shorts and a loose shirt, grabbed a robe, took two large cushions off the sofa, and with cameras swinging from the straps around his neck he walked out of the room and up the tower stairs.

When he got near the top of the tower stairs he was surprised to see the trapdoor open. Carelessness. What if it should rain? He would speak to Granville about it. The stairs narrowed at the top, and he pushed though the opening with the two cushions under one arm and the other hand steadying the cameras so they wouldn't bang against the cowling around the opening. When he got on the roof, he turned left and laid out his cushions carefully end to end and placed his cameras next to them. Since he hadn't gotten much sleep the night before, he decided to stretch out and maybe doze a little and at the same time catch a little sun. He took off his clothing and placed it next to the cameras.

He had barely gotten his eyes closed when he heard a small noise like a rustle. He assumed that it was a bird that might have landed on the tower. It would go away. Then he heard it again, so he turned his head in that direction.

Kerrie was lying totally unclothed on some cushions less than fifteen feet away on the other side of the trap door. She was lying on her stomach with one arm under her head and was facing the other way. The sun lit up her golden red hair like a flaming halo and her fair, pearl-like skin radiated a golden pink. This was someone he knew intimately in a multitude of different ways; but he just had never seen her totally nude. It was like a picture puzzle with many pieces and this was finally the last large piece that completed the total picture of her personality.

She stirred again and then stood up placing her back to the sun. She stretched first one arm outward and then the other, and gave a big yawn. He thought, 'Her body's beautiful and well proportioned. With the flaming aura around her golden red hair, she looks like a goddess.' His body began tingle all over.

After she stretched she held her arms out straight from her shoulders with her hands hanging downward; she had long slender fingers and her hands were graceful. Next she lowered her arms and placed them slightly behind her back. He kept admiring her flaming hair. He didn't think that he had seen it hanging down to full length before; she had always worn it in either a ponytail or that shapeless bun. Today it was in a sort of escallop which hung down over her shoulders to almost the middle of her back.

And he had never seen her bare legs before. Every time they had played tennis she had worn some kind of leggings or full-length slacks to shield her skin from the sun.

Occasionally, she would take a deep breath, or maybe it was a deep sigh, which lifted her breasts slightly, and when she exhaled her chest would slowly lower, and he just lay there drinking in her beauty with his head on his hand with the arm propped up on its elbow.

He thought, 'She is beautiful. A classic beauty.'

After several minutes she knelt and fished around in the big bag that she used as a purse. She took out a plastic bottle of sunscreen lotion and started applying it to her arms, and next she was applying it to her back somewhat unevenly.

He lay motionless, completely enchanted and excited in watching all of her movements. When she was having difficulty getting the liquid on her back, he inadvertently spoke out, "Let me help you with that."

The unexpected voice might have startled her, but it was a familiar voice, a deep part of her. She looked toward him at the same time that she was extending her arm to hand him the bottle.

He rose and walked over to her, took the bottle of lotion and finished applying it to her back. Then he continued down her torso, down the back of her legs, and between her legs.

He then turned her around and began to apply the lotion on her chest. As he was rubbing it on her breasts she closed her eyes and began to feel dizzy. The sky was twirling around her, and she had the sensation that she might spin and go hurtling off the top of the tower. She reached up to steady herself, and when she put her two arms on his shoulders he let the bottle of lotion slip from his hand, and he put his arms around her and pulled her tightly to him.

She felt a giant surge of energy, emanating as an invisible emotional effluvium, a transfer to him of her deepest feelings, totally sapping her senses, and at the same time she was taking from him an equally strong transfer of love, which she eagerly absorbed, and it was changing her into a different form of being, a beautifully different and welcome form.

He likewise felt the intense exchange of emotion, just in holding her. He could feel her becoming a part of his being. The combining of their persons, physically and mentally and emotionally was replacing the loneliness he had endured for the many years. This was someone with whom he could share everything. He respected her, and he wished to care for her and protect her with all of his strength and ability. He had waited a long time to find her; she was worth every moment of the time he had waited.

They could not have told you later how long they just stood there holding each other tightly and absorbing the joy of mutual surrender, which each had much wanted and needed. They kissed each other repeatedly, and the emotional bond kept elevating until they lay down on the cushions together.

Physical union occurred as naturally as if they had been married for years. At one point her hair fell about his face. It smelled clean and pure, like everything about her.

They continued to lie together holding each other for more than two hours, until finally she whispered, "I think I might be getting more sun than I should."

He whispered, "Let's go down to my, I mean our, room. We have much to discuss. And come to think of it, I feel hungry. I haven't eaten a thing all day. Are you hungry?"

"I haven't eaten all day either," she said.

"O.K. I'll go and prowl around the kitchen, and I'll find something."

She started to dress, but he said, "Wait." He went over and picked up his shirt and returned to her, "You wear this - and I'll wear my robe, and we'll not disturb the magic we had to come up here to uncover."

He first went cautiously down the steps to be absolutely sure there was no one in the castle. Then he came back to get her, and they carried everything inside, replacing her sofa cushions as they went by her floor. He settled her in the sitting area of his bedroom, and taking his ring of keys, he headed for the kitchen.

He found a big chunk of roast beef and hacked off some pieces, grabbed some bread, and some cheese, and then headed for the wine cellar and came up with a bottle of champagne and a bottle of red Bordeaux. When he returned to the kitchen he fished around and found eating utensils and a tray, and looking into one of the chill boxes again he grabbed half an apple pie and was going to start upstairs when he remembered napkins, glasses, and plates. When he entered the bedroom he had a napkin draped over one arm and the tray balanced dangerously on a hand above his head, and mimicking her French accent, he announced, "And now my queen, we must celebrate."

She laughed. "Mai oui, Cherie. Merci."

They attacked the foods and wine, and sat there eating and talking about anything that came to their minds, nothing important. Finally, he said, "Could we talk seriously for a few moments about the future - our future?" He had in mind proposing then and there, going to the safe and taking out the large ruby ring that had been worn by the wives of the previous

Lairds, which she had discovered and so honestly surrendered to him. He was going to put it on her finger as an engagement ring, and let it serve that purpose until they had a chance to buy a ring that was more in keeping with current style.

She desperately hoped that he would propose marriage, but she didn't want to start out the relationship with there having been deception on her part in the past. She said, "Before we talk about the future, could we clear up the past? I do have some things to confess."

He wondered, 'What could she possibly have to confess; that she had once gotten a parking ticket? Or that she had once forgotten to add the waiter's tip to the bill in some restaurant?' But then he glanced at Carolyn's picture and said, "Well, there are some things you should know before you get tied up with the likes of me."

Not wanting to rupture the magic of this anxiously awaited closeness, she suggested, "Why don't we just wait until tomorrow to go through all that and for today no confessions?"

Reluctantly he agreed, "Then let's just hold hands and talk. But first let me take this tray out of here. If I keep seeing all this food, I'll start nibbling, and I don't want to gain back the weight I've lost recently."

She knew that she deserved full credit for slimming him down and she gently patted him on his bare stomach, rubbed his stomach some, and said, "I'm proud of your stomach the way it is."

As she was patting and stroking his stomach, he said, "I had better get this tray out of here right now, or it may have to sit there a while longer."

He stood and piled the remains of the meal on the tray, except for the glassware and the bottle of red wine, and went out the door toward the kitchen area. While he was gone, she got up and wandered around the room. She looked at the picture of Carolyn whom she had assumed must have been a first wife that he wanted to tell her about. She glanced at the other objects on the desk and noticed on the side in a flat box three pink envelopes, which had been opened; the return address was the same on all of them and the name was E. Stokesdale, the woman he called a Wonder Woman in his diary. Her reaction was, 'I'm sure that he's been seeing her, but I'm here now and she isn't.'

When the Laird returned she was looking at one of the paintings on the wall. He sat down on the edge of the bed and beckoned her with his index finger. "I want to check something." She walked over and stood between his legs, and he parted the already unbuttoned shirt that she was wearing, and putting his fingertip on the cleavage between her breasts, asked, "Where is that beauty mark you had right here last night? And I want to know if you or Granville was the one that put it there?"

She adopted her Marie Antoinette smile and accent, waved her index finger from side to side and then touched the tip of his nose and said, "Naughty, naughty." She then leaned over and putting her hands on either side of his face gave him a long deep kiss.

The sun had gone down and the room began to take on a chill. She whispered. "Are you beginning to feel chilled?"

He whispered, "No. On the contrary."

She continued, "Maybe we should close a window, or do something to make it warmer in here."

He rose and removed the shirt from her shoulders, pulled the coverlet back from the bed and lifted her onto it. He slid in beside her and pulled a blanket up until only the tops of their heads were protruding. They wrapped their arms around each other tightly, and gradually began to feel more and more like one unit, and soon they were that. After a little more than an hour, she yawned and whispered; "If I fall asleep, don't mistake it for boredom. I just didn't get very much sleep last night."

"Nor did I," he answered. "Let's both go to sleep, just like this."

Suddenly she sat bolt upright. "What if we sleep all night and the servants discovered that I'd been here all night? This is a small town and my reputation would be marked forever!"

He was reluctant to let her go, so he promised, "I'll set the alarm clock for very early, and when we wake up we'll put you in one of the guest rooms down the hall, and I'll come up with some excuse for your not going home, like you broke a leg or something."

She thought for a few moments and said, 'O.K."

He set the alarm, and they both dropped off to sleep. After several hours she awakened and felt too exhilarated to go back to sleep. So she just lay close to him.

The events of the ball and today had happened so fast she wanted to replay them in her mind. She almost couldn't believe that they were there together. But there were still some things to be resolved tomorrow. And the more she thought about it, the more she began to be anxious that maybe he would take it very unkindly that she had been searching for the treasure those months and might say that he would never be able to trust her again.

Trust was so important in marriage. Trust. Her mind shifted back to the pink letters on the desk from that Stokesdale dame - the Wonder Woman - the one he had written was the most exciting person he had ever met. And what about that little filly that was here a week with all the uncle stuff? And how many more fillies did he have parked around other cities with all his travel?

She finally decided that she would have to satisfy her mind on the Stokesdale issue, and quietly slid out of bed. He was sleeping soundly and didn't move. She went over to the desk, felt around, took the letters, and proceeded to the bathroom. She closed the door and turned on the light.

She looked at the dates on the cancellations and opened the oldest one of less than a month ago. The letter read:

"Darling, I beg you not to be angry for my not calling or writing you this whole week. I do hope you can slip away the week of (date). (She thought that was three weeks ago when he was supposed to be doing legal work in the States.) S.T.P. wants us if possible to stay with them for the whole week. Don't tell me you can't. Call me as soon as possible. (And it was signed:) With all my love."

The second letter read:

"My Dearest, The big moment is being set for (date). And you should let me know if that is good. There are so many things that have to be planned. Isn't it exciting."

(Signed) Love and kisses."

And the final letter just last week:

"Darling, Our big day has been set for (date) - (that would be two weeks from now, she noted). So far over two hundred people have responded from the guest list that they will attend. And just to honor us!"

(Signed:) All my love."

Kerrie was thunderstruck. She felt paralyzed and couldn't move for a few minutes. All of today had been just an adventure for him. He obviously was going to marry Madam Stokesdale in the next two weeks. How could she have been so stupid? He hadn't sought her out to propose. He had stumbled on her on the tower roof and had taken advantage of an easy mark. How could she have been so naive? And it came back to her what she had thought before, 'Money always marries money.'

She had to cry. But she wasn't going to cry here. She turned off the bathroom light and quietly opened the door. She dizzily walked over to the bed and looked at him in the moonlight coming through the window, sleeping so peacefully. She wished she could hate him. But she couldn't. 'I love him so much that I can't stand the pain. It would be better to jump off the top of the tower and end the pain right now.' And for a few minutes she debated the possibility and started to move toward the door and was going to climb up the tower steps and get it over with. But she thought of the scandal. She loved him too much to do this to him, despite the Stokesdale marriage. No, she would just disappear somewhere and never be seen again. After being deeply emotionally involved with him and her heritage here at Kirkwood, she couldn't envision any kind of life on the outside. She gathered up her clothing and her handbag. She went over to the bed again for a last look, the last time she would ever see him. She bent over and very gently kissed his hair, and mentally said to him, "Goodbye my love. I'll see you in the next world." She then walked to the closet and exited into the secret passageway, though the underground cave, and out into the world away from Kirkwood forever.

The Laird slept until the alarm went off an hour earlier than usual. He felt great, he thought. He hadn't slept so well in twenty years. He did have a dream, but it wasn't a nightmare. He lay there reflecting on the dream.

It was like most dreams. It didn't make sense as to time and place. First, he was having a wonderful time walking in the woods with Kerrie, and they were holding hands. But it was strange in that when she stopped holding his hand to pick up a wildflower from the ground or a leaf from a tree, he stopped and was totally immobile, like a stone. When she took his hand again he came alive. It happened several times. They were next in a city on a shopping street - shopping - not his favorite sport. He didn't go into the stores. He stood outside and waited. And the same thing occurred. When she released his hand he was like a statue or a window manikin. Several people passed and stopped and looked at him like he was an advertisement for something or a street performer. One woman remarked, "They're making those window dummies more realistic all the time." Another man came up and thought he was an advertisement for suits, and looked under his sleeve for the price tag, and under the lapel of the coat, and then walked away puzzled. When she came out of the stores she took his hand and they walked away very animatedly.

The scene shifted next to a beach, like the beach near the town below the castle. They were both in bathing suits walking along, holding hands, having a good time, and Kerrie suggested that they take a dip in the water. And even though it was a dream, his subconscious mind told him that if he went in the water and she let go of his hand he would sink like a stone. He told her to go ahead and he would wait. She went in for a quick dip alone. He stood there like a statue with one arm extended, the arm that was holding her hand as they parted. Several people passed, looked at him, shook their heads or shrugged their shoulders, and walked on.

Then two girls walked up. They were on holiday and looking for male company. They approached him, and he just stared blankly. One chucked him under the chin. He didn't move. She tickled him under the extended arm. No reaction. The other said, "I'll show you where to tickle him, and I'll guarantee that I'll get a rise out of him." She looked over her shoulder to see if anyone was watching and was about to execute her sure fire technique, when the first girl said, "Look, there's some real live men setting up a volleyball net. Let's go over and stake our claim." And they moved off.

Kerrie had seen the girls hanging around her property, and she came out of the water to reaffirm her ownership and took his hand. He came alive, and they happily walked off.

He knew that you didn't have to have six degrees in psychology to interpret his dream. It was very plain, and he didn't disagree. 'Kerrie is my key to living. Without her I'm a non-person.'

He wondered, 'Why haven't I heard any sound of water from the washroom?' It must have been almost fifteen minutes since he had awakened. 'Maybe she's sick and has a fever'.

He got out of bed and went to the bathroom and looked in. She wasn't there. He searched the bedroom, even looking under the bed and inside the armoires. 'Strange. Could she have slipped out of the room already? Very likely. Maybe she was apprehensive about the servants finding her.' He decided to take a quick shower and to find her and agree on the alibi for her being there.

Eight minutes later he left his room. He never noticed that the door was firmly bolted from the inside and she could not have reset the bolt without a key. The only two keys were on his desk or with Granville. He started down the hall on that level. No Kerrie in any of the bedrooms or the adjoining bathrooms.

He was not going to spend all morning searching all possible rooms without help, so he rang for Granville. Granville came out of the servants' area still buttoning his morning vest. He explained, "Granville, Miss Bramwood was not well yesterday and stayed, but I'm not sure where. Would you please help me find her?"

"Right, Sir. I'll start at the top level, if you don't mind continuing upward from here."

Then the Laird had an inspiration. He went over to the door of the servant's quarters. "Ogier! (Whistle)."

Ogier came running, and he ordered, "Ogier, find Miss Bramwood. Find Kerrie."

The dog put her nose up in the air and ran up the tower steps to the very top to the trapdoor and then bounded down and circled around Kerrie's area on the third floor, and then continued on down to the Laird's room. She circled the room a number of times, and then went over to the closet and stood by the paneling in front of the secret passage that Kerrie had used to exit. (It is also immediately in front of the passageway that has been filled in with gravel.)

The Laird thought, 'It always works in movies, but it sure didn't work this time. Stupid dog,'

Granville returned from checking the rooms in the upper levels, and reported, "No luck, Sir."

The Laird decided to go outdoors and speak to the gardeners who were already at work. He went out followed by Granville and Ogier. When the Laird asked them to look for Miss Bramwood, that she was ill, maybe delirious, and could be wandering around the grounds, they each started in a different direction. Ogier ran about in circles and then came back barking for the Laird to follow her. She took him to the place above the river and the entrance to the underground cave. The dog ran back and forth barking, but when the Laird looked down he could see nothing. He summoned the gardeners and instructed them to look along the edge of the river to see if she might have fallen down the embankment. In less than ten minutes they were back. No luck. He then asked Jeffrey to see if by any chance she was at her house. He went inside and returned to his bedroom and sat at his desk and waited.

He felt confused. What could have happened? He would wait for Jeffrey. As he sat and pondered, his eyes lit on the three letters in pink envelopes. They were out of position, in the wrong place. He picked them up and returned them to his 'Pending Box.' Then he wondered if Kerrie had seen the letters and the return addresses, and could that have been what was disturbing her. No need. They all had to do with the forthcoming opening of the Racing Hall of Fame in Florida, U.S.A.

He tried to remember what was in the letters, and picked the first one up. It started with 'Darling' and signed off with 'All my love.' That's Betsy - she addressed everybody that way. The date she was talking about was indeed the tentative opening date for the Racing Hall of Fame. She had been in contact with the director, S.T.P. (Stanislaus Thaddeus Pryszczinski - everyone called him STP for short) and had kept calling the Laird suggesting that they go together or meet there. She seemed anxious that they be together - why, he couldn't imagine.

After that little episode in London there was no further attempt on the part of either one to reheat the friendship. But she was not indifferent toward him either. She never broke off a relationship totally with any man. She only collected them like a professional soldier collects campaign ribbons. Every time they met at various social functions she always acted like an old friend and had greeted him with an "Al Darling, the Lawman,' and she would lean over to be kissed. Anyone watching would have to conclude they were dear old friends or that he was one of her many admirers, which was exactly what she wanted.

The next letter - same thing, started out 'Dearest' and ended 'Love and Kisses.' Vintage Betsy. And more about the date which had been postponed several times.

The last letter referred to the guest list for the opening reception, and yes they were being honored, and so were a lot of other people.

How many times he had told the younger lawyers on his staff to read every document not only from your own position, but put yourself in the other person's shoes and try to understand what they think it means. And then it hit him like a head on collision. Could she have thought he was going to marry Betsy Stokesdale? He rang for Granville. Then ran into the hallway yelling for him and Jeffrey. Granville came hurrying and Jeffrey was just coming in the door from having checked Kerrie's house.

"Nobody at Miss Bramwood's house, Sir, and I checked the garage and her car's gone."

The Laird started talking fast and seemed so distraught that Granville was afraid he might have a heart attack.

"Jeffrey," he ordered, "Get in the Land Rover and drive down to the town as fast as you can and see if she's anywhere there, and phone me soon as you can. I'll be right here by the phone! Call me on my private line! And don't worry about getting a ticket. I'll pay for it. Go!"

Jeffrey dashed out the door and sped toward the town as fast as he could. He drove up the high street and paused at each intersection to see if her car was on any of the side streets. When he got to the end of the high street, he was going to double back and drive up and down each side street, when he decided to stop at the petrol station and ask if they had seen her. They always opened up early, and if she had any thought of driving some distance, she might have stopped for fuel.

The station owner told him, "She came through a couple of hours ago. Acted strange for her, looked sick. Usually, she's so bright and cheery."

"Did she say where she was going?"

"Said she was headed for Ayr. Had to hurry to catch the morning train."

Jeffrey used the telephone in the station to inform the Laird, and said he was going to speed up to Ayr and see if he could learn more.

When he reached Ayr he drove directly to the petrol station where they occasionally left their cars if they were going somewhere by train. Her car was parked over on the side. He dashed inside and asked the attendant with a tone of urgency, "How long ago did the person leave that Austin over there, and do you know where she went?"

"Miss Bramwood?" the attendant smiled. "Regular customer. Comes in every few weeks when she goes to London. She headed over to the station. I'm sure she was going to take the morning train to London. Who should I say was asking for her when she returns?"

"Jeffrey—," he started to give the man his name.

"Jeffrey? She left a letter for a Jeffrey. She said if she didn't return in a week to drop this in the mail." He reached under the counter and produced an envelope.

Jeffrey looked at the addressee on the envelope and grabbed it. "That's me." He tore open the envelope and read the letter quickly. It said:

'Dear Jeffrey: My car is for you. I wont be needing it any more. You should be able to get a few thousand quid for it. Consider it a gift for your wedding some day to Miss Bayne. I will always have fond thoughts of you. Cherrie Bramwood. P.S. I have enclosed the papers for the car. If you have any trouble getting the ownership transferred over to you, talk with Mr. Cameron MacKim, and I'm sure he can straighten it out. C.B.'

Jeffrey asked to use the phone and dialed the Laird. He was choked up. "Sir, bad news! She's gone to London! And she's left her car here to be given to me! I don't think she's ever coming back, Sir!" Jeffrey had tears in his eyes.

The Laird ran out into the hallway yelling for Granville, who was standing in the hall outside the door. "Granville, she's gone to London. Jeffrey says she's not coming back. I'll explain that later. Do you have any idea where she goes when she visits

London? I never asked her. Maybe we'll have to go over and break into her house and see if we can find out where the place is that she works."

Granville was getting upset now, and he fell completely out of character. "Stay right here, Duncan. I might have something that will help." He dashed up the tower steps and quickly returned carrying a white manila folder.

He opened the folder and handed a piece of paper to the Laird. "I know that you handled the employment of Miss Bramwood, but just to keep things tidied up I did have her fill out our usual employment application. Here's the name and address of the company she works for in London, and here's the name of a next of kin."

"Granville, I'd better leave for London immediately—."

But Granville had left the Laird and dashed into his bedroom and came running out with his ever packed overnight bag, and heading for the front door urged, "Come on, if we hurry, we can catch the Edinburgh express train for London at Newcastle. We'll miss it if we go to Edinburgh. It's only a little over 100 miles to Newcastle, a rough trip. But I think you can do it."

They got into the Laird's Corvette with the racing engine. He had never tried to break records when he raced - just win the race. Today he would push this car for all it would do. And for the next two hours Granville learned what it was like to be in a race, a race against time. The Laird hardly spoke during the entire trip. He was racing now, and concentrating intensely, listening to his engine, watching the road, anticipating every turn, and whipping around every vehicle when there was the minutest space between it and an oncoming car. If a police car had seen them, it wouldn't have had a chance of catching them. Many times Granville was sure that the car was going to miss a turn or go off the road as the Laird kept pushing his speed to the ultimate. They arrived at Newcastle with ten minutes to spare.

The Laird had burned a lot of energy in the race to Newcastle, but he was still full of adrenaline. "Granville, drive the car back to the castle. And don't kill yourself! Drive very slowly for the first ten or fifteen miles until you get the feel of it. The accelerator is extremely sensitive, like a hair trigger on a gun. I'll call you as soon as I learn something. And don't forget to call the Connaught and get me a room for at least tonight and tell them I might be there a few extra days."

Granville helped him get on the train with his bag. "Good luck, Duncan. We'll all be praying for you."

The train ride to London was frustrating for the Laird. Couldn't this thing move faster? To complicate matters they were shunted on a sidetrack and had to delay several hours for a problem somewhere up ahead. Maybe he should have driven all the way to London. When he finally reached London, it was late afternoon. He got into a cab and had it drive to the address of the next of kin. No one answered his ring. He got back in the cab and went to the Connaught and checked in.

He looked in the phone book for a number for the next of kin. Nothing. He called information. No luck. Maybe the information was old. Maybe the person was dead. He skipped dinner. Around 8 p.m. he returned to the flat. It was dark inside and no one answered his ring. He rang the bells of the neighbors on each side. Neither seemed to know anything about the next-door tenant, or so they pretended. He returned to the hotel. He had no luck trying to sleep. His adrenaline was still running heavy.

Finally morning came. He decided to go over to the company and start there.

The reception at the publishing company was courteous but not useful. After being shuffled from the Personnel Department to a couple of others he finally got to the person that was Kerrie's immediate supervisor. He told the Laird that she hadn't been in for several weeks, but she was due any day now. There were deadlines on some things within the next week, and she had never missed a deadline. If he would leave his number he would have her phone him when she came in. He took the supervisor's phone number and left to try the house of the next of kin once more.

The cab drive was slow in the early morning traffic, and he arrived at the house after ten o'clock. His ring was answered by an elderly lady in a wheelchair. At first she was suspicious that he might be selling something, but she sensed his concern for reaching Kerrie, and she decided to be cooperative. The woman talked slowly and deliberately. "She was here last night. Came in very late; I don't know how late. I don't hear very well, and she has her own key. I've known her since she was a child - since she was, let me think, ten years old. Yes, It was ten years old, because that was the year that—."

The Laird interrupted, "Could you tell me where she is now?" He didn't want to hear the history of the British Empire, but the old woman was determined to tell it all her way.

"Like I said, I've known her since she was a small girl, watched her grow up. Folks lived down the street. Her mother and I were the best of friends. Mother suffered from a disease she picked up in Egypt - curse of the mummies it was, I always said. Have you ever been to Egypt?"

He just shook his head no.

"Well I advise you not to go. Can't be too careful. Where was I? Oh yes, talking about Kerrie Bramwood. Fine girl. Knew her since she was a child. Good catch for some man she'd be."

The Laird had an inspiration to get the lady's attention. "Her job. It's about her job. She's supposed to be there this morning by ten o'clock or she might lose it."

That got the old girl's attention. "Oh, Sir, I'm sure she was there by that time. Left here about 8:30 with some books she was going to turn in. She's probably there right now."

And before she could backtrack to the time when Kerrie was ten, he asked, "May I use your telephone?"

The old lady replied, "Nobody calls me anymore, so I had it taken out. But there are all kinds of places to telephone down the street. Would you like to have a cup of tea?"

"No, thank you. You've been very kind. But I must rush to Miss Bramwood's place of work." He reached in his pocket and took out his name card, and laid it on a table, and told the old woman, "If she should return here and I missed her at the company, tell her to wait right here for me."

The lady started again, "Don't you allow those people to make her redundant. She's a wonderful person. Very reliable. Why one time when she was fifteen——." He was gone and wouldn't hear about what Kerrie did when she was fifteen.

He ran down the street to a phone box and called the supervisor at the publishing company. The man said. "Yes, she's been in and ought to be somewhere in the building, probably going over some manuscripts with one of the editors." Back on the street he hailed a cab and asked the driver to hurry to the address of the publisher.

When he got to the publishing company he went directly into the editorial department. In fairly short order he was taken to the desk of a gentlemen who told him, "Miss Bramwood was here and left some completed work. She said something about going up to our Legal Department."

The Laird received directions and hurried up to the Legal Department of the company. The gentleman there accepted his claim that he was her fiancé and told him, "She was here briefly asking about how she could transfer the title to a house that she owned in Scotland to a friend, and I told her it wouldn't be easy. After hearing more of the story I suggested that she sell the house and give the proceeds to her elderly friend. She did get on the telephone with someone, and I overheard her making an appointment with him tomorrow morning to arrange the sale. Name of the person was MacMillan." The Laird recognized the name of the estate agent in the town. He thanked the man and left the building.

He had plenty of time before returning to Kirkwood, and decided to try the home of the next of kin once more in case she might be there. He had noticed an underground station very near the home and this time took the tube and arrived in a much shorter time than it would have taken by cab.

The elderly woman answered the door. She remembered him, and invited him in.

"Has Miss Bramwood returned here since I left a couple of hours ago?" he asked. He noticed his card was still lying on the table.

"Yes. She was here for only a short time. Said she had to rush. She was going back to Scotland; that she had an important appointment there tomorrow morning."

"After that do you expect her to come back here? Did you give her my message, my card?"

The old lady looked confused, "Your card. Oh yes, your card. No she wont be coming back today. She said her company is sending her to work in a foreign country for a while. But when she returns to England, you can bet your Wellies I'll give her that card."

Disappointed, he nevertheless thanked the old lady, and returned to the hotel. He telephoned Granville and had him check the number of the estate agent in the town, and told him if he didn't call back in fifteen minutes that he would catch the next plane to Glasgow and someone should be there to pick him up. He next telephoned the estate agent and confirmed that he did have an appointment with Miss Bramwood the following morning in his office.

CHAPTER XLII

When Kerrie had left the castle that morning she had no interest in continuing life on earth any longer than she had to, but there were three things she would have to do in the following order: (1) go to London and turn in her completed work to the publishing company; (2) transfer the title to her house to the elderly lady at whose home she stayed when in London (the lady was not her next of kin, but a long time friend of her mother). Kerrie had no living relatives, and the old lady had always been kind to her and had refused to accept money for the room, and Kerrie had given her gifts of things she needed instead); and (3) she would purchase a ticket on the overnight ferry to Calais, France. She would only take the identification she needed to get on the boat and after the ferry would be well out in the English Channel, maybe two-thirds of the way - closer to France than England, she would dispose of any remaining identification and slip over the side of the boat into the water. She could swim a few hundred yards, but not five miles. Her body would eventually wash up somewhere in France, but no one would care; it happened every day she was sure.

She only took a small bag when she left for the railway station. As she was leaving her house, she decided that she would take some paper and envelopes and write a few lines to thank people that had been friendly to her.

When she arrived in London she went to the elderly lady's house and dropped her things and left. She wanted no company. She walked the streets until late and then went back to the house, missing the Laird by minutes. She couldn't sleep, so she sat up and wrote her letters.

The first letter was to Baroness Auldlay:

'Dear Lady Auldlay, I'm writing to let you know that I have discontinued my arrangement at Kirkwood, and am leaving the area permanently. I wish to thank you for your many kindnesses, and the friendship of you and your family. Your children are wonderful, and I shall especially miss them. With fond memories, Kerrie Bramwood.'

She next was going to write each of the three children of whom she had become very fond. But she couldn't stop the flow of tears each time she began to think of them, so she added a P.S. to the first letter: 'Please give each of the children a hug for me.'

The next letter was to Granville:

'Dear Granville, You are the nearest I ever had to a brother. I now realize how much you tried to help me in your subtle ways. I am so sorry to be leaving Kirkwood, but I think you will agree that my presence would be very awkward after a few more weeks. Jeffrey worships you, and he is lucky to have a good role model. Maybe in the next world we can act together in a play. Remember you said I was a natural born actress. Marie Antoinette.'

The letter to Jeffrey:

'Dear Jeffrey, I am not that much older than you, but I have always felt much older. If I ever had had a son, I would have wanted him to be like you with your sincerity and dedication to the important things in life. I didn't have time to write more when I left you the note for the car, but I fully expect that you will marry Miss Bayne. She's a wonderful girl and you both deserve each other. Maybe you feel that you aren't ready to get married now for financial reasons, but I have a feeling that Granville has been away from the stage too long and will be going back to it soon (don't tell him I said that). So sell that car right away and go out and get an engagement ring and propose to that girl. Don't take no for an answer, and don't let her defer her answer for even one night.

Most sincerely, C. Bramwood.'

The letter to Mrs. MacDuffie:
'Dear Mrs. MacDuffie, As you probably know by now I will not be coming back to the castle. I will be away from Scotland for the indefinite future. You and your husband and daughters have been a great deal of help to the Laird, and you've done a lot to make the Kirkwood household one of the most notable in our part of Scotland. My best wishes to you and your family always, C. Bramwood.'

A letter to Fergus:
'Dear Fergus - the surrogate Grandfather for everyone at Kirkwood, especially Jeffrey - he hangs on every word you speak. I will miss you terribly. With fond memories, Kerrie Bramwood.'

And finally her letter of resignation to the publishing company, thanking them for the years of a happy relationship.

She didn't write the Laird. What could she have said?
The next morning she skipped breakfast, despite the fact that she hadn't eaten in twenty-four hours, and took the underground to the publishing house. The Laird had left about thirty minutes before she arrived. Her supervisor was in a conference, so she gave her letter of resignation to his secretary and told her she would be in the Editorial Department. She had two pieces of work to discuss briefly with two editors and she indicated to each that all of her comments were either on the manuscripts or the attached notes of comments. Then she went to the Legal Department of the publishing company.

The Legal Department was just one man. She asked him if he could give her a legal form to transfer a house to a friend. He told her that it was not that simple. He suggested that she sell the property and pay the proceeds to the lady. She then telephoned the estate agent in the village below the castle and made an appointment for the following morning to arrange the sale. He assured her he could handle the sale as she wished, but a solicitor would have to handle the conveyance, and she would have to sign the deed. She left the building, again missing the Laird by minutes.

Regretfully, she decided to make the trip all the way back to Scotland. It would be an extra painful day, more time in her life than she had planned, and it wasn't welcome. But she wanted to do it for the old lady, and another twenty-four hours on earth she would have to tolerate. She had no sense of feeling anyway. As she walked down the block to the tube she had to cross the street and near the corner was a wire trash receptacle. She accidentally brushed it with her hand and a protruding piece of wire cut the top of her hand and it started to bleed. A kindly woman pointed it out to her, and she stared at the blood all over the top of her hand thinking she no longer felt any life and it was puzzling to see her hand bleeding. She put a handkerchief around the hand and took the tube back to the neighborhood of the elderly lady.

She told the old woman that she would be living abroad for the indefinite future, but she would write to her. She decided that as soon as the house was sold she would send her the money. She left as soon as she could get away and went to the railway station and took the next available train for Ayr.

When she arrived at Ayr she walked over to the petrol station for her car. It was very late and the station was closed. She fished into her large bag and found the extra set of keys and drove off to her home.

She spent the night sitting in a chair. From time to time she dozed, and when it was finally light she left the house and got into her car.

She had a lot of time before her appointment. She drove past the castle and farther up the hill until she could look back and see the top of the tower. She was going to sit and stare for the last time at the place where she had experienced some of the most beautiful days in her life, where she felt closely attached to someone, to someone she loved deeply. After only a few minutes she drove back down the hill. The pain of reliving those hours was more than she could bear. She felt that she was barely functioning, and with her remaining energy she just wanted to make it to the cross channel ferry.

She proceeded down the hill and a short distance north where there was a stretch of open beach alongside the road, and she parked to watch the waves rolling into the shore. The sea looked very inviting, so quiet, so peaceful, so permanent - a beautiful place to spend eternity.

The tide was slowly receding leaving a velvet carpet of wet sand. It looked so inviting to walk over the carpet and into the fog beyond, into a new quiet peaceful world, a world without hurt and pain.

When it was near 10 A.M. she went into the office of the estate agent. A solicitor was present, and after she agreed to have him represent her, she signed various papers and left.

She was going to go back to the railway station and catch the train to London when she thought that out of a sense of decency she should go to her house and destroy the Green Book. It could fall into the wrong hands and create problems. She still had time, so she returned to her house. She went to her desk intending to cut out the pages and burn them in the fireplace. To her surprise and puzzlement a small black book - Christina Rossetti's book of poetry was resting on top of the Green Book. She couldn't remember putting it there. Her brain was too tired and confused to try to reason how it got there. She knew that the book only belonged in one place and that was on the top floor of the castle on the desk in the bedroom referred to as Christina Rossetti's room. It could create some kind of problem if the book remained in her house. She decided to change her plan and take both books and give them to Mrs. MacOster at the gatehouse and ask her to be sure to give both to the Laird.

When she drove back to the gatehouse the gates were wide open. She rang the bell of the gatehouse several times. No answer. She looked into the yard and saw no one. At first she was going to place the books on the steps of the gatehouse, but decided she had better walk up to the front door of the castle and ring and give them either to Granville or Jeffrey, whoever answered, and leave. If they tried to detain her for any reason, she would say that she had to go home and would return later.

The Laird had been sitting in the Great Hall looking out the window from early morning, hoping she would come. Not only had she left a number of personal things in her work area, but also he simply couldn't believe that she wouldn't stop by at least to say goodbye to some of the people. When she walked down the lane into the courtyard the Laird saw her. He hurried to the front door.

After she rang, he opened the door. She didn't look up, but held out the books and started to say—. She noticed a pair of loafers and slacks. No one except the Laird ever wore loafers and slacks at the castle. He put his arms on top of her shoulders and said in a very concerned tone, "Kerrie. Where have you—." But he never finished. In her state of numbness, heightened by her lack of nourishment for two days, the sight of him was more than her emotions could handle and she fainted. He caught her, picked her up and carried her into his bedroom, yelling on the way, "Mrs. MacDuffie!!! Anybody!!!"

Mrs. MacDuffie came running. "Mrs. MacDuffie get some water, quick!"

She ran into the bathroom and came out with a glass of water, but they couldn't get any into her, and the Laird ordered, "Call Doctor MacLaine and tell him to come quick, he's probably in the clinic."

Doctor MacLaine arrived in his white coat in less than five minutes. Her body was trembling, she seemed to be experiencing chills, and she was unconscious. He felt her head, took her pulse, and noticed her very pale condition. He picked up the phone and gave orders to someone at the clinic and in another few minutes a nurse came in with a plastic tray with some hypodermic needles and vials. MacLaine drew some medicines into a needle and injected it into one of her arms. "She looks dehydrated," he mumbled. He carefully covered her.

Within a few more minutes a nurse came into the room wheeling an I.V. rack and another aide was carrying the solution. The nurse began to put the I.V. into Kerrie's arm, but she stirred and fought to keep it from going in. The Doctor and the Laird helped to hold her, and they just barely got it inserted without causing damage to her arm. She seemed to be calming from the effect of the shot.

Doctor MacLaine asked the Laird, "What happened to her? She looks like she's experienced a trauma of some kind."

Within that brief part of a minute Kerrie half awakened. She stared at the I.V. on her arm with a puzzled expression and said in a pained voice, "No! No! I must not have it!" and she gave a little shriek and tore it from her arm and flung the needle and tube on the floor. Four people couldn't hold her down while they tried again to get the needle into the other arm. They gave up trying.

"How can she have so much strength and yet be so weak, Magnus?" asked the Laird.

"We don't know. I've seen people smaller than her break rawhide shackles on both arms and both legs. Sometimes people can summon superhuman force. I'd like to get some fluids into her, but all we can do is try to get her to drink when she's awake - water, weak tea, juice."

Doctor MacLaine stayed another fifteen minutes. "She's asleep now Duncan. The sedative has taken effect. I'll come back in a few hours, but call me if anything occurs."

The Laird sat holding her hand, and she lay motionless for more than an hour. Sometimes she emitted a sigh, which was more of a soft wail. It sounded like she was in deep pain.

Suddenly she sat up and was wide-awake. The Laird thought, 'Thank God she's coming around.'

She stared at him. "Who are you? Are you here to get a lesson from Coach? Does he know you're coming?"

He responded incredulously, "Kerrie. Its me Duncan."

She turned her head as if in thought. "Duncan. I don't know any Duncan. Have you been here for tennis lessons or consultation before?"

"Kerrie please. Duncan! You do know me." Then he thought he would try another tack. "Sometimes people call me Al - Al Lawman."

He was sure he saw a glimmer of recognition. She uttered a plaintive, "Ooooh," and she fell back asleep or into a coma again.

He rang for Granville. "Ask Doctor MacLaine to come over here right away."

When MacLaine came in he repeated for him what had happened word for word. MacLaine went over to her and checked her vital signs. He shook his head from side to side. "I don't like it. Not good. I'm sure she's had a very serious trauma, and now she's suffering amnesia. How old do you think she sounded?"

"She was talking about tennis lessons, and I would say that had to be at least eight or ten years ago," guessed the Laird.

"Duncan, I'll have to be frank. The result of extreme trauma can be amnesia. One type is anterograde - after the moment of shock - people forget everything and the mind blocks out the incident and much or all that happened afterward for a period - the body's way of protecting the brain from pain or unhappiness.

"The other is retrograde where people forget many things prior to the incident. They can regress to a younger age, even infancy. Or they can assume another identity, like the man who is sure he's Napoleon - again the mind's way of saying it's too painful to be who I really am; I'll be someone else."

"How long might this go on?" queried the Laird in a worried voice.

"No way of telling," answered the Doctor. And after a pause, "It might be just a matter of an hour, or it might be longer. We can only hope. I'm not a psychiatrist. Tomorrow, I'll arrange for a colleague who's at the hospital in Glasgow to take a look at her. He's one of the top men in the country. In the meantime get some paper and keep a log of everything that happens and everything she says."

The Laird stayed with her all night except for the brief periods when the nurse or Mrs. MacDuffie were with her. At one point the sedative seemed to be wearing off and she stirred and woke up with a very pained expression of her face.

She obligingly drank some tea, and promptly went back to sleep. In a little while she was thrashing about the bed, and he summoned the nurse who gave her an injection. It didn't seem to help, and after another twenty minutes or so she returned at his call and gave her an additional amount, remarking, "We can't increase this any more. We're at the limit."

When night came they brought the Laird's food on a tray. Another nurse arrived and said she would sit with her all night. But the Laird insisted that he would stay with her, and the staff would make the nurse comfortable out in the hall. Mrs. MacDuffie insisted that she would stay the night in the hall also in case there was something she could do. Granville and Jeffrey also agreed that they would take turns sitting up in case there was an emergency.

The Laird also had another thought. He was worried that if she woke up when he dozed off she might manage to disappear, so he had Ogier brought in and told the dog, "Guard! Don't let Kerrie get away. Guard!"

The dog looked at the Laird with almost a human look of wonderment, as if to say, 'Is there something wrong with you?' But he obliged and got into a crouching guard position and gave a few feeble growls. Later when the Laird left the room while the nurse was there he returned to find Ogier licking Kerrie's hand, which was hanging over the side of the bed. When the dog saw him returning she more or less resumed her guard position and gave a few more feeble growls. The Laird leaned down and said, "Ogier, Kerrie's sick. You have to help me be sure she doesn't walk out of here and hurt herself." He was quite sure that the dog seemed to give an indication of understanding, because she resumed her guard position, this time with intense concentration.

During the night Kerrie woke up and had a session with herself about the breakup with the assistant professor some years ago. She first started out very angry and then seemed to be resigned. And then she turned to the Laird and said as an aside, "You know it was probably the best thing that could have happened. If he really didn't love me, just think what a terrible marriage it would have made." And again she dropped off into a troubled sleep.

In the morning the Laird wakened to Granville's knock at the door. He hadn't set the alarm. When Granville entered the room it awakened Kerrie. "What time is it," she asked. She looked right past the Laird as if she couldn't see him in the chair by her bedside. "I have to go jogging. I'm going to meet someone jogging."

"You've just finished jogging," answered the Laird to keep her in bed. "You said you were thirsty from jogging and wanted a glass of water." He handed her the water. She looked at him suspiciously, but she accepted the glass and drank the water. Then she stared out into space and didn't respond to any conversation. After ten minutes or so, she fell asleep again.

MacLaine had told them not to give her sedatives in the morning if possible, as the doctor from Glasgow would be in around ten o'clock to examine her. The doctor did arrive shortly before ten and asked the Laird to stay out in the hall while the two doctors examined her.

They were in the room almost an hour. Finally they came out. Both had serious expressions on their faces. The Laird asked, "Did you learn anything? What are her chances of getting better?"

The consulting doctor said, "I believe everything Doctor MacLaine has told you is quite exactly what I would say. She has suffered a serious trauma. While we were with her, she actually came around enough for us to ask her some questions.

"At first she had thought she was in another world. She didn't know me but thought I had just died and entered the next world. I sensed that she seemed to know Doctor MacLaine, and I said, "Of course you know this gentlemen,' and she replied, 'Yes, he brings people into the world and also ushers them out.' She thought that something like twenty-five years had passed by. She said to Doctor MacLaine, 'Of course you know Duncan Fleming.' He said, 'Yes.' She wanted to know if you were still alive and if he had known your wife. I asked the name of your wife, and she said, 'Stokesdale,' and she asked if you had any children. I decided to tell her that Lord Fleming had never married. That seemed to shock her, and she became more rational, but still confused and cryptic in her answers.

"She declined to tell us what the problem is, but it's very clear that she doesn't want to live. She's already planned her death. She wants to get out of bed and go to London. She says she has to buy a ticket for the ferry. She wouldn't say which ferry."

"Isn't there anything you can do? That I can do," pleaded the Laird.

"We can't go into the brain and cut out the problem like a surgeon. It's in the hands of Mother Nature. I'll come back again in three days, but call me if she seems to take a turn for the worse. In the meantime keep her in bed. She's very weak. And try to get some nourishment into her."

"How long might this amnesia last, could it be permanent?" questioned the Laird.

"I don't think so," responded the psychiatrist. "I think this is a type of amnesia brought on by strong emotional trauma. Popular novels have exaggerated the nature of this syndrome. It usually lasts only a few days. I'm more worried about what prompted this behavior and what might follow when she's more rational again. She must be watched very, very closely. There's no doubt that she has a strong self-destructive tendency."

"Can you explain to me why she sometimes sees me when she wakes up and at other times not. And sometimes she reacts to what I say and other times it seems that she doesn't hear at all. Can she hear me when she's sleeping?" asked the Laird.

"Good questions," replied the psychiatrist, "and I wish we had good answers. But the mind is sometimes selective. And yes, we know from experiments that she can hear whatever you say when she's sleeping, but the question is whether her mind chooses to react or simply store the input.

"I'm sorry that I sound negative, Lord Fleming, but I feel obliged to prepare you for the worst. She strongly wants to die. The odds aren't good. All we can do is hope."

After the two doctors left, Kerrie was very restive and kept repeating in her sleep, "I have to get to the ferry. I must go." Again they had to get the nurse to give her an injection, after which time she seemed to rest more peacefully.

Baroness Auldlay came over that day and brought her some vegetable soup. "Tell her I had it made just for her," she instructed Granville, who repeated the comment to the Laird. She didn't insist on seeing the patient, but said she would be back again tomorrow. At the time the Laird wondered how the Baroness knew that Kerrie wasn't well, but he didn't ask.

That night Kerrie wakened a number of times. Twice she was talking in a strong Scottish accent. He tried to write down what she said but couldn't follow fast enough. He tried to get Mrs. MacDuffie in from the hall to interpret, but he wasn't quick enough, as she had relapsed into sleep again. She also had one siege where she awakened feeling very anxious as if she had forgotten to prepare for a test in school - the Laird surmised it was a test at the university. He assuaged her anxiety by telling her the test was postponed; she gave a big sigh and fell back to sleep.

On the third day during the morning she awoke and she was Marie Antoinette - French accent and all, calling for someone to come and do her hair. Granville was in the hall when Mrs. MacDuffie came out and told him, "She thinks she's Marie Antoinette."

Granville grabbed the food tray that was on its way into the room in the hands of the young MacDuffie girl, and approaching the bed, he spoke to her with the French accent he had taught her. "Ah, I see Your Highness is awake. We have brought in your favorite breakfast." He rattled off the actual names of the things on the tray in French, and she accepted the tray and did eat some of the eggs and a bit of toast and drank some coffee - but complained that the coffee was too weak - not strong enough, like real French coffee.

While she was sipping some of the coffee, Fergus was at the bedroom door. Ordinarily, he would never be in the castle other than the servant's quarters and through the rear door. But he wanted to bring Kerrie some flowers, and Granville had said it would be all right if he gave them to her himself.

When she saw him she said in her French accent, "Ah, Feh-goo, dear, loyal Feh-goo. Daffodils - my favorite flower. Thank you so much. You shall be my driver forever throughout eternity." She paused, then continued, "I haven't seen Louis. They won't let me see him. I fear the worst. The court has found me guilty; guilty of treason to France. A queen guilty? Of treason to her own country?" And she put her hand up to her neck and stroked it gently. Then she turned away on her side and went to sleep.

Fergus walked out of the room with tears in his eyes. When he passed Mrs. MacDuffie he whispered to her in Gaelic, "Dona, dona (bad, bad). She wants to die. I can feel it"

She tossed, but slept much of the day. She didn't awaken to take any liquids or other nourishment. The Laird only left her side long enough to shower and change his clothing. Occasionally, he would get up and pace around the room and then return to be at her side. Trays of food went untouched. Granville came in a number of times with phone messages, but he refused to talk with anyone. Baroness Auldlay came by and left some herbal tea, and said she would be back the next day.

The Laird sat alone with her hour after hour. He had a lot of time to think about how much Kerrie had come to mean to him.

If she didn't get well, he resolved to get rid of the castle, and—what? Do what? He couldn't plan in those terms. She had to get well. As he watched her sleeping, he wondered how such torture could rage within someone so beautiful. He didn't know where to start to blame himself, but the blame was his. His life had numerous successes, but it was all overridden and obscured by two major tragedies, first Carolyn's death and now Kerrie's illness, and he felt responsible in large measures for both.

Doctor MacLaine came by and talked with the Laird in low tones at the other end of the bedroom. The Laird told him the entire story of how he was going to propose and how it was delayed and showed him the 'pink letters.'

"I'm not surprised," indicated MacLaine, shaking his head. "Most often severe trauma involves love. Disappointment in love and rejection - which can also be a child rejected or abandoned by a parent. Sometimes it's money or lack of success, but that often translates itself into something like 'I won't be loved by my family or friends if I don't have a lot of money or success in my career.'" He urged the Laird to keep trying to get some liquid and nourishment into her and also into himself. "I don't want to have two patients on my hands, Duncan."

When it got near to dusk, her breathing seemed to stop several times. The Laird went over each time and shook her gently and called out, "Kerrie! Kerrie!" And her breathing would return to normal.

A little later a strange event occurred. Kerrie wakened and raised herself up on one elbow. The window near the bed was open and a large squirrel, he looked like the patriarch of all squirrels, appeared on the ledge; it just stood there erect and looked at her. She looked at the squirrel and said, "I'm ready. I'm coming."

This sent a shock through the Laird. In the coffers in the diary of the Fifteenth Laird he had written about the same exact scene when the Fourteenth Laird had died within just a few minutes after a squirrel had appeared at the same window, and she had also said, "I'm ready. I'm coming."

Kerrie's breathing changed, she was now gasping. The Laird shook his fist at the squirrel and yelled, "Out!!! Get out!!!" He pulled a loafer from his foot and threw it at the animal and missed. He threw the other and missed. The squirrel just stood there. The Laird stepped back a few steps to his desk and picked up an ashtray and hurled it, and it bounced off the stone wall onto the floor. He seized the picture of Carolyn in its crystal frame and hurled it. The frame hit the stone sill and burst into fragments. The picture fell onto the floor. The squirrel jumped onto the drapery, descended to the floor, took the picture in its mouth and ran with it up the drape, onto the sill, and out the window. The Laird grabbed the other picture of his mother and her close friend and the two Courtiss children and was prepared to throw it when the squirrel disappeared. He ran to the window and yelled, "Stay out! And don't come back!" And he added at a feverish pitch, "But if you must take her, take me too!"

He closed the window and locked it and returned to the bedside. She was struggling to breathe. Tears were in his eyes. He felt frightened and desperate, and he yelled at the stone walls, "Robert Semple - Twelve!! Christina!!! I need you!!! Help" He flopped face down on the bed next to Kerrie exhausted.

Christina Rossetti was suddenly standing on the other side of the bed. In an appealing voice she said, "Duncan, she wants to know that you love her and only her. Tell her and keep telling her."

He was next aware of a heavy hand on his shoulder. Expecting to see Granville, he turned. It was Twelve, and he was speaking with his heavy Scottish accent. "Laddie, remember what the Doctor said, that her brain can hear you even if she's not awake. Talk to her."

Then both were gone.

He put his mouth up to her ear. "Kerrie, this is Duncan. Al. Al Lawman. I love you - only you. I want you to be my wife." And he kept repeating it over and over, and over and over.

Her breathing returned to normal, and she stopped her gasping, but her arms and legs kept moving about restlessly.

He kept repeating, "Kerrie, this is Duncan. Al. Al Lawman. I love you - only you. I want you to be my wife."

After a period her breathing became gasping and then seemed to stop. He kept repeating over and over that he loved her. After several hours his voice became hoarse, and it reduced to a whisper, and he kept on repeating. Finally, she seemed to calm down and her breathing was normal, and he fell asleep from exhaustion with his arm across her chest and his mouth at her ear.

When the Laird awakened it was morning and light was streaming in through the windows that hadn't been draped for the night. He remembered how he must have fallen asleep and was afraid for the worst when he opened his eyes. But she was awake and smiling at him, and she began gently to stroke his head.

He looked up at her and she continued to smile. He wasn't sure how to react or what to say. Finally, he asked, "How are you feeling this morning? Did you have a good night's sleep?"

"Duncan, I've had a terrible dream and at the same time it was beautiful. I dreamt that it was dark, and I was somewhere alone in the ocean in the water, miles from shore. I started to drown. Then I heard you calling me from the distance saying you loved me and that you wanted to marry only me. It gave me the strength to keep on trying to swim, and every time I started to sink I heard you calling and it gave me new energy."

He was apprehensive that it might be a momentary interlude, and his voice was still hoarse, but he whispered, "Kerrie, Kerrie. You're the only one I love, and I desperately want you to be well and to marry me as soon as possible."

She whispered, "I accept Al Lawman. With all my heart. Do you think the Laird will object?"

He reached over onto the bedside table where he had placed the ruby ring that he would use to seal their engagement if she should recover. He placed it on her finger, and whispered, "You'll be the most beautiful Lady this castle has ever had, and in accepting this you have to promise not to run off again if we ever have a misunderstanding." He kissed her repeatedly.

There was a gentle rap at the door. It was Granville. The Laird hadn't appeared, and he was checking.

The Laird didn't answer, causing him to enter. When he came in, the Laird was sitting on the edge of the bed, holding Kerrie's hand, and he announced, "Granville, there's going to be a wedding, and we have a lot of things to do."

Granville responded, "Yes Sir. What will be the date?"

Kerrie interrupted, "Could we have breakfast first? I'm starving. I could eat a whole Black Angus steer."

Granville took a few steps toward the open door and called out, "Mrs. MacDuffie. Jeffrey. We need two breakfasts."

Mrs. MacDuffie and Jeffrey came hurrying into the room followed by the nurse on duty and one of the MacDuffie girls.

The Laird said to Granville, "How about some bacon, eggs, kippers, cheese, biscuits, coffee?"

And Granville was relaying the order to Jeffrey two steps behind him, "Bacon, eggs—"

And Jeffrey was relaying the order to the MacDuffie girl that had walked into the room, "For two, bacon, eggs—."

And then Granville announced that Baroness Auldlay would be over in a little while. And Jeffrey was repeating that to the MacDuffie girl, and the Laird was asking when she was coming.

At this point Mrs. MacDuffie had stepped up to the bedside as Kerrie was motioning to her. Kerrie was moving her hand as if she was coming her own hair, and then like she was applying lipstick.

Mrs. MacDuffie got the idea and said, "Gentlemen. Gentlemen." But she couldn't interrupt the cacophony. She caught the eye of her daughter and motioned toward the door with her head, and again with Jeffrey, and she whispered something into Granville's ear. She said to her daughter in a low tone, "Hurry back with the breakfast. They all began moving toward the door and the Laird unconsciously found himself moving along with them into the outer hall.

When the group was on the outside Mrs. MacDuffie closed the door and bolted it from the inside. Hearing the bolt snap shut, the Laird tried to open the door. He rapped several times. No answer.

The Laird announced to everyone in general in his hoarse voice, "Damn. That's my room, and I'm locked out." He turned away from the closed door and said, "Granville, give me your key. Mine's on the desk in the bedroom." Granville wasn't there. He ordered Jeffrey, "Go find Granville and tell him to bring his key for my room."

CHAPTER XLIII

Jeffrey had noticed that Granville had gone through the door into the servant's area, and he went to fetch him. Not finding him in the kitchen area, he went to his personal quarters - no answer to his knock. He next headed into the lower storage area and found Granville sitting on a chair outside the wine cellar. His feet were up on a table, and he was puffing on a cigar.

Jeffrey relayed the order, "The Laird wants you to come with your keys ASAP."

Granville didn't move. He blew a couple of smoke rings and watched each one disappear. He noted that Jeffrey's eyes were glued to the lighted cigar. "I know what you're thinking. His Nibs will take my head off if he sees me smoking inside the castle.

"Jeffrey, pull up that chair and sit down. Let's let him wait a bit. Sometimes it's better to let the pot simmer than to keep stirring it." And then as an aside, "that line's from a play I was in years ago called The Consequences of Truth."

Jeffrey reluctantly pulled up the chair and sat on the edge of the seat opposite Granville. He was nervous about the delay.

Granville continued, waving his cigar in the air as he spoke. "Things are going very well. Not quite on schedule, and not exactly as scripted, but - very well."

Jeffrey interrupted, "Give me your keys, and I'll run them up."

"No. No. Stay put," instructed Granville in an unconcerned voice. "I have something to tell you - an announcement."

Jeffrey waited while he blew another smoke ring.

"Jeffrey, within a few days we shall have a Lady of the castle, of whom I approve most heartily. In a few more weeks we shall have a large wedding reception, and after that I will be, shall we say, retiring. I've been away from the boards too long, and my wife and I shall be doing some other things."

Jeffrey stood up and looked at him in amazement. "You never told me you had a wife."

"I should have said my fiancée. Sit down. We're getting married after the Laird and Lady have their big wedding reception. And if you're wondering whom I will be marrying, it's the widow Mrs. MacCrackan.

"For you, more importantly, is the fact that I shall be recommending to the Laird that you be promoted Butler of Kirkwood Castle. Ordinarily, someone your age might be considered too young by at least a dozen or so years. But I believe there's always a time for exceptions, and you have accumulated under my tutorship all the necessary qualifications. However, there are a few things you might have noticed, but about which we have not spoken.

"The Butler has a very powerful position in a large household such as this. All incoming communications and many outgoing communications go through his hands. You must think of yourself not only involved in housekeeping and other functional necessities, but rather a member of a family in which you are an adjunct to the head. And you are to be concerned about the quality of life of everyone from the Laird and Lady on down to the maids. And in due course there may be children in the household, and you can do much to influence their favorable development.

"What I mean specifically is that you can accelerate worthwhile outside friendships of the Laird and his family by the way you handle or don't handle invitations, mail - which sometimes gets mislaid, phone calls which can be answered that the Laird's schedule is very difficult for the next several months or vice versa.

"I can see I'm not making myself clear. Let's be more specific. Since I have been butler to the Laird, now over five years, he's been besieged by matchmakers trying to get him to the altar. As you have undoubtedly noticed, the Laird's a very unusual person - when he focuses his attention on something, magical things happen. He can make two and two add up to five or even ten.

"I've been concerned that he makes many people around him happy, but he deserves more out of life himself. I must confess I've steered more than a few totally unsuitable ladies away from him. So I've stayed on with him in the hope that I could help him some way, somehow to solve that important aspect of his future. Frankly, I haven't seen anyone appropriate for him, until recently when Miss Bramwood came to join us at the castle. In many subtle little ways I've elevated her importance in our tight little family structure, and I've helped her relationship with the Laird to flower, and now that it's on track, I'm going to go back to my chosen profession.

"I'll confess to you, and only you, that originally Duncan Fleming and I were social friends. At one point he was in a pinch and badly needed a butler for a very large affair at the old manor house, and I offered to handle it for him on the condition that we both act our relative roles at complete arm's length. Overall it's worked pretty well. I've missed a few things here and there, but if I must say so myself, it has been quite exemplary.

"You, however, will do even better than I have. You're a professional. I'm just an actor. And by the way, as a profession, being a butler isn't a bad life. If you put together a good team, things run quite smoothly. And you get room and board and your clothing provided and you can save virtually 100% of your income - after taxes that is. I should tell you that if you ask the Laird what to do with your savings, he's a very shrewd investor. More than doubled my savings in the five plus years I've been with him."

Granville glanced at his watch. "In the next thirty minutes, Baroness Auldlay should be arriving. So I'd better go upstairs and dress more appropriately to receive her at the door. In the meantime, here's the key to the Laird's room. Tell him you found me indisposed - better left undescribed. He'll forget the delay. He has only one thing on his mind now and that's the health of his fiancée and the forthcoming wedding."

Jeffrey got up shaking his head as if he was trying to return to his senses, and walked out the door to deliver the key to the Laird. He turned back and asked Granville, "How did you know that Baroness Auldlay was coming?"

"Because my good friend, I telephoned her butler and suggested it. I neglected to mention to you that in the better households in the area there's a tight little clique of butlers who cooperate very carefully and subtly with each other behind the scenes. I'll introduce you to this group shortly. Most of them are older than you; but that makes no difference. If people are competent and relevant, age is not a barrier.

"You might recall that some months ago, our Laird and Miss Bramwood began playing tennis at the Auldlay estate - all arranged by me with their butler. And don't think our costume ball production was all impromptu. It was very carefully cleared ahead of time with the Baroness, and she was, shall we say, a co-conspirator. Also, in the recent days with our Lady's illness, who but her closest friend would come to see her every day? It might have taken a little prompting to put them in their respective roles, but once in it they both have handled their parts beautifully. By the way that entire Auldlay family is twenty-four carat. I don't mean they have a lot of money; I mean that they are genuine people, the type that our Laird and Miss Bramwood should have as close friends."

He gestured at Jeffrey, waving him out the door, looked at the remaining stub of the cigar and snuffed it out carefully in the ashtray. He rose and went to change so as to be ready to admit the Baroness on her arrival.

Jeffrey took the key up to the Laird, who failed to gain admittance to his room. Mrs. MacDuffie had bolted the door from the inside. But when she heard him trying the key, she did ask him to be patient, as Miss Bramwood is dressing. So he paced up and down the hall for the next half hour. He was still apprehensive about her recovery being permanent.

When they opened the door to admit him, Kerrie was sitting on the sofa on the far end of the room in an exquisite, pale green, dressing gown of Chinese silk. Aside from its high collar, it could have been a ball gown, and it was perfect for her coloring. Her hair was still damp and it fell in generous curls on her shoulders and back. All in all she looked very regal, despite her recent illness.

"Beautiful," exclaimed the Laird. "Where'd you get the gown?"

"It was in the armoire of clothing from Sixteen's Lady," replied Mrs. MacDuffie. She neglected to mention that Granville had specifically instructed that they have this gown in readiness for when Miss Bramwood recovered.

A cart with the breakfast followed into the room on the Laird's heels, and the pair indulged in a long silence while they caught up on neglected dining. They only exchanged smiles and an occasional wink.

Shortly after they were finished, Granville entered the room. "Lady Auldlay has come by unexpectedly. Shall I admit her or say that Miss Bramwood is indisposed?"

The Laird looked at Kerrie who nodded affirmatively, and said, "By all means admit her, but maybe you can get this trolley out of here first." With the hot coffee, his voice was starting to recover.

When the Baroness walked in she went directly to Kerrie and sat down on the sofa and embraced her. "We've all been so worried, Kerrie Dear. And the children have wanted to come over to see you. I've been trying to tell them that you were getting better and not to worry, but they wanted to come and see for themselves. And you know that little imp of a Susan, only eight years old, she was most insistent that she wanted to see for herself. And I said, 'Don't you trust Mother?' And she said, 'Oh, yes Mother, we trust you, but we still want to see for ourselves. Don't forget you used to tell us there was a Tooth Fairy and an Easter Bunny and a Santa Claus." And at that point

Kerrie and the Baroness burst out into laughter, and it took them more than a minute to regain their breath and be able to speak.

Even the Laird had to smile at the story. He was pleased to see Kerrie relax and take pleasure in a story about the children. When their laughter subsided, he said, "Lady Auldlay, we would like you to be the first to know that Miss Bramwood and I are going to be married. And we'd like your advice as to how we should handle all of this. We'd like to have a large formal reception when she's stronger, but for a variety of reasons we'd like to tie the knot as soon as possible."

"Praise be to the Almighty," said the Baroness, lifting her arms and looking upward. "It's about time and now I can stop holding my breath. And stop calling me Lady, both of you, my name's Valerie. That's what my close friends call me."

Valerie thought for a few moments. "I think it would work very well if you had a small wedding right here at Kirkwood, and made a public announcement of the wedding with the indication that the reception will follow in a few weeks. Why don't you let me help and handle all of this? I'll work it out with Kerrie."

Ignoring the Laird the Baroness and Kerrie got into a deep two-way conversation. After a bit he excused himself and said he would be phoning MacKim to get started on the legal arrangements for the marriage.

CHAPTER XLIV

After the Baroness left the Laird rejoined Kerrie in the bedroom. She had already had an exhausting day, but she wanted to talk and clean the slate a little before taking a rest.

"I think we had better go into the Great Hall and have a discussion, as we shouldn't spend too much time in here alone until after the wedding," suggested Kerrie. "But first I want to show you a couple of things."

The Laird couldn't imagine what she would show him in the privacy of his own room, but he closed the door and watched as she removed the two squirrels from the posts at the foot of the bed. She showed him the contents, and said, "Here's where I found the ruby ring I'm wearing."

She went over to the closet and opened the entrance to the secret passageway that she had used so often in recent months. The Laird sat dumfounded. After closing the entrance she asked for the Laird to ring for Granville, and when he appeared she asked if he could locate the little Green Book that she had in her hand when she came to the castle a few days ago.

After a short wait Granville returned and handed her the Green book. "This was the only book I could find. It was on the small table in the entry hall." She thanked him, and Kerrie and the Laird walked together into the Great Hall.

She immediately launched into the story of her heritage, and how she had decided to find a suspected treasure in the castle and how she had searched those many weeks, and she openly confessed how her original plan had been abandoned when she found herself uncontrollably in love with him.

She interrupted her narrative to ask, "Does anyone ever call you Alan?"

He thought for a moment. "No, I don't recall that anyone ever did."

"I like Alan. First of all it reminds me of someone I fell in love with at first sight named Al Lawman - it's almost a blend of the two words, and Duncan sounds so formal, and I can't imagine myself calling you Dunk, and certainly not Dunkie, so I would like to call you Alan. And every time I say Alan, I will mean Darling. I wouldn't feel comfortable saying Darling in front of the servants."

She continued on with her narrative. He wanted her to tell it all right down to the reason she left and ran to London and up until the moment she returned to the castle.

Suddenly she stopped and sat upright. "I forgot that I signed papers to sell the house across the road, and now I wish I hadn't. It really was part of the castle grounds at one time and was built for my ancestor, who by the way was also a Cherrie Bramwood."

The Laird stood up. "Let me get MacKim on the phone and see if he can undo the paperwork. I also think that it's an important part of the history of our castle, and I greatly prefer that it not be sold."

He managed to reach MacKim and when he hung up he assured her that MacKim was going to get to it right away.

He took Kerrie's two hands. "I have two reactions to everything you've just told me. First I'm sorry that you didn't find a treasure. I would have been happy for you to have it. You deserve it, and morally this whole place and everything in it should have been yours. However, from a selfish viewpoint, we might never have been sitting here together if you'd found the treasure. So all's well that ends well. But you've gotten me off on a line of thinking that there may be something, and we'll search for it together. The money in the bedpost might have just been the petty cash, and there could be a bigger cache somewhere. And the Kirkwood emerald, there is a strong likelihood that it's hidden somewhere in the castle."

It was now the Laird's turn to relate his past. He told her first of the background of the Stokesdale letters, and gently admonished her never to jump to conclusions too rapidly again. He also suggested that they go together to the opening of the Racing Hall of Fame, and it would be an opportunity to get her into the States where he's still a legal resident and to complete any and all formalities connected with their marriage. He also told the complete story of his relationship with Carolyn and the children, and how he was now their substitute father.

When he finished the story about Carolyn and the children, she had a tear in the corner of each eye. "Those poor children. That poor girl. She needs a mother or at least a sister. I want to help you take care of them. And since they're our children, they ought to be present at our wedding ceremony."

The Laird looked at his watch. "It's still too early to reach them, but I'll call later and tell them to hop over here on the next available flight."

For the few days until the marriage Kerrie stayed at the castle and slept in a bedroom in the old section down the hall from the Laird's room. (Whether Kerrie and the Laird communicated during the night through the connecting secret passageway, the world will never know.) Kerrie recovered rapidly in the ensuing days. Doctor MacLaine said that her strong physical condition was much in her favor and within a few weeks she would be fully back to normal.

Each member of the staff approached her and said how happy they were that she was well and would become the mistress of Kirkwood Castle. Mrs. MacDuffie said she was glad now to have a true mistress in the castle.

Kerrie took Granville aside for a serious conversation. She wanted him to make a list of all the things that he thought she should be doing now that she would be the actual mistress in the castle. Granville chuckled. "For some months you've been in absolute charge of everything of importance that's been happening in the castle. All you have to do is keep doing what you've been doing. The Laird has been informed of things about which he wants to be informed, but basically all he does is sign the checks and enjoy hearing about it." Granville debated about whether to announce his resignation during this conversation, but decided to wait until after the wedding and the reception later. He would also let Jeffrey handle all the details for the reception as proof of his ability to handle the position of butler.

CHAPTER XLV

The wedding took place on the castle lawn a few days later. Fergus and the gardeners arranged an arbor of flowers for the place of the ceremony and laid a path of fresh cut flowers for the bride to walk upon from the front door to the arbor. Baroness Auldlay handled the announcement to the newspapers. It read:

"Kirkwood Castle, Ayrshire, Scotland. Today Miss Kerrie Bramwood and Laird Duncan Alan Fleming were married in a private ceremony conducted by the Reverend Malcolm MacTaggart. Vows were exchanged in the castle garden, and the couple were attended only by a few close personal friends, Lord and Lady Auldlay and members of their family, Miss Saundra Morthland, and from the United States Miss Victoria Courtiss and Mr. Darwood Courtiss V. The Lady Fleming had been unwell recently, and a reception for friends is expected to be held within a few weeks."

Victoria Courtiss and her brother Darwood were delighted to attend the wedding for several reasons. The first thing Victoria did when they arrived at the castle when she was greeted by Kerrie was to give her a warm embrace, and she enthused, "After I met you that week when I visited the castle, I've been hoping and praying every day that Uncle Dunk would ask you to be his wife."

The four young people Ramsay and Rhonda Auldlay and Victoria and Darwood hit it off famously from the first moment - the boys with each other, the girls with each other, and the girls with their new male friends. They spent every moment possible with each other those few days and the old Vauxhall was on the road frequently between their homes. They parted reluctantly and each affirmed that they couldn't wait until the year-end holidays to be together again.

The wedding announcement had been sent to the local and London papers that checked their files and noted the Laird's racing history, and it was picked up by the wire services and appeared in several American papers, including that of the Laird's home city. Someone gave a clipping of the news item to the father of the Courtiss children. He immediately dispatched a letter to the Laird:

"Duncan, It's been a while since we've crossed paths. I was interested in the enclosed clipping and noted that my children are staying with you. I miss them very much and plan to drop by on one of my frequent trips to Europe. I know they will be happy to see me. I'm working on some very rich real estate deals (You know me, even though I don't need the money, I can't keep my finger out of business), and if you would like to double your money in six months, please send me your check for $100,000. Make the check out to me personally, as we haven't decided on which of the corporations to use for this particular little beauty. I'll expect to hear from you shortly. This will be subscribed so quickly that I don't want you to miss it. Your old pal. Dar."

The Laird thought, 'Oh yes. A good way to say goodbye to money. Permanently.' He didn't reply to the letter.

A couple of weeks later he got another letter:

"Duncan, As I warned you, the real estate deal filled in fast. You ought to see the list of smart people who grabbed at the chance to be in it. If you want to get in, I'll let you have a part of one of my shares. I feel obligated to let other investors see that I am heavily committed personally to the transaction. I can only spare a half share for $50,000. Make the check out to me personally. Dar.

P.S. If I don't receive your check, I'll assume that this letter was never received, and I'll dash over to see you and the children personally."

The Laird was amused. 'A veiled threat to come over here. He'll never get past the castle gate. And if we put out the word, he wont be able to get the time of day in the town or even a place to sleep for a number of miles in any direction.'

The last communication he received was a priority letter via Federal Express:

"Duncan, Am on my way to visit you on the first available flight. Will let you know the details so you can have someone meet me at the airport. Our books are all tied up with the auditors. They are working on a massive refund from the IRS (seven figures). Please arrange for me to pick up a ticket from the airline. Will reimburse you later. Dar."

The Laird's reaction was, 'That's his last artless attempt. He's run out of money even for an air ticket.'

Some days afterward Granville reported, "Sir, A Mr. Courtiss telephoned you a number of times from the United States. Something about an urgent real estate deal. But I neglected to mention it, and somehow I've mislaid his return number. I assume that isn't a problem?"

CHAPTER XLVI

The wedding announcement triggered a flood of gifts to the castle from numerous friends in England as well as the United States. The Laird half-complained to his wife, "I almost wish we had kept our marriage a secret. We might have to put an addition on the castle as big as the castle just to house all these gifts."

The Laird's gift to his bride was the construction of tennis courts on the far south side of the gardens, close to the river. With the help of Baron Auldlay who contacted a number of his friends she found a 1937 Bentley racing car, much in need of restoration. It was given with the plea that he never works on it after dinnertime. The Baron was surprised how many vintage cars were standing about neglected in the garages and old carriage houses of his friends and acquaintances, and he suggested to the Laird that they ought to start a vintage car museum in one of the abandoned warehouses down by the seafront in the town. He was pretty sure he could get a lot of the cars donated or at least placed on permanent loan. He offered to pay for the renovation of the building personally. Needless to say the Laird was excited to be involved with anything concerned with automobiles, and another project was launched.

In the days immediately after the wedding the married couple spent a lot of time in their bedchamber together. They took their meals in the Great Hall, but immediately afterward returned to their room. One might conclude that this was normal for a healthy newlywed couple, but as this routine went on for a week, even the young MacDuffie girls, who were hoping for marriages in their futures, were mildly worried for themselves and asked their mother, "Is this what happens when people are first married? Mightn't this be physically too much for a bride, all day for a week, especially one who's been ill recently?"

In truth the married pair were spending a great deal of time exploring the cave area below the castle and the secret passageway. Kerrie took the Laird over every inch of what she had explored in seeking the treasure. He had no new ideas as to where they might look.

At the end of the ten-day period, the Laird was visited by a close friend from the United States. Despite all the excitement at the castle the visit hadn't been postponed, as they were not only good friends, but the castle was big enough that visitors could be swallowed up and only show up for a few hours at dinner and lunch and need not be a burden to the host and hostess. The friend's avocation was heraldry. The Laird asked him to look at a photocopy of the coat of arms from the Green Book about the castle. The shield displayed a chevron between three thistles and the motto was 'Look Up. Look Up.'

The visitor advised, "Before I came to visit, I checked the references for the coat of arms of Semple. The arms of Semple consist of a chevron between three bugle horns. And the motto is Courage. If you say this was from some document about the Semples and the castle, I would say that someone is trying to send a message. I'd look around here for thistles, and I'd look upward for them."

The Laird remembered the message from the Twelfth Laird in that séance months ago telling him to advise the person in the castle with red hair to 'Look up.' A coincidence???

The visitor also asked them where the well was located in the castle. The Laird had never seen any sign of a well in the castle. The visitor insisted that no one would have built a castle without an interior water supply. Another unsolved mystery. But it was put at the far end of the long list of questions regarding the castle, because the local council water supply came right into the property.

The Laird and his new Lady went back down into the cave and shone a torch on the ceiling. After careful study they began to see a number of thistle-like images of different sizes, and some very faint. Some might have been scratched in whole or part, taking advantage of natural shapes in the overhead. Kerrie said, "Look Alan. The bottom of the stems takes you along a path, and the path follows my yarn. It doesn't go to the portcullis. It takes you right to the place where you can crawl through the wall to reach the inside."

They kept tracking all the overhead signs. Two new possible passages were discovered. Where there seemed to be a waterfall, a barrier, between the cave and the direction toward Kerrie's house on the other side of the road, there was an indication that there was something overhead in that direction. The Laird climbed up on some rocks and expected to find an opening through which he might crawl and gain access to another room beyond the waterfall that completely filled the opening of what might have been a doorway. No luck. It was impossible to get through the small openings in the side of the wall.

Kerrie called to him, "Reach in the opening behind that stem of the thistle and see if you can feel anything"

He reached in and felt around. "Only a large round stone in here and there's a stream of water running along a sort of trough or gutter. I think it must be the water that's falling through the door-like opening over there."

"See if you can move the stone around."

He pushed the stone to the left and to the right. "It seems to fit over a hole," he announced.

"Alan! You've just shut off the waterfall in the opening. Come down here. I think we can enter that doorway and off to the side we might be able to slide through an opening and go beyond this part of the cave."

He climbed down. At the top of the opening water was still trickling down slightly, but he could see in the recess above what appeared to be two long pieces of cast iron, leaving a slot between them and it was from there the water had fallen. It was not a natural formation; obviously man made.

They slipped into the opening and moved sideways a few feet and entered another section of cave. Searching carefully, they found more thistles that led them directly to a wooden door, not obvious from where they had entered.

"This has to go into the lower part of my house," exclaimed Kerrie. "I never knew this was here. And frankly I doubt if my parents did."

They carefully moved the doorway back and found themselves staring at the shelves of a basement storage cabinet. The cabinet had been set firmly in place.

"We'll check it out from the inside of my house," said Kerrie. "At least I hope it's still my house."

They retraced their steps and moved the stone, again creating the waterfall in the opening.

"The information I'm going to share with you soon about the Thirteenth Laird would suggest that he was the one who engineered this barrier, and I suspect he may have been a frequent visitor to my house," Kerrie announced.

They retraced their steps back to the entranceway of the passageway beneath the castle. The Laird was still looking up and said, "Oh, oh, Kerrie. I think there's something else over here." He pointed toward the north wall; beyond which was the part of the cave that undoubtedly had the opening that was totally blocked off by the collapsed outside entrance.

The stems pointed to a sizable opening. But it looked like so many of the other holes, that from below there were no obvious connections to the other side. He climbed up some rocks and said, "I'm going to take this on faith and slide into this opening, and I'm sure it'll take me somewhere."

"Please be careful," Kerrie admonished.

In a few moments his head reappeared at the opening, and he called down, "Come on up and through. I've got two surprises for you."

She climbed up and slid into the opening, and he helped her down a pile of stones onto the cave floor.

"See. There's one set of stems that takes us right to this opening that we just came through. There's another set that leads right to that door over there that must go to the passageway inside the castle that's blocked up. I'd open it, but I'm afraid that a few tons of gravel might come sliding out on top of us.

Now look over here." He led her around to the left into an alcove and shone his torch on a bier made out of stone and on it a wooden coffin. Behind it was a pile of stones forming a small altar on which was the stub of a candle.

The coffin was not a simple pine box. It appeared to be oak with carving along the edges, and on the top the Semple coat of arms. The Laird said, "Kerrie dear. Turn around. I'm going to open the lid and see if there's anything in here."

She turned. He felt under the edge of the lid and found a wooden bolt, which moved easily. He lifted the lid. "Kerrie, don't look but I think I see a corpse with red hair in what looks like the discolored remains of a white wedding dress, and at its feet the corpse of an infant." He closed the top and moved the wooden bolt back into place.

Kerrie was ashen. "Alan, I feel faint. I think you're going to have to hold me up for a minute." He helped her walk over and sit on a large stone and held her until color started to come back into her face.

"Alan - Darling, we both know that all the Semples for over 200 years are accounted for in the cemetery at the bottom of the hill, except one - my great-great-great grandmother, Cherrie Bramwood - the one who bore a son to the Thirteenth Laird. The one for whom he built the house I lived in across the road. She reportedly disappeared and the rumor has always been that she was disposed of. But all of this happened within a few days. Her disappearance. His sudden death. He was going to adopt his son - my Bramwood named ancestor - and had instructed his lawyer to do it - remember I said there was a letter. And now a further mystery. Is that Cherrie Bramwood? What about the wedding dress? What about the baby? It makes me shudder. She has red hair. It makes me feel like I'm lying there."

The Laird put his arms around her shoulders. "No. You're right here with me now. Very much alive. And we both have a long life together to look forward to. But let's start with Doc MacLaine and have him examine the body and see if he can give us more information."

The next day Doctor MacLaine came over at mid-morning and sat with Kerrie and the Laird in the small drawing room. He listened as they explained how they had discovered the casket in the cave below. When they finished he stroked his chin and gave a short sigh. "Yes. I don't have to look. Many of the so-called skeletons in the cupboards, particularly anything to do with the Lairds and the castle, have been passed down from my ancestors to me. That is most probably Cherrie Bramwood, and the baby is the one she was carrying.

"Thirteen didn't know it when he first married, but his wife had an obsession that she would bear a child by divine intervention, in other words virgin birth - like in the bible, and that her progeny would be something special. So the marriage in effect was never consummated. The Thirteenth Laird had all the normal human drives and the then Cherrie Bramwood, who worked in the castle and reportedly was a beautiful girl, became his paramour and bore him a son. The castle grounds extended in all directions in those years and the house across the road was built on castle property for Miss Bramwood and the son.

"Apparently, he wanted to recognize his son and adopt him as his legal heir, which was not uncommon in those days, but his legal wife objected, and he honored her wishes until she died. Shortly after she died several things happened.

"The story passed on down to me by my father was that Thirteen was going to marry Miss Bramwood and adopt the son, who was then in his teens, as soon as possible. However, the then butler for a long time had amorous intentions toward Miss Bramwood and wanted to share in her favors and invited her to the castle one day when the Laird was out. She appeared, undoubtedly expecting to see the Laird and was led to a bedchamber. She rejected his advances, and he tried to force himself on her. The struggle knocked her to the floor causing a skull fracture, and it also induced labor for a second child she was carrying who was still quite a bit from full term.

"The Laird returned to find the butler raving like a maniac and his soon to be wife near delivery. My ancestor was called and delivered the baby. It only lived a few hours, as it was too premature, and we didn't have the techniques then that we have now. However, the baby was baptized and a marriage was performed. Miss Bramwood, the new Lady Semple, died the next day. The butler committed suicide the same day, and Thirteen died of a massive coronary occlusion a few days later.

"I had heard that the body of Miss Bramwood, the Lady Semple, had disappeared, but I didn't know that she was interred in a cave below the castle. Reportedly, the boy was educated by the next Laird and that property, I understand, has always been maintained as if it were part of the Kirkwood property.

"And now the story gets confusing and there seems to be several versions. But the one I think is close to the truth is as follows. Apparently, Thirteen told Fourteen, a distant relative, that he wished the boy to succeed him as heir and had started legal proceedings. When he died unexpectedly she found herself the legal heir and ignored his wishes. The marriage to Miss Bramwood was also kept a secret and the then minister insisted that the marriage had never taken place. My ancestor hadn't been a witness. However, this later must have caused some neuroses on the part of Fourteen for which she was treated without success. She insisted that at night she heard voices in the walls and a baby crying. She also put up all the money for the new church building down in the town - maybe to erase whatever was bothering her conscience." He lifted up his hands and dropped them on his lap as if to say, 'There it is.'

The Laird shook his head. "That's quite a story."

"And it explains a lot," added Kerrie.

"I haven't mentioned it," said the Laird, "but a number of times I thought I heard footsteps in the passageway leading down to this area and a sound like a small baby crying. Every time I opened the door to the passageway the sounds stopped. I assumed that the crying was a cat somewhere and the footsteps were the building creaking - which it does sometimes. I can understand why Fourteen had the passageway filled with that stone rubble."

"What do you think we ought to do with the remains of my grandmother and baby?" asked Kerrie.

"It raises all kinds of legal questions," MacLaine explained. "Technically you can't bury someone without a permit and a certifying death certificate. In this case the world doesn't even know that a corpse exists. Why don't you let me come back with some gloves and things, and I'll take a look first, and then you can decide what to do."

It was agreed that they would wait and MacLaine left and returned in a half hour. While he was gone they talked about his narrative and the Laird observed, "That explains why the secret passageway to the cave on that side is filled with rubble. Fourteen must have heard or thought she heard the footsteps of Cherrie Bramwood, The Lady Semple, and also the baby crying and had it filled to quell her fears that their ghosts might be coming up that passageway. I also suspect that building the new church might have been the result of a little quid pro quo for expunging the record of the marriage. We ought to ask Malcolm MacTaggart to check the archives in the church and see if he can find any record of these events."

When MacLaine returned, the Laird alone escorted him down through the secret passageway and into the cave area with the coffin. He held the torch while the doctor examined the two corpses.

"It's been amazingly dry down here all these years and the bodies are like mummies, the skin like parchment. This was a red haired woman in her late twenties or early thirties would be my guess, and the baby was obviously premature. The woman is in an elaborate wedding dress and the baby is wearing what looks like a baptismal gown." MacLaine held up a gold ring. "I don't believe in burying jewelry and things of value with the deceased. I think your wife ought to have this as a keepsake. I'll clean it up with alcohol first." He slipped it into a small plastic bag.

"What to do about all this?" mused the Laird. "I think my wife would feel better if we moved the coffin into the family mausoleum in the cemetery. In my desk I have the key for it. But the exit to the outside of the cave over there has collapsed, looks like a section ten or twelve feet long, and I don't know how we'd ever get the coffin out of here, and I don't fancy handling the remains and pushing them through the opening in the wall"

"I can't advise you as to what to do," said MacLaine, "and I'm going to forget that I ever saw anything here. But you might get a couple of former coal miners from up the way and have them open up the collapsed entrance and shore it up temporarily and move the coffin out one night. I'll help you and maybe you can get at least one or two trusted friends, and we'll put it in the back of your small truck and place it in the mausoleum. Afterward you can pull the timbers out with some ropes and close the entry again."

That plan was temporarily placed on the agenda until the Laird confirmed it with Kerrie.

The next morning the Reverend MacTaggart made one of his frequent visits and the Laird approached him. "Malcolm, my wife and Sandy are trying to nail down dates of the births, deaths, and so forth of the former lairds. We've run into a snag, which suggests that the Thirteenth Laird might have married twice. Could you check your records?"

"How about tomorrow? Soon enough?" replied MacTaggart.

Sandy was standing there listening. She flashed a beautiful smile, and said quietly, "How about today, Malcolm?'

Without hesitating, he said, "Of course Sandy, today. I wasn't thinking. I'll get back to you on this today before you leave."

"Why don't you go do it right now, before you forget?" said Sandy sweetly.

"Of course. Before I forget," echoed MacTaggart and he left to return to the church.

An hour later the minister returned carrying a grimy and worn oversized book. The Laird and Lady and Sandy were assembled, and he opened the book to a page and showed them the entry recording the burial of the Thirteenth Laird. Sandwiched between entries of the burial of the previous virginal Lady Semple and one Humphrey Lydiard, butler at Kirkwood Castle, were two entries that were completely crossed out; it looked as if ink were painted over the two entries with a brush.

"Peculiar," said MacTaggart. "There are any number of other entries with mistakes where the then minister just ran a line through them, but these are totally obliterated."

"Malcolm, we think there should be both a marriage and a baptism there, and we'll be perfectly frank and say that we think this marriage was to my wife's ancestor," affirmed the Laird.

"It does look very strange," commented MacTaggart. "Another place I could check is to go to the cathedral in Glasgow. In those years duplicates of all vital statistics had to be sent there. Sometimes those things weren't carefully filed, but I can give it a shot." He looked at Sandy. "If I go this afternoon, will that be soon enough?"

Sandy nodded approvingly.

Late that afternoon Sandy had left and the Laird and Lady were having tea when the Laird received an excited telephone call from the minister who was still in Glasgow. "Would you believe? I found the entries for those dates. The Thirteenth Laird did marry a Miss Cherrie Bramwood, same name as your wife, and he also baptized a newborn infant that died the same day. They'll be mailing you certified copies of these records within the week."

When he told Kerrie, she said, "After all these years of wondering if all of this was fact or fiction. I can't tell you how it puts a big wonder inside of me to rest."

A few days later Kerrie shared all of this with her closest friend, the Baroness Auldlay. When they had the large wedding reception a few weeks afterward the Baroness said she thought they ought to issue another press release, and she would handle it for them. She crafted the press announcement:

"Lost 'Princess' Returns to Family Castle: The Laird and Lady of Kirkwood Castle, Mr. and Mrs. Duncan Alan Fleming, who were married only a few weeks ago, discovered in researching old castle records that the Lady Fleming is a direct descendant of the Thirteenth Laird, and that by manipulation within the family his successor deprived the rightful heir from succeeding to the Kirkwood Estate, which in turn would have been the current Lady Fleming."

The rest of the release mentioned how the happy couple is glad that it happened this way, or they wouldn't have found each other. The Laird's prominence in automobile racing was also mentioned.

As she had hoped the story was picked up by the national and international news wire services, and requests for photos and interviews poured in. Several magazines wanted exclusive interviews.

CHAPTER XLVII

The week after the wedding, the Laird and Lady flew to the United States, and after several days of visits in the Laird's home city which were filled with dinners and luncheons with friends and his law partners, they went to Florida for the opening of the Racing Hall of Fame. Regina Godfrey had visited the castle shortly after the wedding and with a local dressmaker began immediately on a new wardrobe suitable for the Lady. She used a number of the antique fabrics for certain gowns, and she told Kerrie, "I had all these in mind for you months ago when I first saw them. I was just waiting for the Laird to wake up and propose to you."

Granville was very interested in their attending the opening of the Racing Hall of Fame and he asked Mrs. Godfrey to create a suitable outfit for the Lady, something dignified, but something eye catching for any publicity photos that might be taken. He then talked with Kerrie, explaining how to pose and what to do in front of the T.V. cameras. From his long involvement in the theatre, he had a good feel for publicity photos, what to do and what not to do.

Because of the news announcement released by Baroness Auldlay, the members of the news media at the opening of the Racing Hall of Fame were anxious to photo and interview the Laird and his new Lady. For the Florida climate she had a simple sheath dress with a décolleté front and short sleeves. She wore a pearl choker and a pearl bracelet. After she posed with the Laird the first few times and shared her beautiful smile with the cameramen, they followed her all about the exhibit. There was a ribbon cutting, but several press people wanted a reenactment of the ribbon cutting only with Kerrie.

Betsy Stokesdale was there and she was most annoyed. Her plan of being on the arm of the Laird had misfired. She was a small player in the whole display, but she had originally schemed that if she could be with the Laird it would magnify her chances of being in the publicity shots. She had also planned to hint that there was a romantic involvement.

After being grossly ignored and following the crowd as they moved about, she finally trapped one cameraman who had lagged behind to change the film in his camera. "I'm Betty Stokes, one of the women in the display in the ladies section. Wouldn't you like to get a shot of me over there?" She flashed him a dazzling smile.

The cameraman looked at her. "Would you please throw this in the trash can when you go out the door, Missus?" He handed her the paper wrapping from the film, and hurried after the crowd following Lady Fleming.

Without exception the T.V. news and the printed media showed Kerrie's picture and even the Laird at her side seemed to be dimmed out. The next issue of Racing Magazine, which was devoted entirely to the opening showed her alone on the cover. Having his wife displayed in public like this both pleased and annoyed the Laird, but he reasoned that it would soon pass and be forgotten.

While they had been in the United States the Laird spotted a news item in the local papers. The father of the Courtiss children was found dead on the street in the Skid Row section. The paper slanted the story as if he was murdered, "and it's time the police did something about crime in the streets." Acting on instinct, the Laird phoned the local morgue and confirmed his belief that the body might be there. He went to the morgue and posed as attorney for the family, which in a way he was.

The attendant showed him the body and dryly commented, "Another Skid Row bum. We get a couple of these a week. Stunk so much we had to fumigate it before we could do our procedures. I don't think this was an ordinary mugging. The body had multiple fractures. My guess is he owed some big boys money - maybe for drugs."

Courtiss had lost weight and was emaciated. The attendant took out a plastic bag and said these were his valuables, or what was left of them: two dollars and thirty-five cents, an expired driver's license, an expired credit card, a pawn ticket for a watch, and a snapshot of a man and a woman in a salacious pose.

"What the hell's that?" asked the Laird.

The attendant turned the snapshot over. On the back was a phone number. "Sir, my guess is that you're looking at the business card of a cheap house of prostitution. Here's a copy of the autopsy report. He tested positive for AIDS."

The Laird signed a form for the release of the body and had an undertaker pick it up and cremate it and place the urn in the family mausoleum. He knew well that Courtiss had been profligate up until his last days. He had regularly given Duncan Fleming as a reference for credit, and amazingly obtained it in many directions despite the lack of a recommendation, and later inquiries would come into the law firm as to his whereabouts. He had also lost his home on foreclosure, and despite the money that flowed to him for the children's care and education, it wasn't enough. His death may have been more than a casual mugging. Duncan resolved not to tell his children and burden them with the shame that was not of their making. If it ever came up, he would say that as far as he knew their father died of natural causes.

While they were on the trip to and from America, they had a lot of time together to replay and discuss the events of the last weeks and the treasure hunt and plans for the future. Two things came out of it.

"Alan, I've been thinking about what your friend said about the well. It has to be in the old part of the castle and that means the dungeon area. We should check it when we get home. It just could have a connection with the treasure."

The other thing was, "Kerrie, while I was in the States, I alerted my law partners that I would be dropping out of active day to day participation. I will become, as they say in the profession, 'Of Counsel.' Trying to practice law at a remote location is not easy and not fair to the clients. Also, Preston Auldlay has been getting me more and more involved in his company's affairs, and he strongly wants me to take a part time position with his holding company as Assistant to the Chairman and as a Member of the Board of Directors in their closely held family company. He says he needs me desperately as a confidante and general advisor - not in legal matters. Interestingly, our young people and theirs, as you know, have hit it off famously, and the Baron and Baroness agreed that they wouldn't be at all unhappy if those friendships flowered and something happened one day."

"By the way, Alan, mentioning Valerie, I hope you're planning to continue your Thursday chess sessions with Doctor MacLaine. Valerie has asked me to join a little group of four, now five, who meet every Thursday afternoon. They talk about projects in the county, and she thinks I would fit in nicely. I think you know all these ladies, Nicholson, Crowe, and MacGoldrick?"

The Laird reviewed in his own mind - all these women ran superb households, had fine children and devoted husbands. Each was very attractive in a classical way, and he had the impression that every community project in which they were involved was worthwhile and successful. He said, "Kerrie, you'll fit into that group perfectly. You're all examples of my concept of the perfect wife."

"When had you decided that, Alan?"

Without hesitating he answered, "After the first few times I met you."

She gave him a small kiss on the cheek.

During one of the long discussions, Kerrie asked him, "Alan, what would you have done, if I hadn't come back to the castle that day after I signed those papers to sell my house?"

The Laird smiled. "I knew you were in town and exactly where and when. I didn't want to forcibly abduct you, and I was hoping some way somehow, you would find your way back to the castle."

"Yes, but what if I hadn't come?"

"I have to confess,' he admitted, "that while you were in the estate sales office signing the papers to sell your house, our loyal, trustworthy, honest, Assistant Butler, Gardener, and General Factotum - one Jeffrey - had siphoned the gasoline out of your tank and you had barely a teacupful left. If you hadn't gone to the castle, you wouldn't have gotten as far as the town limit, and both he and Granville were standing very close by to offer assistance, and soon I would appear on the scene as a White Knight to save you and also to try and talk some sense into your head."

"Oh," was all she said.

There was silence for a while, and then Kerrie mentioned, "It was clever of you to have someone put Christina Rossetti's book into my house."

The Laird knit his brow. "I have no idea how that book got there. None of us had a key to get into your house."

CHAPTER XLVIII

Their return trip was booked through London as the Laird wanted to visit his stockbrokers and place Kerrie's name on the account, and while there they planned to visit the office of K.T. and C.L. Hoare and Company, Dealers in Old Coins and Precious Metals. The numerous letters that they had found in the coffers strongly suggested there were a lot of transactions between the former lairds and this dealer.

They were warmly received at the offices of K.T. and C.L. Hoare and Company and ushered immediately to the partners' room. Both of the brothers were present. They had followed the news in the London papers and were pleased to meet the present Lords of Kirkwood. Inasmuch as Lady Fleming was a direct descendant of the former lairds they were quite open about their previous business dealings with the family.

"Our firm and its predecessor has been privileged to deal with the Lairds of Kirkwood for the better part of two centuries. Usually, once a year in the autumn the Laird would visit and bring a sizable amount of gold coins, which were sold, for cash. In earlier times there was some silver and also jewelry which we usually referred to other dealers."

His brother interceded at this point. He had walked over to a filing cabinet and pulled out a large envelope. "This is a record of the transactions over the years. You may look at it if you wish. However, one item of particular interest, which we handled for the Laird almost twenty years ago, was the sale of a large emerald brooch. It went at auction anonymously at Christies, purchased by a Middle East oil sheik. We did have a paste copy made of the piece which I suspect is somewhere about the castle. It would have limited value for resale. Here's a copy of the auction booklet and the receipt for the transaction. As you can see it went for almost a half million pounds. You might like to have photocopies of these."

Kerrie and the Laird exchanged knowing looks.

"We should let you know," offered the Laird, "that we believe that the family reserves of gold coins was probably fully depleted."

"We were advised of that when the emerald was sold," acknowledged one of the brothers, "but we have appreciated your business over the years nevertheless, and if we can serve you in the future in any way, please let us know."

They exchanged a few more pleasantries with the two partners and took their leave, so as to reach the castle sometime in the late afternoon.

While they were in the taxi headed back to the airport the Laird said, "This helps to solve one mystery in part, but it strongly suggests that the paste copy of the emerald is still somewhere about the castle premises. It would be nice to have the original, but we really don't need it for the value, and if the copy were really a good copy, no one would dare suspect that my beautiful wife would be wearing some kind of imitation. It also indicates very clearly that the vast treasure of the Semples had run out, and at some point they would be hard pressed to retain ownership of Kirkwood."

"Circumstances change, Alan. In Medieval times a castle and its entire staff and army of knights, archers, and so forth could be supported on twenty pounds yearly, but of course a lot of their food was grown on nearby lands. A small handful of those gold coins was all they needed to live very well for a year."

CHAPTER XLIX

When they arrived back at the castle, they were greeted by the entire staff plus Sandy Morthland. Granville told them that Councilor MacKim wanted to see them when they returned, and he would be by first thing the next morning.

The couple was weary from their trip and the time change, but Sandy reported that she had exciting news - she had deciphered the code used so generously by the Thirteenth Laird - the Judge - the father of Robert Bramwood, Kerrie's ancestor. It was agreed that after the Laird and Lady had a chance to freshen up and have a brief nap Sandy would join them for dinner together with the Reverend MacTaggart.

After the dinner and when coffee had been served Sandy put on a pair of dark horn rimmed glasses. "Malcolm, would you please move the easel with the flip chart over near the table. Thank you."

Addressing the Lord and Lady, she continued, "We're now going to have a session on how the code of Robert Semple, Thirteenth Laird, was deciphered. As Kerrie knows, this code and its solution have almost taken over my life for months; it became a compulsion. I've awakened in the middle of the night thinking about it and was unable to go back to sleep. I even dreamt about it. But one night while you were gone, I awakened and sat bolt upright. There it was. Why hadn't I arrived at the solution sooner? I had the key.

"What the Thirteenth Laird had done, as was reportedly common in so many of these codes, was to make a strip of paper with the letters A through Z plus two punctuation marks. So what little Saundra did was to make up horizontal strips and try to match them up to see if A was always an F or a T, or whatever. No luck, just a lot of confusion.

"So then I looked for the most often repeated combinations, and they were these: (she pointed to her flip chart).

?ZPNHTA	-	7 letters - Cherrie?
G?AGMZK!	-	8 letters - Kirkwood?
NEMAHC	-	6 letters - Robert?

"It also struck me early on that it would be too simple for Thirteen to just substitute one letter for another. If we look at Cherrie the two R's are different, but in Kirkwood the two K's are the same as every fourth letter. That put me into the possibility of three substitutions for each letter alternately. But yet not so simple. He started each sentence with the first substitution and continued, so that these same words might be different if they appeared elsewhere in a sentence.

"And about the time I started to pursue this line of thinking, the thought that woke me out of a sound sleep was that in more than two decades of diaries - invariably more than one book for each year, Thirteen had inadvertently written three dates in code. And of course they followed in sequence of the other dates in plain language. The first one I saw was March. So now we confirmed these letters, albeit with variations: (she turned over a page on the easel).

> `C-h-e-r-r-i-e
> K-i-r-k-w-o-o-d
> R-o-b-e-r-t

and they were consistent.

"The next date I found in code was October, and now we were able to confirm, again with the same variations.

> C-h-e-r-r-i-e
> K-i-r-k-w-o-o-d
> R-o-b-e-r-t

"The third date that I found in code was December which confirmed the D in Kirkwood, and now we were in business. What the Laird had done was to use three strips of letters, changing after each letter and then repeating. Fortunately, he didn't scramble the letters. I've deciphered a number of the pages, and actually it isn't too hard. You mentally shift for each letter like using a foreign language, except it's easier as you only have 28 items in each 'language,' and it actually goes pretty fast.

"One of the computer geniuses in my brother's company made a little program for me to accomplish the transcription automatically. It works quite efficiently.

Sandy paused, pushed the glasses to the top of her head, "Any questions so far?" There were none. She replaced the glasses.

"I have here a number of pages of things I've translated from the code. And I did rather skip around in time. I'll let you read these pages at your leisure, but for the moment a few summary comments. First off Thirteen writes soon after his marriage about the mental problems of his new wife. She was determined to have a child by virgin birth; it was an obsession. He writes about his desperation, and I think at that point he really was devoted to her. He consulted numerous medical practitioners, but she refused to cooperate and became increasingly difficult.

"After a number of years of this unfortunate marriage, he had a severe bout with influenza, and servants tended him twenty four hours around the clock. It seems that one Cherrie Bramwood drew the night duty, and after he was fairly well recovered he wrote of wooing her into his bed and even prolonged his presumed recovery to continue the clandestine, nocturnal relationship. Interesting, from the earliest entries, he writes that Cherrie is very intelligent, a good listener, and he could confide his innermost thoughts to her.

"He built the house across the street for her, and apparently relieved her of any household duties and kept her there attended by a maid. Within a year she bore him the son Robert."

She continued, "It's very obvious that Thirteen was very fond of the boy Robert - almost daily entries about everything he did as he was developing in those first ten years. I shared some of this with one of the faculty at Edinburgh University who is a

314

specialist in child development, and she said Thirteen was a most accurate observer, and that there is virtually nothing like this from those years, and she would like to use it as a case study.

"Also, and I'm repeating, it's very certain that Thirteen was deeply in love with Cherrie Bramwood. Apparently, she was more than the mother of the child; she was a close companion and confidante. There is one section where he was struggling with the decision in a legal case, and he writes that she influenced him to take a more humanitarian view.

"There's also a discussion about one other legal case that I transcribed. This was about the trial of the Earl of Bodenloch for the alleged murder of his wife. The judge wrote that despite the jury finding him not guilty, in his mind there was no question that the Earl did it. He believed that the jury was swayed by the man's prominence. Also he felt that the prosecutors could have done a better job of presenting the evidence. The murder was never solved. Anyway, this is supposedly the Scottish equivalent of the murder of Edwin Drood, about which Charles Dickens wrote."

Putting down her papers on the table and pushing them together in a neat stack, she then fished about and pulled out another handful. "Here's what I was looking for, the entries for the last few days.

"There's quite a bit here, and I'll paraphrase. On this entry he writes that he returned to Kirkwood a day early after holding court all week in Glasgow. He found Miss Bramwood in the midst of labor pains on a bed in the castle and the butler completely out of his mind. He sent for Doctor MacLaine - surely the ancestor of our present Doctor MacLaine - who gave the butler a sedative and delivered the baby, a little girl, premature - only six months. The baby lived only a few hours, but the minister had been summoned and baptized it. He wrote that Miss Bramwood was diagnosed as having a concussion and some internal injuries, but she was able to relate about the struggle with the butler. The butler committed suicide that night - hung himself in the stable. The next day Miss Bramwood seemed to be recovering and the minister came and married them. Later that day she suffered internal hemorrhaging and died.

"The next entries indicate how Thirteen was suffering from extreme pain in his chest and left arm. He wrote that the stress of all the recent events caused him to be very tired. He mentions that the proceedings were under way with his lawyer for the adoption of Robert who would become the next Laird. And then the sentence of the last entry was never finished. There's an inkblot on the page. He must have died shortly afterward."

Sandy took off her glasses, placed them on the table, rose, and made an abbreviated curtsy. "And there my Lord and Lady is the report for today."

Kerrie got up from her chair and went over and kissed Sandy on the cheek and hugged her, and in a voice heavy with emotion said, "Thank you, Sandy."

The Laird also rose and kissed Sandy on the cheek. "I thank you too. That was absolutely brilliant, Sandy."

Kerrie prompted, "You should also kiss her once more on the other cheek, Alan. I've neglected to mention that Sandy and I have been comparing our ancestries, and from her line a cousin married a Semple - the Tenth Laird, which makes us something like sixth cousins, once or twice removed, and by marriage you're Sandy's distant cousin too."

Dutifully, the Laird kissed Sandy again on both cheeks, murmuring the word, "Cousin."

To his surprise she returned a hardy kiss on the cheek, saying "Three times, Cousin, like the Russians do it."

The Laird's reaction was, 'This young lady is a far cry from the shy, detached Sandy that I first met.'

The minister cautioned the Laird, "Ahem. Careful, Duncan. Only one kiss to a customer."

The Laird responded, "O.K. Malcolm. It's your turn."

Sandy shifted her weigh to her right foot, placed her hand on her hip and thrust it in the direction of the minister and placed her cheek sideways awaiting such from the minister, but he just blushed and didn't move. Tapping the toe of one foot, she said to the Laird, "I don't think he heard what you said, Duncan. You have to repeat it."

The next morning MacKim arrived as scheduled, and he was all smiles. "Good news." He placed the keys to Kerrie's house on the table. Opening his briefcase, he took out some papers. "Here's your original agreement to sell the property.

"The day you signed the offer to sell, the estate agent marched right over to your neighbor who had been wanting this property for years, and offered it to him at a figure which in my opinion was well below a fair market price. But when the solicitor got into the case, he found that the property could not be sold without first offering it to the Laird of Kirkwood because of a right of preemption. So, the sale had not taken place."

MacKim closed his briefcase. "I'll leave these papers with you and of course the keys."

After he left the Laird said, "You know, I've never been in your house."

Kerrie protested, "It's not my fault that you were never in the house."

"What do you mean by that?" he asked, knitting his brow.

"If you had kissed me at my door that night after the costume ball, I would have invited you in."

"Yes," he replied. "If you had invited me in I would have kissed you inside the house, many times over, but I couldn't do it right there in front of Fergus. But that's history. Let's go and visit the Bramwood love nest."

They walked out the castle and up the lane and down the road and were unlocking her door in five minutes. When they got inside, Kerrie glanced about. "It doesn't look like anything's been touched. It's all here, such as it is."

The Laird stood and didn't speak. Then he walked about and looked into each of the rooms. In her living room on the mantle was a large picture of him in a frame, as there was next to her bed on a small table. In the room she used as an office was another. Mounted on a section of the wall was a large bulletin board with numerous clippings of him, some from his racing days. In short he felt the place was almost a shrine for one Duncan Alan Fleming. He took her in his arms and very tenderly kissed her, and all he could say was, "I wish you had invited me in here that night after the costume ball."

They went into the lower level and looked for the entrance from the cave. It was there as expected, but at some point in time someone had built a storage cabinet over the doorway, which in itself was not an obvious door. For the indefinite future they decided to leave it as is.

"And now let's go back and find the well in the castle," suggested Kerrie. "That keeps popping back into my mind."

They returned to the castle, and proceeded directly down into the dungeon area. They weren't there very long when the Laird said, "Don't look Miss Semple, or I should say 'do look.' Look up at the ceiling. If you look closely, there's a circle of thistles, very subtle, but there.

"I've wondered why this was a dirt floor, and obviously they didn't want to cover the well, just in case it was ever needed. I'm sure we've found it. Stay here while I get a shovel."

He walked to the rear of the dungeon and out into the new section of the castle and after a few minutes returned with a trowel. "I had to go out through the garage entrance and get this from the gardeners. They wanted to come in and help with any digging, but I told them you wanted to putter in some flower pots."

He got down on the floor and scraped away six inches of earth and hit a solid oak cover a little over two and one-half feet in diameter. After most of the earth was cleared away he lifted it to reveal the water below. The well looked to be seven or eight feet deep, and like much of the rest of the cave the wall was filled with holes of different sizes, a couple of them fairly large. Water was flowing in silently near the top from a hole. They stood and studied it.

"This must be the same water as in the Kirkwhapple Burn outside, but it has to be part of an underground water system, like the waterfall in the cave," mused the Laird. "It doesn't overflow, because water seeks its own level. So it continuously flows in here and slowly drains out to somewhere, probably toward the ocean, and stays in balance. Nature is sometimes amazing."

"Mother nature is often amazing," agreed Kerrie, "but I don't think she carves perfectly square holes for water to flow through."

The Laird bent over and looked closely. "You're right. That opening looks like it was carved into a square by a stonemason. I would guess they slowly enlarged the opening size until the flow came into balance."

Kerrie was staring into space and thinking when her eyes focused on a squirrel carved out of stone standing on a bracket on the wall. Its base was about the same size as the opening in the well. "Alan, do you think anyone would ever have reason to stop the flow of water in a well, maybe to clean it out or to retrieve something that fell into it?"

"Oh, they might," he speculated.

"See that squirrel? I think the base is a stopper for the opening."

The Laird looked at it for a moment, and then walked over and picked it up. "Heavy," he said. And he carefully slid it into the opening. The flow of water stopped and only the squirrel's head was protruding.

"A perfect fit," he observed. As they watched, the water level slowly receded and finally the well was empty. "It's almost like a water closet, except that it works more slowly."

They stood looking at the last of the water receding. The Laird suggested, "I guess we should leave it like we found it," and started to withdraw the squirrel. Then he stopped and looked at Kerrie.

"This might be ridiculous, but the word 'ridiculous' is almost becoming commonplace in the daily vocabulary around here. I'm suddenly reminded about something I read years ago about a well somewhere in France. During some kind of war or siege, a person hid in a well in a sort of anteroom and was never discovered. That hole on the side down below is large enough for a person to crawl into. Maybe, just maybe, there's an anteroom down there and that's where the family vault is. I'm going down and take a look. I think I can work my way down there by using some of the smaller holes for my feet."

Kerrie asked, "How would that supposed room stay dry?"

He was part way down in the well and he stopped. "The dungeon is below ground level. It might be like the letter 'J,' but anyway we'll find out."

"Be careful," she admonished.

He got to the bottom, bent over, and then all she saw of him was the lower part of his body and then he was out of sight. A few minutes later he climbed back out of the hole. When he straightened up, he was smiling smugly. He held out his hand. "Here." He handed her three gold coins. "Before you do a dance, we've found the treasure, but there's not much left. I suspect the value of these pieces is worth more in antique or numismatic value than in the metal value. I think there are probably a few hundred of these. No jewelry.

"There are about twenty small wooden chests which must have been used to carry the stuff originally - small enough to push through the opening. All of them are empty, except one. There's a small room up there, amazingly dry. There's some air circulation coming from the cracks, like in the rest of the cave. You can't stand up in there. I'm going to go back and bring out one of the little chests, and for now if it's O.K. with you, let's leave the coins in there. And I think when I climb back out you ought to come down and take a quick look for yourself."

He returned to the bottom of the well and disappeared and when he returned he brought out a handsomely carved little wooden chest with metal bands around it. "I'll bet these are hundreds of years old. As I think about it, the Lairds lived off the MacBroom treasure for centuries - no income tax, wages were cheap, prices low. But no matter how you slice it, nothing lasts forever and if Seventeen had even found the treasure, he would have eventually run out of resources. Those MacBrooms must have really been rascals to have acquired all that booty."

Kerrie waved a finger in front of her and pretended to be indignant. "Be careful what you say about the MacBrooms. I've got some of that blood in me you know."

"Come to think of it, the way little you handled those big furniture removers that day, I think that was the pirate blood in you. You had them half scared to death."

"Just for that remark, matey," she said. "When we get in bed tonight I'm going to keelhaul you."

"I'm not sure what that means in bed," he remarked, "but I think I'm going to like it."

The Laird returned the chest to its hiding place and next Kerrie climbed down and took a look at the room. After she climbed back onto the dungeon floor, he took the stone squirrel out of the well and they watched it refill the well to the level of the inflow and then to a very slow stream. He replaced the oak lid and pushed the dirt back in place and walked about over it until it looked like the rest of the floor.

CHAPTER L

The next morning Kerrie was awakened at daybreak by the noise of the Laird walking about the bedroom. As usual, he was wearing only his pajama trousers. He had a tape measure in his hand. She half rose in bed.

"Alan, what are you doing with that tape measure at this hour of the morning?" She covered a big yawn with her hand.

"Treasure hunting, my Dear - the daily sport here at Kirkwood."

She yawned again. "But why so early in the morning?"

"Because I wanted to surprise you with something green, like an emerald, when you woke up."

"I'll be just as surprised at eight o'clock as now. Come on back to bed."

The Laird opened the secret passageway that was filled with rubble and deliberately banged the paneling against the sidewall.

"What on earth are you doing now?" called Kerrie.

"Still working on the same project, but I think I'm getting warmer."

She turned over and tried to go back to sleep.

Next he noisily dragged a very odd chair across the floor. It looked like a two- seater highchair, but it had no tray.

At this point Kerrie was ready to give up trying to sleep, and she half sat up. "And what are you doing with that chair?"

"There aren't any chairs in the passageway, and I thought it could use at least one if we ever choose to come and sit in here, or better yet, if we needed a ladder and didn't have one handy."

She got out of bed and moved to his side. As usual, she was wearing an extra large T-shirt with 'WIMBLEDON' printed on it, which covered all of her essentials, barely.

"You see here, my dear Watson, or rather Miss Semple, or my Dearest, I've looked at that odd shaped chair in my room for months and wondered who in their right mind would make something like that. The seat is too high to sit on comfortably, and it certainly isn't a highchair, yet it has this stout little cross piece like a footrest.

"So now we take this little monstrosity and put it into the passageway against the wall at the very top of the stairs, and voila. It fits perfectly into place and even the feet lock the chair into these little holes on the edges. And now I ask my valued assistant to hold this torch while I climb onto the facsimile ladder, and I will search in these various holes for something of value.

"Aha! Here it is where it should be." He pulled out several small felt bags and handed them to Kerrie. He climbed down and they emptied the bags on the desk. First the imitation emerald, then a large string of oriental pearls, and a dozen more pieces of expensive looking jewelry.

Kerrie's first words were, "Alan, you put those there, because I checked those holes myself. I stood on the safe and could reach those holes from there."

"Yes, my dear. I'm sure you checked them. But, you have to reach into the holes with your right hand. If you stand on the safe and lean far over, you have to balance yourself with your right hand so that you don't fall, and you cannot reach into the far left with your left hand. But you can reach far in with your right arm if you use something like that chair for a ladder."

Kerrie kissed him. "Darling, you're brilliant. But I'm going back to bed. We can look at these things after breakfast."

"Let me check those holes a bit more," said the Laird, walking back to the passageway.

He climbed up the chair again and reached around and started tossing bundles of English pounds down onto the floor.

Kerrie called from the bed, "What are you doing now?"

"Making a cash withdrawal from the Semple Federal Reserve Bank," answered the Laird. "It looks like more than twenty bundles of probably 100 notes of 100 pounds to each bundle. Over 200,000 pounds."

Kerrie was out of bed watching him again.

The Laird climbed down. "I think that's all there is in those various holes. This is probably what remained from the proceeds of the sale of the emerald. This cash and the notes in the bedpost would have kept the Sixteenth Laird going only another five or six years; maybe a couple more if they were frugal. There's no doubt that the Semple fortune was running out."

Kerrie pushed a few of the bundles on the floor aside with her foot and closed the door to the passageway. "Alan, there are more important things in life than money. Right now I'm going back to bed. She walked away towing the drawstring and untying the bow on his pajama trousers.

He yielded. "I didn't realize I was so tired. I guess I'll have to go back to bed for a couple more hours too."

EPILOGUE

The Laird discontinued his law practice, except for an occasional consultation for an old client. He joined the Auldlay holding company as Assistant to the Chairman and soon found himself spending more time than originally envisioned, but it was productive. At the end of their first year of marriage it became obvious that a family was on its way, and in due course was born Duncan Robert Semple Fleming, who one day would be the 19th Laird.

Granville married Trish. She sold her pub, and they undertook to run the restaurants in the restored fortress on the waterfront. One was for formal dining, and it had a steady clientele - some of the best food in all of Scotland was the usual comment. Another part of the fortress was set up as a restaurant with entertainment - pure Scots entertainment (folk music and singing, pipes, Highland dancing, Robert Burns recitations, and skits). This was very popular with the tourists along the beaches, and Granville was in his element as the director.

Jeffrey became the butler of Kirkwood Castle, and he did marry the young city librarian. They established housekeeping in the Bramwood home across the road. The mother moved in with them and part of the house was dedicated to the Kirkwood archives and by arrangement scholars could explore the archives for research purposes.

Eventually, Victoria Courtiss became engaged to Ramsay Auldlay and they married when he finished school in England, and they both attended the University of Pennsylvania while he did graduate work in business administration. At the U. of P. at the same time were his brother-in-law, 'Dunk' Courtiss and his fiancée Rhonda Auldlay.

Sandy Morthland married the Reverend Malcolm MacTaggart, despite numerous other proposals to her. He left the ministry and they devote much of their time to his pet project of running a camp for gifted children on her property in the

Highlands. During the winter months she is a regular visitor at Kirkwood where she assists The Lady Fleming in the unending task of sorting out the loads of documents and either copying them or donating them to libraries and museums. Over time Sandy become the mother of four children.

The Lady Fleming divides her time between running the castle household, plus its special projects, and also with Valerie Auldlay and the tight little circle of five women with whom she has become active in the numerous charitable projects in the county. She still lets the Laird win at tennis, and he thinks she continues to improve with practice.